I0595481

George Saintsbury, Thomas Love Peacock

The Misfortunes of Elphin and Rhododaphne

George Saintsbury, Thomas Love Peacock

The Misfortunes of Elphin and Rhododaphne

ISBN/EAN: 9783337380229

Printed in Europe, USA, Canada, Australia, Japan

Cover: Foto ©Andreas Hilbeck / pixelio.de

More available books at **www.hansebooks.com**

THE
MISFORTUNES OF ELPHIN

AND

RHODODAPHNE

BY

THOMAS LOVE PEACOCK

ILLUSTRATED BY F. H. TOWNSEND

WITH AN INTRODUCTION BY GEORGE SAINTSBURY

London

MACMILLAN AND CO., LIMITED

NEW YORK: THE MACMILLAN COMPANY

1897

All rights reserved

INTRODUCTION

The Misfortunes of Elphin occupies a curious position among Peacock's books. I myself prefer it to almost all of them, and I know some others who think with me ; but it has been by no means a general favourite, though every one, I think, has acknowledged the merit of the 'War Song of Dinas Vawr.' It is not difficult to account for this comparative want of popularity. The scenery and subject are remote ; and the shortness of the book does not give the author time to make them familiar. The poetry is of a stamp at least as unfamiliar, and still more difficult to bring home to English readers ; for high as Welsh poetry stands by consent even of those who do not invariably admire Celtic things, its whole scheme, imagery, language and prosody appear to be even more difficult to transplant into English than the vague and doubtful fragments of Gaelic, and the abundant and genuine stores of Irish.

But I should imagine that the chief stumbling-blocks have been, first, the pervading irony of the thing, and, secondly, the additional offence of ironic treatment of a romantic subject. It must be added, too, that, with one exception, Peacock does not seem to have cared to exert that gift for slight but sufficient projection of character which he had discovered in *Nightmare Abbey*, had made still better use of in *Maid Marian*, and was to show almost throughout *Crotchet Castle*. Except Seithenyn the immortal, all the figures are but shadowy, and most of them are but the shadows of shades. Gwythno is simply an early Welsh René of Anjou ; Elphin and Angharad, Taliesin and Melanghel, respectable and amiable nonentities ; Maelgon, Rhûn, Melvas, bold bad men with a pleasantly incisive fashion of speech ; Arthur and Gwenyvar (except at the moment when she slaps Gwenvach's face) cyphers.[1] It seems as if the author had relapsed upon the system of types rather than individualities.

Yet after admitting this and making allowance for it, the book seems to me amply endowed with charm and interest. In the first place it is here first that we see, full-blown and splendid, that extraordinary Peacockian style, the beginnings of which appear in *Nightmare Abbey*, and which, as has been noted, makes great advances, but does not attain to perfection, in *Maid Marian*. In the author's two first books this style, both in conversation and in narrative, is intermittently perceptible, if indeed it is perceptible at all. In both Peacock writes sometimes quite ill; generally in a sufficient but not very remarkable manner; seldom very well.

---

[1] Although these introductions are not scholastic dissertations it may be permitted to point out that the Arthurian part of the story has a good deal of literary interest. The 'Celticists' have in vain endeavoured (since they relinquished the treacherous help of persons like the late M. de la Villemarqué) to assign a *direct* Celtic origin to the best known and most poetical parts of the canonical Arthurian legend. In the escapade of Melvas, however, and the detention of Guinevere in the 'Isle of Glass,' critical charity, as well as partisan enthusiasm has sometimes been inclined to see the origin of the 'Melleagraunce' episodes of Malory and of the *Chevalier à la Charette* of Chrestien much earlier. The original authority for this experience of the Queen, who, as M. Paulin Paris demurely says, *était très sujette à être enlevée*, seems to be the Latin *Vita Gildae* attributed to Caradoc of Lancarvan, the contemporary of Geoffrey of Monmouth.

Here, after the successive progresses just referred to, his style is absolutely full-grown. As with all the best styles, it is not particularly easy to indicate with precision the exact *nuances* which make up its effect. It has something of Sallust, something of Tacitus, something of Lucian, and something of Voltaire, and his models and imitators. If any one puts these together he will anticipate, and if he reads *Elphin* he will find, a peculiar sort of ironic antithesis in the clauses, and a crisp cadence in the whole sentence. That this may have been partly brought about by an attempt to render, and that it was very successful in rendering, the sententiousness of the Welsh manner is very probable; but it is noticeable, though not to the same extent, in *Maid Marian* and even in *Nightmare Abbey*, where there could have been no such influence or object. And it continued, softened a little from the tension here shown, to mark Peacock till the last. It is not a 'snip-snap' style, and though it is full of epigram, the epigram is not fired off pointblank at the reader with an obvious 'there's one for you' from the writer. It slips easily off the pen, and is accompanied by the best Swiftian or Lucianic absence of insistence and waiting for applause. Further, the descriptive passages, already very good in *Maid Marian*, are even better here; and Peacock has nowhere excelled the departure from Seithenyn's castle and the picture of Caer Lleon. Indeed I do not think it excessive to say that *The Misfortunes of Elphin*, taking it all round, is his best-written book.

It will, however, of course depend on how far the reader can enjoy the austerer kind of irony whether he will enjoy this writing or not, for it cannot be said that *The Misfortunes of Elphin* is a book by any means over-flowing with the milk of human kindness. Peacock's old attacks on the Lakers are indeed mostly dropped (though there is still a laureate who is a parasite and something worse, as in *Maid Marian*), and those on Lord Brougham have scarcely begun. The satire on humanity is more general than personal; but it is severe enough and very little relieved. The characters of the book who are virtuous are not interesting, and those who are interesting cannot by the farthest stretch of imagination or charity be called virtuous. Very sentimental or very rigidly moral persons can hardly be expected to be much in love with the delightful reprobate Seithenyn, who is the pillar and mainstay of the book. It is impossible to defend the conduct of this bibulous prince. He ought not to have neglected the embankment. He ought not, when remonstrated with on the subject, to have indulged in attempts to defend his conduct which were flippant if they were not serious, and painfully sophistical if they were. When the catastrophe had come, his neglect not merely to attempt any atonement for it, but even to ascertain the fate of his daughter and his household, was reprehensible in the highest degree. Although the manners of the time may justify his acceptance of the position of King Ednyfed's butler, they do not excuse the levity with which he transfers his services to the slayer of his master and benefactor. Even the comparatively beneficent part which he plays in the latest scenes, appears to have been dictated partly by the same levity and partly by self-interest; and his unblushing practice in and confession of habitual intoxication cannot but have blunted such very rudimentary principles of honour and honesty as his general conduct shows him to have originally possessed.

But if it is impossible for Propriety to defend Seithenyn, it is equally impossible for Taste and Sense not to regard him with prodigious admiration and affection. From his very first appearance, when he is quite (and the land of Gwaelod very nearly) half seas over, but still in state and dignity, to his very last, when he takes place under Sir Bedivere (but I do not think he followed his chief to Lyonesse), his magnificently apolaostic temperament displays itself in a series of *actes et paroles* equally magnificent. There is no bad blood in Seithenyn, though there may be a certain amount of selfishness; and difficult as it may be to arrange an exact Organon of his peculiar logic, he strikes me as being as good a reasoner as many logicians and others who have attained very high repute in the world, as well as infinitely more amusing. He, quite as well as Friar Michael, might have been the mouthpiece of that famous formula as to 'making a joke of things' which has been quoted in the general Introduction to this series as expressing Peacock's most abiding conviction; and he is never false to his own principles. With what courtesy, combined with what topsy-turviness of argument, does he defend the policy of 'Can't you let it alone,' against the arguments of Elphin and the blunter assertions of Teithrin at his first appearance! 'It was half rotten when I was born, and that is a conclusive reason why it should be three parts rotten when I die' strikes us now (it is the fate of political reasoning) as a caricature not so much of Tory arguments of the kind, which have long ceased to be heard, as of 'progressive' fallacies of another kind; but it is still beautiful. Although the proceeding of leaping into the sea with a drawn sword to stop a flood may not seem from the point of view of common sense and engineering entirely rational, it is heroic, it is logical (for this *was* 'the enemy'), and it is warranted by the example of Marcus (not, as some say, Quintus) Curtius. And when, after many years, we meet Seithenyn again, how admirably true to himself is he ! There is, perhaps, a little less of the absolute quaintness combined with dignity which previously distinguished him ; a butler, even in the days when butlers were sometimes princes, could not be entirely the same in manner as a prince who was the head of an Embankment Commission. It was not necessary for years to bring Seithenyn the philosophic mind, for he had always had it; but they had made his wisdom milder and mellower, while not impairing in the very least the marvellous topsy-turviness of his logic. I still, after years of reading, have been unable, as I was unable ten years ago, to find anything in literature quite so beautiful as his demonstration that he is not dead ; and though you may very frequently hear things not at all unlike it in life, that enhances instead of depreciating its value. I believe that he did kill two or three of the followers of King Melvas. There is no trace of cowardice in Seithenyn ; a coward could not have been guilty, even in words, of the unblushing impudence of the parenthetical reference to King Elphin ('what he is king of you shall tell me at leisure'), considering that the speaker was responsible for the circumscription of Elphin's kingdom. A coward's impudence is never really humorous in this way. Parolles and Bessus and Bobadil we laugh at, not with. Pistol would not have said this ; and though Falstaff might, no person of intelligence now takes Falstaff for a coward. And we should find reasons, if we had space to set them forth, for equal admiration of Seithenyn at Avallon and at Caer Lleon.

I do not remember to have seen it anywhere noticed in connection with the satire on the Tory and especially the Canningite position towards Reform in *Elphin*—satire which is of course chiefly to be found in Seithenyn's defence of the embankment—that it is of a very double-edged nature. The Radicals who were made sore by *Crotchet Castle* must have been rather hasty and short-sighted if they took unmixed delight in this its forerunner by no long time, even though it did on the surface seem to make for them. The invading ocean is quite as susceptible of being taken as a text as the rotten embankment; and the whole tone and gust of the book are exceedingly unlike those of a fervent believer in progress of any kind, for all its gibes at kings and queens, at bishops and archbishops, at high-born hereditary commissioners, at war, at taxation, and so forth.

Something has been said above, though in little more than allusion, of the verse here, which stands of course by itself, being all either imitated or translated from actual Welsh originals. Nothing approaches the 'Dinas Vawr' song, which has a diabolical lightness and swing about it quite unlike anything that is to be found elsewhere. It is probably the succinctest piece of humorous modern poetry in the world: there is not a line, not a word to spare. 'The Circling of the Mead-horns' is a very good drinking song, but inferior, I think, to the less archaic performances of the other novels. The rest, as noted above, must be regarded rather as experiments in the introduction of Welsh poetry to English readers than as independent historical compositions. The best, I think, is Merlin's 'Apple-trees'; but most suffer a little from that singular habit common to all nations in a state of imperfect development, but apparently commonest and lasting longest among Celts, of making verse a medium for things which would be much better said in prose.

Such things, however, can in no case interpose any serious obstacle in reading, because they can be skipped without the slightest difficulty; and they may add an ornament and relish for some tastes. Indeed it is so certain that almost every reader according to his idiosyncrasy will either like

The Misfortunes of Elphin extremely or be quite unable to get on with it, that details of this sort matter very little—much less than in any of the other books. The only thing to fear in the case of a book, still so little read, is that its antique garb may serve to deter some readers who are fit readers from attempting it. Here the office of an introducer comes in with special appropriateness ; and he may without officiousness give his assurance that not the most brand-new modern story in appearance can be freer from anything really out of date than *The Misfortunes of Elphin*. For irony of the true kind never faileth : and this is pure irony.

As the *Misfortunes* by themselves would have been hardly of bulk sufficient for a volume, it has been thought that it might not be disagreeable to readers to have Peacock's longest poem, a verse-novel itself, added to the now complete reissue of his prose novels. *Rhododaphne*, though it has not lacked fit admiration, has never been popular, but it is a very interesting example of that section of the Romantic poetry of the first quarter of this century which was written by men who were not first of all poets. In this section *Rhododaphne* takes very high rank. Peacock's scholarship (a point in which he was far superior to all his great poetical contemporaries, including even Coleridge, as far as exactness is concerned) may have a little 'sicklied o'er' his strictly poetical vein ; and his eighteenth-century peculiarities also appear. But it is an immense advance on his only other long poem, *The Genius of the Thames*, published six years earlier, and we have little difficulty in seeing in it the great contagion of Shelley, in whose company at Marlow Peacock had just (1817) been living. The poem is exactly contemporary with *Nightmare Abbey*, which Shelley had in a very different way also inspired. It is pleasant to read the two together, and to observe how entirely the note of persiflage

is kept out of the poem, how omnipresent it is in the
novel. But this contrast is almost as well presented by the
actual conjunction. It is, of course, only a very superficial
criticism to which irony and sentiment seem incompatible.
But their incompatibility is an inveterate popular error;
and it cannot be quite useless to remind readers from time
to time that no one is less unlikely than the author of a
Rhododaphne to be the author also of a *Misfortunes of
Elphin.*

GEORGE SAINTSBURY.

CONTENTS

THE MISFORTUNES OF ELPHIN

CHAPTER I

THE PROSPERITY OF GWAELOD 3

CHAPTER II

THE DRUNKENNESS OF SEITHENYN . . . 10

CHAPTER III

THE OPPRESSION OF GWENHIDWY . . 16

CHAPTER IV

THE LAMENTATIONS OF GWYTHNO 28

CHAPTER V

THE PRIZE OF THE WEIR . . . 34

CHAPTER VI

THE EDUCATION OF TALIESIN . . . 40

CHAPTER VII

THE HUNTINGS OF MAELGON . . . 51

CHAPTER VIII

PAGE

THE LOVE OF MELANGHEL . 60

CHAPTER IX

THE SONGS OF DIGANWY . . . 65

CHAPTER X

THE DISAPPOINTMENT OF RHÛN . 74

CHAPTER XI

THE HEROES OF DINAS VAWR . 81

CHAPTER XII

THE SPLENDOUR OF CAER LLEON . . 91

CHAPTER XIII

THE GHOSTLINESS OF AVALLON . 98

CHAPTER XIV

THE RIGHT OF MIGHT . . 110

CHAPTER XV

THE CIRCLE OF THE BARDS . . 117

CHAPTER XVI

THE JUDGMENTS OF ARTHUR . . 126

CONTENTS

RHODODAPHNE

	PAGE
PREFACE	135
CANTO I	141
CANTO II	155
CANTO III	169
CANTO IV	183
CANTO V	197
CANTO VI	209
CANTO VII	229
NOTES	257

LIST OF ILLUSTRATIONS

	PAGE
They began their march . . . *Frontispiece*	
He heard, or seemed to hear, words, ' Beware of the oppression of Gwenhidwy '.	7
The cupbearers reeled off with their lord . .	17
' Thus, thus I prove the falsehood ' . . .	25
In the coracle lay a sleeping child, clothed in splendid apparel	36
Initiated him in these mysteries . . .	44
Elphin was impressed into royal favour . . .	50
' Whither lead you, my friend ? My horse can no longer keep his footing '	54
She gave him a supper . . .	57
One of ' the Three Chaste Kisses of the island of Britain ' .	63
Rhûn and his bard returned to the banks of the Mawddach, where they resolved themselves into an ambuscade .	72
The cataracts thunder down the steep . . .	76
The hoarse voice of Teithrin ap Tathral sounded in their ears from without, ' Foxes ! you have been seen through, and you are fairly trapped '	79
' I am the man '	84
' I swore I would not budge from the water unless my two barrels went with me '	87
A face, as round and as red as the setting sun in November, shone forth in the aperture . . .	100
And strikes up, ' I'd be a butterfly ' . . .	103

PAGE

'I will take a simple and single draught of what happens to be here' 108

'Obey the king : first drink, then speak' . . 113

This slap is recorded in the Bardic Triads as one of the Three Fatal Slaps 127

RHODODAPHNE

From Ladon's shores Anthemion came   145

Unconsciously the flower he took   .   152

He stood as if he listened still   .   162

'If round my footsteps dwell unholy sign or evil spell'   .   166

'O maid ! I have another love !'   .   178

'Oh, thou art dead !'   190

And fled o'er plain and steep, with frantic tread, as Passion's aimless impulse led   194

'There sit !'—cried one in rugged tone   202

Anthemion, with the opening day, from deep entrancement on the sands stood up   213

Up that image rose, and spake, as from a trumpet   .   220

Anthemion took the cup, and quaffed   224

'Now art thou mine !'   .   .   227

Those feelings came and passed away, and left him lorn   .   232

They plied, throughout the enchanted hall, their servile ministries   235

Or stalked around the garden-dells in lion-guise   .   238

Satyrs and Fauns would start around .   241

The bath concludes the day .   .   .   244

And lodged in Rhododaphne's breast .   .   .   247

He fell, as falls a wounded bird   .   .   251

And on his lips impressed a kiss   255

Quod non exspectes ex transverso fit,
Et suprà nos Fortuna negotia curat :
Quare da nobis vina Falerna, puer.

Petronius Arbiter.

CHAPTER I

THE PROSPERITY OF GWAELOD

Regardless of the sweeping whirlwind's sway,
That, hush'd in grim repose, expects his evening prey.
GRAY.

IN the beginning of the sixth century, when Uther Pendragon held the nominal sovereignty of Britain over a number of petty kings, Gwythno Garanhir was king of Caredigion. The most valuable portion of his dominions was the Great Plain of Gwaelod, an extensive tract of level land, stretching along that part of the sea-coast which now belongs to the counties of Merioneth and Cardigan. This district was populous and highly cultivated. It contained sixteen fortified towns, superior to all the towns and cities of the Cymry, excepting Caer Lleon upon Usk; and, like Caer Lleon, they bore in their architecture, their language, and their manners, vestiges of past intercourse with the Roman lords of the world. It contained also one of the three privileged ports of the isle of Britain, which was called the Port of Gwythno. This port, we may believe if we please, had not been unknown to the Phoenicians and Carthaginians, when they visited the island for metal, accommodating the inhabitants, in return, with luxuries which they would not otherwise have dreamed of, and which they could very well have done without; of course, in arranging the exchange of what they denominated equivalents, imposing on their simplicity, and taking advantage of their ignorance, according to the approved practice of civilised nations; which they called imparting the blessings of Phoenician and Carthaginian light.

3

An embankment of massy stone protected this lowland country from the sea, which was said, in traditions older than the embankment, to have, in occasional spring-tides, paid short but unwelcome visits to the interior inhabitants, and to have, by slow aggressions, encroached considerably on the land. To prevent the repetition of the first of these inconveniences, and to check the progress of the second, the people of Gwaelod had built the stony rampart, which had withstood the shock of the waves for centuries, when Gwythno began his reign.

Gwythno, like other kings, found the business of governing too light a matter to fill up the vacancy of either his time or his head, and took to the more solid pursuits of harping and singing : not forgetting feasting, in which he was glorious ; nor hunting, wherein he was mighty. His several pursuits composed a very harmonious triad. The chase conduced to the good cheer of the feast, and to the good appetite which consumed it ; the feast inspired the song ; and the song gladdened the feast and celebrated the chase.

Gwythno and his subjects went on together very happily. They had little to do with him but to pay him revenue, and he had little to do with them but to receive it. Now and then they were called on to fight for the protection of his sacred person, and for the privilege of paying revenue to him rather than to any of the kings in his vicinity, a privilege of which they were particularly tenacious. His lands being far more fertile, and his people, consequently, far more numerous, than those of the rocky dwellers on his borders, he was always victorious in the defensive warfare to which he restricted his military achievements ; and, after the invaders of his dominions had received two or three inflictions of signal chastisement, they limited their aggressions to coming quietly in the night, and vanishing before morning with cattle : an heroic operation, in which the pre-eminent glory of Scotland renders the similar exploits of other nations not worth recording.

Gwythno was not fond of the sea : a moonstruck bard had warned him to beware of the oppression of Gwenhidwy ;[1] and he thought he could best do so by keeping as far as possible out of her way. He had a palace built of choice slate stone on the rocky banks of the Mawddach, just above the point

---

[1] *Gwen-hudiw*, ' the white alluring one ' ; the name of a mermaid. Used figuratively for the elemental power of the sea.

where it quitted its native mountains and entered the plain of Gwaelod. Here, among green woods and sparkling waters, he lived in festal munificence, and expended his revenue in encouraging agriculture, by consuming a large quantity of produce.

Watch-towers were erected along the embankment, and watchmen were appointed to guard against the first approaches of damage or decay. The whole of these towers, and their companies of guards, were subordinate to a central castle, which commanded the seaport already mentioned, and wherein dwelt Prince Seithenyn ap Seithyn Saidi, who held the office of Arglwyd Gorwarcheidwad yr Argae Breninawl, which signifies, in English, Lord High Commissioner of Royal Embankment; and he executed it as a personage so denominated might be expected to do : he drank the profits, and left the embankment to his deputies, who left it to their assistants, who left it to itself.

The condition of the head, in a composite as in a simple body, affects the entire organisation to the extremity of the tail, excepting that, as the tail in the figurative body usually receives the largest share in the distribution of punishment, and the smallest in the distribution of reward, it has the stronger stimulus to ward off evil, and the smaller supply of means to indulge in diversion ; and it sometimes happens that one of the least regarded of the component parts of the said tail will, from a pure sense of duty, or an inveterate love of business, or an oppressive sense of ennui, or a development of the organ of order, or some other equally cogent reason, cheerfully undergo all the care and labour, of which the honour and profit will redound to higher quarters.

Such a component portion of the Gwaelod High Commission of Royal Embankment was Teithrin ap Tathral, who had the charge of a watch-tower where the embankment terminated at the point of Mochres, in the high land of Ardudwy. Teithrin kept his portion of the embankment in exemplary condition, and paced with daily care the limits of his charge ; but one day, by some accident, he strayed beyond them, and observed symptoms of neglect that filled him with dismay. This circumstance induced him to proceed till his wanderings brought him round to the embankment's southern termination in the high land of Caredigion. He met with abundant hospitality at the towers of his colleagues, and at the castle of Seithenyn : he was supposed to be walking for his amusement ; he was asked no questions, and he carefully abstained from asking any. He examined and observed in silence ; and, when he had completed his observations, he hastened to the palace of Gwythno.

Preparations were making for a high festival, and Gwythno was composing an ode.   Teithrin knew better than to interrupt him in his *awen*.[1]

Gwythno had a son named Elphin, who is celebrated in history as the most expert of fishers.   Teithrin, finding the king impracticable, went in search of the young prince.

Elphin had been all the morning fishing in the Mawddach, in a spot where the river, having quitted the mountains and not yet entered the plain, ran in alternate streams and pools sparkling through a pastoral valley.   Elphin sat under an ancient ash, enjoying the calm brightness of an autumnal noon, and the melody and beauty of the flying stream, on which the shifting sunbeams fell chequering through the leaves.   The monotonous music of the river, and the profound stillness of the air, had contributed to the deep abstraction of a meditation into which Elphin had fallen.   He was startled into attention by a sudden rush of the wind through the trees, and during the brief interval of transition from the state of reverie to that of perfect consciousness, he heard, or seemed to hear, in the gust that hurried by him, the repetition of the words, ' Beware of the oppression of Gwenhidwy.'   The gust was momentary : the leaves ceased to rustle, and the deep silence of nature returned.

The prophecy, which had long haunted the memory and imagination of his father, had been often repeated to Elphin, and had sometimes occupied his thoughts, but it had formed no part of his recent meditation, and he could not persuade himself that the words had not been actually spoken near him. He emerged from the shade of the trees that fringed the river, and looked round him from the rocky bank.

At this moment Teithrin ap Tathral discovered and approached him.

Elphin knew him not, and inquired his name.   He answered, ' Teithrin ap Tathral.'

----

[1] The rapturous and abstracted state of poetical inspiration.

He heard, or seemed to hear, words, ' Beware of the oppression of Gwenhidwy.'

'And what seek you here?' said Elphin.

'I seek,' answered Teithrin, 'the Prince of Gwaelod, Elphin ap Gwythno Garanhir.'

'You spoke,' said Elphin, 'as you approached.' Teithrin answered in the negative.

'Assuredly you did,' said Elphin. 'You repeated the words, "Beware of the oppression of Gwenhidwy."'

Teithrin denied having spoken the words; but their mysterious impression made Elphin listen readily to his information and advice; and the result of their conference was a determination, on the part of the Prince, to accompany Teithrin ap Tathral on a visit of remonstrance to the Lord High Commissioner.

They crossed the centre of the enclosed country to the privileged Port of Gwythno, near which stood the castle of Seithenyn. They walked towards the castle along a portion of the embankment, and Teithrin pointed out to the Prince its dilapidated condition. The sea shone with the glory of the setting sun; the air was calm; and the white surf, tinged with the crimson of sunset, broke lightly on the sands below. Elphin turned his eyes from the dazzling splendour of ocean to the green meadows of the Plain of Gwaelod; the trees, that in the distance thickened into woods; the wreaths of smoke rising from among them, marking the solitary cottages, or the populous towns; the massy barrier of mountains beyond, with the forest rising from their base; the precipices frowning over the forest; and the clouds resting on their summits, reddened with the reflection of the west. Elphin gazed earnestly on the peopled plain, reposing in the calm of evening between the mountains and the sea, and thought, with deep feelings of secret pain, how much of life and human happiness was entrusted to the ruinous mound on which he stood.

CHAPTER II

THE DRUNKENNESS OF SEITHENYN

The three immortal drunkards of the isle of Britain : Ceraint of Essyllwg ;
Gwrtheyrn Gwrthenau ; and Seithenyn ap Seithyn Saidi.—TRIADS
OF THE ISLE OF BRITAIN.

THE sun had sunk beneath the waves when they reached the castle of Seithenyn. The sound of the harp and the song saluted them as they approached it. As they entered the great hall, which was already blazing with torchlight, they found his highness, and his highness's household, convincing themselves and each other, with wine and wassail, of the excellence of their system of virtual superintendence ; and the following jovial chorus broke on the ears of the visitors :

THE CIRCLING OF THE MEAD HORNS

Fill the blue horn, the blue buffalo horn .
Natural is mead in the buffalo horn :
As the cuckoo in spring, as the lark in the morn,
So natural is mead in the buffalo horn.

As the cup of the flower to the bee when he sips,
Is the full cup of mead to the true Briton's lips :
From the flower-cups of summer, on field and on tree,
Our mead cups are filled by the vintager bee.

Seithenyn [1] ap Seithyn, the generous, the bold,
Drinks the wine of the stranger from vessels of gold ; [2]
But we from the horn, the blue silver-rimmed horn,
Drink the ale and the mead in our fields that were born.

---

[1] The accent is on the second syllable : Seithényn.
[2] Gwin . . . o cur . . . ANEURIN.

The ale-froth is white, and the mead sparkles bright;
They both smile apart, and with smiles they unite : [1]
The mead from the flower, and the ale from the corn,
Smile, sparkle, and sing in the buffalo horn.

The horn, the blue horn, cannot stand on its tip;
Its path is right on from the hand to the lip :
Though the bowl and the wine-cup our tables adorn,
More natural the draught from the buffalo horn.

But Seithenyn ap Seithyn, the generous, the bold,
Drinks the bright-flowing wine from the far-gleaming gold :
The wine, in the bowl by his lip that is worn,
Shall be glorious as mead in the buffalo horn.

The horns circle fast, but their fountains will last,
As the stream passes ever, and never is past :
Exhausted so quickly, replenished so soon,
They wax and they wane like the horns of the moon.

Fill high the blue horn, the blue buffalo horn ;
Fill high the long silver-rimmed buffalo horn :
While the roof of the hall by our chorus is torn,
Fill, fill to the brim, the deep silver-rimmed horn.

Elphin and Teithrin stood some time on the floor of the
hall before they attracted the attention of Seithenyn, who,
during the chorus, was tossing and flourishing his golden
goblet. The chorus had scarcely ended when he noticed them,
and immediately roared aloud, 'You are welcome all four.'

Elphin answered, 'We thank you : we are but two.'

'Two or four,' said Seithenyn, 'all is one. You are welcome
all. When a stranger enters, the custom in other places is to
begin by washing his feet. My custom is, to begin by washing
his throat. Seithenyn ap Seithyn Saidi bids you welcome.'

Elphin, taking the wine-cup, answered, 'Elphin ap Gwythno
Garanhir thanks you.'

Seithenyn started up. He endeavoured to straighten himself into perpendicularity, and to stand steadily on his legs.
He accomplished half his object by stiffening all his joints but
those of his ankles, and from these the rest of his body vibrated
upwards with the inflexibility of a bar. After thus oscillating

---

[1] The mixture of ale and mead made *bradawd*, a favourite drink of the
Ancient Britons.

for a time, like an inverted pendulum, finding that the attention requisite to preserve his rigidity absorbed all he could collect of his dissipated energies, and that he required a portion of them for the management of his voice, which he felt a dizzy desire to wield with peculiar steadiness in the presence of the son of the king, he suddenly relaxed the muscles that perform the operation of sitting, and dropped into his chair like a plummet. He then, with a gracious gesticulation, invited Prince Elphin to take his seat on his right hand, and proceeded to compose himself into a dignified attitude, throwing his body back into the left corner of his chair, resting his left elbow on its arm and his left cheekbone on the middle of the back of his left hand, placing his left foot on a footstool, and stretching out his right leg as straight and as far as his position allowed. He had thus his right hand at liberty, for the ornament of his eloquence and the conduct of his liquor.

Elphin seated himself at the right hand of Seithenyn. Teithrin remained at the end of the hall : on which Seithenyn exclaimed, 'Come on, man, come on. What, if you be not the son of a king, you are the guest of Seithenyn ap Seithyn Saidi. The most honourable place to the most honourable guest, and the next most honourable place to the next most honourable guest ; the least honourable guest above the most honourable inmate ; and, where there are but two guests, be the most honourable who he may, the least honourable of the two is next in honour to the most honourable of the two, because they are no more but two ; and, where there are only two, there can be nothing between. Therefore sit, and drink. GWIN O EUR : wine from gold.'

Elphin motioned Teithrin to approach, and sit next to him.

Prince Seithenyn, whose liquor was 'his eating and his drinking solely,' seemed to measure the gastronomy of his guests by his own ; but his groom of the pantry thought the strangers might be disposed to eat, and placed before them a choice of provision, on which Teithrin ap Tathral did vigorous execution.

'I pray your excuses,' said Seithenyn, 'my stomach is weak, and I am subject to dizziness in the head, and my memory is not so good as it was, and my faculties of attention are somewhat impaired, and I would dilate more upon the topic, whereby you should hold me excused, but I am troubled with a feverishness and parching of the mouth, that very much injures my speech, and impedes my saying all I would say, and will say before I have done, in token of my loyalty and fealty to your highness and your highness's house. I must just moisten my lips, and I will then proceed with my observations. Cupbearer, fill.'

'Prince Seithenyn,' said Elphin, ' I have visited you on a subject of deep moment. Reports have been brought to me, that the embankment, which has been so long entrusted to your care, is in a state of dangerous decay.'

'Decay,' said Seithenyn, 'is one thing, and danger is another. Everything that is old must decay. That the embankment is old, I am free to confess; that it is somewhat rotten in parts, I will not altogether deny; that it is any the worse for that, I do most sturdily gainsay. It does its business well : it works well : it keeps out the water from the land, and it lets in the wine upon the High Commission of Embankment. Cupbearer, fill. Our ancestors were wiser than we : they built it in their wisdom ; and, if we should be so rash as to try to mend it, we should only mar it.'

'The stonework,' said Teithrin, 'is sapped and mined : the piles are rotten, broken, and dislocated : the floodgates and sluices are leaky and creaky.'

'That is the beauty of it,' said Seithenyn. 'Some parts of it are rotten, and some parts of it are sound.'

'It is well,' said Elphin, 'that some parts are sound : it were better that all were so.'

'So I have heard some people say before,' said Seithenyn ; 'perverse people, blind to venerable antiquity : that very unamiable sort of people who are in the habit of indulging their reason. But I say, the parts that are rotten give elasticity to those that are sound : they give them elasticity, elasticity, elasticity. If it were all sound, it would break by its own obstinate stiffness : the soundness is checked by the rottenness, and the stiffness is balanced by the elasticity. There is nothing so dangerous as innovation. See the waves in the equinoctial storms, dashing and clashing, roaring and pouring, spattering and battering, rattling and battling against it. I would not be so presumptuous as to say, I could build anything that would stand against them half an hour ; and here this immortal old work, which God forbid the finger of modern mason should bring into jeopardy, this immortal work has stood for centuries, and will stand for centuries more, if we let it alone. It is well : it works well : let well alone. Cupbearer, fill. It was half rotten when I was born, and that is a conclusive reason why it should be three parts rotten when I die.'

The whole body of the High Commission roared approbation.

'And after all,' said Seithenyn, 'the worst that could happen would be the overflow of a spring-tide, for that was the worst that happened before the embankment was thought of; and, if the high water should come in, as it did before, the low water would go out again, as it did before. We should be no deeper in it than our ancestors were, and we could mend as easily as they could make.'

'The level of the sea,' said Teithrin, 'is materially altered.

'The level of the sea!' exclaimed Seithenyn. 'Who ever heard of such a thing as altering the level of the sea? Alter the level of that bowl of wine before you, in which, as I sit here, I see a very ugly reflection of your very good-looking face. Alter the level of that : drink up the reflection : let me see the face without the reflection, and leave the sea to level itself.'

'Not to level the embankment,' said Teithrin.

'Good, very good,' said Seithenyn. 'I love a smart saying, though it hits at me. But, whether yours is a smart saying or no, I do not very clearly see ; and, whether it hits at me or no, I do not very sensibly feel. But all is one. Cupbearer, fill.'

'I think,' pursued Seithenyn, looking as intently as he could at Teithrin ap Tathral, 'I have seen something very like you before. There was a fellow here the other day very like you : he stayed here some time : he would not talk : he did nothing but drink : he used to drink till he could not stand, and then he went walking about the embankment. I suppose he thought it wanted mending ; but he did not say anything. If he had, I should have told him to embank his own throat, to keep the liquor out of that. That would have posed him : he could not have answered that : he would not have had a word to say for himself after that.'

'He must have been a miraculous person,' said Teithrin, 'to walk when he could not stand.'

'All is one for that,' said Seithenyn. 'Cupbearer, fill.'

'Prince Seithenyn,' said Elphin, 'if I were not aware that wine speaks in the silence of reason, I should be astonished at your strange vindication of your neglect of duty, which I take shame to myself for not having sooner known and remedied. The wise bard has well observed, "Nothing is done without the eye of the king."'

'I am very sorry,' said Seithenyn, 'that you see things in a wrong light ; but we will not quarrel for three reasons : first, because you are the son of the king, and may do and say what you please, without any one having a right to be displeased : second, because I never quarrel with a guest, even if he grows riotous in his cups : third, because there is nothing to quarrel about ; and perhaps that is the best reason of the three ; or rather the first is the best, because you are the son of the king ; and the third is the second, that is, the second best, because there is nothing to quarrel about ; and the second is nothing to the purpose, because, though guests will grow riotous in their cups, in spite of my good orderly example, God forbid I should say, that is the case with you. And I completely agree in the truth of your remark, that reason speaks in the silence of wine.'

Seithenyn accompanied his speech with a vehement swinging of his right hand : in so doing, at this point, he dropped his cup : a sudden impulse of rash volition, to pick it dexterously up before he resumed his discourse, ruined all his devices for maintaining dignity ; in stooping forward from his chair, he lost his balance, and fell prostrate on the floor.

The whole body of the High Commission arose in simultaneous confusion, each zealous to be the foremost in uplifting his fallen chief. In the vehemence of their uprise, they hurled the benches backward and the tables forward ; the crash of cups and bowls accompanied their overthrow ; and rivulets of liquor ran gurgling through the hall. The household wished to redeem the credit of their leader in the eyes of the Prince ; but the only service they could render him was to participate his discomfiture ; for Seithenyn, as he was first in dignity, was also, as was fitting, hardest in skull ; and that which had impaired his equilibrium had utterly destroyed theirs. Some fell, in the first impulse, with the tables and benches ; others were tripped up by the rolling bowls ; and the remainder fell at different points of progression, by jostling against each other, or stumbling over those who had fallen before them.

CHAPTER III

> Nid meddw y dyn a allo
> Cwnu ei hun a rhodio,
> Ac yved rhagor ddiawd :
> Nid yw hyny yn veddwdawd.

> Not drunk is he, who from the floor
> Can rise alone, and still drink more ;
> But drunk is he, who prostrate lies,
> Without the power to drink or rise.

A SIDE door, at the upper end of the hall, to the left of Seithenyn's chair, opened, and a beautiful young girl entered the hall, with her domestic bard, and her attendant maidens.

It was Angharad, the daughter of Seithenyn. The tumult had drawn her from the solitude of her chamber, apprehensive that some evil might befall her father in that incapability of self-protection to which he made a point of bringing himself by set of sun. She gracefully saluted Prince Elphin, and directed the cupbearers (who were bound, by their office, to remain half sober till the rest of the company were finished off, after which they indemnified themselves at leisure), she directed the cupbearers to lift up Prince Seithenyn, and bear him from the hall. The cupbearers reeled off with their lord, who had already fallen asleep, and who now began to play them a pleasant march with his nose, to inspirit their progression.

Elphin gazed with delight on the beautiful apparition, whose gentle and serious loveliness contrasted so strikingly with the broken trophies and fallen heroes of revelry that lay scattered at her feet.

16

The cupbearers reeled off with their lord.

'Stranger,' she said, 'this seems an unfitting place for you : let me conduct you where you will be more agreeably lodged.'

'Still less should I deem it fitting for you, fair maiden,' said Elphin.

She answered, 'The pleasure of her father is the duty of Angharad.'

Elphin was desirous to protract the conversation, and this very desire took from him the power of speaking to the purpose. He paused for a moment to collect his ideas, and Angharad stood still, in apparent expectation that he would show symptoms of following, in compliance with her invitation.

In this interval of silence, he heard the loud dashing of the sea, and the blustering of the wind through the apertures of the walls.

This supplied him with what has been, since Britain was Britain, the alpha and omega of British conversation. He said, 'It seems a stormy night.'

She answered, 'We are used to storms : we are far from the mountains, between the lowlands and the sea, and the winds blow round us from all quarters.'

There was another pause of deep silence. The noise of the sea was louder, and the gusts pealed like thunder through the apertures. Amidst the fallen and sleeping revellers, the confused and littered hall, the low and wavering torches, Angharad, lovely always, shone with single and surpassing loveliness. The gust died away in murmurs, and swelled again into thunder, and died away in murmurs again ; and, as it died away, mixed with the murmurs of ocean, a voice, that seemed one of the many voices of the wind, pronounced the ominous words, 'Beware of the oppression of Gwenhidwy.'

They looked at each other, as if questioning whether all had heard alike.

'Did you not hear a voice ?' said Angharad, after a pause.

'The same,' said Elphin, 'which has once before seemed to say to me, "Beware of the oppression of Gwenhidwy."'

Teithrin hurried forth on the rampart : Angharad turned pale, and leaned against a pillar of the hall. Elphin was amazed and awed, absorbed as his feelings were in her. The sleepers on the floor made an uneasy movement, and uttered an inarticulate cry.

Teithrin returned. 'What saw you ?' said Elphin.

Teithrin answered, 'A tempest is coming from the west, The moon has waned three days, and is half hidden in clouds, just visible above the mountains : the bank of clouds is black in the west ; the scud is flying before them ; and the white waves are rolling to the shore.'

'This is the highest of the spring-tides,' said Angharad, 'and they are very terrible in the storms from the west, when the spray flies over the embankment, and the breakers shake the tower which has its foot in the surf.'

'Whence was the voice,' said Elphin, 'which we heard erewhile ?   Was it the cry of a sleeper in his drink, or an error of the fancy, or a warning voice from the elements ? '

' It was surely nothing earthly,' said Angharad, 'nor was it an error of the fancy, for we all heard the words, " Beware of the oppression of Gwenhidwy."   Often and often, in the storms of the spring-tides, have I feared to see her roll her power over the fields of Gwaelod.'

' Pray heaven she do not to-night,' said Teithrin.

' Can there be such a danger ? ' said Elphin.

' I think,' said Teithrin, ' of the decay I have seen, and I fear the voice I have heard.'

A long pause of deep silence ensued, during which they heard the intermitting peals of the wind, and the increasing sound of the rising sea, swelling progressively into wilder and more menacing tumult, till, with one terrific impulse, the whole violence of the equinoctial tempest seemed to burst upon the shore.   It was one of those tempests which occur once in several centuries, and which, by their extensive devastations, are chronicled to eternity ; for a storm that signalises its course with extraordinary destruction, becomes as worthy of celebration as a hero for the same reason.   The old bard seemed to be of this opinion ; for the turmoil which appalled Elphin, and terrified Angharad, fell upon his ears as the sound of inspiration : the *awen* came upon him ; and, seizing his harp, he mingled his voice and his music with the uproar of the elements :

THE SONG OF THE FOUR WINDS[1]

Wind from the north : the young spring day
Is pleasant on the sunny mead ;

---

[1] This poem is a specimen of a numerous class of ancient Welsh poems, in which each stanza begins with a repetition of the predominant idea,

THE OPPRESSION OF GWENHIDWY

The merry harps at evening play ;
The dance gay youths and maidens lead :
The thrush makes chorus from the thorn :
The mighty drinker fills his horn.

Wind from the east : the shore is still ;
The mountain-clouds fly tow'rds the sea ;
The ice is on the winter-rill ;
The great hall fire is blazing free :
The prince's circling feast is spread :
Drink fills with fumes the brainless head.

Wind from the south : in summer shade
'Tis sweet to hear the loud harp ring ;
Sweet is the step of comely maid,
Who to the bard a cup doth bring :
The black crow flies where carrion lies :
Where pig-nuts lurk, the swine will work.

Wind from the west : the autumnal deep
Rolls on the shore its billowy pride :
He, who the rampart's watch must keep,
Will mark with awe the rising tide :
The high spring-tide, that bursts its mound,
May roll o'er miles of level ground.

Wind from the west : the mighty wave
Of ocean bounds o'er rock and sand ;
The foaming surges roar and rave
Against the bulwarks of the land :
When waves are rough, and winds are high,
Good is the land that's high and dry.

Wind from the west : the storm-clouds rise ;
The breakers rave ; the whirl-blasts roar,
The mingled rage of seas and skies
Bursts on the low and lonely shore :
When safety's far, and danger nigh,
Swift feet the readiest aid supply.

Wind from the west——

---

and terminates with a proverb, more or less applicable to the subject. In some poems, the sequence of the main images is regular and connected, and the proverbial terminations strictly appropriate ; in others, the sequency of the main images is loose and incoherent, and the proverbial termination has little or nothing to do with the subject of the stanza. The basis of the poem in the text is in the Englynion of Llwyarch Hên.

His song was cut short by a tremendous crash. The tower, which had its foot in the sea, had long been sapped by the waves ; the storm had prematurely perfected the operation, and the tower fell into the surf, carrying with it a portion of the wall of the main building, and revealing, through the chasm, the white raging of the breakers beneath the blackness of the midnight storm. The wind rushed into the hall, extinguishing the torches within the line of its course, tossing the grey locks and loose mantle of the bard, and the light white drapery and long black tresses of Angharad. With the crash of the falling tower, and the simultaneous shriek of the women, the sleepers started from the floor, staring with drunken amazement ; and, shortly after, reeling like an Indian from the wine-rolling Hydaspes,[1] in staggered Seithenyn ap Seithyn.

Seithenyn leaned against a pillar, and stared at the sea through the rifted wall, with wild and vacant surprise. He perceived that there was an innovation, and he felt that he was injured : how, or by whom, he did not quite so clearly discern. He looked at Elphin and Teithrin, at his daughter, and at the members of his household, with a long and dismal aspect of blank and mute interrogation, modified by the struggling consciousness of puzzled self-importance, which seemed to require from his chiefship some word of command in this incomprehensible emergency. But the longer he looked, the less clearly he saw ; and the longer he pondered, the less he understood. He felt the rush of the wind ; he saw the white foam of the sea ; his ears were dizzy with their mingled roar. He remained at length motionless, leaning against the pillar, and gazing on the breakers with fixed and glaring vacancy.

‘ The sleepers of Gwaelod,’ said Elphin, ‘ they who sleep in peace and security, trusting to the vigilance of Seithenyn, what will become of them ? ’

‘ Warn them with the beacon fire,’ said Teithrin, ‘ if there be fuel on the summit of the landward tower.’

‘ That of course has been neglected too,’ said Elphin.

‘ Not so,’ said Angharad, ‘ that has been my charge.’

[1] In the fourteenth and fifteenth books of the *Dionysiaca* of Nonnus, Bacchus changes the river Astacis into wine ; and the multitudinous army of water-drinking Indians, proceeding to quench their thirst in the stream, become franticly drunk, and fall an easy prey to the Bacchic invaders. In the thirty-fifth book, the experiment is repeated on the Hydaspes. ‘ *Ainsi conquesta Bacchus l'Inde,*’ as Rabelais has it.

Teithrin seized a torch, and ascended the eastern tower, and, in a few minutes, the party in the hall beheld the breakers reddening with the reflected fire, and deeper and yet deeper crimson tinging the whirling foam, and sheeting the massy darkness of the bursting waves.

Seithenyn turned his eyes on Elphin. His recollection of him was extremely faint, and the longer he looked on him he remembered him the less. He was conscious of the presence of strangers, and of the occurrence of some signal mischief, and associated the two circumstances in his dizzy perceptions with a confused but close connection. He said at length, looking sternly at Elphin, 'I do not know what right the wind has to blow upon me here; nor what business the sea has to show itself here; nor what business you have here: but one thing is very evident, that either my castle or the sea is on fire; and I shall be glad to know who has done it, for terrible shall be the vengeance of Seithenyn ap Seithyn. Show me the enemy,' he pursued, drawing his sword furiously, and flourishing it over his head, 'Show me the enemy; show me the enemy.'

An unusual tumult mingled with the roar of the waves; a sound, the same in kind, but greater in degree, with that produced by the loose stones of the beach, which are rolled to and fro by the surf.

Teithrin rushed into the hall, exclaiming, 'All is over! the mound is broken; and the spring-tide is rolling through the breach.'

Another portion of the castle wall fell into the mining waves, and, by the dim and thickly-clouded moonlight, and the red blaze of the beacon fire, they beheld a torrent pouring in from the sea upon the plain, and rushing immediately beneath the castle walls, which, as well as the points of the embankment that formed the sides of the breach, continued to crumble away into the waters.

'Who has done this?' vociferated Seithenyn. 'Show me the enemy.'

'There is no enemy but the sea,' said Elphin, 'to which you, in your drunken madness, have abandoned the land. Think, if you can think, of what is passing in the plain. The storm drowns the cries of your victims; but the curses of the perishing are upon you.'

'Show me the enemy,' vociferated Seithenyn, flourishing his sword more furiously.

Angharad looked deprecatingly at Elphin, who abstained from further reply.

'There is no enemy but the sea,' said Teithrin, 'against which your sword avails not.'

'Who dares to say so?' said Seithenyn. 'Who dares to say that there is an enemy on earth against whom the sword of Seithenyn ap Seithyn is unavailing? Thus, thus I prove the falsehood.'

And, springing suddenly forward, he leaped into the torrent, flourishing his sword as he descended.

'Oh, my unhappy father!' sobbed Angharad, veiling her face with her arm on the shoulder of one of her female attendants, whom Elphin dexterously put aside, and substituted himself as the supporter of the desolate beauty.

'We must quit the castle,' said Teithrin, 'or we shall be buried in its ruins. We have but one path of safety, along the summit of the embankment, if there be not another breach between us and the high land, and if we can keep our footing in this hurricane. But there is no alternative. The walls are melting away like snow.'

The bard, who was now recovered from his *awen*, and beginning to be perfectly alive to his own personal safety, conscious at the same time that the first duty of his privileged order was to animate the less gifted multitude by examples of right conduct in trying emergencies, was the first to profit by Teithrin's admonition, and to make the best of his way through the door that opened to the embankment, on which he had no sooner set his foot than he was blown down by the wind, his harp-strings ringing as he fell. He was indebted to the impediment of his harp for not being rolled down the mound into the waters which were rising within.

Teithrin picked him up, and admonished him to abandon his harp to its fate, and fortify his steps with a spear. The bard murmured objections: and even the reflection that he could more easily get another harp than another life, did not reconcile him to parting with his beloved companion. He got over the difficulty by slinging his harp, cumbrous as it was, to his left side, and taking a spear in his right hand.

Angharad, recovering from the first shock of Seithenyn's

'*Thus, thus I prove the falsehood.*'

catastrophe, became awake to the imminent danger. The spirit of the Cymric female, vigilant and energetic in peril, disposed her and her attendant maidens to use their best exertions for their own preservation. Following the advice and example of Elphin and Teithrin, they armed themselves with spears, which they took down from the walls.

Teithrin led the way, striking the point of his spear firmly into the earth, and leaning from it on the wind: Angharad followed in the same manner: Elphin followed Angharad, looking as earnestly to her safety as was compatible with moderate care of his own: the attendant maidens followed Elphin; and the bard, whom the result of his first experiment had rendered unambitious of the van, followed the female train. Behind them went the cupbearers, whom the accident of sobriety had qualified to march: and behind them reeled and roared those of the bacchanal rout who were able and willing to move; those more especially who had wives or daughters to support their tottering steps. Some were incapable of locomotion, and others, in the heroic madness of liquor, sat down to await their destiny, as they finished the half-drained vessels.

The bard, who had somewhat of a picturesque eye, could not help sparing a little leisure from the care of his body, to observe the effects before him: the volumed blackness of the storm; the white bursting of the breakers in the faint and scarcely perceptible moonlight; the rushing and rising of the waters within the mound; the long floating hair and waving drapery of the young women; the red light of the beacon fire falling on them from behind; the surf rolling up the side of the embankment, and breaking almost at their feet; the spray flying above their heads; and the resolution with which they impinged the stony ground with their spears, and bore themselves up against the wind.

Thus they began their march. They had not proceeded far, when the tide began to recede, the wind to abate somewhat of its violence, and the moon to look on them at intervals through the rifted clouds, disclosing the desolation of the inundated plain, silvering the tumultuous surf, gleaming on the distant mountains, and revealing a lengthened prospect of their solitary path, that lay in its irregular line like a ribbon on the deep.

CHAPTER IV

THE LAMENTATIONS OF GWYTHNO

οὐ παύσομαι τὰς Χάριτας
Μούσαις συγκαταμιγνύς,
ἡδίσταν συζυγίαν.
EURIPIDES.

Not, though grief my age defaces,
Will I cease, in concert dear,
Blending still the gentle graces
With the muses more severe.

KING GWYTHNO had feasted joyously, and had sung his new
ode to a chosen party of his admiring subjects, amidst their,
of course, enthusiastic applause. He heard the storm raging
without, as he laid himself down to rest : he thought it a very
hard case for those who were out in it, especially on the sea ;
congratulated himself on his own much more comfortable
condition ; and went to sleep with a pious reflection on the
goodness of Providence to himself.

He was roused from a pleasant dream by a confused and
tumultuous dissonance, that mingled with the roar of the
tempest. Rising with much reluctance, and looking forth from
his window, he beheld in the moonlight a half-naked multitude,
larger than his palace thrice multiplied could have contained,
pressing round the gates, and clamouring for admission and
shelter ; while beyond them his eye fell on the phenomenon
of stormy waters, rolling in the place of the fertile fields from
which he derived his revenue.

Gwythno, though a king and his own laureate, was not
without sympathy for the people who had the honour and
happiness of victualling his royal house, and he issued forth on

28

his balcony full of perplexities and alarms, stunned by the sudden sense of the half-understood calamity, and his head still dizzy from the effects of abruptly-broken sleep, and the vapours of the overnight's glorious festival.

Gwythno was altogether a reasonably good sort of person, and a poet of some note. His people were somewhat proud of him on the latter score, and very fond of him on the former; for even the tenth part of those homely virtues, that decorate the memories of 'husbands kind and fathers dear' in every churchyard, are matters of plebeian admiration in the persons of royalty; and every tangible point in every such virtue so located, becomes a convenient peg for the suspension of love and loyalty. While, therefore, they were unanimous in consigning the soul of Seithenyn to a place that no well-bred divine will name to a polite congregation, they overflowed, in the abundance of their own griefs, with a portion of sympathy for Gwythno, and saluted him, as he issued forth on his balcony, with a hearty *Duw cadw y Brenin*, or God save the King, which he returned with a benevolent wave of the hand; but they followed it up by an intense vociferation for food and lodging, which he received with a pitiful shake of the head.

Meanwhile the morning dawned: the green spots, that peered with the ebbing tide above the waste of waters, only served to indicate the irremediableness of the general desolation.

Gywthno proceeded to hold a conference with his people, as deliberately as the stormy state of the weather and their minds, and the confusion of his own, would permit. The result of the conference was, that they should use their best exertions to catch some stray beeves, which had escaped the inundation, and were lowing about the rocks in search of new pastures. This measure was carried into immediate effect: the victims were killed and roasted, carved, distributed, and eaten, in a very Homeric fashion, and washed down with a large portion of the contents of the royal cellars; after which, having more leisure to dwell on their losses, the fugitives of Gwaelod proceeded to make loud lamentation, all collectively for home and for country, and severally for wife or husband, parent or child, whom the flood had made its victims.

In the midst of these lamentations arrived Elphin and Angharad, with her bard and attendant maidens, and Teithrin ap Tathral. Gwythno, after a consultation, despatched Teithrin and Angharad's domestic bard on an embassy to the court of Uther Pendragon, and to such of the smaller kings as lay in the way, to solicit such relief as their several majesties might be able and willing to afford to a king in distress. It is said that the bard, finding a royal bardship vacant in a more prosperous court, made the most of himself in the market, and stayed where he was better fed and lodged than he could expect to be in Caredigion ; but that Teithrin returned, with many valuable gifts, and most especially one from Merlin, being a hamper, which multiplied an hundredfold by morning whatever was put into it overnight, so that, for a ham and a flask put by in the evening, an hundred hams and an hundred flasks were taken out in the morning. It is at least certain that such a hamper is enumerated among the thirteen wonders of Merlin's art, and, in the authentic catalogue thereof, is called the Hamper of Gwythno.

Be this as it may, Gwythno, though shorn of the beams of his revenue, kept possession of his palace. Elphin married Angharad, and built a salmon-weir on the Mawddach, the produce of which, with that of a series of beehives, of which his princess and her maidens made mead, constituted for some time the principal wealth and subsistence of the royal family of Caredigion.

King Gwythno, while his son was delving or fishing, and his daughter spinning or making mead, sat all day on the rocks, with his harp between his knees, watching the rolling of ocean over the locality of his past dominion, and pouring forth his soul in pathetic song on the change of his own condition, and the mutability of human things. Two of his songs of lamentation have been preserved by tradition : they are the only relics of his muse which time has spared.

GWYDDNAU EI CANT

PAN DDOAI Y MOR DROS CANTREV Y GWAELAWD

A SONG OF GWYTHNO GARANHIR

ON THE INUNDATION OF THE SEA OVER THE PLAIN OF GWAELOD

Stand forth, Seithenyn : winds are high :
Look down beneath the lowering sky ;

THE LAMENTATIONS OF GWYTHNO

Look from the rock : what meets thy sight ?
Nought but the breakers rolling white.

Stand forth, Seithenyn : winds are still :
Look from the rock and heathy hill
For Gwythno's realm : what meets thy view ?
Nought but the ocean's desert blue.

Curst be the treacherous mound, that gave
A passage to the mining wave :
Curst be the cup, with mead-froth crowned,
That charmed from thought the trusted mound.

A tumult, and a cry to heaven !
The white surf breaks ; the mound is riven :
Through the wide rift the ocean-spring
Bursts with tumultuous ravaging.

The western ocean's stormy might
Is curling o'er the rampart's height :
Destruction strikes with want and scorn
Presumption, from abundance born.

The tumult of the western deep
Is on the winds, affrighting sleep :
It thunders at my chamber-door ;
It bids me wake, to sleep no more.

The tumult of the midnight sea
Swells inland, wildly, fearfully :
The mountain-caves respond its shocks
Among the unaccustomed rocks.

The tumult of the vext sea-coast
Rolls inland like an armed host :
It leaves, for flocks and fertile land,
But foaming waves and treacherous sand.

The wild sea rolls where long have been
Glad homes of men, and pastures green :
To arrogance and wealth succeed
Wide ruin and avenging need.

Seithenyn, come : I call in vain :
The high of birth and weak of brain
Sleeps under ocean's lonely roar
Between the rampart and the shore.

The eternal waste of waters, spread
Above his unrespected head,
The blue expanse, with foam besprent,
Is his too glorious monument.

ANOTHER SONG OF GWYTHNO

I love the green and tranquil shore ;
I hate the ocean's dizzy roar,
Whose devastating spray has flown
High o'er the monarch's barrier-stone.

Sad was the feast, which he who spread
Is numbered with the inglorious dead ;
The feast within the torchlit hall,
While stormy breakers mined the wall.

To him repentance came too late :
In cups the chatterer met his fate :
Sudden and sad the doom that burst
On him and me, but mine the worst.

I love the shore, and hate the deep :
The wave has robbed my nights of sleep :
The heart of man is cheered by wine ;
But now the wine-cup cheers not mine.

The feast, which bounteous hands dispense,
Makes glad the soul, and charms the sense :
But in the circling feast I know
The coming of my deadliest foe.

Blest be the rock, whose foot supplied
A step to them that fled the tide ;
The rock of bards, on whose rude steep
I bless the shore, and hate the deep.

' The sigh of Gwythno Garanhir when the breakers ploughed
up his land '[1] is the substance of a proverbial distich, which
may still be heard on the coast of Merioneth and Cardigan, to
express the sense of an overwhelming calamity.   The curious
investigator may still land on a portion of the ancient stony
rampart ; which stretches, off the point of Mochres, far out
into Cardigan Bay, nine miles of the summit being left dry,

---

[1] Ochenaid Gwyddnau Garanhir
    Pan droes y don dros ei dir.

in calm weather, by the low water of the spring-tides ; and
which is now called Sarn Badrig, or St. Patrick's Causeway.

Thus the kingdom of Caredigion fell into ruin : its people
were destroyed, or turned out of house and home ; and its
royal family were brought to a condition in which they found
it difficult to get loaves to their fishes.   We, who live in more
enlightened times, amidst the 'gigantic strides of intellect,'
when offices of public trust are so conscientiously and zealously
discharged, and so vigilantly checked and superintended, may
wonder at the wicked negligence of Seithenyn ; at the sophisms
with which, in his liquor, he vindicated his system, and pronounced the eulogium of his old dilapidations, and at the blind
confidence of Gwythno and his people in this virtual guardian
of their lives and property : happy that our own public
guardians are too virtuous to act or talk like Seithenyn, and
that we ourselves are too wise not to perceive, and too free not
to prevent it, if they should be so disposed.

CHAPTER V

Weave a circle round him thrice,
And close your eyes with holy dread;
For he on honey-dew hath fed,
And drank the milk of paradise.
COLERIDGE.

PRINCE ELPHIN constructed his salmon-weir on the Mawddach at the point where the fresh water met the top of the spring-tides. He built near it a dwelling for himself and Angharad, for which the old king Gwythno gradually deserted his palace. An amphitheatre of rocky mountains enclosed a pastoral valley. The meadows gave pasture to a few cows; and the flowers of the mountain-heath yielded store of honey to the bees of many hives, which were tended by Angharad and her handmaids. Elphin had also some sheep, which wandered on the mountains. The worst was, they often wandered out of reach; but, when he could not find his sheep, he brought down a wild goat, the venison of Gwyneth. The woods and turbaries supplied unlimited fuel. The straggling cultivators who had escaped from the desolation of Gwaelod, and settled themselves above the level of the sea, on a few spots propitious to the plough, still acknowledged their royalty, and paid them tribute in corn. But their principal wealth was fish. Elphin was the first Briton who caught fish on a large scale, and salted them for other purposes than home consumption.

The weir was thus constructed: a range of piles crossed the river from shore to shore, slanting upwards from both shores, and meeting at an angle in the middle of the river. A little

In the coracle lay a sleeping child, clothed in splendid apparel.

down the stream a second range of piles crossed the river in the same manner, having towards the middle several wide intervals with light wicker gates, which, meeting at an angle, were held together by the current, but were so constructed as to yield easily to a very light pressure from below. These gates gave all fish of a certain magnitude admission to a chamber, from which they could neither advance nor retreat, and from which, standing on a narrow bridge attached to the lower piles, Elphin baled them up at leisure. The smaller fish passed freely up and down the river through the interstices of the piles. This weir was put together in the early summer, and taken to pieces and laid by in the autumn.

Prince Elphin, one fine July night, was sleepless and troubled in spirit. His fishery had been beyond all precedent unproductive, and the obstacle which this circumstance opposed to his arrangements for victualling his little garrison kept him for the better half of the night vigilant in unprofitable cogitation. Soon after the turn of midnight, when dreams are true, he was startled from an incipient doze by a sudden cry of Angharad, who had been favoured with a vision of a miraculous draught of fish. Elphin, as a drowning man catches at a straw, caught at the shadowy promise of Angharad's dream, and at once, beneath the clear light of the just-waning moon, he sallied forth with his princess to examine his weir.

The weir was built across the stream of the river, just above the flow of the ordinary tides ; but the spring-tide had opened the wicker gates, and had floated up a coracle [1] between a pair of them, which closing, as the tide turned, on the coracle's nose, retained it within the chamber of the weir, at the same time that it kept the gates sufficiently open to permit the escape of any fish that might have entered the chamber. The great prize, which undoubtedly might have been there when Angharad dreamed of it, was gone to a fish.

Elphin, little pleased, stepped on the narrow bridge, and opened the gates with a pole that terminated piscatorially in a hook. The coracle began dropping down the stream. Elphin arrested its course, and guided it to land.

In the coracle lay a sleeping child, clothed in splendid apparel. Angharad took it in her arms. The child opened its eyes, and stretched its little arms towards her with a smile ;

[1] A small boat of basketwork, sheathed with leather.

and she uttered, in delight and wonder at its surpassing beauty, the exclamation of ' Taliesin !' 'Radiant brow !'

Elphin, nevertheless, looked very dismal on finding no food, and an additional mouth ; so dismal, that his physiognomy on that occasion passed into a proverb : 'As rueful as Elphin when he found Taliesin.'[1]

In after years, Taliesin, being on the safe side of prophecy, and writing after the event, addressed a poem to Elphin, in the character of the foundling of the coracle, in which he supposes himself, at the moment of his discovery, to have addressed Elphin as follows :

DYHUDDIANT ELFFIN

THE CONSOLATION OF ELPHIN

Lament not, Elphin : do not measure
By one brief hour thy loss or gain :
Thy weir to-night has borne a treasure,
Will more than pay thee years of pain.
St. Cynllo's aid will not be vain :
Smooth thy bent brow, and cease to mourn :
Thy weir will never bear again
Such wealth as it to-night has borne.

The stormy seas, the silent rivers,
The torrents down the steeps that spring,
Alike of weal or woe are givers,
As pleases heaven's immortal king.
Though frail I seem, rich gifts I bring,
Which in Time's fulness shall appear,
Greater than if the stream should fling
Three hundred salmon in thy weir.

Cast off this fruitless sorrow, loading
With heaviness the unmanly mind :
Despond not ; mourn not ; evil boding
Creates the ill it fears to find.
When fates are dark, and most unkind
Are they who most should do thee right,
Then wilt thou know thine eyes were blind
To thy good fortune of to-night.

---

[1] Mor drist ac Elffin pan gavod Taliesin.

Though, small and feeble, from my coracle
To thee my helpless hands I spread,
Yet in me breathes a holy oracle
To bid thee lift thy drooping head.
When hostile steps around thee tread,
A spell of power my voice shall wield,
That, more than arms with slaughter red,
Shall be thy refuge and thy shield.

Two years after this event, Angharad presented Elphin with a daughter, whom they named Melanghel. The fishery prospered; and the progress of cultivation and population among the more fertile parts of the mountain districts brought in a little revenue to the old king.

CHAPTER VI

THE EDUCATION OF TALIESIN

The three objects of intellect: the true, the beautiful, and the beneficial.

The three foundations of wisdom: youth, to acquire learning; memory, to retain learning; and genius, to illustrate learning.—TRIADS OF WISDOM.

The three primary requisites of poetical genius: an eye, that can see nature; a heart, that can feel nature; and a resolution, that dares follow nature.—TRIADS OF POETRY.

AS Taliesin grew up, Gwythno instructed him in all the knowledge of the age, which was of course not much, in comparison with ours. The science of political economy was sleeping in the womb of time. The advantage of growing rich by getting into debt and paying interest was altogether unknown: the safe and economical currency, which is produced by a man writing his name on a bit of paper, for which other men give him their property, and which he is always ready to exchange for another bit of paper, of an equally safe and economical manufacture, being also equally ready to render his own person, at a moment's notice, as impalpable as the metal which he promises to pay, is a stretch of wisdom to which the people of those days had nothing to compare. They had no steam-engines, with fires as eternal as those of the nether world, wherein the squalid many, from infancy to age, might be turned into component portions of machinery for the benefit of the purple-faced few. They could neither poison the air with gas, nor the waters with its dregs: in short, they made their money of metal, and breathed pure air, and drank pure water, like unscientific barbarians.

Of moral science they had little; but morals, without science, they had about the same as we have. They had a number of fine precepts, partly from their religion, partly from their bards, which they remembered in their liquor, and forgot in their business.

Political science they had none. The blessings of virtual representation were not even. dreamed of; so that, when any of their barbarous metallic currency got into their pockets or coffers, it had a chance to remain there, subjecting them to the inconvenience of unemployed capital. Still they went to work politically much as we do. The powerful took all they could get from their subjects and neighbours; and called something or other sacred and glorious, when they wanted the people to fight for them. They repressed disaffection by force, when it showed itself in an overt act; but they encouraged freedom of speech, when it was, like Hamlet's reading, 'words, words, words.'

There was no liberty of the press, because there was no press; but there was liberty of speech to the bards, whose persons were inviolable, and the general motto of their order was Y GWIR YN ERBYN Y BYD: the Truth against the World. If many of them, instead of acting up to this splendid profession, chose to advance their personal fortunes by appealing to the selfishness, the passions, and the prejudices of kings, factions, and the rabble, our free press gentry may afford them a little charity out of the excess of their own virtue.

In physical science, they supplied the place of knowledge by converting conjectures into dogmas; an art which is not yet lost. They held that the earth was the centre of the universe; that an immense ocean surrounded the earth; that the sky was a vast frame resting on the ocean; that the circle of their contact was a mystery of infinite mist; with a great deal more of cosmogony and astronomy, equally correct and profound, which answered the same purpose as our more correct and profound astronomy answers now, that of elevating the mind, as the eidouranion lecturers have it, to sublime contemplations.

Medicine was cultivated by the Druids, and it was just as much a science with them as with us; but they had not the wit or the means to make it a flourishing trade; the principal means to that end being women with nothing to do, articles which especially belong to a high state of civilisation.

The laws lay in a small compass: every bard had those of his own community by heart. The king, or chief, was the judge; the plaintiff and defendant told their own story; and the cause was disposed of in one hearing. We may well boast of the progress of light, when we turn from this picture to the statutes at large, and the Court of Chancery; and we may indulge in a pathetic reflection on our sweet-faced myriads of 'learned friends,' who would be under the unpleasant necessity of suspending themselves by the neck, if this barbaric 'practice of the courts' were suddenly revived.

The religion of the time was Christianity grafted on Druidism. The Christian faith had been very early preached in Britain. Some of the Welsh historians are of opinion that it was first preached by some of the apostles: most probably by St. John. They think the evidence inconclusive with respect to St. Paul. But, at any rate, the faith had made considerable progress among the Britons at the period of the arrival of Hengist; for many goodly churches, and, what was still better, richly-endowed abbeys, were flourishing in many places. The British clergy were, however, very contumacious towards the see of Rome, and would only acknowledge the spiritual authority of the archbishopric of Caer Lleon, which was, during many centuries, the primacy of Britain. St. Augustin, when he came over, at a period not long subsequent to that of the present authentic history, to preach Christianity to the Saxons, who had for the most part held fast to their Odinism, had also the secondary purpose of making them instruments for teaching the British clergy submission to Rome: as a means to which end, the newly-converted Saxons set upon the monastery of Bangor Iscoed, and put its twelve hundred monks to the sword. This was the first overt act in which the Saxons set forth their new sense of a religion of peace. It is alleged, indeed, that these twelve hundred monks supported themselves by the labour of their own hands. If they did so, it was, no doubt, a gross heresy; but whether it deserved the castigation it received from St. Augustin's proselytes, may be a question in polemics.

As the people did not read the Bible, and had no religious tracts, their religion, it may be assumed, was not very pure. ·The rabble of Britons must have seen little more than the superficial facts, that the lands, revenues, privileges, and so forth, which once belonged to Druids and so forth, now belonged to abbots, bishops, and so forth, who, like their

Initiated him in these mysteries.

extruded precursors, walked occasionally in a row, chanting unintelligible words, and never speaking in common language but to exhort the people to fight; having, indeed, better notions than their predecessors of building, apparel, and cookery; and a better knowledge of the means of obtaining good wine, and of the final purpose for which it was made.

They were observant of all matters of outward form, and tradition even places among them personages who were worthy to have founded a society for the suppression of vice. It is recorded, in the Triads, that 'Gwrgi Garwlwyd killed a male and female of the Cymry daily, and devoured them; and, on the Saturday, he killed two of each, that he might not kill on the Sunday.' This can only be a type of some sanctimonious hero, who made a cloak of piety for oppressing the poor.

But, even among the Britons, in many of the least populous and most mountainous districts, Druidism was still struggling with Christianity. The lamb had driven the wolf from the rich pastures of the valleys to the high places of the wilderness, where the rites and mysteries of the old religion flourished in secrecy, and where a stray proselyte of the new light was occasionally caught and roasted for the glory of Andraste.

Taliesin, worshipping Nature in her wildest solitudes, often strayed away for days from the dwelling of Elphin, and penetrated the recesses of Eryri,[1] where one especial spot on the banks of Lake Ceirionydd became the favourite haunt of his youth. In these lonely recesses, he became familiar with Druids, who initiated him in their mysteries, which, like all other mysteries, consisted of a quantity of allegorical mummery, pretending to be symbolical of the immortality of the soul, and of its progress through various stages of being; interspersed with a little, too literal, ducking and singeing of the aspirant, by way of trying his mettle, just enough to put him in fear, but not in risk of his life.

That Taliesin was thoroughly initiated in these mysteries is evident from several of his poems, which have neither head nor tail, and which, having no sense in any other point of view, must necessarily, as a learned mythologist has demonstrated, be assigned to the class of theology in which an occult sense can be found or made for them, according to the

[1] Snowdon.

views of the expounder.   One of them, a shade less obscure than its companions, unquestionably adumbrates the Druidical doctrine of transmigration.   According to this poem, Taliesin had been with the cherubim at the fall of Lucifer, in Paradise at the fall of man, and with Alexander at the fall of Babylon ; in the ark with Noah, and in the milky way with Tetragrammaton ; and in many other equally marvellous or memorable conditions : showing that, though the names and histories of the new religion were adopted, its doctrines had still to be learned ; and, indeed, in all cases of this description, names are changed more readily than doctrines, and doctrines more readily than ceremonies.

When any of the Romans or Saxons, who invaded the island, fell into the hands of the Britons, before the introduction of Christianity, they were handed over to the Druids, who sacrificed them, with pious ceremonies, to their goddess Andraste.   These human sacrifices have done much injury to the Druidical character, amongst us, who never practise them in the same way.   They lacked, it must be confessed, some of our light, and also some of our prisons.   They lacked some of our light, to enable them to perceive that the act of coming, in great multitudes, with fire and sword, to the remote dwellings of peaceable men, with the premeditated design of cutting their throats, ravishing their wives and daughters, killing their children, and appropriating their worldly goods, belongs, not to the department of murder and robbery, but to that of legitimate war, of which all the practitioners are gentlemen, and entitled to be treated like gentlemen.   They lacked some of our prisons, in which our philanthropy has provided accommodation for so large a portion of our own people, wherein, if they had left their prisoners alive, they could have kept them from returning to their countrymen, and being at their old tricks again immediately.   They would also, perhaps, have found some difficulty in feeding them, from the lack of the county rates, by which the most sensible and amiable part of our nation, the country squires, contrive to coop up, and feed, at the public charge, all who meddle with the wild animals of which they have given themselves the monopoly.   But as the Druids could neither lock up their captives, nor trust them at large, the darkness of their intellect could suggest no alternative to the process they adopted, of putting them out of the way, which they did with all the sanctions of religion and law. If one of these old Druids could have slept, like the seven sleepers of Ephesus, and awaked, in the nineteenth century, some fine morning near Newgate, the exhibition of some half-dozen funipendulous forgers might have shocked the tender bowels of his humanity as much as one of his wicker baskets of captives in the flames shocked those of Caesar ; and it would, perhaps, have been difficult to convince him that paper credit was not an idol, and one of a more sanguinary character than his Andraste. The Druids had their view of these matters, and we have ours ; and it does not comport with the steam-engine speed of our march of mind to look at more than one side of a question.

The people lived in darkness and vassalage. They were lost in the grossness of beef and ale. They had no pamphlet-eering societies to demonstrate that reading and writing are better than meat and drink ; and they were utterly destitute of the blessings of those 'schools for all,' the house of correction, and the treadmill, wherein the autochthonal justice of our agrestic kakistocracy now castigates the heinous sins which were then committed with impunity, of treading on old foot-paths, picking up dead wood, and moving on the face of the earth within sound of the whir of a partridge.

The learning of the time was confined to the bards. It consisted in a somewhat complicated art of versification ; in a great number of pithy apophthegms, many of which have been handed down to posterity under the title of the Wisdom of Catog ; in an interminable accumulation of Triads, in which form they bound up all their knowledge, physical, traditional, and mythological ; and in a mighty condensation of mysticism, being the still-cherished relics of the Druidical rites and doctrines.

The Druids were the sacred class of the bardic order. Before the change of religion, it was by far the most numerous class ; for the very simple reason, that there was most to be got by it : all ages and nations having been sufficiently en-lightened to make the trade of priest more profitable than that of poet. During this period, therefore, it was the only class that much attracted the notice of foreigners. After the change of religion, the denomination was retained as that of the second class of the order. The Bardd Braint, or Bard of Presidency, was of the ruling order, and wore a robe of sky-blue. The Derwydd, or Druid, wore a robe of white. The Ovydd, or Ovate, was of the class of initiation, and wore a robe of green. The Awenyddion, or disciples, the candidates for admission into the Bardic order, wore a variegated dress of the three colours, and were passed through a very severe moral and intellectual probation.

Gwythno was a Bardd Braint, or Bard of Presidency, and as such he had full power in his own person, without the intervention of a Bardic Congress, to make his Awenydd or disciple, Taliesin, an Ovydd or Ovate, which he did accordingly. Angharad, under the old king's instructions, prepared the green robe of the young aspirant's investiture. He afterwards acquired the white robe amongst the Druids of Eryri.

In all Bardic learning, Gwythno was profound. All that he knew he taught to Taliesin. The youth drew in the draughts of inspiration among the mountain forests and the mountain streams, and grew up under the roof of Elphin, in the perfection of genius and beauty.

E

Elphin was impressed into royal favour.

CHAPTER VII

THE HUNTINGS OF MAELGON

αἰεὶ τὸ μὲν ζῇ, τὸ δὲ μεθίσταται κακόν,
τὸ δ' ἐκπέφηνεν αὐτίκ' ἐξ ἀρχῆς νέον.
EURIPIDES.

> One ill is ever clinging ;
> One treads upon its heels ;
> A third, in distance springing,
> Its fearful front reveals.

GWYTHNO slept, not with his fathers, for they were under the
sea, but as near to them as was found convenient, within the
sound of the breakers that rolled over their ancient dwellings.
Elphin was now king of Caredigion, and was lord of a large
but thinly-peopled tract of rock, mountain, forest, and bog.
He held his sovereignty, however, not, as Gwythno had done
during the days of the glory of Gwaelod, by that most indis-
putable sort of right which consists in might, but by the more
precarious tenure of the absence of inclination in any of his
brother kings to take away anything he had.

Uther Pendragon, like Gwythno, went the way of all flesh,
and Arthur reigned in Caer Lleon, as king of the kings of
Britain. Maelgon Gwyneth was then king of that part of
North Wales which bordered on the kingdom of Caredigion.

Maelgon was a mighty hunter, and roused the echoes of
the mountains with horn and with hound. He went forth to
the chase as to war, provisioned for days and weeks, supported
by bard and butler, and all the apparel of princely festivity.
He pitched his tents in the forest of Snowdon, by the shore of
lake or torrent ; and, after hunting all the day, he feasted half
the night. The light of his torches gleamed on the foam of

51

the cataracts, and the sound of harp and song was mingled with their midnight roar.

When not thus employed, he was either feasting in his castle of Diganwy, on the Conwy, or fighting with any of the neighbouring kings who had anything which he wanted, and which he thought himself strong enough to take from them.

Once, towards the close of autumn, he carried the tumult of the chase into the recesses of Meirion. The consonance, or dissonance, of men and dogs outpealed the noise of the torrents among the rocks and woods of the Mawddach. Elphin and Teithrin were gone after the sheep or goats in the mountains; Taliesin was absent on the borders of his favourite lake; Angharad and Melanghel were alone. The careful mother, alarmed at the unusual din, and knowing, by rumour, of what materials the Nimrods of Britain were made, fled, with her daughter and handmaids, to the refuge of a deeply-secluded cavern, which they had long before noted as a safe retreat from peril. As they ascended the hills that led to the cavern, they looked back, at intervals, through the openings of the woods, to the growing tumult on the opposite side of the valley. The wild goats were first seen, flying in all directions, taking prodigious leaps from crag to crag, now and then facing about, and rearing themselves on their hind legs, as if in act to butt, and immediately thinking better of it, and springing away on all fours among the trees. Next, the more rare spectacle of a noble stag presented itself on the summit of a projecting rock, pausing a moment to snuff the air, then bounding down the most practicable slope to the valley. Next, on the summit which the stag had just deserted, appeared a solitary huntsman, sitting on a prancing horse, and waking a hundred echoes with the blast of his horn. Next rushed into view the main body of the royal company, and the two-legged and four-legged avalanche came thundering down on the track of the flying prey: not without imminent hazard of broken necks; though the mountain-bred horses, which possessed by nature almost the surefootedness of mules, had finished their education under the first professors of the age.

The stag swam the river, and stood at bay before the dwelling of Elphin, where he was in due time despatched by the conjoint valour of dog and man. The royal train burst into the solitary dwelling, where, finding nothing worthy of

' Whither lead you, my friend?   My horse can no longer keep his footing.'

much note, excepting a large store of salt salmon and mead, they proceeded to broil and tap, and made fearful havoc among the family's winter provision. Elphin and Teithrin, returning to their expected dinner, stood aghast on the threshold of their plundered sanctuary. Maelgon condescended to ask them who they were; and, learning Elphin's name and quality, felt himself bound to return his involuntary hospitality by inviting him to Diganwy. So strong was his sense of justice on this head, that, on Elphin's declining the invitation, which Maelgon ascribed to modesty, he desired two of his grooms to take him up and carry him off.

So Elphin was impressed into royal favour, and was feasted munificently in the castle of Diganwy. Teithrin brought home the ladies from the cavern, and, during the absence of Elphin, looked after the sheep and goats, and did his master's business as well as his own.

One evening, when the royal 'nowle' was 'tottie of the must,' while the bards of Maelgon were singing the praises of their master, and of all and everything that belonged to him, as the most eximious and transcendent persons and things of the superficial garniture of the earth, Maelgon said to Elphin, 'My bards say that I am the best and bravest of kings, that my queen is the most beautiful and chaste of women, and that they themselves, by virtue of belonging to me, are the best and wisest of bards. Now what say you on these heads?'

This was a perplexing question to Elphin, who, nevertheless, answered: 'That you are the best and bravest of kings I do not in the least doubt; yet I cannot think that any woman surpasses my own wife in beauty and chastity; or that any bard equals my bard in genius and wisdom.'

'Hear you him, Rhûn?' said Maelgon.

'I hear,' said Rhûn, 'and mark.'

Rhûn was the son of Maelgon, and a worthy heir-apparent of his illustrious sire. Rhûn set out the next morning on an embassy very similar to Tarquin's, accompanied by only one attendant. They lost their way and each other, among the forests of Meirion. The attendant, after riding about some time in great trepidation, thought he heard the sound of a harp, mixed with the roar of the torrents, and following its indications, came at length within sight of an oak-fringed precipice, on the summit of which stood Taliesin, playing and singing to the winds and waters. The attendant could not approach him without dismounting; therefore, tying his horse to a branch, he ascended the rock, and, addressing the young bard, inquired his way to the dwelling of Elphin. Taliesin, in return, inquired his business there; and, partly by examination, partly by divination, ascertained his master's name, and the purport of his visit.

Taliesin deposited his harp in a dry cavern of the rock, and undertook to be the stranger's guide. The attendant remounted his horse, and Taliesin preceded him on foot. But the way by which he led him grew more and more rugged, till the stranger called out, 'Whither lead you, my friend? My horse can no longer keep his footing.' 'There is no other way,' said Taliesin. 'But give him to my management, and do you follow on foot.' The attendant consented. Taliesin mounted the horse, and presently struck into a more practicable track; and immediately giving the horse the reins, he disappeared among the woods, leaving the unfortunate equerry to follow as he might, with no better guide than the uncertain recollection of the sound of his horse's heels.

Taliesin reached home before the arrival of Rhûn, and warned Angharad of the mischief that was designed her.

Rhûn, arriving at his destination, found only a handmaid dressed as Angharad, and another officiating as her attendant. The fictitious princess gave him a supper, and everything else he asked for; and, at parting in the morning, a lock of her hair, and a ring, which Angharad had placed on her finger.

After riding a short distance on his return, Rhûn met his unlucky attendant, torn, tired, and half-starved, and cursing some villain who had stolen his horse. Rhûn was too happy in his own success to have a grain of sympathy for his miserable follower, whom he left to find his horse and his way, or either, or neither, as he might, and returned alone to Diganwy.

Maelgon exultingly laid before Elphin the proof of his wife's infidelity. Elphin examined the lock of hair, and listened to the narration of Rhûn. He divined at once the trick that had been put upon the prince; but he contented himself with saying, 'I do not believe that Rhûn has received the favours of Angharad; and I still think that no wife in Britain, not even the queen of Maelgon Gwyneth, is more chaste or more beautiful than mine.'

She gave him a supper.

Hereupon Maelgon waxed wroth.   Elphin, in a point which much concerned him, held a belief of his own, different from that which his superiors in worldly power required him to hold. Therefore Maelgon acted as the possessors of worldly power usually act in similar cases : he locked Elphin up within four stone walls, with an intimation that he should keep him there till he pronounced a more orthodox opinion on the question in dispute.

CHAPTER VIII

THE LOVE OF MELANGHEL

ἀλλὰ τεαῖς παλάμῃσι μαχήμονα θύρσον ἀείρων,
αἰθέρος ἄξια ῥέξον· ἐπεὶ Διὸς ἄμβροτος αὐλὴ
οὔ σε πόνων ἀπάνευθε δεδέξεται· οὐδέ σοι Ὧραι
μήπω ἀεθλεύσαντι πύλας πετάσωσιν Ὀλύμπου.

Grasp the bold thyrsus ; seek the field's array ;
And do things worthy of ethereal day :
Not without toil to earthborn man befalls
To tread the floors of Jove's immortal halls :
Never to him, who not by deeds has striven,
Will the bright Hours roll back the gates of heaven.
IRIS TO BACCHUS, in the 13th Book of the
DIONYSIACA OF NONNUS.

THE household of Elphin was sufficiently improsperous during the absence of its chief. The havoc which Maelgon's visitation had made in their winter provision, it required the utmost exertions of their collective energies to repair. Even the young princess Melanghel sallied forth, in the garb of a huntress, to strike the deer or the wild goat among the wintry forests, on the summits of the bleak crags, or in the valleys of the flooded streams.

Taliesin, on these occasions, laid aside his harp, and the robe of his order, and accompanied the princess with his hunting spear, and more succinctly apparelled.

Their retinue, it may be supposed, was neither very numerous nor royal, nor their dogs very thoroughbred. It sometimes happened that the deer went one way, the dogs another ; the attendants, losing sight of both, went a third, leaving Taliesin, who never lost sight of Melanghel, alone with her among the hills.

60

One day, the ardour of the chase having carried them far beyond their ordinary bounds, they stood alone together on Craig Aderyn, the Rock of Birds, which overlooks the river Dysyni. This rock takes its name from the flocks of birds which have made it their dwelling, and which make the air resonant with their multitudinous notes. Around, before, and above them rose mountain beyond mountain, soaring above the leafless forests, to lose their heads in mist; beneath them lay the silent river; and along the opening of its narrow valley, they looked to the not-distant sea.

'Prince Llywarch,' said Taliesin, 'is a bard and a warrior: he is the son of an illustrious line. Taliesin is neither prince nor warrior: he is the unknown child of the waters.'

'Why think you of Llywarch?' said Melanghel, to whom the name of the prince was known only from Taliesin, who knew it only from fame.

'Because,' said Taliesin, 'there is that in my soul which tells me that I shall have no rival among the bards of Britain: but, if its princes and warriors seek the love of Melanghel, I shall know that I am but a bard, and not as Llywarch.'

'You would be Prince Taliesin,' said Melanghel, smiling, 'to make me your princess. Am I not a princess already? and such an one as is not on earth, for the land of my inheritance is under the sea, under those very waves that now roll within our view; and, in truth, you are as well qualified for a prince as I am for a princess, and have about as valuable a dominion in the mists and the clouds as I have under the waters.'

Her eyes sparkled with affectionate playfulness, while her long black hair floated loosely in the breeze that pressed the folds of her drapery against the matchless symmetry of her form.

'Oh, maid!' said Taliesin, 'what shall I do to win your love?'

'Restore me my father,' said Melanghel, with a seriousness as winning as her playfulness had been fascinating.

'That will I do,' said Taliesin, 'for his own sake. What shall I do for yours?'

'Nothing more,' said Melanghel; and she held out her hand to the youthful bard. Taliesin seized it with rapture, and pressed it to his lips; then, still grasping her hand, and throwing his left arm round her, he pressed his lips to hers.

Melanghel started from him, blushing, and looked at him a moment with something like severity ; but he blushed as much as she did, and seemed even more alarmed at her displeasure than she was at his momentary audacity. She reassured him with a smile ; and, pointing her spear in the direction of her distant home, she bounded before him down the rock.

This was the kiss of Taliesin to the daughter of Elphin, which is celebrated in an inedited triad, as one of ‘ the Three Chaste Kisses of the Island of Britain.’

One of ' the Three Chaste Kisses of the island of Britain.'

CHAPTER IX

THE SONGS OF DIGANWY

Three things that will always swallow, and never be satisfied : the sea ;
a burial-ground ; and a king.—TRIADS OF WISDOM.

THE hall of Maelgon Gwyneth was ringing with music and
revelry, when Taliesin stood on the floor, with his harp, in the
midst of the assembly, and, without introduction or preface,
struck a few chords, that, as if by magic, suspended all other
sounds, and fixed the attention of all in silent expectation.
He then sang as follows :

CANU Y MEDD

THE MEAD SONG OF TALIESIN

The King of kings upholds the heaven,
And parts from earth the billowy sea :
By Him all earthly joys are given ;
He loves the just, and guards the free.
Round the wide hall, for thine and thee,
With purest draughts the mead-horns foam,
Maelgon of Gwyneth !   Can it be
That here a prince bewails his home ?

The bee tastes not the sparkling draught
Which mortals from his toils obtain ;
That sends, in festal circles quaffed,
Sweet tumult through the heart and brain.
The timid, while the horn they drain,
Grow bold ; the happy more rejoice ;
The mourner ceases to complain ;
The gifted bard exalts his voice.

To royal Elphin life I owe,
Nurture and name, the harp, and mead :
Full, pure, and sparkling be their flow,
The horns to Maelgon's lips decreed :
For him may horn to horn succeed,
Till, glowing with their generous fire,
He bid the captive chief be freed,
Whom at his hands my songs require.

Elphin has given me store of mead,
Mead, ale, and wine, and fish, and corn ;
A happy home ; a splendid steed,
Which stately trappings well adorn.
To-morrow be the auspicious morn
That home the expected chief shall lead ;
So may King Maelgon drain the horn
In thrice three million feasts of mead.

'I give you,' said Maelgon, 'all the rights of hospitality, and as many horns as you please of the mead you so well and justly extol. If you be Elphin's bard, it must be confessed he spoke truth with respect to you, for you are a much better bard than any of mine, as they are all free to confess : I give them that liberty.'

The bards availed themselves of the royal indulgence, and confessed their own inferiority to Taliesin, as the king had commanded them to do. Whether they were all as well convinced of it as they professed to be, may be left to the decision of that very large class of literary gentlemen who are in the habit of favouring the reading public with their undisguised opinions.

'But,' said Maelgon, 'your hero of Caredigion indulged himself in a very unjustifiable bravado with respect to his queen ; for he said she was as beautiful and as chaste as mine. Now Rhûn has proved the contrary, with small trouble, and brought away trophies of his triumph ; yet still Elphin persists in his first assertion, wherein he grossly disparages the queen of Gwyneth ; and for this I hold him in bondage, and will do, till he make recantation.'

'That he will never do,' said Taliesin. 'Your son received only the favours of a handmaid, who was willing, by stratagem, to preserve her lady from violence. The real Angharad was concealed in a cavern.'

Taliesin explained the adventure of Rhûn, and pronounced

an eulogium on Angharad, which put the king and prince into a towering passion.

Rhûn secretly determined to set forth on a second quest ; and Maelgon swore by his mead-horn he would keep Elphin till doomsday.   Taliesin struck his harp again, and, in a tone of deep but subdued feeling, he poured forth the

SONG OF THE WIND [1]

The winds that wander far and free,
Bring whispers from the shores they sweep ;
Voices of feast and revelry ;
Murmurs of forests and the deep ;

Low sounds of torrents from the steep
Descending on the flooded vale ;
And tumults from the leaguered keep,
Where foes the dizzy rampart scale.

The whispers of the wandering wind
Are borne to gifted ears alone ;
For them it ranges unconfined,
And speaks in accents of its own.

It tells me of Deheubarth's throne ;
The spider weaves not in its shield : [2]
Already from its towers is blown
The blast that bids the spoiler yield.

---

[1] This poem has little or nothing of Taliesin's ' Canu y Gwynt,' with the exception of the title.   That poem is apparently a fragment ; and, as it now stands, is an incoherent and scarcely intelligible rhapsody.   It contains no distinct or explicit idea, except the proposition that it is an unsafe booty to carry off fat kine, which may be easily conceded in a case where nimbleness of heel, both in man and beast, must have been of great importance.   The idea from which, if from anything in the existing portion of the poem, it takes its name, that the whispers of the wind bring rumours of war from Deheubarth, is rather implied than expressed.

[2] The spider weaving in suspended armour is an old emblem of peace and inaction.   Thus Bacchylides, in his fragment on Peace :

ἐν δὲ σιδαροδέτοις πόρπαξιν
αἰθᾶν ἀραχνᾶν ἔργα πέλονται.

Euripides, in a fragment of ' Erechtheus ' :

κείσθω δόρυ μοι μίτον ἀμφιπλέκειν
ἀράχναις.

Ill with his prey the fox may wend,
When the young lion quits his lair :
Sharp sword, strong shield, stout arm, should tend
On spirits that unjustly dare.
To me the wandering breezes bear
The war-blast from Caer Lleon's brow ;
The avenging storm is brooding there
To which Diganwy's towers shall bow.

' If the wind talks to you,' said Maelgon, ' I may say, with the proverb, you talk to the wind ; for I am not to be sung, or cajoled, or vapoured, or bullied out of my prisoner. And as to your war-blasts from Caer Lleon, which I construe into a threat that you will stir up King Arthur against me, I can tell you for your satisfaction, and to spare you the trouble of going so far, that he has enough to do with seeking his wife, who has been carried off by some unknown marauder, and with fighting the Saxons, to have much leisure or inclination to quarrel with a true Briton, who is one of his best friends, and his heir-pre-sumptive ; for, though he is a man of great prowess, and more-over, saving his reverence and your presence, a cuckold, he has not yet favoured his kingdom with an heir-apparent. And I request you to understand that when I extolled you above my bards, I did so only in respect of your verse and voice, melody and execution, figure and action, in short, of your manner ; for your matter is naught ; and I must do my own bards the justice to say that, however much they may fall short of you in the requisites aforesaid, they know much better than you do, what is fitting for bards to sing, and kings to hear.'

And Nonnus, whom no poetical image escaped (*Dionysiaca*, L. xxxviii.) :

 οὐ φόνος, οὐ τότε δῆρις· ἔκειτο δὲ τηλόθι χάρμης
Βακχιὰς ἐξαέτηρος ἀραχνιόωσα βοείη.

And Beaumont and Fletcher, in the ' Wife for a Month' :

Would'st thou live so long, till thy sword hung by,
And lazy spiders filled the hilt with cobwebs ?

A Persian poet says, describing ruins :

The spider spreads the veil in the palace of the Caesars.

And among the most felicitous uses of this emblem, must never be for-gotten Hogarth's cobweb over the lid of the charity-box.

The bards, thus encouraged, recovered from the first shock of Maelgon's ready admission of Taliesin's manifest superiority, and struck up a sort of consecutive chorus, in a series of pennillion, or stanzas, in praise of Maelgon and his heirship-presumptive, giving him credit for all the virtues of which the reputation was then in fashion ; and, amongst the rest, they very loftily celebrated his justice and magnanimity.

Taliesin could not reconcile his notions of these qualities with Maelgon's treatment of Elphin. He changed his measure and his melody, and pronounced, in impassioned numbers, the poem which a learned Welsh historian calls 'The Indignation of the Bards,' though, as the indignation was Taliesin's, and not theirs, he seems to have made a small mistake in regard to the preposition.

THE INDIGNATION OF TALIESIN WITH THE BARDS OF MAELGON GWYNETH

> False bards the sacred fire pervert,
> Whose songs are won without desert ;
> Who falsehoods weave in specious lays,
> To gild the base with virtue's praise.
>
> From court to court, from tower to tower,
> In warrior's tent, in lady's bower,
> For gold, for wine, for food, for fire,
> They tune their throats at all men's hire.
>
> Their harps re-echo wide and far
> With sensual love, and bloody war,
> And drunkenness, and flattering lies :
> Truth's light may shine for other eyes.
>
> In palaces they still are found,
> At feasts, promoting senseless sound :
> He is their demigod at least,
> Whose only virtue is his feast.
>
> They love to talk ; they hate to think ;
> All day they sing ; all night they drink :
> No useful toils their hands employ ;
> In boisterous throngs is all their joy.
>
> The bird will fly, the fish will swim,
> The bee the honeyed flowers will skim ;

Its food by toil each creature brings,
Except false bards and worthless kings.

Learning and wisdom claim to find
Homage and succour from mankind ;
But learning's right, and wisdom's due,
Are falsely claimed by slaves like you.

True bards know truth, and truth will show ;
Ye know it not, nor care to know :
Your king's weak mind false judgment warps ;
Rebuke his wrong, or break your harps.

I know the mountain and the plain ;
I know where right and justice reign ;
I from the tower will Elphin free ;
Your king shall learn his doom from me.

A spectre of the marsh shall rise,
With yellow teeth, and hair, and eyes,
From whom your king in vain aloof
Shall crouch beneath the sacred roof.

He through the half-closed door shall spy
The Yellow Spectre sweeping by ;
To whom the punishment belongs
Of Maelgon's crimes and Elphin's wrongs.

By the name of the Yellow Spectre, Taliesin designated a
pestilence, which afterwards carried off great multitudes of the
people, and, amongst them, Maelgon Gwyneth, then sovereign
of Britain, who had taken refuge from it in a church.

Maelgon paid little attention to Taliesin's prophecy, but he
was much incensed by the general tenor of his song.

'If it were not,' said Maelgon, 'that I do not choose to add
to the number of the crimes of which you so readily accuse
me, that of disregarding the inviolability of your bardship, I
would send you to keep company with your trout-catching king,
and you might amuse his salmon-salting majesty with telling
him as much truth as he is disposed to listen to ; which, to
judge by his reception of Rhûn's story of his wife, I take to be
exceedingly little.   For the present, you are welcome to de-
part ; and, if you are going to Caer Lleon, you may present
my respects to King Arthur, and tell him, I hope he will beat
the Saxons, and find his wife ; but I hope, also, that the cutting

Rhûn and his bard returned to the banks of the Mawddach, where they resolved themselves into an ambuscade.—p. 74.

me off with an heir-apparent will not be the consequence of his finding her, or (which, by the bye, is more likely) of his having lost her.'

Taliesin took his departure from the hall of Diganwy, leaving the bards biting their lips at his rebuke, and Maelgon roaring with laughter at his own very excellent jest.

CHAPTER X

THE DISAPPOINTMENT OF RHÛN

παρθένε, πῶς μετάμειψας ἐρευθαλέην σέο μορφήν ;
εἰαρινὴν δ' ἀκτῖνα τίς ἔσβεσε σεῖο προσώπου ;
οὐκετι σῶν μελέων ἀμαρύσσεται ἄργυφος ἄιγλη·
οὐκέτι δ', ὡς τὸ πρόσθε, τεαὶ γελόωσιν ὀπωπαί.

Sweet maid, what grief has changed thy roseate grace,
And quenched the vernal sunshine of thy face?
No more thy light form sparkles as it flies,
Nor laughter flashes from thy radiant eyes.
VENUS TO PASITHEA, in the 33rd Book of the
DIONYSIACA OF NONNUS.

TALIESIN returned to the dwelling of Elphin, auguring that, in consequence of his information, Rhûn would pay it another visit. In this anticipation he was not mistaken, for Rhûn very soon appeared, with a numerous retinue, determined, apparently, to carry his point by force of arms. He found, however, no inmate in the dwelling but Taliesin and Teithrin ap Tathral.

Rhûn stormed, entreated, promised, and menaced, without success. He perlustrated the vicinity, and found various caverns, but not the one he sought. He passed many days in the search, and, finally, departed ; but, at a short distance, he dismissed all his retinue, except his bard of all work, or laureate-expectant, and, accompanied by this worthy, returned to the banks of the Mawddach, where they resolved themselves into an ambuscade. It was not long before they saw Taliesin issue from the dwelling, and begin ascending the hill. They followed him at a cautious distance ; first up a steep ascent of the forest-covered rocks ; then along a small space of densely-wooded tableland, to the edge of a dingle ; and, again, by a

74

The cataracts thunder down the steep.

slight descent, to the bed of a mountain stream, in a spot where the torrent flung itself, in a series of cataracts, down the rift of a precipitous rock, that towered high above their heads. About half-way up the rock, near the base of one of these cataracts, was a projecting ledge, or natural platform of rock, behind which was seen the summit of the opening of a cave. Taliesin paused, and looked around him, as if to ascertain that he was unobserved ; and then, standing on a projection of the rock below, he mingled, in spontaneous song, the full power of his voice with the roar of the waters.

TALIESIN

Maid of the rock ! though loud the flood,
My voice will pierce thy cell :
No foe is in the mountain wood ;
No danger in the dell :
The torrents bound along the glade ;
Their path is free and bright ;
Be thou as they, O mountain maid !
In liberty and light.

Melanghel appeared on the rocky platform, and answered the song of her lover :

MELANGHEL

The cataracts thunder down the steep ;
The woods all lonely wave :
Within my heart the voice sinks deep
That calls me from my cave.
The voice is dear, the song is sweet,
And true the words must be :
Well pleased I quit the dark retreat,
To wend away with thee.

TALIESIN

Not yet ; not yet : let nightdews fall,
And stars be bright above,
Ere to her long-deserted hall
I guide my gentle love.
When torchlight flashes on the roof,
No foe will near thee stray :
Even now his parting courser's hoof
Rings from the rocky way.

MELANGHEL

Yet climb the path, and comfort speak,
To cheer the lonely cave,
Where woods are bare, and rocks are bleak,
And wintry torrents rave.
A dearer home my memory knows,
A home I still deplore ;
Where firelight glows, while winds and snows
Assail the guardian door.

Taliesin vanished a moment from the sight of Rhûn, and almost immediately reappeared by the side of Melanghel, who had now been joined by her mother. In a few minutes he returned, and Angharad and Melanghel withdrew.

Rhûn watched him from the dingle, and then proceeded to investigate the path by which he had gained the platform. After some search he discovered it, ascended to the platform, and rushed into the cavern.

They here found a blazing fire, a half-finished dinner, materials of spinning and embroidering, and other signs of female inhabitancy ; but they found not the inhabitants. They searched the cavern to its depth, which was not inconsiderable ; much marvelling how the ladies had vanished. While thus engaged, they heard a rushing sound, and a crash on the rocks, as of some ponderous body. The mystery of this noise was very soon explained to them, in a manner that gave an unusual length to their faces, and threw a deep tinge of blue into their rosy complexions. A ponderous stone, which had been suspended like a portcullis at the mouth of the cavern, had been dropped by some unseen agency, and made them as close prisoners as Elphin.

They were not long kept in suspense as to how this matter had been managed. The hoarse voice of Teithrin ap Tathral sounded in their ears from without, 'Foxes ! you have been seen through, and you are fairly trapped. Eat and drink. You shall want nothing but to get out ; which you must want some time ; for it is sworn that no hand but Elphin's shall raise the stone of your captivity.'

'Let me out,' vociferated Rhûn, 'and on the word of a prince——' but, before he could finish the sentence, the retreating steps of Teithrin were lost in the roar of the torrent.

The hoarse voice of Teithrin ap Tathral sounded in their ears from without,
'Foxes! you have been seen through, and you are fairly trapped.'

CHAPTER XI

THE HEROES OF DINAS VAWR

L'ombra sua torna ch'era dipartita.
DANTE.

While there is life there is hope.
ENGLISH PROVERB.

PRINCE RHÛN being safe in schistous bastile, Taliesin commenced his journey to the court of King Arthur. On his way to Caer Lleon, he was received with all hospitality, entertained with all admiration, and dismissed with all honour, at the castles of several petty kings, and, amongst the rest, at the castle of Dinas Vawr, on the Towy, which was then garrisoned by King Melvas, who had marched with a great force out of his own kingdom, on the eastern shores of the Severn, to levy contributions in the country to the westward, where, as the pleasure of his company had been altogether unlooked for, he had got possession of a good portion of movable property. The castle of Dinas Vawr presenting itself to him as a convenient hold, he had taken it by storm ; and having cut the throats of the former occupants, thrown their bodies into the Towy, and caused a mass to be sung for the good of their souls, he was now sitting over his bowl, with the comfort of a good conscience, enjoying the fruits of the skill and courage with which he had planned and accomplished his scheme of ways and means for the year.

The hall of Melvas was full of magnanimous heroes, who were celebrating their own exploits in sundry choruses, especially in that which follows, which is here put upon record as being the quintessence of all the war-songs that ever were written, and the sum and substance of all the appetencies, tendencies, and consequences of military glory :

THE WAR-SONG OF DINAS VAWR

The mountain sheep are sweeter,
But the valley sheep are fatter ;
We therefore deemed it meeter
To carry off the latter.
We made an expedition ;
We met a host, and quelled it ;
We forced a strong position,
And killed the men who held it.

On Dyfed's richest valley,
Where herds of kine were brousing,
We made a mighty sally,
To furnish our carousing.
Fierce warriors rushed to meet us ;
We met them, and o'erthrew them :
They struggled hard to beat us ;
But we conquered them, and slew them.

As we drove our prize at leisure,
The king marched forth to catch us :
His rage surpassed all measure,
But his people could not match us.
He fled to his hall-pillars ;
And, ere our force we led off,
Some sacked his house and cellars,
While others cut his head off.

We there, in strife bewild'ring,
Spilt blood enough to swim in :
We orphaned many children,
And widowed many women.
The eagles and the ravens
We glutted with our foemen ;
The heroes and the cravens,
The spearmen and the bowmen.

We brought away from battle,
And much their land bemoaned them,
Two thousand head of cattle,
And the head of him who owned them :
Ednyfed, king of Dyfed,
His head was borne before us ;
His wine and beasts supplied our feasts,
And his overthrow, our chorus.

As the doughty followers of Melvas, having sung themselves hoarse with their own praises, subsided one by one into drunken sleep, Taliesin, sitting near the great central fire, and throwing around a scrutinising glance on all the objects in the hall, noticed a portly and somewhat elderly personage, of an aspect that would have been venerable if it had been less rubicund and Bacchic, who continued plying his potations with undiminished energy, while the heroes of the festival dropped round him, like the leaves of autumn. This figure excited Taliesin's curiosity. The features struck him with a sense of resemblance to objects which had been somewhere familiar to him ; but he perplexed himself in vain with attempts at definite recollections. At length, when these two were almost the sole survivors of the evening, the stranger approached him with a golden goblet, which he had just replenished with the choicest wine of the vaults of Dinas Vawr, and pronounced the oracular monosyllable, 'Drink !' to which he subjoined emphatically, 'GWIN O EUR: wine from gold. That is my taste. Ale is well ; mead is better ; wine is best. Horn is well ; silver is better ; gold is best.'

Taliesin, who had been very abstemious during the evening, took the golden goblet, and drank to please the inviter ; in the hope that he would become communicative, and satisfy the curiosity his appearance had raised.

The stranger sat down near him, evidently in that amiable state of semi-intoxication which inflates the head, warms the heart, lifts up the veil of the inward man, and sets the tongue flying, or rather tripping, in the double sense of nimbleness and titubancy.

The stranger repeated, taking a copious draught, 'My taste is wine from gold.'

'I have heard those words,' said Taliesin, 'GWIN O EUR, repeated as having been the favourite saying of a person whose memory is fondly cherished by one as dear to me as a mother, though his name, with all others, is the byword of all that is disreputable.'

'I cannot believe,' said the stranger, 'that a man whose favourite saying was GWIN O EUR, could possibly be a disreputable person, or deserve any other than that honourable remembrance, which, you say, only one person is honest enough to entertain for him.'

'His name,' said Taliesin, 'is too unhappily notorious throughout Britain by the terrible catastrophe of which his GWIN O EUR was the cause.'

'And what might that be?' said the stranger.

'The inundation of Gwaelod,' said Taliesin.

'You speak then,' said the stranger, taking an enormous

potation, 'of Seithenyn, Prince Seithenyn, Seithenyn ap Seithyn Saidi, Arglwyd Gorwarcheidwad yr Argae Breninawl?'

'I seldom hear his name,' said Taliesin, 'with any of those sounding additions; he is usually called Seithenyn the Drunkard.'

The stranger goggled about his eyes in an attempt to fix them steadily on Taliesin, screwed up the corners of his mouth, stuck out his nether lip, pursed up his chin, thrust forward his right foot, and elevated his golden goblet in his right hand:

then, in a tone which he intended to be strongly becoming of his impressive aspect and imposing attitude, he muttered, ' Look at me.'

Taliesin looked at him accordingly, with as much gravity as he could preserve.

After a silence, which he designed to be very dignified and solemn, the stranger spoke again : ' I am the man.'

' What man ? ' said Taliesin.

' The man,' replied his entertainer, ' of whom you have spoken so disparagingly : Seithenyn ap Seithyn Saidi.'

' Seithenyn,' said Taliesin, ' has slept twenty years under the waters of the western sea, as King Gwythno's *Lamentations* have made known to all Britain.'

' They have not made it known to me,' said Seithenyn, ' for the best of all reasons, that one can only know the truth ; for, if that which we think we know is not truth, it is something which we do not know. A man cannot know his own death ; for, while he knows anything, he is alive ; at least, I never heard of a dead man who knew anything, or pretended to know anything ; if he had so pretended, I should have told him to his face he was no dead man.'

' Your mode of reasoning,' said Taliesin, ' unquestionably corresponds with what I have heard of Seithenyn's ; but how is it possible Seithenyn can be living ? '

' Everything that is, is possible, says Catog the Wise,' answered Seithenyn, with a look of great sapience. ' I will give you proof that I am not a dead man ; for, they say, dead men tell no tales : now I will tell you a tale, and a very interesting one it is. When I saw the sea sapping the tower, I jumped into the water, and just in the nick of time. It was well for me that I had been so provident as to empty so many barrels, and that somebody, I don't know who, but I suppose it was my daughter, had been so provident as to put the bungs into them, to keep them sweet ; for the beauty of it was that, when there was so much water in the case, it kept them empty ; and when I jumped into the sea, the sea was just making a great hole in the cellar, and they were floating out by dozens. I don't know how I managed it, but I got one arm over one, and the other arm over another : I nipped them pretty tight ; and, though my legs were under water, the good liquor I had in me kept me warm. I could not help thinking, as I had nothing else to think of just then that touched me so nearly, that if I had left them full, and myself empty, as a sober man would have done, we should all three, that is, I and the two barrels, have gone to the bottom together, that is to say, separately; for we should never have come together, except at the bottom, perhaps; when no one of us could have done the other any good; whereas they have done me much good, and I have requited it; for, first, I did them the service of emptying them; and then they did me the service of floating me with the tide, whether the ebb, or the flood, or both, is more than I can tell, down to the coast of Dyfed, where I was picked up by fishermen; and such was my sense of gratitude, that, though I had always before detested an empty barrel, except as a trophy, I swore I would not budge from the water unless my two barrels went with me; so we were all marched inland together, and were taken into the service of King Ednyfed, where I stayed till his castle was sacked, and his head cut off, and his beeves marched away with, by the followers of King Melvas, of whom I killed two or three; but they were too many for us; therefore, to make the best of a bad bargain, I followed leisurely in the train of the beeves, and presented myself to King Melvas, with this golden goblet, saying GWIN O EUR. He was struck with my deportment, and made me his chief butler; and now my two barrels are the two pillars of his cellar, where I regularly fill them from affection, and as regularly empty them from gratitude, taking care to put the bungs in them, to keep them sweet.'

'But all this while,' said Taliesin, 'did you never look back to the Plain of Gwaelod, to your old king, and, above all, to your daughter?'

'Why, yes,' said Seithenyn, 'I did in a way. But as to the Plain of Gwaelod, that was gone, buried under the sea, along with many good barrels, which I had been improvident enough to leave full: then, as to the old king, though I had a great regard for him, I thought he might be less likely to feast me in his hall than to set up my head on a spike over his gate: then, as to my daughter——'

Here he shook his head, and looked maudlin; and dashing two or three drops from his eye, he put a great many into his mouth.

' I swore I would not budge from the water unless my two barrels went with me.'

'Your daughter,' said Taliesin, 'is the wife of King Elphin, and has a daughter, who is now as beautiful as her mother was.'

'Very likely,' said Seithenyn, 'and I should be very glad to see them all ; but I am afraid King Elphin, as you call him (what he is king of, you shall tell me at leisure), would do me a mischief. At any rate, he would stint me in liquor. No ! If they will visit me, here I am. Fish, and water, will not agree with me. I am growing old, and need cordial nutriment. King Melvas will never want for beeves and wine ; nor, indeed, for anything else that is good. I can tell you what,' he added, in a very low voice, cocking his eye, and putting his finger on his lips, 'he has got in this very castle the finest woman in Britain.'

'That I doubt,' said Taliesin.

'She is the greatest, at any rate,' said Seithenyn, 'and ought to be the finest.'

'How the greatest ? ' said Taliesin.

Seithenyn looked round, to observe if there were any listener near, and fixed a very suspicious gaze on the rotund figure of a fallen hero, who lay coiled up like a maggot in a filbert, and snoring with an energy that, to the muddy apprehensions of Seithenyn, seemed to be counterfeit. He determined, by a gentle experiment, to ascertain if his suspicions were well founded ; and proceeded, with what he thought great caution, to apply the point of his foot to the most bulging portion of the fat sleeper's circumference. But he greatly miscalculated his intended impetus, for he impinged his foot with a force that overbalanced himself, and hurled him headlong over his man, who instantly sprang on his legs, shouting 'To arms !' Numbers started up at the cry ; the hall rang with the din of arms, and with the vociferation of questions, which there were many to ask, and none to answer. Some stared about for the enemy ; some rushed to the gates ; others to the walls. Two or three, reeling in the tumult and the darkness, were jostled over the parapet, and went rolling down the precipitous slope of the castle hill, crashing through the bushes, and bellowing for some one to stop them, till their clamours were cut short by a plunge into the Towy, where the conjoint weight of their armour and their liquor carried them at once to the bottom. The rage which would have fallen on

the enemy, if there had been one, was turned against the
author of the false alarm ; but, as none could point him out,
the tumult subsided by degrees, through a descending scale of
imprecations, into the last murmured malediction of him whom
the intensity of his generous anger kept longest awake.   By
this time, the rotund hero had again coiled himself up into his
ring ; and Seithenyn was stretched in a right line, as a
tangent to the circle, in a state of utter incapacity to elucidate
the mystery of King Melvas's possession of the finest woman
in Britain.

CHAPTER XII

THE SPLENDOUR OF CAER LLEON

The three principal cities of the isle of Britain : Caer Llion upon Wysg in Cymru ; Caer Llundain in Lloegr ; and Caer Evrawg in Deifr and Brynaich.[1]—TRIADS OF THE ISLE OF BRITAIN.

THE sunset of a bright December day was glittering on the waves of the Usk, and on the innumerable roofs, which, being composed chiefly of the glazed tiles of the Romans, reflected the light almost as vividly as the river, when Taliesin descended one of the hills that border the beautiful valley in which then stood Caer Lleon, the metropolis of Britain, and in which now stands, on a small portion of the selfsame space, a little insignificant town, possessing nothing of its ancient glory but the unaltered name of Caer Lleon.

The rapid Usk flowed then, as now, under the walls : the high wooden bridge, with its slender piles, was then much the same as it is at this day ; it seems to have been never regularly rebuilt, but to have been repaired, from time to time, on the original Roman model. The same green and fertile meadows, the same gently-sloping wood-covered hills, that now meet the eye of the tourist, then met the eye of Taliesin ; except that the woods on one side of the valley were then only the skirts of an extensive forest, which the nobility and beauty of Caer Lleon made frequently re-echo to the clamours of the chase.

The city, which had been so long the centre of the Roman supremacy, which was now the seat of the most illustrious

---

[1] Caer Lleon upon Usk in Cambria . London in Loegria : and York in Deïra and Bernicia.

sovereign that had yet held the sceptre of Britain, could not be approached by the youthful bard, whose genius was destined to eclipse that of all his countrymen, without feelings and reflections of deep interest. The sentimental tourist (who, perching himself on an old wall, works himself up into a soliloquy of philosophical pathos, on the vicissitudes of empire and the mutability of all sublunary things, interrupted only by an occasional peep at his watch, to ensure his not overstaying the minute at which his fowl, comfortably roasting at the nearest inn, has been promised to be ready) has, no doubt, many fine thoughts well worth recording in a dapper volume; but Taliesin had an interest in the objects before him too deep to have a thought to spare, even for his dinner. The monuments of Roman magnificence, and of Roman domination, still existing in comparative freshness; the arduous struggle in which his countrymen were then engaged with the Saxons, and which, notwithstanding the actual triumphs of Arthur, Taliesin's prophetic spirit told him would end in their being dispossessed of all the land of Britain, except the wild region of Wales (a result which political sagacity might have apprehended from their disunion, but which, as he told it to his countrymen in that memorable prophecy which every child of the Cymry knows, has established for him, among them, the fame of a prophet); the importance to himself and his benefactors of the objects of his visit to the city, on the result of which depended the liberation of Elphin, and the success of his love for Melanghel; the degree in which these objects might be promoted by the construction he had put on Seithenyn's imperfect communication respecting the lady in Dinas Vawr,—furnished, all together, more materials for absorbing thought than the most zealous peregrinator, even if he be at once poet, antiquary, and philosopher, is likely to have at once in his mind, on the top of the finest old wall on the face of the earth.

Taliesin passed, in deep musing, through the gates of Caer Lleon; but his attention was speedily drawn to the objects around him. From the wild solitudes in which he had passed his earlier years, the transition to the castles and cities he had already visited, furnished much food to curiosity; but the ideas of them sank into comparative nothingness before the magnificence of Caer Lleon.

He did not stop in the gateway to consider the knotty question, which has since puzzled so many antiquaries, whether the name of Caer Lleon signifies the City of Streams, the City of Legions, or the City of King Lleon? He saw a river filled with ships, flowing through fine meadows, bordered by hills and forests; walls of brick, as well as of stone; a castle, of impregnable strength; stately houses, of the most admirable architecture; palaces, with gilded roofs; Roman temples, and Christian churches; a theatre, and an amphitheatre. The public and private buildings of the departed Romans were in excellent preservation; though the buildings, and especially the temples, were no longer appropriated to their original purposes. The king's butler, Bedwyr, had taken possession of the Temple of Diana, as a cool place of deposit for wine; he had recently effected a stowage of vast quantities therein, and had made a most luminous arrangement of the several kinds, under the judicious and experienced superintendence of Dyvrig, the ex-Archbishop of Caer Lleon, who had just then nothing else to do, having recently resigned his see in favour of King Arthur's uncle, David, who is, to this day, illustrious as the St. David in whose honour the Welshmen annually adorn their hats with a leek. This David was a very respectable character in his way: he was a man of great sanctity and simplicity; and, in order to eschew the vanities of the world, which were continually present to him in Caer Lleon, he removed the metropolitan see, from Caer Lleon, to the rocky, barren, woodless, streamless, meadowless, tempest-beaten point of Mynyw, which was afterwards called St. David's. He was the mirror and pattern of a godly life; teaching by example, as by precept; admirable in words, and excellent in deeds; tall in stature, handsome in aspect, noble in deportment, affable in address, eloquent and learned, a model to his followers, the life of the poor, the protector of widows, and the father of orphans. This makes altogether a very respectable saint; and it cannot be said that the honourable leek is unworthily consecrated. A long series of his Catholic successors maintained, in great magnificence, a cathedral, a college, and a palace; keeping them all in repair, and feeding the poor into the bargain, from the archi-episcopal, or, when the primacy of Caer Lleon had merged in that of Canterbury, from the episcopal, revenues: but these things were reformed altogether by one of the first Protestant bishops, who, having a lady that longed for the gay world, and wanting more than all the revenues for himself and his family, first raised the wind by selling off the lead from the roof of his palace, and then obtained permission to remove from it, on the plea that it was not watertight. The immediate successors of this bishop, whose name was Barlow, were in every way worthy of him ; the palace and college have, consequently, fallen into incurable dilapidation, and the cathedral has fallen partially into ruins, and, most impartially, into neglect and defacement.

To return to Taliesin, in the streets of Caer Lleon. Plautus and Terence were not heard in the theatre, nor to be heard of in its neighbourhood ; but it was thought an excellent place for an Eisteddfod, or Bardic Congress, and was made the principal place of assembly of the Bards of the island of Britain. This is what Ross of Warwick means, when he says there was a noble university of students in Caer Lleon.

The mild precepts of the new religion had banished the ferocious sports to which the Romans had dedicated the amphitheatre, and, as Taliesin passed, it was pouring forth an improved and humanised multitude, who had been enjoying the pure British pleasure of baiting a bear.

The hot baths and aqueducts, the stoves of 'wonderful artifice,' as Giraldus has it, which diffused hot air through narrow spiracles, and many other wonders of the place, did not all present themselves to a first observation. The streets were thronged with people, especially of the fighting order, of whom a greater number flocked about Arthur than he always found it convenient to pay. Horsemen, with hawks and hounds, were returning from the neighbouring forest, accompanied by beautiful huntresses, in scarlet and gold.

Taliesin, having perlustrated the city, proceeded to the palace of Arthur. At the gates he was challenged by a formidable guard, but passed by his bardic privilege. It was now very near Christmas, and when Taliesin entered the great hall, it was blazing with artificial light, and glowing with the heat of the Roman stoves.

Arthur had returned victorious from the great battle of Badon Hill, in which he had slain with his own hand four hundred and forty Saxons ; and was feasting as merrily as an honest man can be supposed to do while his wife is away.

Kings, princes, and soldiers of fortune, bards and prelates, ladies superbly apparelled, and many of them surpassingly beautiful; and a most gallant array of handsome young cup-bearers, marshalled and well drilled by the king's butler, Bedwyr, who was himself a petty king, were the chief components of the illustrious assembly.

Amongst the ladies were the beautiful Tegau Eurvron; Dywir the Golden-haired; Enid, the daughter of Yniwl; Garwen, the daughter of Henyn; Gwyl, the daughter of Enddaud; and Indeg, the daughter of Avarwy Hir, of Maelienydd. Of these, Tegau Eurvron, or Tegau of the Golden Bosom, was the wife of Caradoc, and one of the Three Chaste Wives of the island of Britain. She is the heroine who, as the lady of Sir Cradock, is distinguished above all the ladies of Arthur's court, in the ballad of the 'Boy and the Mantle.'

Amongst the bards were Prince Llywarch, then in his youth, afterwards called Llywarch Hên, or Llywarch the Aged; Aneurin, the British Homer, who sang the fatal battle of Cattraëth, which laid the foundation of the Saxon ascendency, in heroic numbers, which the gods have preserved to us, and who was called the Monarch of the Bards, before the days of the glory of Taliesin; and Merddin Gwyllt, or Merlin the Wild, who was so deep in the secrets of nature, that he obtained the fame of a magician, to which he had at least as good a title as either Friar Bacon or Cornelius Agrippa.

Amongst the petty kings, princes, and soldiers of fortune, were twenty-four marchawg, or cavaliers, who were the counsellors and champions of Arthur's court. This was the heroic band, illustrious, in the songs of chivalry, as the Knights of the Round Table. Their names and pedigrees would make a very instructive and entertaining chapter; and would include the interesting characters of Gwalchmai ap Gwyar the Courteous, the nephew of Arthur; Caradoc, 'Colofn Cymry,' the Pillar of Cambria, whose lady, as above noticed, was the mirror of chastity; and Trystan ap Tallwch, the lover of the beautiful Essyllt, the daughter, or, according to some, the wife, of his uncle March ap Meirchion: persons known to all the world, as Sir Gawain, Sir Cradock, and Sir Tristram.

On the right hand of King Arthur sate the beautiful Indeg, and on his left the lovely Garwen. Taliesin advanced, along the tesselated floor, towards the upper end of the hall, and, kneeling before King Arthur, said, 'What boon will King Arthur grant to him who brings news of his queen?'

'Any boon,' said Arthur, 'that a king can give.'

'Queen Gwenyvar,' said Taliesin, 'is the prisoner of King Melvas, in the castle of Dinas Vawr.'

The mien and countenance of his informant satisfied the king that he knew what he was saying; therefore, without further parlance, he broke up the banquet, to make preparations for assailing Dinas Vawr.

But, before he began his march, King Melvas had shifted his quarters, and passed beyond the Severn to the isle of Avallon, where the marshes and winter-floods assured him some months of tranquillity and impunity.

King Arthur was highly exasperated, on receiving the intelligence of Melvas's movement; but he had no remedy, and was reduced to the alternative of making the best of his Christmas with the ladies, princes, and bards who crowded his court.

The period of the winter solstice had been always a great festival with the northern nations, the commencement of the lengthening of the days being, indeed, of all points in the circle of the year, that in which the inhabitants of cold countries have most cause to rejoice. This great festival was anciently called Yule—whether derived from the Gothic *Iola*, to make merry; or from the Celtic *Hiaul*, the sun; or from the Danish and Swedish *Hiul*, signifying wheel or revolution, December being *Hiul-month*, or the month of return; or from the Cimbric word *Ol*, which has the important signification of ALE, is too knotty a controversy to be settled here; but Yule had been long a great festival with both Celts and Saxons, and, with the change of religion, became the great festival of Christmas, retaining most of its ancient characteristics while England was Merry England: a phrase which must be a mirifical puzzle to any one who looks for the first time on its present most lugubrious inhabitants.

The mistletoe of the oak was gathered by the Druids with great ceremonies, as a symbol of the season. The mistletoe continued to be so gathered, and to be suspended in halls and kitchens, if not in temples, implying an unlimited privilege of kissing: which circumstance, probably, led a learned antiquary to opine that it was the forbidden fruit.

The Druids, at this festival, made, in a capacious cauldron, a mystical brewage of carefully-selected ingredients, full of occult virtues, which they kept from the profane, and which was typical of the new year and of the transmigration of the soul. The profane, in humble imitation, brewed a bowl of spiced ale, or wine, throwing therein roasted crabs ; the hissing of which, as they plunged, piping hot, into the liquor, was heard with much unction at midwinter, as typical of the conjunct benignant influences of fire and strong drink. The Saxons called this the Wassail-bowl, and the brewage of it is reported to have been one of the charms with which Rowena fascinated Vortigern.

King Arthur kept his Christmas so merrily, that the memory of it passed into a proverb : [1] 'As merry as Christmas in Caer Lleon.'

Caer Lleon was the merriest of places, and was commonly known by the name of Merry Caer Lleon ; which the English ballad-makers, for the sake of the smoother sound, and confounding Cambria with Cumbria, most ignorantly or audaciously turned into Merry Carlisle ; thereby emboldening a northern antiquary to set about proving that King Arthur was a Scotchman ; according to the old principles of harry and foray, which gave Scotchmen a right to whatever they could find on the English border ; though the English never admitted their title to anything there, excepting a halter in Carlisle.

The chase, in the neighbouring forest ; tilting in the amphitheatre ; trials of skill in archery, in throwing the lance and riding at the quintain, and similar amusements of the morning, created good appetites for the evening feasts ; in which Prince Cei, who is well known as Sir Kay, the seneschal, superintended the viands, as King Bedwyr did the liquor ; having each a thousand men at command, for their provision, arrangement, and distribution ; and music worthy of the banquet was provided and superintended by the king's chief harper, Geraint, of whom a contemporary poet observes, that when he died the gates of heaven were thrown wide open, to welcome the ingress of so divine a musician.

[1] 'Mor llawen ag Ngdolig yn Nghaerlleon.'

CHAPTER XIII

THE GHOSTLINESS OF AVALLON

Poco più poco meno, tutti al mondo vivono d'impostura : e chi è di buon gusto, dissimula quando occorre, gode quando può crede quel che vuole, ride de' pazzi, e figura un mondo a suo gusto.—GOLDONI.

'WHERE is the young bard,' said King Arthur, after some nights of Christmas had passed by, ' who' brought me the news of my queen, and to whom I promised a boon, which he has not yet claimed?'

None could satisfy the king's curiosity. Taliesin had disappeared from Caer Lleon. He knew the power and influence of Maelgon Gwyneth ; and he was aware that King Arthur, however favourably he might receive his petition, would not find leisure to compel the liberation of Elphin till he had enforced from Melvas the surrender of his queen. It occurred to him that her restoration might be effected by peaceable means ; and he knew that, if he could be in any degree instrumental to this result, it would greatly strengthen his claims on the king. He engaged a small fishing-vessel, which had just landed a cargo for the Christmas feasts of Caer Lleon, and set sail for the isle of Avallon. At that period, the spring-tides of the sea rolled round a cluster of islands, of which Avallon was one, over the extensive fens, which wiser generations have embanked and reclaimed.

The abbey of Avallon, afterwards called Glastonbury, was, even then, a comely and commodious pile, though not possessing any of that magnificence which the accumulated wealth of ages subsequently gave to it. A large and strongly-fortified castle, almost adjoining the abbey, gave to the entire place the air of a stronghold of the church militant. King Melvas was

A face, as round and as red as the setting sun in November, shone forth in the aperture.

one of the pillars of the orthodoxy of those days : he was called
the Scourge of the Pelagians ; and extended the shield of his
temporal might over the spiritual brotherhood of Avallon, who,
in return, made it a point of conscience not to stint him in
absolutions.

Some historians pretend that a comfortable nunnery was
erected at a convenient distance from the abbey, that is to say,
close to it ; but this involves a nice question in monastic
antiquity, which the curious may settle for themselves.

It was about midway between nones and vespers when
Taliesin sounded, on the gate of the abbey, a notice of his
wish for admission. A small trap-door in the gate was
cautiously opened, and a face, as round and as red as the
setting sun in November, shone forth in the aperture.

The topographers who have perplexed themselves about
the origin of the name of Ynys Avallon, ‘ the island of apples,’
had not the advantage of this piece of meteoroscopy : if they
could have looked on this archetype of a Norfolk beefin, with
the knowledge that it was only a sample of a numerous fraternity, they would at once have perceived the fitness of the
appellation. The brethren of Avallon were the apples of the
church. It was the oldest monastic establishment in Britain ;
and consequently, as of reason, the most plump, succulent,
and rosy. It had, even in the sixth century, put forth the
fruits of good living, in a manner that would have done honour
to a more enlightened age. It went on steadily improving in
this line till the days of its last abbot, Richard Whiting, who
built the stupendous kitchen, which has withstood the ravages
of time and the Reformation ; and who, as appears by
authentic documents, and, amongst others, by a letter signed
with the honoured name of Russell, was found guilty, by a
right worshipful jury, of being suspected of great riches, and
of an inclination to keep them ; and was accordingly sentenced
to be hanged forthwith, along with his treasurer and sub-
treasurer, who were charged with aiding and abetting him in
the safe custody of his cash and plate ; at the same time that
the Abbot of Peterborough was specially reprieved from the
gallows, on the ground that he was the said Russell’s particular
friend. This was a compendium of justice and mercy according to the new light of King Henry the Eighth. The abbot’s
kitchen is the most interesting and perfect portion of the

existing ruins. These ruins were overgrown with the finest ivy in England, till it was, not long since, pulled down by some Vandal, whom the Society of Antiquaries had sent down to make drawings of the walls, which he executed literally, by stripping them bare, that he might draw the walls, and nothing else. Its shade no longer waves over the musing moralist, who, with folded arms, and his back against a wall, dreams of the days that are gone; or the sentimental cockney, who, seating himself with much gravity on a fallen column, produces a flute from his pocket, and strikes up 'I'd be a butterfly.'

From the phenomenon of a blushing fruit that was put forth in the abbey gate of Avallon issued a deep, fat, gurgling voice, which demanded of Taliesin his name and business.

'I seek the abbot of Avallon,' said Taliesin.

'He is confessing a penitent,' said the ghostly brother, who was officiating in turn as porter.

'I can await his leisure,' said Taliesin, 'but I must see him.'

'Are you alone?' said the brother.

'I am,' said Taliesin.

The gate unclosed slowly, just wide enough to give him admittance. It was then again barred and barricaded.

The ghostly brother, of whom Taliesin had now a full view, had a figure corresponding with his face, and wanted nothing but a pair of horns and a beard in ringlets, to look like an avatar of Bacchus. He maintained, however, great gravity of face, and decorum of gesture, as he said to Taliesin, 'Hospitality is the rule of our house; but we are obliged to be cautious in these times, though we live under powerful protection. Those bloody Nimrods, the Saxons, are athirst for the blood of the righteous. Monsters that are born with tails.'

Taliesin had not before heard of this feature of Saxon conformation, and expressed his astonishment accordingly.

'How?' said the monk. 'Did not a rabble of them fasten goats' tails to the robe of the blessed preacher in Riw, and did he not, therefore, pray that their posterity might be born with tails? And it is so. But let that pass. Have they not ..... monasteries, plundered churches, and put holy brethren to the sword? The blood of the saints calls for vengeance.'

'And will have it,' said Taliesin, 'from the hand of Arthur.'

The name of Arthur evidently discomposed the monk, who,

And strikes up ' I'd be a butterfly.'

desiring Taliesin to follow him, led the way across the hall of the abbey, and along a short wide passage, at the end of which was a portly door.

The monk disappeared through this door, and, presently returning, said, 'The abbot requires your name and quality.'

'Taliesin, the bard of Elphin ap Gwythno Garanhir,' was the reply.

The monk disappeared again, and, returning, after a longer pause than before, said, 'You may enter.'

The abbot was a plump and comely man, of middle age, having three roses in his complexion : one in full blossom on each cheek, and one in bud on the tip of his nose.

He was sitting at a small table, on which stood an enormous vase and a golden goblet ; and opposite to him sat the penitent of whom the round-faced brother had spoken, and in whom Taliesin recognised his acquaintance of Dinas Vawr, who called himself Seithenyn ap Seithyn.

The abbot and Seithenyn sat with their arms folded on the table, leaning forward towards each other, as if in momentous discussion.

The abbot said to Taliesin, 'Sit'; and to his conductor, 'Retire, and be silent.'

'Will it not be better,' said the monk, 'that I cross my lips with the sign of secrecy?'

'It is permitted,' said the abbot.

Seithenyn held forth the goblet to the monk, who swallowed the contents with much devotion. He then withdrew, and closed the door.

'I bid you most heartily welcome,' said Seithenyn to Taliesin. 'Drink off this, and I will tell you more. You are admitted to this special sitting at my special instance. I told the abbot I knew you well. Now I will tell you what I know. You have told King Arthur that King Melvas has possession of Queen Gwenyvar, and, in consequence, King Arthur is coming here, to sack and raze the castle and abbey, and cut every throat in the isle of Avallon. I have just brought the abbot this pleasant intelligence, and, as I knew it would take him down a cup or two, I have also brought what I call my little jug, to have the benefit of his judgment on a piece of rare wine which I have broached this morning : there is no better in Caer Lleon. And now we are holding council on the emergency. But I must say you abuse your bardic privilege, to enjoy people's hospitality, worm out their secrets, and carry the news to the enemy. It was partly to give you this candid opinion that I have prevailed on the abbot to admit you to this special sitting. Therefore drink. GWIN O EUR : Wine from gold.'

'King Arthur is not a Saxon, at any rate,' sighed the abbot, winding up his fainting spirits with a draught. 'Think not, young stranger, that I am transgressing the laws of temperance: my blood runs so cold when I think of the bloodthirsty Saxons, that I take a little wine medicinally, in the hope of warming it ; but it is a slow and tedious remedy.'

'Take a little more,' said Seithenyn. 'That is the true quantity. Wine is my medicine ; and my quantity is a little more. A little more.'

'King Arthur,' said Taliesin, 'is not a Saxon ; but he does not brook injuries lightly. It were better for your abbey that he came not here in arms. The aiders and abettors of Melvas, even though they be spiritual, may not carry off the matter without some share of his punishment, which is infallible.'

'That is just what I have been thinking,' said Seithenyn.

'God knows,' said the abbot, 'we are not abettors of Melvas, though we need his temporal power to protect us from the Saxons.'

'How can it be otherwise,' said Taliesin, 'than that these Saxon despoilers should be insolent and triumphant, while the princes of Britain are distracted with domestic broils : and for what ?'

'Ay,' said Seithenyn, 'that is the point. For what ? For a woman, or some such rubbish.'

'Rubbish, most verily,' said the abbot. 'Women are the flesh which we renounce with the devil.'

'Holy father,' said Taliesin, 'have you not spiritual influence with Melvas, to persuade him to surrender the queen without bloodshed, and, renewing his allegiance to Arthur, assist him in his most sacred war against the Saxon invaders ?'

'A righteous work,' said the abbot; 'but Melvas is headstrong and difficult.'

'Screw yourself up with another goblet,' said Seithenyn ; 'you will find the difficulty smooth itself off wonderfully. Wine from gold has a sort of double light, that illuminates a dark path miraculously.'

'I will take a simple and single draught of what happens to be here.'

The abbot sighed deeply, but adopted Seithenyn's method of throwing light on the subject.

'The anger of King Arthur,' said Taliesin, 'is certain, and its consequences infallible. The anger of King Melvas is doubtful, and its consequences to you cannot be formidable.'

'That is nearly true,' said the abbot, beginning to look resolute, as the rosebud at his nose-tip deepened into damask.

'A little more,' said Seithenyn, 'and it will become quite true.'

By degrees the proposition ripened into absolute truth. The abbot suddenly inflated his cheeks, started on his legs, and stalked bolt upright out of the apartment, and forthwith out of the abbey, followed by Seithenyn, tossing his goblet in the air, and catching it in his hand, as he went.

The round-faced brother made his appearance almost immediately. 'The abbot,' he said, 'commends you to the hospitality of the brotherhood. They will presently assemble to supper. In the meanwhile, as I am thirsty, and content with whatever falls in my way, I will take a simple and single draught of what happens to be here.'

His draught was a model of simplicity and singleness ; for, having uplifted the ponderous vase, he held it to his lips, till he had drained it of the very copious remnant which the abrupt departure of the abbot had caused Seithenyn to leave in it.

Taliesin proceeded to enjoy the hospitality of the brethren, who set before him a very comfortable hot supper, at which he quickly perceived that, however dexterous King Elphin might be at catching fish, the monks of Avallon were very far his masters in the three great arts of cooking it, serving it up, and washing it down ; but he had not time to profit by their skill and experience in these matters, for he received a pressing invitation to the castle of Melvas, which he obeyed immediately.

CHAPTER XIV

THE RIGHT OF MIGHT

The three triumphs of the bards of the isle of Britain : the triumph of learning over ignorance ; the triumph of reason over error ; and the triumph of peace over violence.—TRIADS OF BARDISM.

'FRIEND SEITHENYN,' said the abbot, when, having passed the castle gates, and solicited an audience, he was proceeding to the presence of Melvas, 'this task, to which I have accinged myself, is arduous, and in some degree awful ; being, in truth, no less than to persuade a king to surrender a possession, which he has inclination to keep for ever, and power to keep, at any rate, for an indefinite time.'

'Not so very indefinite,' said Seithenyn ; 'for with the first song of the cuckoo (whom I mention on this occasion as a party concerned) King Arthur will batter his castle about his ears, and, in all likelihood, the abbey about yours.'

The abbot sighed heavily.

'If your heart fail you,' said Seithenyn, 'another cup of wine will set all to rights.'

'Nay, nay, friend Seithenyn,' said the abbot, 'that which I have already taken has just brought me to the point at which the heart is inspirited, and the wit sharpened, without any infraction of the wisdom and gravity which become my character, and best suit my present business.'

Seithenyn, however, took an opportunity of making signs to some cupbearers, and, when they entered the apartment of Melvas, they were followed by vessels of wine and goblets of gold.

King Melvas was a man of middle age, with a somewhat round, large, regular-featured face, and an habitual smile of extreme self-satisfaction, which he could occasionally convert into a look of terrific ferocity, the more fearful for being rare. His manners were, for the most part, pleasant. He did much mischief, not for mischief's sake, nor yet for the sake of excitement, but for the sake of something tangible. He had a total and most complacent indifference to everything but his own will and pleasure. He took what he wanted wherever he could find it, by the most direct process, and without any false pretence. He would have disdained the trick which the chroniclers ascribe to Hengist, of begging as much land as a bull's hide would surround, and then shaving it into threads, which surrounded a goodly space. If he wanted a piece of land, he encamped upon it, saying, 'This is mine.' If the former possessor could eject him, so ; it was not his : if not, so ; it remained his. Cattle, wine, furniture, another man's wife, whatever he took a fancy to, he pounced upon and appropriated. He was intolerant of resistance ; and, as the shortest way of getting rid of it, and not from any blood-thirstiness of disposition, or, as the phrenologists have it, development of the organ of destructiveness, he always cut through the resisting body, longitudinally, horizontally, or diagonally, as he found most convenient. He was the arch-marauder of West Britain. The abbey of Avallon shared largely in the spoil, and they made up together a most harmonious church and state. He had some respect for King Arthur ; wished him success against the Saxons ; knew the superiority of his power to his own ; but he had heard that Queen Gwenyvar was the most beautiful woman in Britain ; was, therefore, satisfied of his own title to her, and, as she was hunting in the forest, while King Arthur was absent from Caer Lleon, he seized her, and carried her off.

'Be seated, holy father,' said Melvas ; 'and you, also, Seithenyn, unless the abbot wishes you away.'

But the abbot's heart misgave him, and he assented readily to Seithenyn's stay.

Melvas. Now, holy father, to your important matter of private conference.

Seithenyn. He is tongue-tied, and a cup too low.

The Abbot. Set the goblet before me, and I will sip in moderation.

Melvas. Sip, or not sip, tell me your business.

The Abbot. My business, of a truth, touches the lady your prisoner, King Arthur's queen.

Melvas. She is my queen, while I have her, and no prisoner. Drink, man, and be not afraid. Speak your mind: I will listen, and weigh your words.

The Abbot. This queen——

Seithenyn. Obey the king: first drink, then speak.

The Abbot. I drink to please the king.

Melvas. Proceed.

The Abbot. This queen, Gwenyvar, is as beautiful as Helen, who caused the fatal war that expelled our forefathers from Troy: and I fear she will be a second Helen, and expel their posterity from Britain.[1] The infidel Saxons, to whom the cowardly and perfidious Vortigern gave footing in Britain, have prospered even more by the disunion of her princes than either by his villany, or their own valour. And now there is no human hope against them but in the arms of Arthur. And how shall his arms prosper against the common enemy, if he be forced to turn them on the children of his own land for the recovery of his own wife?

Melvas. What do you mean by his own? That which he has, is his own: but that which I have, is mine. I have the wife in question, and some of the land. Therefore they are mine.

The Abbot. Not so. The land is yours under fealty to him.

Melvas. As much fealty as I please, or he can force me, to give him.

The Abbot. His wife, at least, is most lawfully his.

Melvas. The winner makes the law, and his law is always against the loser. I am so far the winner; and, by my own law, she is lawfully mine.

The Abbot. There is a law above all human law, by which she is his.

Melvas. From that it is for you to absolve me; and I dispense my bounty according to your indulgence.

---

[1] According to the British Chronicles, Brutus, the great-grandson of Æneas, having killed his father, Silvius, to fulfil a prophecy, went to Greece, where he found the posterity of Helenus, the son of Priam; collected all of the Trojan race within the limits of Greece; and, after some adventures by land and sea, settled them in Britain, which was before uninhabited, 'except by a few giants.'

'*Obey the king: first drink, then speak.*'

The Abbot.   There are limits we must not pass.

Melvas.   You set up your landmark, and I set up mine. They are both movable.

The Abbot.   The Church has not been niggardly in its indulgences to King Melvas.

Melvas.   Nor King Melvas in his gifts to the Church.

The Abbot.   But, setting aside this consideration, I would treat it as a question of policy.

Seithenyn.   Now you talk sense.   Right without might is the lees of an old barrel, without a drop of the original liquor.

The Abbot.   I would appeal to you, King Melvas, by your love to your common country, by your love of the name of Britain, by your hatred of the infidel Saxons, by your respect for the character of Arthur ; will you let your passion for a woman, even though she be a second Helen, frustrate, or even impede, the great cause, of driving these spoilers from a land in which they have no right even to breathe ?

Melvas.   They have a right to do all they do, and to have all they have.   If we can drive them out, they will then have no right here.   Have not you and I a right to this good wine, which seems to trip very merrily over your ghostly palate ?   I got it by seizing a good ship, and throwing the crew overboard, just to remove them out of the way, because they were troublesome.   They disputed my right, but I taught them better.   I taught them a great moral lesson, though they had not much time to profit by it.   If they had had the might to throw me overboard, I should not have troubled myself about their right, any more, or, at any rate, any longer, than they did about mine.

Seithenyn.   The wine was lawful spoil of war.

The Abbot.   But if King Arthur brings his might to bear upon yours, I fear neither you nor I shall have a right to this wine, nor to anything else that is here.

Seithenyn.   Then make the most of it while you have it.

The Abbot.   Now, while you have some months of security before you, you may gain great glory by surrendering the lady ; and, if you be so disposed, you may no doubt claim, from the gratitude of King Arthur, the fairest princess of his court to wife, and an ample dower withal.

Melvas.   That offers something tangible.

Seithenyn. Another ray from the golden goblet will set it in a most luminous view.

The Abbot. Though I should advise the not making it a condition, but asking it, as a matter of friendship, after the first victory that you have helped him to gain over the Saxons.

Melvas. The worst of those Saxons is, that they offer nothing tangible, except hard knocks. They bring nothing with them. They come to take; and lately they have not taken much. But I will muse on your advice; and, as it seems, I may get more by following than rejecting it, I shall very probably take it, provided that you now attend me to the banquet in the hall.

Seithenyn. Now you talk of the hall and the banquet, I will just intimate that the finest of all youths, and the best of all bards, is a guest in the neighbouring abbey.

Melvas. If so, I have a clear right to him, as a guest for myself.

The abbot was not disposed to gainsay King Melvas's right. Taliesin was invited accordingly, and seated at the left hand of the king, the abbot being on the right. Taliesin summoned all the energies of his genius to turn the passions of Melvas into the channels of Anti-Saxonism, and succeeded so perfectly, that the king and his whole retinue of magnanimous heroes were inflamed with intense ardour to join the standard of Arthur; and Melvas vowed most solemnly to Taliesin, that another sun should not set, before Queen Gwenyvar should be under the most honourable guidance on her return to Caer Lleon.

CHAPTER XV

THE CIRCLE OF THE BARDS

The three dignities of poetry : the union of the true and the wonderful ;
the union of the beautiful and the wise ; and the union of art and nature.
—TRIADS OF POETRY.

AMONGST the Christmas amusements of Caer Lleon, a grand
Bardic Congress was held in the Roman theatre, when the
principal bards of Britain contended for the pre-eminence in
the art of poetry, and in its appropriate moral and mystical
knowledge. The meeting was held by daylight. King Arthur
presided, being himself an irregular bard, and admitted, on
this public occasion, to all the efficient honours of a Bard of
Presidency.

To preside in the Bardic Congress was long a peculiar
privilege of the kings of Britain. It was exercised in the
seventh century by King Cadwallader. King Arthur was
assisted by twelve umpires, chosen by the bards, and confirmed by the king.

The Court, of course, occupied the stations of honour, and
every other part of the theatre was crowded with a candid and
liberal audience.

The bards sate in a circle on that part of the theatre
corresponding with the portion which we call the stage.

Silence was proclaimed by the herald ; and, after a grand
symphony, which was led off in fine style by the king's harper,
Geraint, Prince Cei came forward, and made a brief oration,
to the effect that any of the profane, who should be irregular
and tumultuous, would be forcibly removed from the theatre,
to be dealt with at the discretion of the officer of the guard.
Silence was then a second time proclaimed by the herald.

Each bard, as he stood forward, was subjected to a number of interrogatories, metrical and mystical, which need not be here reported. Many bards sang many songs. Amongst them, Prince Llywarch sang

GORWYNION Y GAUAV

THE BRILLIANCIES OF WINTER

Last of flowers, in tufts around
Shines the gorse's golden bloom :
Milk-white lichens clothe the ground
'Mid the flowerless heath and broom :
Bright are holly-berries, seen
Red, through leaves of glossy green.

Brightly, as on rocks they leap,
Shine the sea-waves, white with spray ;
Brightly, in the dingles deep,
Gleams the river's foaming way ;
Brightly through the distance show
Mountain-summits clothed in snow.

Brightly, where the torrents bound,
Shines the frozen colonnade,
Which the black rocks, dripping round,
And the flying spray have made :
Bright the ice-drops on the ash
Leaning o'er the cataract's dash.

Bright the hearth, where feast and song
Crown the warrior's hour of peace,
While the snow-storm drives along,
Bidding war's worse tempest cease ;
Bright the hearth-flame, flashing clear
On the up-hung shield and spear.

Bright the torchlight of the hall
When the wintry night-winds blow ;
Brightest when its splendours fall
On the mead-cup's sparkling flow :
While the maiden's smile of light
Makes the brightness trebly bright.

Close the portals ; pile the hearth ;
Strike the harp ; the feast pursue ;

THE CIRCLE OF THE BARDS

Brim the horns : fire, music, mirth,
Mead and love, are winter's due.
Spring to purple conflict calls
Swords that shine on winter's walls.

Llywarch's song was applauded, as presenting a series of images with which all present were familiar, and which were all of them agreeable.

Merlin sang some verses of the poem which is called

AVALLENAU MYRDDIN

MERLIN'S APPLE-TREES

Fair the gift to Merlin given,
Apple-trees seven score and seven ;
Equal all in age and size ;
On a green hill-slope, that lies
Basking in the southern sun,
Where bright waters murmuring run.

Just beneath the pure stream flows ;
High above the forest grows ;
Not again on earth is found
Such a slope of orchard ground :
Song of birds, and hum of bees,
Ever haunt the apple-trees.

Lovely green their leaves in spring ;
Lovely bright their blossoming :
Sweet the shelter and the shade
By their summer foliage made :
Sweet the fruit their ripe boughs hold,
Fruit delicious, tinged with gold.

Gloyad, nymph with tresses bright,
Teeth of pearl, and eyes of light,
Guards these gifts of Ceidio's son,
Gwendol, the lamented one,
Him, whose keen-edged sword no more
Flashes 'mid the battle's roar.

War has raged on vale and hill :
That fair grove was peaceful still.
There have chiefs and princes sought
Solitude and tranquil thought :

There have kings, from courts and throngs,
Turned to Merlin's wild-wood songs.

Now from echoing woods I hear
Hostile axes sounding near :
On the sunny slope reclined,
Feverish grief disturbs my mind,
Lest the wasting edge consume
My fair spot of fruit and bloom.

Lovely trees, that long alone
In the sylvan vale have grown,
Bare, your sacred plot around,
Grows the once wood-waving ground :
Fervent valour guards ye still ;
Yet my soul presages ill.

Well I know, when years have flown,
Briars shall grow where ye have grown :
Them in turn shall power uproot ;
Then again shall flowers and fruit
Flourish in the sunny breeze,
On my new-born apple-trees.

This song was heard with much pleasure, especially by those of the audience who could see, in the imagery of the apple-trees, a mystical type of the doctrines and fortunes of Druidism, to which Merlin was suspected of being secretly attached, even under the very nose of St. David.

Aneurin sang a portion of his poem on the Battle of Cattraeth ; in which he shadowed out the glory of Vortimer, the weakness of Vortigern, the fascinations of Rowena, the treachery of Hengist, and the vengeance of Emrys.

THE MASSACRE OF THE BRITONS

Sad was the day for Britain's land,
A day of ruin to the free,
When Gorthyn [1] stretched a friendly hand
To the dark dwellers of the sea. [2]

But not in pride the Saxon trod,
Nor force nor fraud oppressed the brave,

---

[1] Gwrtheyrn ; Vortigern.   [2] Hengist and Horsa.

THE CIRCLE OF THE BARDS

Ere the grey stone and flowery sod
Closed o'er the blessed hero's grave.[1]

The twice-raised monarch [2] drank the charm,
The love-draught of the ocean-maid : [3]
Vain then the Briton's heart and arm,
Keen spear, strong shield, and burnished blade.

'Come to the feast of wine and mead,'
Spake the dark dweller of the sea : [4]
'There shall the hours in mirth proceed ;
There neither sword nor shield shall be.'

Hard by the sacred temple's site,
Soon as the shades of evening fall,
Resounds with song and glows with light
The ocean-dweller's rude-built hall.

The sacred ground, where chiefs of yore
The everlasting fire adored,
The solemn pledge of safety bore,
And breathed not of the treacherous sword.

The amber wreath his temples bound ;
His vest concealed the murderous blade ;
As man to man, the board around,
The guileful chief his host arrayed.

None but the noblest of the land,
The flower of Britain's chiefs, were there :
Unarmed, amid the Saxon band,
They sate, the fatal feast to share.

Three hundred chiefs, three score and three,
Went, where the festal torches burned
Before the dweller of the sea :
They went ; and three alone returned.

Till dawn the pale sweet mead they quaffed :
The ocean-chief unclosed his vest ;
His hand was on his dagger's haft,
And daggers glared at every breast.

---

[1] Gwrthevyr : Vortimer, who drove the Saxons out of Britain.

[2] Vortigern, who was, on the death of his son Vortimer, restored to the throne from which he had been deposed.

[3] Ronwen : Rowena.   [4] Hengist.

But him, at Eidiol's [1] breast who aimed,
The mighty Briton's arm laid low :
His eyes with righteous anger flamed ;
He wrenched the dagger from the foe ;

And through the throng he cleft his way,
And raised without his battle-cry ;
And hundreds hurried to the fray,
From towns, and vales, and mountains high.

But Britain's best blood dyed the floor
Within the treacherous Saxon's hall ;
Of all, the golden chain who wore,
Two only answered Eidiol's call.

Then clashed the sword ; then pierced the lance ;
Then by the axe the shield was riven ;
Then did the steed on Cattraeth prance,
And deep in blood his hoofs were driven.

Even as the flame consumes the wood,
So Eidiol rushed along the field ;
As sinks the snow-bank in the flood,
So did the ocean-rovers yield.

The spoilers from the fane he drove ;
He hurried to the rock-built tower,
Where the base king, [2] in mirth and love,
Sate with his Saxon paramour. [2]

The storm of arms was on the gate,
The blaze of torches in the hall,
So swift, that ere they feared their fate,
The flames had scaled their chamber wall.

They died : for them no Briton grieves ;
No planted flower above them waves ;
No hand removes the withered leaves
That strew their solitary graves.

And time the avenging day brought round
That saw the sea-chief vainly sue :
To make his false host bite the ground
Was all the hope our warrior knew.

---

[1] Eidiol or Emrys : Emrys Wledig : Ambrosius.
[2] Vortigern and Rowena.

THE CIRCLE OF THE BARDS

> And evermore the strife he led,
> Disdaining peace, with princely might,
> Till, on a spear, the spoiler's [1] head
> Was reared on Caer-y-Cynan's height.

The song of Aneurin touched deeply on the sympathies of the audience, and was followed by a grand martial symphony, in the midst of which Taliesin appeared in the Circle of Bards. King Arthur welcomed him with great joy, and sweet smiles were showered upon him from all the beauties of the court.

Taliesin answered the metrical and mystical questions to the astonishment of the most proficient ; and, advancing, in his turn, to the front of the circle, he sang a portion of a poem which is now called HANES TALIESIN, The History of Taliesin; but which shall be here entitled

THE CAULDRON OF CERIDWEN

> The sage Ceridwen was the wife
> Of Tegid Voël, of Pemble Mere :
> Two children blest their wedded life,
> Morvran and Creirwy, fair and dear :
> Morvran, a son of peerless worth,
> And Creirwy, loveliest nymph of earth :
> But one more son Ceridwen bare,
> As foul as they before were fair.
>
> She strove to make Avagddu wise ;
> She knew he never could be fair :
> And, studying magic mysteries,
> She gathered plants of virtue rare :
> She placed the gifted plants to steep
> Within the magic cauldron deep,
> Where they a year and day must boil,
> Till three drops crown the matron's toil.
>
> Nine damsels raised the mystic flame ;
> Gwion the Little near it stood :
> The while for simples roved the dame
> Through tangled dell and pathless wood.
> And, when the year and day had past,
> The dame within the cauldron cast
> The consummating chaplet wild,
> While Gwion held the hideous child.

---

[1] Hengist.

But from the cauldron rose a smoke
That filled with darkness all the air :
When through its folds the torchlight broke,
Nor Gwion, nor the boy, was there.
The fire was dead, the cauldron cold,
And in it lay, in sleep uprolled,
Fair as the morning-star, a child,
That woke, and stretched its arms, and smiled.

What chanced her labours to destroy,
She never knew ; and sought in vain
If 'twere her own misshapen boy,
Or little Gwion, born again :
And, vext with doubt, the babe she rolled
In cloth of purple and of gold,
And in a coracle consigned
Its fortunes to the sea and wind.

The summer night was still and bright,
The summer moon was large and clear,
The frail bark, on the spring-tide's height,
Was floated into Elphin's weir.
The baby in his arms he raised :
His lovely spouse stood by, and gazed,
And, blessing it with gentle vow,
Cried 'TALIESIN !' 'Radiant brow !'

And I am he : and well I know
Ceridwen's power protects me still ;
And hence o'er hill and vale I go,
And sing, unharmed, whate'er I will.
She has for me Time's veil withdrawn :
The images of things long gone,
The shadows of the coming days,
Are present to my visioned gaze.

And I have heard the words of power,
By Ceirion's solitary lake,
That bid, at midnight's thrilling hour,
Eryri's hundred echoes wake.
I to Diganwy's towers have sped,
And now Caer Lleon's halls I tread,
Demanding justice, now, as then,
From Maelgon, most unjust of men.

The audience shouted with delight at the song of Taliesin,
and King Arthur, as President of the Bardic Congress, con-
ferred on him, at once, the highest honours of the sitting.

Where Taliesin picked up the story which he told of himself, why he told it, and what he meant by it, are questions not easily answered. Certain it is, that he told this story to his contemporaries, and that none of them contradicted it. It may, therefore, be presumed that they believed it ; as any one who pleases is most heartily welcome to do now.

Besides the single songs, there were songs in dialogue, approaching very nearly to the character of dramatic poetry ; and pennillion, or unconnected stanzas, sung in series by different singers, the stanzas being complete in themselves, simple as Greek epigrams, and presenting in succession moral precepts, pictures of natural scenery, images of war or of festival, the lamentations of absence or captivity, and the complaints or triumphs of love. This pennillion-singing long survived among the Welsh peasantry almost every other vestige of bardic customs, and may still be heard among them on the few occasions on which rack-renting, tax-collecting, common-enclosing, methodist-preaching, and similar developments of the light of the age, have left them either the means or inclination of making merry.

CHAPTER XVI

THE JUDGMENTS OF ARTHUR

Three things to which success cannot fail where they shall justly be : discretion, exertion, and hope.—TRIADS OF WISDOM.

KING ARTHUR had not long returned to his hall, when Queen Gwenyvar arrived, escorted by the Abbot of Avallon and Seithenyn ap Seithyn Saidi, who had brought his golden goblet, to gain a new harvest of glory from the cellars of Caer Lleon.

Seithenyn assured King Arthur, in the name of King Melvas, and on the word of a king, backed by that of his butler, which, truth being in wine, is good warranty even for a king, that the queen returned as pure as on the day King Melvas had carried her off.

'None here will doubt that,' said Gwenvach, the wife of Modred. Gwenyvar was not pleased with the compliment, and, almost before she had saluted King Arthur, she turned suddenly round, and slapped Gwenvach on the face, with a force that brought more crimson into one cheek than blushing had ever done into both. This slap is recorded in the Bardic Triads as one of the Three Fatal Slaps of the Island of Britain. A terrible effect is ascribed to this small cause ; for it is said to have been the basis of that enmity between Arthur and Modred which terminated in the battle of Camlan, wherein all the flower of Britain perished on both sides : a catastrophe more calamitous than any that ever before or since happened in Christendom, not even excepting that of the battle of Roncesvalles ; for, in the battle of Camlan, the Britons ex-hausted their own strength, and could no longer resist the

This slap is recorded in the Bardic Triads as one of the Three Fatal Slaps.

progress of the Saxon supremacy. This, however, was a later result, and comes not within the scope of the present veridicous narrative.

Gwenvach having flounced out of the hall, and the tumult occasioned by this little incident having subsided, Queen Gwenyvar took her ancient seat by the side of King Arthur, who proceeded to inquire into the circumstances of her restoration. The Abbot of Avallon began an oration, in praise of his own eloquence, and its miraculous effects on King Melvas; but he was interrupted by Seithenyn, who said, 'The abbot's eloquence was good and well timed; but the chief merit belongs to this young bard, who prompted him with good counsel, and to me, who inspirited him with good liquor. If he had not opened his mouth pretty widely when I handed him this golden goblet, exclaiming GWIN O EUR, he would never have had the heart to open it to any other good purpose. But the most deserving person is this very promising youth, in whom I can see no fault, but that he has not the same keen perception as my friend the abbot has of the excellent relish of wine from gold. To be sure, he plied me very hard with strong drink in the hall of Dinas Vawr, and thereby wormed out of me the secret of Queen Gwenyvar's captivity; and, afterwards, he pursued us to Avallon, where he persuaded me and the abbot, and the abbot persuaded King Melvas, that it would be better for all parties to restore the queen peaceably: and then he clenched the matter with the very best song I ever heard in my life. And, as my young friend has a boon to ask, I freely give him all my share of the merit, and the abbot's into the bargain.'

'Allow me, friend GWIN O EUR,' said the abbot, 'to dispose of my own share of merit in my own way. But, such as it is, I freely give it to this youth, in whom, as you say, I can see no fault, but that his head is brimful of Pagan knowledge.'

Arthur paid great honour to Taliesin, and placed him on his left hand at the banquet. He then said to him, 'I judge, from your song of this morning, that the boon you require from me concerns Maelgon Gwyneth. What is his transgression, and what is the justice you require?'

Taliesin narrated the adventures of Elphin in such a manner as gave Arthur an insight into his affection for Melanghel; and he supplicated King Arthur to command and enforce the liberation of Elphin from the Stone Tower of Diganwy.

Before King Arthur could signify his assent, Maelgon Gwyneth stalked into the hall, followed by a splendid retinue. He had been alarmed by the absence of Rhûn, had sought him in vain on the banks of the Mawddach, had endeavoured to get at the secret by pouncing upon Angharad and Melanghel, and had been baffled in his project by the vigilance of Teithrin ap Tathral. He had, therefore, as a last resort, followed Taliesin to Caer Lleon, conceiving that he might have had some share in the mysterious disappearance of Rhûn.

Arthur informed him that he was in possession of all the circumstances, and that Rhûn, who was in safe custody, would be liberated on the restoration of Elphin.

Maelgon boiled with rage and shame, but had no alternative but submission to the will of Arthur.

King Arthur commanded that all the parties should be brought before him. Caradoc was charged with the execution of this order, and, having received the necessary communications and powers from Maelgon and Taliesin, he went first to Diganwy, where he liberated Elphin, and then proceeded to give effect to Teithrin's declaration, that 'no hand but Elphin's should raise the stone of Rhûn's captivity.' Rhûn, while his pleasant adventure had all the gloss of novelty upon it, and his old renown as a gay deceiver was consequently in such dim eclipse, was very unwilling to present himself before the ladies of Caer Lleon; but Caradoc was peremptory, and carried off the crestfallen prince, together with his bard of all work, who was always willing to go to any court, with any character, or none.

Accordingly, after a moderate lapse of time, Caradoc reappeared in the hall of Arthur, with the liberated captives, accompanied by Angharad and Melanghel, and Teithrin ap Tathral.

King Arthur welcomed the new-comers with a magnificent festival, at which all the beauties of his court were present, and, addressing himself to Elphin, said, 'We are all debtors to this young bard: my queen and myself for her restoration to me; you for your liberation from the Stone Tower of Diganwy. Now, if there be, amongst all these ladies, one whom he would choose for his bride, and in whose eyes he may find favour, I will give the bride a dowry worthy of the noblest princess in Britain.'

Taliesin, thus encouraged, took the hand of Melanghel, who did not attempt to withdraw it, but turned to her father a blushing face, in which he read her satisfaction and her wishes. Elphin immediately said, ' I have nothing to give him but my daughter ; but her I most cordially give him.'

Taliesin said, ' I owe to Elphin more than I can ever repay : life, honour, and happiness.'

Arthur said, ' You have not paid him ill ; but you owe nothing to Maelgon and Rhûn, who are your debtors for a lesson of justice, which I hope they will profit by during the rest of their lives. Therefore Maelgon shall defray the charge of your wedding, which shall be the most splendid that has been seen in Caer Lleon.'

Maelgon looked exceedingly grim, and wished himself well back in Diganwy.

There was a very pathetic meeting of recognition between Seithenyn and his daughter ; at the end of which he requested her husband's interest to obtain for him the vacant post of second butler to King Arthur. He obtained this honourable office ; and was so zealous in the fulfilment of its duties, that, unless on actual service with a detachment of liquor, he never was a minute absent from the Temple of Diana.

At a subsequent Bardic Congress, Taliesin was unanimously elected Pen Beirdd, or Chief of the Bards of Britain. The kingdom of Caredigion flourished under the protection of Arthur, and, in the ripeness of time, passed into the hands of Avaon, the son of Taliesin and Melanghel.

RHODODAPHNE

OR

THE THESSALIAN SPELL

Rogo vos, oportet, credatis, sunt mulieres plus sciae, sunt
nocturnae, et quod sursum est deorsum faciunt.—PETRONIUS.

Rogo vos, oportet, credatis, sunt mulieres plus sciae, sunt
nocturnae, et quod sursum est deorsum faciunt.—PETRONIUS.

PREFACE

The ancient celebrity of Thessalian magic is familiar, even from Horace, to every classical reader. The *Metamorphoses* of Apuleius turn entirely upon it, and the following passage in that work might serve as the text of a long commentary on the subject. 'Considering that I was now in the middle of Thessaly, celebrated by the accordant voice of the world as the birthplace of the magic art, I examined all things with intense curiosity. Nor did I believe anything which I saw in that city (Hypata) to be what it appeared; but I imagined that every object around me had been changed by incantation from its natural shape; that the stones of the streets, and the waters of the fountains, were indurated and liquefied human bodies; and that the trees which surrounded the city, and the birds which were singing in their boughs, were equally human beings, in the disguise of leaves and feathers. I expected the statues and images to walk, the walls to speak; I anticipated prophetic voices from the cattle, and oracles from the morning sky.'

According to Pliny, Menander, who was skilled in the subtleties of learning, composed a Thessalian drama, in which he comprised the incantations and magic ceremonies of women drawing down the moon. Pliny considers the belief in magic as the combined effect of the operations of three powerful causes, medicine, superstition, and the mathematical arts. He does not mention music, to which the ancients (as is shown by the fables of Orpheus, Amphion, the Sirens, etc.) ascribed the most miraculous powers: but, strictly speaking, it was included in the mathematical arts, as being a science of numerical proportion.

The belief in the supernatural powers of music and pharmacy

ascends to the earliest ages of poetry. Its most beautiful forms are the Circe of Homer, and Medea in the days of her youth, as she appears in the third book of Apollonius.

Lucian's treatise on the Syrian Goddess contains much wild and wonderful imagery; and his *Philopseudes*, though it does not mention Thessalian magic in particular, is a compendium of almost all the ideas entertained by the ancients of supernatural power, distinct from, and subordinate to, that of the gods; though the gods were supposed to be drawn from their cars by magic, and compelled, however reluctantly, to yield it a temporary obedience. These subjects appear to have been favourite topics with the ancients in their social hours, as we may judge from the *Philopseudes*, and from the tales related by Niceros and Trimalchio at the feast given by the latter in the *Satyricon* of Petronius. Trimalchio concludes his marvellous narrative by saying (in the words which form the motto of this poem): 'You must of necessity believe that there are women of supernatural science, framers of nocturnal incantations, who can turn the world upside down.'

It will appear from these references, and more might have been made if it had not appeared superfluous, that the power ascribed by the ancients to Thessalian magic is by no means exaggerated in the following poem, though its forms are in some measure diversified.

The opening scene of the poem is in the Temple of Love at Thespia, a town of Boeotia, near the foot of Mount Helicon. That Love was the principal deity of Thespia we learn from Pausanias; and Plutarch, in the beginning of his Erotic dialogue, informs us that a festival in honour of this deity was celebrated by the Thespians with great splendour every fifth year. They also celebrated a quinquennial festival in honour of the Muses, who had a sacred grove and temple in Helicon. Both these festivals are noticed by Pausanias, who mentions likewise the three statues of Love (though without any distinguishing attributes), and those of Venus and Phryne by Praxiteles. The Winged Love of Praxiteles, in Pentelican marble, which he gave to his mistress Phryne, who bestowed it on her native Thespia, was held in immense admiration by the ancients. Cicero speaks of it as the great and only attraction of Thespia.

The time is an intermediate period between the age of the

Greek tragedians, who are alluded to in the second canto, and that of Pausanias, in whose time the Thespian altar had been violated by Nero, and Praxiteles's statue of Love removed to Rome, for which outrageous impiety, says Pausanias, he was pursued by the just and manifest vengeance of the gods, who, it would seem, had already terrified Claudius into restoring it, when Caligula had previously taken it away.

The second song in the fifth canto is founded on the Homeric hymn, 'Bacchus, or the Pirates.' Some other imitations of classical passages, but for the most part interwoven with unborrowed ideas, will occur to the classical reader.

The few notes subjoined are such as seemed absolutely necessary to explain or justify the text. Those of the latter description might, perhaps, have been more numerous, if much deference had seemed due to that species of judgment, which, having neither light nor tact of its own, can only see and feel through the medium of authority.

> σοφὸς ὁ πολλὰ εἰδὼς φυᾷ·
> μαθόντες δὲ λάβροι
> παγγλωσσίᾳ, κόρακες ὥς, ἄκραντα γαρύετον
> Διὸς πρὸς ὄρνιχα θεῖον.
>
> Pind. *Olymp.* ii.

THE bards and sages of departed Greece
Yet live, for mind survives material doom ;
Still, as of yore, beneath the myrtle bloom
They strike their golden lyres, in sylvan peace.
Wisdom and Liberty may never cease,
Once having been, to be : but from the tomb
Their mighty radiance streams along the gloom
Of ages evermore without decrease.
Among those gifted bards and ságes old,
Shunning the living world, I dwell, and hear,
Reverent, the creeds they held, the tales they told :
And from the songs that charmed their latest ear,
A yet ungathered wreath, with fingers bold,
I weave, of bleeding love and magic mysteries drear.

CANTO I

CANTO I

THE rose and myrtle blend in beauty
Round Thespian Love's hypæthric fane ;
And there alone, with festal duty
Of joyous song and choral train,
From many a mountain, stream, and vale,
And many a city fair and free,
The sons of Greece commingling hail
Love's primogenial deity.
    Central amid the myrtle grove
That venerable temple stands :
Three statues, raised by gifted hands,
Distinct with sculptured emblems fair,
His threefold influence imaged bear,
Creative, Heavenly, Earthly Love.[1]
The first, of stone and sculpture rude,
From immemorial time has stood ;
Not even in vague tradition known
The hand that raised that ancient stone.
Of brass the next, with holiest thought,
The skill of Sicyon's artist wrought.[2]
The third, a marble form divine,
That seems to move, and breathe, and smile,
Fair Phryne to this holy shrine
Conveyed, when her propitious wile
Had forced her lover to impart
The choicest treasure of his art.[3]
Her, too, in sculptured beauty's pride,
His skill has placed by Venus' side ;
Nor well the enraptured gaze descries
Which best might claim the Hesperian prize.
    Fairest youths and maids assembling

Dance the myrtle bowers among :
Harps to softest numbers trembling
Pour the impassioned strain along,
Where the poet's gifted song
Holds the intensely listening throng.
Matrons grave and sages grey
Lead the youthful train to pay
Homage on the opening day
Of Love's returning festival :
Every fruit and every flower
Sacred to his gentler power,
Twined in garlands bright and sweet,
They place before his sculptured feet,
And on his name they call :
From thousand lips, with glad acclaim,
Is breathed at once that sacred name ;
And music, kindling at the sound,
Wafts holier, tenderer strains around :
The rose a richer sweet exhales ;
The myrtle waves in softer gales ;
Through every breast one influence flies ;
All hate, all evil passion dies ;
The heart of man, in that blest spell,
Becomes at once a sacred cell,
Where Love, and only Love, can dwell.[4]
   From Ladon's shores Anthemion came,
Arcadian Ladon, loveliest tide
Of all the streams of Grecian name
Through rocks and sylvan hills that glide.
The flower of all Arcadia's youth
Was he : such form and face, in truth,
As thoughts of gentlest maidens seek
In their day-dreams : soft glossy hair
Shadowed his forehead, snowy-fair,
With many a hyacinthine cluster :
Lips, that in silence seemed to speak,
Were his, and eyes of mild blue lustre :
And even the paleness of his cheek,
The passing trace of tender care,
Still shewed how beautiful it were
If its own natural bloom were there.

From Ladon's shores Anchemion came.

L

His native vale, whose mountains high
The barriers of his world had been,
His cottage home, and each dear scene
His haunt from earliest infancy,
He left, to Love's fair fane to bring
His simple wild-flower offering.
She with whose life his life was twined,
His own Calliroë, long had pined
With some strange ill, and none could find
What secret cause did thus consume
That peerless maiden's roseate bloom :
The Asclepian sage's skill was vain ;
And vainly have their vows been paid
To Pan, beneath the odorous shade
Of his tall pine ; and other aid
Must needs be sought to save the maid :
And hence Anthemion came, to try
In Thespia's old solemnity,
If such a lover's prayers may gain
From Love in his primæval fane.

He mingled in the votive train,
That moved around the altar's base.
Every statue's beauteous face
Was turned towards that central altar.
Why did Anthemion's footsteps falter ?
Why paused he, like a tale-struck child,
Whom darkness fills with fancies wild ?
A vision strange his sense had bound :
It seemed the brazen statue frowned—
The marble statue smiled.
A moment, and the semblance fled :
And when again he lifts his head,
Each sculptured face alone presents
Its fixed and placid lineaments.

He bore a simple wild-flower wreath :
Narcissus, and the sweet-briar rose ;
Vervain, and flexile thyme, that breathe
Rich fragrance ; modest heath, that glows
With purple bells ; the amaranth bright,
That no decay nor fading knows,
Like true love's holiest, rarest light ;

And every purest flower, that blows
In that sweet time, which Love most blesses,
When spring on summer's confines presses.
  Beside the altar's foot he stands,
And murmurs low his suppliant vow,
And now uplifts with duteous hands
The votive wild-flower wreath, and now—
At once, as when in vernal night
Comes pale frost or eastern blight,
Sweeping with destructive wing
Banks untimely blossoming,
Droops the wreath, the wild-flowers die;
One by one on earth they lie,
Blighted strangely, suddenly.
  His brain swims round; portentous fear
Across his wildered fancy flies:
Shall death thus seize his maiden dear?
Does Love reject his sacrifice?
He caught the arm of a damsel near,
And soft sweet accents smote his ear:
—'What ails thee, stranger?   Leaves are sear,
And flowers are dead, and fields are drear,
And streams are wild, and skies are bleak,
And white with snow each mountain's peak,
When winter rules the year;
And children grieve, as if for aye
Leaves, flowers, and birds were past away:
But buds and blooms again are seen,
And fields are gay, and hills are green,
And streams are bright, and sweet birds sing;
And where is the infant's sorrowing?'—
  Dimly he heard the words she said,
Nor well their latent meaning drew;
But languidly he raised his head,
And on the damsel fixed his view.
Was it a form of mortal mould
That did his dazzled sense impress?
Even painful from its loveliness!
Her bright hair, in the noonbeams glowing,
A rosebud wreath above confined,
From whence, as from a fountain, flowing,

Long ringlets round her temples twined,
And fell in many a graceful fold,
Streaming in curls of feathery lightness
Around her neck's marmoreal whiteness.
Love, in the smile that round her lips,
Twin roses of persuasion, played,
—Nectaries of balmier sweets than sips
The Hymettian bee,—his ambush laid ;
And his own shafts of liquid fire
Came on the soul with sweet surprise,
Through the soft dews of young desire
That trembled in her large dark eyes ;
But in those eyes there seemed to move
A flame, almost too bright for love,
That shone, with intermitting flashes,
Beneath their long deep-shadowy lashes.
—'What ails thee, youth ? '—her lips repeat,
In tones more musically sweet
Than breath of shepherd's twilight reed,
From far to woodland echo borne,
That floats like dew o'er stream and mead,
And whispers peace to souls that mourn.
—'What ails thee, youth ? '—'A fearful sign
For one whose dear sake led me hither :
Love repels me from his shrine,
And seems to say : That maid divine
Like these ill-omened flowers shall wither.'—
—'Flowers may die on many a stem ;
Fruits may fall from many a tree ;
Not the more for loss of them
Shall this fair world a desert be :
Thou in every grove wilt see
Fruits and flowers enough for thee.
Stranger ! I with thee will share
The votive fruits and flowers I bear,
Rich in fragrance, fresh in bloom ;
These may find a happier doom :
If they change not, fade not now,
Deem that Love accepts thy vow.'—
    The youth, mistrustless, from the maid
Received, and on the altar laid

The votive wreath : it did not fade ;
And she on his her offering threw.
Did fancy cloud Anthemion's view ?
Or did those sister garlands fair
Indeed entwine and blend again,
Wreathed into one, even as they were,
Ere she, their brilliant sweets to share,
Unwove their flowery chain ?
She fixed on him her radiant eyes,
And—'Love's propitious power,'—she said,—
'Accepts thy second sacrifice.
The sun descends tow'rds ocean's bed.
Day by day the sun doth set,
And day by day the sun doth rise,
And grass with evening dew-drops wet
The morning radiance dries :
And what if beauty slept, where peers
That mossy grass ? and lover's tears
Were mingled with that evening dew ?
The morning sun would dry them too.
Many a loving heart is near,
That shall its plighted love forsake :
Many lips are breathing here
Vows a few short days will break :
Many, lone amidst mankind,
Claim from Love's unpitying power
The kindred heart they ne'er shall find :
Many, at this festal hour,
Joyless in the joyous scene,
Pass, with idle glance unmoved,
Even those whom they could best have loved,
Had means of mutual knowledge been :
Some meet for once and part for aye,
Like thee and me, and scarce a day
Shall each by each remembered be :
But take the flower I give to thee,
And till it fades remember me.'—
  Anthemion answered not : his brain
Was troubled with conflicting thought :
A dim and dizzy sense of pain
That maid's surpassing beauty brought ;

Unconsciously the flower he took.

And strangely on his fancy wrought
Her mystic moralisings, fraught
With half-prophetic sense, and breathed
In tones so sweetly wild.
Unconsciously the flower he took,
And with absorbed admiring look
Gazed, as with fascinated eye
The lone bard gazes on the sky,
Who, in the bright clouds rolled and wreathed
Around the sun's descending car,
Sees shadowy rocks sublimely piled,
And phantom standards wide unfurled,
And towers of an aërial world
Embattled for unearthly war.
So stood Anthemion, till among
The mazes of the festal throng
The damsel from his sight had past ;
Yet well he marked that once she cast
A backward look, perchance to see
If he watched her still so fixedly.

CANTO II

CANTO II

DOES Love so weave his subtle spell,
So closely bind his golden chain,
That only one fair form may dwell
In dear remembrance, and in vain
May other beauty seek to gain
A place that idol form beside
In feelings all pre-occupied ?
Or does one radiant image, shrined
Within the inmost soul's recess,
Exalt, expand, and make the mind
A temple, to receive and bless
All forms of kindred loveliness ?

HOWBEIT, as from those myrtle bowers,
And that bright altar crowned with flowers,
Anthemion turned, as thought's wild stream
Its interrupted course resumed,
Still, like the phantom of a dream,
Before his dazzled memory bloomed
The image of that maiden strange :
Yet not a passing thought of change
He knew, nor once his fancy strayed
From his long-loved Arcadian maid.
Vaguely his mind the scene retraced,
Image on image wildly driven,
As in his bosom's fold he placed
The flower that radiant nymph had given.
With idle steps, at random bent,
Through Thespia's crowded ways he went ;
And on his troubled ear the strains

Of choral music idly smote ;
And with vacant eye he saw the trains
Of youthful dancers round him float,
As the musing bard from his sylvan seat
Looks on the dance of the noontide heat,
Or the play of the watery flowers, that quiver
In the eddies of a lowland river.
　　Around, beside him, to and fro,
The assembled thousands hurrying go.
These the palaestric sports invite,
Where courage, strength, and skill contend ;
The gentler Muses those delight,
Where throngs of silent listeners bend,
While rival bards, with lips of fire,
Attune to love the impassioned lyre ;
Or where the mimic scene displays
Some solemn tale of elder days,
Despairing Phaedra's vengeful doom,
Alcestis' love too dearly tried,
Or Haemon dying on the tomb
That closes o'er his living bride.[5]
　　But choral dance, and bardic strain,
Palaestric sport, and scenic tale,
Around Anthemion spread in vain
Their mixed attractions : sad and pale
He moved along, in musing sadness,
Amid all sights and sounds of gladness.
　　A sudden voice his musings broke.
He looked ; an aged man was near,
Of rugged brow, and eye severe.
—'What evil,'—thus the stranger spoke,—
'Has this our city done to thee,
Ill-omened boy, that thou should'st be
A blot on our solemnity ?
Or what Alastor bade thee wear
That laurel-rose, to Love profane,
Whose leaves, in semblance falsely fair
Of Love's maternal flower, contain
For purest fragrance deadliest bane ?[6]
Art thou a scorner ? dost thou throw
Defiance at his power ?　Beware !

Full soon thy impious youth may know
What pangs his shafts of anger bear ;
For not the sun's descending dart,
Nor yet the lightning-brand of Jove,
Fall like the shaft that strikes the heart
Thrown by the mightier hand of Love.'—
—' O stranger ! not with impious thought
My steps this holy rite have sought.
With pious heart and offerings due
I mingled in the votive train ;
Nor did I deem this flower profane ;
Nor she, I ween, its evil knew,
That radiant girl, who bade me cherish
Her memory till its bloom should perish. —
—'Who, and what, and whence was she ? —
—' A stranger till this hour to me.'—
—' O youth, beware ! that laurel-rose
Around Larissa's evil walls
In tufts of rank luxuriance grows,
'Mid dreary valleys, by the falls
Of haunted streams ; and magic knows
No herb or plant of deadlier might,
When impious footsteps wake by night
The echoes of those dismal dells,
What time the murky midnight dew
Trembles on many a leaf and blossom,
That draws from earth's polluted bosom
Mysterious virtue, to imbue
The chalice of unnatural spells.
Oft, those dreary rocks among,
The murmurs of unholy song,
Breathed by lips as fair as hers
By whose false hands that flower was given,
The solid earth's firm breast have riven,
And burst the silent sepulchres,
And called strange shapes of ghastly fear,
To hold, beneath the sickening moon,
Portentous parle, at night's deep noon,
With beauty skilled in mysteries drear.
O youth ! Larissa's maids are fair ;
But the daemons of the earth and air

Their spells obey, their councils share,
And wide o'er earth and ocean bear
Their mandates to the storms that tear
The rock-enrooted oak, and sweep
With whirlwind wings the labouring deep.
Their words of power can make the streams
Roll refluent on their mountain-springs,
Can torture sleep with direful dreams,
And on the shapes of earthly things,
Man, beast, bird, fish, with influence strange,
Breathe foul and fearful interchange,
And fix in marble bonds the form
Erewhile with natural being warm,
And give to senseless stones and stocks
Motion, and breath, and shape that mocks,
As far as nicest eye can scan,
The action and the life of man.
Beware ! yet once again beware !
Ere round thy inexperienced mind,
With voice and semblance falsely fair,
A chain Thessalian magic bind,
Which never more, O youth ! believe,
Shall either earth or heaven unweave.'—
    While yet he spoke, the morning scene,
In more portentous hues arrayed,
Dwelt on Anthemion's mind : a shade
Of deeper mystery veiled the mien
And words of that refulgent maid.
The frown, that, ere he breathed his vow,
Dwelt on the brazen statue's brow ;
His votive flowers, so strangely blighted ;
The wreath her beauteous hands untwined
To share with him, that, self-combined,
Its sister tendrils reunited,
Strange sympathy ! as in his mind
These forms of troubled memory blended
With dreams of evil undefined,
Of magic and Thessalian guile,
Now by the warning voice portended
Of that mysterious man, awhile,
Even when the stranger's speech had ended,

He stood as if he listened still.

He stood as if he listened still.
At length he said :—' O reverend stranger !
Thy solemn words are words of fear.
Not for myself I shrink from danger ;
But there is one to me more dear
Than all within this earthly sphere,
And many are the omens ill
That threaten her : to Jove's high will
We bow ; but if in human skill
Be aught of aid or expiation
That may this peril turn away,
For old Experience holds his station
On that grave brow, O stranger ! say.' —
—' O youth ! experience sad indeed
Is mine ; and should I tell my tale,
Therein thou might'st too clearly read
How little may all aid avail
To him, whose hapless steps around
Thessalian spells their chains have bound :
And yet such counsel as I may
I give to thee.   Ere close of day
Seek thou the planes, whose broad shades fall
On the stream that laves yon mountain's base :
There on thy Natal Genius call [7]
For aid, and with averted face
Give to the stream that flower, nor look
Upon the running wave again ;
For, if thou should'st, the sacred plane
Has heard thy suppliant vows in vain ;
Nor then thy Natal Genius can,
Nor Phoebus, nor Arcadian Pan,
Dissolve thy tenfold chain.'—
　　The stranger said, and turned away.
Anthemion sought the plane-grove's shade.
'Twas near the closing hour of day.
The slanting sunbeam's golden ray,
That through the massy foliage made
Scarce here and there a passage, played
Upon the silver-eddying stream,
Even on the rocky channel throwing
Through the clear flood its golden gleam.

The bright waves danced beneath the beam
To the music of their own sweet flowing.
The flowering sallows on the bank,
Beneath the o'ershadowing plane-trees wreathing
In sweet association, drank
The grateful moisture, round them breathing
Soft fragrance through the lonely wood.
There, where the mingling foliage wove
Its closest bower, two altars stood,
This to the Genius of the Grove,
That to the Naiad of the Flood.
So light a breath was on the trees,
That rather like a spirit's sigh
Than motion of an earthly breeze,
Among the summits broad and high
Of those tall planes its whispers stirred ;
And save that gentlest symphony
Of air and stream, no sound was heard,
But of the solitary bird,
That aye, at summer's evening hour,
When music save her own is none,
Attunes, from her invisible bower,
Her hymn to the descending sun.
    Anthemion paused upon the shore :
All thought of magic's impious lore,
All dread of evil powers, combined
Against his peace, attempered ill
With that sweet scene ; and on his mind
Fair, graceful, gentle, radiant still,
The form of that strange damsel came ;
And something like a sense of shame
He felt, as if his coward thought
Foul wrong to guileless beauty wrought.
At length—'O radiant girl !'—he said,—
' If in the cause that bids me tread
These banks, be mixed injurious dread
Of thy fair thoughts, the fears of love
Must with thy injured kindness plead
My pardon for the wrongful deed.
Ye Nymphs and Sylvan Gods, that rove
The precincts of this sacred wood !

'If round my footsteps dwell unholy sign or evil spell.'

Thou, Achelöus' gentle daughter,
Bright Naiad of this beauteous water !
And thou, my Natal Genius good !
Lo ! with pure hands the crystal flood
Collecting, on these altars blest,
Libation holiest, brightest, best,
I pour.   If round my footsteps dwell
Unholy sign or evil spell,
Receive me in your guardian sway ;
And thou, O gentle Naiad ! bear
With this false flower those spells away,
If such be lingering there.'—
    Then from the stream he turned his view,
And o'er his back the flower he threw.
Hark ! from the wave a sudden cry,
Of one in last extremity,
A voice as of a drowning maid !
The echoes of the sylvan shade
Gave response long and drear.
He starts : he does not turn.   Again !
It is Calliroë's cry !   In vain
Could that dear maiden's cry of pain
Strike on Anthemion's ear ?
At once, forgetting all beside,
He turned to plunge into the tide,
But all again was still :
The sun upon the surface bright
Poured his last line of crimson light,
Half-sunk behind the hill :
But through the solemn plane-trees past
The pinions of a mightier blast,
And in its many-sounding sweep,
Among the foliage broad and deep,
Aërial voices seemed to sigh,
As if the spirits of the grove
Mourned, in prophetic sympathy
With some disastrous love.

CANTO III

CANTO III

By living streams, in sylvan shades,
Where winds and waves symphonious make
Sweet melody, the youths and maids
No more with choral music wake
Lone Echo from her tangled brake,
On Pan, or Sylvan Genius, calling,
Naiad or Nymph, in suppliant song :
No more by living fountain, falling
The poplar's circling bower among,
Where pious hands have carved of yore
Rude bason for its lucid store
And reared the grassy altar nigh,
The traveller, when the sun rides high,
For cool refreshment lingering there,
Pours to the Sister Nymphs his prayer.
Yet still the green vales smile : the springs
Gush forth in light : the forest weaves
Its own wild bowers ; the breeze's wings
Make music in their rustling leaves ;
But 'tis no spirit's breath that sighs
Among their tangled canopies :
In ocean's caves no Nereid dwells :
No Oread walks the mountain-dells :
The streams no sedge-crowned Genii roll
From bounteous urn : great Pan is dead :
The life, the intellectual soul
Of vale, and grove, and stream, has fled
For ever with the creed sublime
That nursed the Muse of earlier time.

THE broad moon rose o'er Thespia's walls,
And on the light wind's swells and falls
Came to Anthemion's ear the sounds
Of dance, and song, and festal pleasure,
As slowly tow'rds the city's bounds
He turned, his backward steps to measure.
But with such sounds his heart confessed
No sympathy : his mind was pressed
With thoughts too heavy to endure
The contrast of a scene so gay ;
And from the walls he turned away,
To where, in distant moonlight pure,
Mount Helicon's conspicuous height
Rose in the dark-blue vault of night.
Along the solitary road
Alone he went ; for who but he
On that fair night would absent be
From Thespia's joyous revelry ?
The sounds that on the soft air flowed
By slow degrees in distance died :
And now he climbed the rock's steep side,
Where frowned o'er sterile regions wide
Neptunian Ascra's ruined tower : [8]
Memorial of gigantic power :
But thoughts more dear and more refined
Awakening, in the pensive mind,
Of him, the Muses' gentlest son,
The shepherd-bard of Helicon,
Whose song, to peace and wisdom dear,
The Aonian Dryads loved to hear.
By Aganippe's fountain-wave
Anthemion passed : the moonbeams fell
Pale on the darkness of the cave,
Within whose mossy rock-hewn cell
The sculptured form of Linus stood,
Primaeval bard.   The Nymphs for him
Through every spring, and mountain flood,
Green vale, and twilight woodland dim,
Long wept : all living nature wept
For Linus ; when, in minstrel strife,
Apollo's wrath from love and life

The child of music swept.
  The Muses' grove is nigh.   He treads
Its sacred precincts.   O'er him spreads
The palm's aërial canopy,
That, nurtured by perennial springs,
Around its summit broad and high
Its light and branchy foliage flings,
Arching in graceful symmetry.
Among the tall stems jagg'd and bare
Luxuriant laurel interweaves
An undershade of myriad leaves,
Here black in rayless masses, there
In partial moonlight glittering fair;
And wheresoe'er the barren rock
Peers through the grassy soil, its roots
The sweet andrachne strikes, to mock [9]
Sterility, and profusely shoots
Its light boughs, rich with ripening fruits.
The moonbeams, through the chequering shade,
Upon the silent temple played,
The Muses' fane.   The nightingale,
Those consecrated bowers among,
Poured on the air a warbled tale,
So sweet, that scarcely from her nest,
Where Orpheus' hallowed relics rest,
She breathes a sweeter song.[10]
  A scene, whose power the maniac sense
Of passion's wildest mood might own!
Anthemion felt its influence:
His fancy drank the soothing tone
Of all that tranquil loveliness;
And health and bloom returned to bless
His dear Calliroë, and the groves
And rocks where pastoral Ladon roves
Bore record of their blissful loves.
  List! there is music on the wind!
Sweet music! seldom mortal ear
On sounds so tender, so refined,
Has dwelt.   Perchance some Muse is near,
Euterpe, or Polymnia bright,
Or Erato, whose gentle lyre

Responds to love and young desire !
It is the central hour of night :
The time is holy, lone, severe,
And mortals may not linger here !
   Still on the air those wild notes fling
Their airy spells of voice and string,
In sweet accordance, sweeter made
By response soft from caverned shade.
He turns to where a lovely glade
Sleeps in the open moonlight's smile,
A natural fane, whose ample bound
The palm's columnar stems surround,
A wide and stately peristyle ;
Save where their interrupted ring
Bends on the consecrated cave,
From whose dark arch, with tuneful wave,
Libethrus issues, sacred spring.
Beside its gentle murmuring,
A maiden, on a mossy stone,
Full in the moonlight, sits alone :
Her eyes, with humid radiance bright,
As if a tear had dimmed their light,
Are fixed upon the moon ; her hair
Flows long and loose in the light soft air ;
A golden lyre her white hands bear ;
Its chords, beneath her fingers fleet,
To such wild symphonies awake,
Her sweet lips breathe a song so sweet,
That the echoes of the cave repeat
Its closes with as soft a sigh,
As if they almost feared to break
The magic of its harmony.
   Oh ! there was passion in the sound,
Intensest passion, strange and deep ;
Wild breathings of a soul, around
Whose every pulse one hope had bound,
One burning hope, which might not sleep.
But hark ! that wild and solemn swell !
And was there in those tones a spell,
Which none may disobey ? For lo !
Anthemion from the sylvan shade

Moves with reluctant steps and slow,
And in the lonely moonlight glade
He stands before the radiant maid.
   She ceased her song, and with a smile
She welcomed him, but nothing said :
And silently he stood the while,
And tow'rds the ground he drooped his head,
As if he shrunk beneath the light
Of those dark eyes so dazzling bright.
At length she spoke :—'The flower was fair
I bade thee till its fading wear :
And didst thou scorn the boon,
Or died the flower so soon ? '—
   —'It did not fade,
O radiant maid !
But Thespia's rites its use forbade,
To Love's vindictive power profane :
If soothly spoke the reverend seer,
Whose voice rebuked, with words severe,
Its beauty's secret bane.'—
—'The world, O youth ! deems many wise,
Who dream at noon with waking eyes,
While spectral fancy round them flings
Phantoms of unexisting things ;
Whose truth is lies, whose paths are error,
Whose gods are fiends, whose heaven is terror ;
And such a slave has been with thee,
And thou, in thy simplicity,
Hast deemed his idle sayings truth.
The flower I gave thee, thankless youth !
The harmless flower thy hand rejected,
Was fair : my native river sees
Its verdure and its bloom reflected
Wave in the eddies and the breeze.
My mother felt its beauty's claim,
And gave, in sportive fondness wild,
Its name to me, her only child.'—
   'Then RHODODAPHNE is thy name ? '—
Anthemion said : the maiden bent
Her head in token of assent.
—'Say once again, if sooth I deem,

Penëus is thy native stream ? '—
—' Down Pindus' steep Penëus falls,
And swift and clear through hill and dale
It flows, and by Larissa's walls,
And through wild Tempe, loveliest vale ;
And on its banks the cypress gloom
Waves round my father's lonely tomb.
My mother's only child am 1 :
Mid Tempe's sylvan rocks we dwell ;
And from my earliest infancy,
The darling of our cottage-dell
For its bright leaves and clusters fair,
My namesake flower has bound my hair.
With costly gift and flattering song,
Youths, rich and valiant, sought my love.
They moved me not.   I shunned the throng
Of suitors, for the mountain-grove
Where Sylvan Gods and Oreads rove.
The Muses, whom I worship here,
Had breathed their influence on my being,
Keeping my youthful spirit clear
From all corrupting thoughts, and freeing
My footsteps from the crowd, to tread
Beside the torrent's echoing bed,
Mid wind-tost pines, on steeps aërial,
Where elemental Genii throw
Effluence of natures more ethereal
Than vulgar minds can feel or know.
Oft on those steeps, at earliest dawn,
The world in mist beneath me lay,
Whose vapoury curtains, half withdrawn,
Revealed the flow of Therma's bay,
Red with the nascent light of day ;
Till full from Athos' distant height
The sun poured down his golden beams
Scattering the mists like morning dreams,
And rocks and lakes and isles and streams
Burst, like creation, into light.
In noontide bowers the bubbling springs,
In evening vales the winds that sigh
To eddying rivers murmuring by,

N

' O maid ! I have another love ! '

Have heard to these symphonious strings
The rocks and caverned glens reply.
Spirits that love the moonlight hour
Have met me on the shadowy hill:
Dream'st thou of Magic ? of the power
That makes the blood of life run chill,
And shakes the world with daemon skill ?
Beauty is Magic ; grace and song ;
Fair form, light motion, airy sound :
Frail webs ! and yet a chain more strong
They weave the strongest hearts around,
Than e'er Alcides' arm unbound :
And such a chain I weave round thee,
Though but with mortal witchery.'—
    His eyes and ears had drank the charm.
The damsel rose, and on his arm
She laid her hand.   Through all his frame
The soft touch thrilled like liquid flame ;
But on his mind Calliroë came
All pale and sad, her sweet eyes dim
With tears which for herself and him
Fell : by that modest image mild
Recalled, inspired, Anthemion strove
Against the charm that now beguiled
His sense, and cried, in accents wild,
—'O maid ! I have another love !'—
But still she held his arm, and spoke
Again in accents thrilling sweet :
—'In Tempe's vale a lonely oak
Has felt the storms of ages beat :
Blasted by the lightning-stroke,
A hollow, leafless, branchless trunk
It stands ; but in its giant cell
A mighty sylvan power doth dwell,
An old and holy oracle.
Kneeling by that ancient tree,
I sought the voice of destiny,
And in my ear these accents sunk :
" Waste not in loneliness thy bloom :
With flowers the Thespian altar dress :
The youth whom Love's mysterious doom

Assigns to thee, thy sight shall bless
With no ambiguous loveliness ;
And thou, amid the joyous scene,
Shalt know him, by his mournful mien,
And by the paleness of his cheek,
And by the sadness of his eye,
And by his withered flowers, and by
The language thy own heart shall speak."
And I did know thee, youth ! and thou
Art mine, and I thy bride must be.
Another love ! the gods allow
No other love to thee or me !'
   She gathered up her glittering hair,
And round his neck its tresses threw,
And twined her arms of beauty rare
Around him, and the light curls drew
In closer bands : ethereal dew
Of love and young desire was swimming
In her bright eyes, albeit not dimming
Their starry radiance, rather brightning
Their beams with passion's liquid lightning.
She clasped him to her throbbing breast,
And on his lips her lips she prest,
And cried the while
With joyous smile :
—'These lips are mine ; the spells have won them,
Which round and round thy soul I twine ;
And be the kiss I print upon them
Poison to all lips but mine !'—
   Dizzy awhile Anthemion stood,
With thirst-parched lips and fevered blood,
In those enchanting ringlets twined :
The fane, the cave, the moonlight wood,
The world, and all the world enshrined,
Seemed melting from his troubled mind :
But those last words the thought recalled
Of his Calliroë, and appalled
His mind with many a nameless fear
For her, so good, so mild, so dear.
With sudden start of gentle force
From Rhododaphne's arms he sprung,

And swifter than the torrent's course
From rock to rock in tumult flung,
Adown the steeps of Helicon,
By spring, and cave, and tower, he fled,
But turned from Thespia's walls, and on
Along the rocky way, that led
Tow'rds the Corinthian Isthmus, sped,
Impatient to behold again
His cottage-home by Ladon's side,
And her, for whose dear sake his brain
Was giddy with foreboding pain,
Fairest of Ladon's virgin train,
His own long-destined bride.

CANTO IV

CANTO IV

Magic and mystery, spells Circaean,
The Siren voice, that calmed the sea,
And steeped the soul in dews Lethaean ;
The enchanted chalice, sparkling free
With wine, amid whose ruby glow
Love couched, with madness linked and woe ;
Mantle and zone, whose woof beneath
Lurked wily grace, in subtle wreath
With blandishment and young desire
And soft persuasion intertwined,
Whose touch, with sympathetic fire,
Could melt at once the sternest mind ;
Have passed away : for vestal Truth
Young Fancy's foe, and Reason chill,
Have chased the dreams that charmed the youth
Of nature and the world, which still,
Amid that vestal light severe,
Our colder spirits leap to hear
Like echoes from a fairy hill.
Yet deem not so.   The Power of Spells
Still lingers on the earth, but dwells
In deeper folds of close disguise,
That baffle Reason's searching eyes :
Nor shall that mystic Power resign
To Truth's cold sway his webs of guile,
Till woman's eyes have ceased to shine,
And woman's lips have ceased to smile,
And woman's voice has ceased to be
The earthly soul of melody.

A night and day had passed away :
A second night.   A second day
Had risen.   The noon on vale and hill
Was glowing, and the pensive herds
In rocky pool and sylvan rill
The shadowy coolness sought.   The birds
Among their leafy bowers were still,
Save where the red-breast on the pine,
In thickest ivy's sheltering nest,
Attuned a lonely song divine,
To soothe old Pan's meridian rest.[11]
The stream's eternal eddies played
In light and music ; on its edge
The soft light air scarce moved the sedge :
The bees a pleasant murmuring made
On thymy bank and flowery hedge :
From field to field the grasshopper
Kept up his joyous descant shrill ;
When once again the wanderer,
With arduous travel faint and pale,
Beheld his own Arcadian vale.

From Oryx, down the sylvan way,
With hurried pace the youth proceeds.
Sweet Ladon's waves beside him stray
In dear companionship : the reeds
Seem, whispering on the margin clear,
The doom of Syrinx to rehearse,
Ladonian Syrinx, name most dear
To music and Maenalian verse.
It is the Aphrodisian grove.
Anthemion's home is near.   He sees
The light smoke rising from the trees
That shade the dwelling of his love.
Sad bodings, shadowy fears of ill,
Pressed heavier on him, in wild strife
With many-wandering hope, that still
Leaves on the darkest clouds of life
Some vestige of her radiant way :
But soon those torturing struggles end ;
For where the poplar silver-grey
And dark associate cedar blend

Their hospitable shade, before
One human dwelling's well-known door,
Old Pheidon sits, and by his side
His only child, his age's pride,
Herself, Anthemion's destined bride.
    She hears his coming tread.   She flies
To meet him.   Health is on her cheeks,
And pleasure sparkles in her eyes,
And their soft light a welcome speaks
More eloquent than words.   Oh, joy !
The maid he left so fast consuming,
Whom death, impatient to destroy,
Had marked his prey, now rosy-blooming,
And beaming like the morning star
With loveliness and love, has flown
To welcome him : his cares fly far,
Like clouds when storms are overblown ;
For where such perfect transports reign
Even memory has no place for pain.
    The poet's task were passing sweet,
If, when he tells how lovers meet,
One half the flow of joy, that flings
Its magic on that blissful hour,
Could touch, with sympathetic power,
His lyre's accordant strings.
It may not be.   The lyre is mute,
When venturous minstrelsy would suit
Its numbers to so dear a theme :
But many a gentle maid, I deem,
Whose heart has known and felt the like,
Can hear, in fancy's kinder dream,
The chords I dare not strike.
    They spread a banquet in the shade
Of those old trees.   The friendly board
Calliroë's beauteous hands arrayed,
With self-requiting toil, and poured
In fair-carved bowl the sparkling wine.
In order due Anthemion made
Libation, to Olympian Jove,
Arcadian Pan, and Thespian Love,
And Bacchus, giver of the vine.

The generous draught dispelled the sense
Of weariness.   His limbs were light :
His heart was free : Love banished thence
All forms but one most dear, most bright :
And ever with insatiate sight
He gazed upon the maid, and listened,
Absorbed in ever new delight,
To that dear voice, whose balmy sighing
To his full joy blest response gave,
Like music doubly-sweet replying
From twilight echo's sylvan cave ;
And her mild eyes with soft rays glistened,
Imparting and reflecting pleasure ;
For this is Love's terrestrial treasure,
That in participation lives,
And evermore, the more it gives,
Itself abounds in fuller measure.
  Old Pheidon felt his heart expand
With joy that from their joy had birth,
And said :—' Anthemion ! Love's own hand
Is here, and mighty on the earth
Is he, the primogenial power,
Whose sacred grove and antique fane
Thy prompted footsteps, not in vain,
Have sought ; for, on the day and hour
Of his incipient rite, most strange
And sudden was Calliroë's change.
The sickness under which she bowed,
Swiftly, as though it ne'er had been,
Passed, like the shadow of a cloud
From April's hills of green.
And bliss once more is yours ; and mine
In seeing yours, and more than this ;
For ever, in our children's bliss,
The sun of our past youth doth shine
Upon our age anew.   Divine
No less than our own Pan must be
To us Love's bounteous deity ;
And round our old and hallowed pine
The myrtle and the rose must twine
Memorial of the Thespian shrine.'—

'*Oh, thou art dead!*'

'Twas strange indeed, Anthemion thought,
That, in the hour when omens dread
Most tortured him, such change was wrought ;
But love and hope their lustre shed
On all his visions now, and led
His memory from the mystic train
Of fears which that strange damsel wove
Around him in the Thespian fane
And in the Heliconian grove.
    Eve came, and twilight's balmy hour :
Alone, beneath the cedar bower,
The lovers sate, in converse dear
Retracing many a backward year,
Their infant sports in field and grove,
Their mutual tasks, their dawning love,
Their mingled tears of past distress,
Now all absorbed in happiness ;
And oft would Fancy intervene,
To throw, on many a pictured scene
Of life's untrodden path, such gleams
Of golden light, such blissful dreams,
As in young Love's enraptured eye
Hope almost made reality.
    So in that dear accustomed shade,
With Ladon flowing at their feet,
Together sate the youth and maid,
In that uncertain shadowy light
When day and darkness mingling meet.
Her bright eyes ne'er had seemed so bright,
Her sweet voice ne'er had seemed so sweet,
As then they seemed.   Upon his neck
Her head was resting, and her eyes
Were raised to his, for no disguise
Her feelings knew ; untaught to check,
As in these days more worldly wise,
The heart's best purest sympathies.
    Fond youth ! her lips are near to thine :
The ringlets of her temples twine
Against thy cheek : oh ! more or less
Than mortal wert thou not to press
Those ruby lips !   Or does it dwell

Upon thy mind, that fervid spell
Which Rhododaphne breathed upon
Thy lips erewhile in Helicon?
Ah! pause, rash boy! bethink thee yet:
And canst thou then the charm forget?
Or dost thou scorn its import vain
As vision of a fevered brain?
    Oh! he has kissed Calliroë's lips!
And with the touch the maid grew pale,
And sudden shade of strange eclipse
Drew o'er her eyes its dusky veil.
As droops the meadow-pink its head,
By the rude scythe in summer's prime
Cleft from its parent stem, and spread
On earth to wither ere its time,
Even so the flower of Ladon faded,
Swifter than, when the sun hath shaded
In the young storm his setting ray,
The western radiance dies away.
    He pressed her heart: no pulse was there.
Before her lips his hand he placed:
No breath was in them.   Wild despair
Came on him, as, with sudden waste,
When snows dissolve in vernal rain,
The mountain-torrent on the plain
Descends; and with that fearful swell
Of passionate grief, the midnight spell
Of the Thessalian maid recurred,
Distinct in every fatal word:
—'These lips are mine; the spells have won them,
Which round and round thy soul I twine;
And be the kiss I print upon them
Poison to all lips but mine!'—
—'Oh, thou art dead, my love!'—he cried—
'Art dead, and I have murdered thee!'—
He started up in agony.
The beauteous maiden from his side
Sunk down on earth.   Like one who slept
She lay, still, cold, and pale of hue;
And her long hair all loosely swept
The thin grass, wet with evening dew.

O

And fled o'er plain and steep, with frantic tread, as Passion's aimless impulse led.

He could not weep ; but anguish burned
Within him like consuming flame.
He shrieked : the distant rocks returned
The voice of woe.   Old Pheidon came
In terror forth : he saw ; and wild
With misery fell upon his child,
And cried aloud, and rent his hair.
Stung by the voice of his despair,
And by the intolerable thought
That he, how innocent soe'er,
Had all this grief and ruin wrought,
And urged perchance by secret might
Of magic spells, that drew their chain
More closely round his phrensied brain,
Beneath the swiftly-closing night
Anthemion sprang away, and fled
O'er plain and steep, with frantic tread,
As Passion's aimless impulse led.

CANTO V

CANTO V

Though Pity's self has made thy breast
Its earthly shrine, O gentle maid !
Shed not thy tears, where Love's last rest
Is sweet beneath the cypress shade ;
Whence never voice of tyrant power,
Nor trumpet-blast from rending skies,
Nor winds that howl, nor storms that lower,
Shall bid the sleeping sufferer rise.
But mourn for them, who live to keep
Sad strife with fortune's tempests rude ;
For them, who live to toil and weep
In loveless, joyless solitude ;
Whose days consume in hope, that flies
Like clouds of gold that fading float,
Still watched with fondlier lingering eyes
As still more dim and more remote.
Oh ! wisely, truly, sadly sung
The bard by old Cephisus' side [12]
(While not with sadder, sweeter tongue,
His own loved nightingale replied) :
—' Man's happiest lot is NOT TO BE ;
And when we tread life's thorny steep,
Most blest are they, who, earliest free,
Descend to death's eternal sleep.'—

Long, wide, and far, the youth has strayed,
Forlorn, and pale, and wild with woe,
And found no rest.   His loved, lost maid,
A beauteous, sadly-smiling shade,
Is ever in his thoughts, and slow
Roll on the hopeless, aimless hours

Sunshine, and grass, and woods, and flowers,
Rivers, and vales, and glittering homes
Of busy men, where'er he roams,
Torment his sense with contrast keen,
Of that which is, and might have been.
　The mist that on the mountains high
Its transient wreath light-hovering flings,
The clouds and changes of the sky,
The forms of unsubstantial things,
The voice of the tempestuous gale,
The rain-swoln torrent's turbid moan,
And every sound that seems to wail
For beauty past and hope o'erthrown,
Attemper with his wild despair;
But scarce his restless eye can bear
The hills, and rocks, and summer streams
The things that still are what they were
When life and love were more than dreams.
　It chanced, along the rugged shore,
Where giant Pelion's piny steep
O'erlooks the wide Aegean deep,
He shunned the steps of humankind,
Soothed by the multitudinous roar
Of ocean, and the ceaseless shock
Of spray, high-scattering from the rock
In the wail of the many-wandering wind.
A crew, on lawless venture bound,
Such men as roam the seas around,
Hearts to fear and pity strangers,
Seeking gold through crimes and dangers,
Sailing near, the wanderer spied.
Sudden, through the foaming tide,
They drove to land, and on the shore
Springing, they seized the youth, and bore
To their black ship, and spread again
Their sails, and ploughed the billowy main.
　Dark Ossa on their watery way
Looks from his robe of mist; and, grey
With many a deep and shadowy fold,
The sacred mount, Olympus old,
Appears: but where with Therma's sea

‘ There sit !’—cried one in rugged tone.

Penëus mingles tranquilly,
They anchor with the closing light
Of day, and through the moonless night
Propitious to their lawless toil,
In silent bands they prowl for spoil.
    Ere morning dawns, they crowd on board,
And to their vessel's secret hoard
With many a costly robe they pass,
And vase of silver, gold, and brass.
A young maid too their hands have torn
From her maternal home, to mourn
Afar, to some rude master sold,
The crimes and woes that spring from gold.
—'There sit !'—cried one in rugged tone,—
'Beside that boy.   A well-matched pair
Ye seem, and will, I doubt not, bear,
In our good port, a value rare.
There sit, but not to wail and moan :
The lyre, which in those fingers fair
We leave, whose sound through night's thick shade
To unwished ears thy haunt bewrayed,
Strike ; for the lyre, by beauty played,
To glad the hearts of men was made.'—
    The damsel by Anthemion's side
Sate down upon the deck.   The tide
Blushed with the deepening light of morn.
A pitying look the youth forlorn
Turned on the maiden.   Can it be ?
Or does his sense play false ?   Too well
He knows that radiant form.   'Tis she,
The magic maid of Thessaly,
'Tis Rhododaphne ! By the spell,
That ever round him dwelt, opprest,
He bowed his head upon his breast,
And o'er his eyes his hand he drew,
That fatal beauty's sight to shun.
Now from the orient heaven the sun
Had clothed the eastward waves with fire :
Right from the west the fair breeze blew :
The full sails swelled, and sparkling through
The sounding sea the vessel flew :

With wine and copious cheer the crew
Caroused : the damsel o'er the lyre
Her rapid fingers lightly flung,
And thus, with feigned obedience, sung.
—'The Nereid's home is calm and bright,
The ocean-depths below,
Where liquid streams of emerald light
Through caves of coral flow.
She has a lyre of silver strings
Framed on a pearly shell,
And sweetly to that lyre she sings
The shipwrecked seaman's knell.
    The ocean-snake in sleep she binds ;
The dolphins round her play :
His purple conch the Triton winds
Responsive to the lay :
Proteus and Phorcys, sea-gods old,
Watch by her coral cell,
To hear, on watery echoes rolled,
The shipwrecked seaman's knell.'—
—' Cease ! '—cried the chief in accents rude—
'From songs like these mishap may rise.
Thus far have we our course pursued
With smiling seas and cloudless skies.
From wreck and tempest, omens ill,
Forbear ; and sing, for well 1 deem
Those pretty lips possess the skill,
Some ancient tale of happier theme ;
Some legend of imperial Jove,
In uncouth shapes disguised by love ;
Or Hercules, and his hard toils ;
Or Mercury, friend of craft and spoils ;
Or Jove-born Bacchus, whom we prize
O'er all the Olympian deities.'—
    He said, and drained the bowl.   The crew
With long coarse laugh applauded.   Fast
With sparkling keel the vessel flew,
For there was magic in the breeze
That urged her through the sounding seas.
By Chanastraeum's point they past,
And Ampelos.   Grey Athos, vast

With woods far-stretching to the sea,
Was full before them, while the maid
Again her lyre's wild strings assayed,
In notes of bolder melody :

—'Bacchus by the lonely ocean
Stood in youthful semblance fair :
Summer winds, with gentle motion,
Waved his black and curling hair.
Streaming from his manly shoulders
Robes of gold and purple dye
Told of spoil to fierce beholders
In their black ship sailing by.
On the vessel's deck they placed him
Strongly bound in triple bands ;
But the iron rings that braced him
Melted, wax-like, from his hands.
Then the pilot spake in terror :
—"'Tis a god in mortal form !
Seek the land ; repair your error
Ere his wrath invoke the storm."—
—"Silence !"—cried the frowning master,—
" Mind the helm : the breeze is fair :
Coward ! cease to bode disaster :
Leave to men the captive's care."—
While he speaks and fiercely tightens
In the full free breeze the sail,
From the deck wine bubbling lightens,
Winy fragrance fills the gale.
Gurgling in ambrosial lustre
Flows the purple-eddying wine :
O'er the yard-arms trail and cluster
Tendrils of the mantling vine :
Grapes, beneath the broad leaves springing,
Blushing as in vintage-hours,
Droop, while round the tall mast clinging
Ivy twines its buds and flowers,
Fast with graceful berries blackening :—
Garlands hang on every oar :
Then in fear the cordage slackening,
One and all they cry,—"To shore !"—

Bacchus changed his shape, and glaring
With a lion's eyeballs wide,
Roared : the pirate-crew, despairing,
Plunged amid the foaming tide.
Through the azure depths they flitted
Dolphins by transforming fate :
But the god the pilot pitied,
Saved, and made him rich and great.'—

   The crew laid by their cups, and frowned.
A stern rebuke the leader gave.
With arrowy speed the ship went round
Nymphaeum.   To the ocean-wave
The mountain-forest sloped, and cast
O'er the white surf its massy shade.
They heard, so near the shore they past,
The hollow sound the sea-breeze made,
As those primaeval trees it swayed.
—'Curse on thy songs !'—the leader cried,—
'False tales of evil augury !'—
—'Well hast thou said,'—the maid replied,—
'They augur ill to thine and thee.'—
   She rose, and loosed her radiant hair,
And raised her golden lyre in air.
The lyre, beneath the breeze's wings,
As if a spirit swept the strings,
Breathed airy music, sweet and strange,
In many a wild phantastic change.
Most like a daughter of the Sun [13]
She stood : her eyes all radiant shone
With beams unutterably bright ;
And her long tresses, loose and light,
As on the playful breeze they rolled,
Flamed with rays of burning gold.
His wondering eyes Anthemion raised
Upon the maid : the seamen gazed
In fear and strange suspense, amazed.
   From the forest-depths profound
Breathes a low and sullen sound :
'Tis the woodland spirit's sigh,
Ever heard when storms are nigh.

On the shore the surf that breaks
With the rising breezes makes
More tumultuous harmony.
Louder yet the breezes sing :
Round and round, in dizzy ring,
Sea-birds scream on restless wing :
Pine and cedar creak and swing
To the sea-blast's murmuring.
Far and wide on sand and shingle
Eddying breakers boil and mingle :
Beetling cliff and caverned rock
Roll around the echoing shock,
Where the spray, like snow-dust whirled,
High in vapoury wreaths is hurled.
   Clouds on clouds, in volumes driven,
Curtain round the vault of heaven.
—'To shore ! to shore !' the seamen cry.
The damsel waved her lyre on high,
And to the powers that rule the sea
It whispered notes of witchery.
Swifter than the lightning-flame
The sudden breath of the whirlwind came.
Round at once in its mighty sweep
The vessel whirled on the whirling deep.
Right from shore the driving gale
Bends the mast and swells the sail :
Loud the foaming.ocean raves :
Through the mighty waste of waves
Speeds the vessel swift and free,
Like a meteor of the sea.
   Day is ended.   Darkness shrouds
The shoreless seas and lowering clouds.
Northward now the tempest blows :
Fast and far the vessel goes :
Crouched on deck the seamen lie ;
One and all, with charmed eye,
On the magic maid they gaze :
Nor the youth with less amaze
Looks upon her radiant form
Shining by the golden beams
Of her refulgent hair, that streams

Like waving star-light on the storm ;
And hears the vocal blast that rings
Among her lyre's enchanted strings.
    Onward, onward flies the bark,
Through the billows wild and dark.
From her prow the spray she hurls ;
O'er her stern the big wave curls ;
Fast before the impetuous wind
She flies—the wave bursts far behind.
    Onward, onward flies the bark,
Through the raging billows :—Hark !
'Tis the stormy surge's roar
On the Aegean's northern shore.
Tow'rds the rocks, through surf and surge,
The destined ship the wild winds urge.
High on one gigantic wave
She swings in air.   From rock and cave
A long loud wail of fate and fear
Rings in the hopeless seaman's ear.
Forward, with the breaker's dash,
She plunges on the rock.   The crash
Of the dividing bark, the roar
Of waters bursting on the deck,
Are in Anthemion's ear : no more
He hears or sees : but round his neck
Are closely twined the silken rings
Of Rhododaphne's glittering hair,
And round him her bright arms she flings,
And cinctured thus in loveliest bands
The charmed waves in safety bear
The youth and the enchantress fair,
And leave them on the golden sands.

CANTO VI

Hast thou, in some safe retreat,
Waked and watched, to hear the roar
Of breakers on the wind-swept shore?
Go forth at morn.   The waves, that beat
Still rough and white when blasts are o'er,
May wash, all ghastly, to thy feet
Some victim of the midnight storm.
From that drencbed garb and pallid form
Shrink not : but fix thy gaze, and see
Thy own congenial destiny.
For him, perhaps, an anxious wife
On some far coast o'erlooks the wave :
A child, unknowing of the strife
Of elements, to whom he gave
His last fond kiss, is at her breast :
The skies are clear, the seas at rest
Before her, and the hour is nigh
Of his return : but black the sky
To him, and fierce the hostile main,
Have been.   He will not come again.
But yesterday, and life, and health,
And hope, and love, and power, and wealth,
Were his : to-day, in one brief hour,
Of all his wealth, of all his power,
He saved not, on his shattered deck,
A plank, to waft him from the wreck.
Now turn away, and dry thy tears,
And build long schemes for distant years !
Wreck is not only on the sea.
The warrior dies in victory :
The ruin of his natal roof

O'erwhelms the sleeping man : the hoof
Of his prized steed has struck with fate
The horseman in his own home gate :
The feast and mantling bowl destroy
The sensual in the hour of joy.
The bride from her paternal porch
Comes forth among her maids : the torch,
That led at morn the nuptial choir,
Kindles at night her funeral pyre.
Now turn away, indulge thy dreams,
And build for distant years thy schemes !

On Thracia's coast the morn was grey.
Anthemion, with the opening day,
From deep entrancement on the sands
Stood up.   The magic maid was there
Beside him on the shore.   Her hands
Still held the golden lyre : her hair
In all its long luxuriance hung
Unringleted, and glittering bright
With briny drops of diamond light :
Her thin wet garments lightly clung
Around her form's rare symmetry.
Like Venus risen from the sea
She seemed : so beautiful : and who
With mortal sight such form could view,
And deem that evil lurked beneath ?
Who could approach those starry eyes,
Those dewy coral lips, that breathe
Ambrosial fragrance, and that smile
In which all Love's Elysium lies,
Who this could see, and dream of guile,
And brood on wrong and wrath the while ?
If there be one, who ne'er has felt
Resolve, and doubt, and anger melt,
Like vernal night-frosts, in one beam
Of Beauty's sun, 'twere vain to deem,
Between the Muse and him could be
A link of human sympathy.
    Fain would the youth his lips unclose
In keen reproach for all his woes

Anthemion, with the opening day, from deep entrancement on the sands stood up.

And his Calliroë's doom.   In vain:
For closer now the magic chain
Of the inextricable spell
Involved him, and his accents fell
Perplexed, confused, inaudible.
And so awhile he stood.   At length,
In painful tones, that gathered strength
With feeling's faster flow, he said:
—'What would'st thou with me, fatal maid?
That ever thus, by land and sea,
Thy dangerous beauty follows me?'—
    She speaks in gentle accents low,
While dim through tears her bright eyes move:
—'Thou askest what thou well dost know;
I love thee, and I seek thy love.'—
    —'My love!   It sleeps in dust for ever
Within my lost Calliroë's tomb:
The smiles of living beauty never
May my soul's darkness re-illume.
We grew together, like twin flowers,
Whose opening buds the same dews cherish;
And one is reft, ere noon-tide hours,
Violently; one remains, to perish
By slow decay; as I remain
Even now, to move and breathe in vain.
The late, false love, that worldlings learn,
When hearts are hard, and thoughts are stern,
And feelings dull, and Custom's rule
Omnipotent, that love may cool,
And waste, and change: but this—which flings
Round the young soul its tendril rings,
Strengthening their growth and grasp with years,
Till habits, pleasures, hopes, smiles, tears,
All modes of thinking, feeling, seeing,
Of two congenial spirits, blend
In one inseparable being,—
Deem'st thou this love can change or end?
There is no eddy on the stream,
No bough that light winds bend and toss,
No chequering of the sunny beam
Upon the woodland moss,

No star in evening's sky, no flower
Whose beauty odorous breezes stir,
No sweet bird singing in the bower,
Nay, not the rustling of a leaf,
That does not nurse and feed my grief
By wakening thoughts of her.
All lovely things a place possessed
Of love in my Calliroë's breast:
And from her purer, gentler spirit,
Did mine the love and joy inherit,
Which that blest maid around her threw.
With all I saw, and felt, and knew,
The image of Calliroë grew,
Till all the beauty of the earth
Seemed as to her it owed its birth,
And did but many forms express
Of her reflected loveliness.
The sunshine and the air seemed less
The sources of my life: and how
Was she torn from me?   Earth is now
A waste, where many echoes tell
Only of her I loved—how well
Words have no power to speak :—and thou—
Gather the rose-leaves from the plain
Where faded and defiled they lie,
And close them in their bud again,
And bid them to the morning sky
Spread lovely as at first they were :
Or from the oak the ivy tear,
And wreathe it round another tree
In vital growth : then turn to me,
And bid my spirit cling on thee,
As on my lost Calliroë!'—
    —'The Genii of the earth, and sea,
And air, and fire, my mandates hear.
Even the dread Power, thy Ladon's fear,
Arcadian Daemogorgon, knows [14]
My voice : the ivy or the rose,
Though torn and trampled on the plain,
May rise, unite, and bloom again,
If on his aid I call : thy heart

Alone resists and mocks my art.'—
—'Why lov'st thou me, Thessalian maid?
Why hast thou, cruel beauty, torn
Asunder two young hearts, that played
In kindred unison so blest,
As they had filled one single breast
From life's first opening morn?
Why lov'st thou me?   The kings of earth
Might kneel to charms and power like thine:
But I, a youth of shepherd birth—
As well the stately mountain-pine
Might coil around the eglantine,
As thou thy radiant being twine
Round one so low, so lost as mine.'—
—'Sceptres and crowns, vain signs that move
The souls of slaves, to me are toys.
I need but love: I seek but love:
And long, amid the heartless noise
Of cities, and the woodland peace
Of vales, through all the scenes of Greece
I sought the fondest and the fairest
Of Grecian youths, my love to be:
And such a heart and form thou bearest,
And my soul sprang at once to thee,
Like an arrow to its destiny.
Yet shall my lips no spell repeat,
To bid thy heart responsive beat
To mine: thy love's spontaneous smile,
Nor forced by power, nor won by guile,
I claim: but yet a little while,
And we no more may meet.
For I must find a dreary home,
And thou, where'er thou wilt, shalt roam:
But should one tender thought awake
Of Rhododaphne, seek the cell,
Where she dissolved in tears doth dwell
Of blighted hope, and she will take
The wanderer to her breast, and make
Such flowers of bliss around him blow,
As kings would yield their thrones to know.'—
—'It must not be.   The air is laden

With sweetness from thy presence born :
Music and light are round thee, maiden,
As round the Virgin Power of Morn :
I feel, I shrink beneath, thy beauty :
But love, truth, woe, remembrance, duty,
All point against thee, though arrayed
In charms whose power no heart could shun
That ne'er had loved another maid
Or any but that loveliest one,
Who now, within my bosom's void,
A sad pale shade, by thee destroyed,
Forbids all other love to bind
My soul : thine least of womankind.'—
   Faltering and faint his accents broke,
As those concluding words he spoke.
No more she said, but sadly smiled,
And took his hand ; and like a child
He followed her.   All waste and wild,
A pathless moor before them lies.
Beyond, long chains of mountains rise :
Their summits with eternal snow
Are crowned : vast forests wave below,
And stretch, with ample slope and sweep,
Down to the moorlands and the deep.
Human dwelling see they none,
Save one cottage, only one,
Mossy, mildewed, frail, and poor,
Even as human home can be,
Where the forest skirts the moor,
By the inhospitable sea.
There, in tones of melody,
Sweet and clear as Dian's voice
When the rocks and woods rejoice
In her steps the chace impelling,
Rhododaphne, pausing, calls.
Echo answers from the walls :
Mournful response, vaguely telling
Of a long-deserted dwelling.
Twice her lips the call repeat,
Tuneful summons, thrilling sweet.
Still the same sad accents follow,

Up that image rose, and spake, as from a trumpet.

Cheerless echo, faint and hollow.
Nearer now, with curious gaze,
The youth that lonely cot surveys.
Long grass chokes the path before it.
Twining ivy mantles o'er it,
On the low roof blend together
Beds of moss and stains of weather,
Flowering weeds that trail and cluster,
Scaly lichen, stone-crop's lustre,
All confused in radiance mellow,
Red, grey, green, and golden yellow.
Idle splendour ! gleaming only
Over ruins rude and lonely,
When the cold hearth-stone is shattered,
When the ember-dust is scattered,
When the grass that chokes the portal
Bends not to the tread of mortal.

The maiden dropped Anthemion's hand,
And forward, with a sudden bound,
She sprung.   He saw the door expand,
And close, and all was silence round,
And loneliness : and forth again
She came not.   But within this hour,
A burthen to him, and a chain,
Had been her beauty and her power :
But now, thus suddenly forsaken,
In those drear solitudes, though yet
His early love remained unshaken,
He felt within his breast awaken
A sense of something like regret.

But he pursued her not : his love,
His murdered love, such step forbade.
He turned his doubtful feet, to rove
Amid that forest's maze of shade.
Beneath the matted boughs, that made
A noonday twilight, he espied
No trace of man ; and far and wide
Through fern and tangling briar he strayed,
Till toil, and thirst, and hunger weighed
His nature down, and cold and drear
Night came, and no relief was near.

But now at once his steps emerge
Upon the forest's moorland verge,
Beside the white and sounding surge.
For in one long self-circling track,
His mazy path had led him back,
To where that cottage old and lone
Had stood : but now to him unknown
Was all the scene.   Mid gardens, fair
With trees and flowers of fragrance rare,
A rich and ample pile was there,
Glittering with myriad lights, that shone
Far-streaming through the dusky air.
   With hunger, toil, and weariness,
Outworn, he cannot choose but pass
Tow'rds that fair pile.   With gentle stress
He strikes the gate of polished brass.
Loud and long the portal rings,
As back with swift recoil it swings,
Disclosing wide a vaulted hall,
With many columns bright and tall
Encircled.   Throned in order round,
Statues of daemons and of kings
Between the marble columns frowned
With seeming life : each throne beside,
Two humbler statues stood, and raised
Each one a silver lamp, that wide
With many-mingling radiance blazed.
   High-reared on one surpassing throne,
A brazen image sate alone,
A dwarfish shape, of wrinkled brow,
With sceptred hand and crowned head.
No sooner did Anthemion's tread
The echoes of the hall awake,
Than up that image rose, and spake,
As from a trumpet :—'What would'st thou ?'—
   Anthemion, in amaze and dread,
Replied :—'With toil and hunger worn,
I seek but food, and rest till morn.'—
The image spake again, and said :
—'Enter : fear not : thou art free
To my best hospitality.'—

Anthemion took the cup, and quaffed.

Spontaneously, an inner door
Unclosed.   Anthemion from the hall
Passed to a room of state, that wore
Aspect of destined festival.
Of fragrant cedar was the floor,
And round the light-pilastered wall
Curtains of crimson and of gold
Hung down in many a gorgeous fold.
Bright lamps, through that apartment gay
Adorned like Cytherëa's bowers
With vases filled with odorous flowers,
Diffused an artificial day.
A banquet's sumptuous order there,
In long array of viands rare,
Fruits, and ambrosial wine, was spread.
A golden boy, in semblance fair
Of actual life, came forth, and led
Anthemion to a couch, beside
That festal table, canopied
With cloth by subtlest Tyrian dyed,
And ministered the feast : the while,
Invisible harps symphonious wreathed
Wild webs of soul-dissolving sound,
And voices, alternating round,
Songs, as of choral maidens, breathed.
   Now to the brim the boy filled up
With sparkling wine a crystal cup.
Anthemion took the cup, and quaffed,
With reckless thirst, the enchanted draught.
That instant came a voice divine,
A maiden voice :—'Now art thou mine !'—
   The golden boy is gone.   The song
And the symphonious harps no more
Their Siren minstrelsy prolong.
One crimson curtain waves before
His sight, and opens.   From its screen,
The nymph of more than earthly mien,
The magic maid of Thessaly,
Came forth, her tresses loosely streaming,
Her eyes with dewy radiance beaming,
Her form all grace and symmetry,

In silken vesture light and free
As if the woof were air, she came,
And took his hand, and called his name.
　　—'Now art thou mine!'—again she cried,—
'My love's indissoluble chain
Has found thee in that goblet's tide,
And thou shalt wear my flower again.'—
She said, and in Anthemion's breast
She placed the laurel-rose: her arms
She twined around him, and imprest
Her lips on his, and fixed on him
Fond looks of passionate love: her charms
With tenfold radiance on his sense
Shone through the studied negligence
Of her light vesture.　His eyes swim
With dizziness.　The lamps grow dim,
And tremble, and expire.　No more.
Darkness is there, and Mystery:
And Silence keeps the golden key
Of Beauty's bridal door.

'Now art thou mine!'

CANTO VII

Those feelings came and passed away, and left him lorn.

First, fairest, best, of powers supernal,
Love waved in heaven his wings of gold,
And from the depths of Night eternal,
Black Erebus, and Chaos old,
Bade light, and life, and beauty rise
Harmonious from the dark disguise
Of elemental discord wild,
Which he had charmed and reconciled.
Love first in social bonds combined
The scattered tribes of humankind,
And bade the wild race cease to roam,
And learn the endearing name of home.
From Love the sister arts began,
That charm, adorn, and soften man.
To Love the feast, the dance, belong,
The temple-rite, the choral song ;
All feelings that refine and bless,
All kindness, sweetness, gentleness.
Him men adore, and gods admire,
Of delicacy, grace, desire,
Persuasion, bliss, the bounteous sire ;
In hopes, and toils, and pains, and fears,
Sole dryer of our human tears ;
Chief ornament of heaven, and king
Of earth, to whom the world doth sing
One chorus of accordant pleasure,
Of which he taught and leads the measure.
He kindles in the inmost mind
One lonely flame—for once—for one—
A vestal fire, which, there enshrined,

Lives on, till life itself be done.
All other fires are of the earth,
And transient : but of heavenly birth
Is Love's first flame, which howsoever
Fraud, power, woe, chance, or fate, may sever
From its congenial source, must burn
Unquenched, but in the funeral urn.

   AND thus Anthemion knew and felt,
As in that palace on the wild,
By daemon art adorned, he dwelt
With that bright nymph, who ever smiled
Refulgent as the summer morn
On eastern ocean newly born.
Though oft, in Rhododaphne's sight,
A phrensied feeling of delight,
With painful admiration mixed
Of her surpassing beauty, came
Upon him, yet of earthly flame
That passion was.   Even as betwixt
The night-clouds transient lightnings play,
Those feelings came and passed away,
And left him lorn.   Calliroë ever
Pursued him like a bleeding shade,
Nor all the magic nymph's endeavour
Could from his constant memory sever
The image of that dearer maid.
   Yet all that love and art could do
The enchantress did.   The pirate-crew
Her power had snatched from death, and pent
Awhile in ocean's bordering caves,
To be her ministers and slaves :
And there, by murmured spells, she sent
On all their shapes phantastic change.
In many an uncouth form and strange,
Grim dwarf, or bony Aethiop tall,
They plied, throughout the enchanted hall,
Their servile ministries, or sate ·
Gigantic mastiffs in the gate,
Or stalked around the garden-dells
In lion-guise, gaunt centinels.

They plied, throughout the enchanted hall, their servile ministries.

Or stalked around the garden-dells in lion-guise.

And many blooming youths and maids,
A joyous Bacchanalian train
(That mid the rocks and piny shades
Of mountains, through whose wild domain
Oeagrian Hebrus, swift and cold,
Impels his waves o'er sands of gold,
Their orgies led), by secret force
Of her far-scattered spells compelled,
With song, and dance, and shout, their course
Tow'rds that enchanted dwelling held.
    Oft, 'mid those palace-gardens fair,
The beauteous nymph (her radiant hair
With mingled oak and vine leaves crowned)
Would grasp the thyrsus ivy-bound,
And fold, her festal vest around,
The Bacchic nebris, leading thus
The swift and dizzy thiasus :
And as she moves, in all her charms,
With springing feet and flowing arms,
'Tis strange in one fair shape to see
How many forms of grace can be.
The youths and maids, her beauteous train,
Follow fast in sportive ring,
Some the torch and mystic cane,
Some the vine-bough, brandishing ;
Some, in giddy circlets fleeting,
The Corybantic timbrel beating :
Maids, with silver flasks advancing,
Pour the wine's red-sparkling tide,
Which youths, with heads recumbent dancing,
Catch in goblets as they glide :
All upon the odorous air
Lightly toss their leafy hair,
Ever singing, as they move,
—' Io Bacchus ! son of Jove !'—
And oft, the Bacchic fervours ending,
Among those garden-bowers they stray,
Dispersed, where fragrant branches blending
Exclude the sun's meridian ray,
Or on some thymy bank repose,
By which a tinkling rivulet flows,

Where birds, on each o'ershadowing spray,
Make music through the live-long day.
The while, in one sequestered cave,
Where roses round the entrance wave,
And jasmin sweet and clustering vine
With flowers and grapes the arch o'ertwine,
Anthemion and the nymph recline,
While in the sunny space, before
The cave, a fountain's lucid store
Its crystal column shoots on high,
And bursts, like showery diamonds flashing,
So falls, and with melodious dashing
Shakes the small pool.   A youth stands by,
A tuneful rhapsodist, and sings,
Accordant to his changeful strings,
High strains of ancient poesy.
And oft her golden lyre she takes,
And such transcendent strains awakes,
Such floods of melody, as steep
Anthemion's sense in bondage deep
Of passionate admiration : still
Combining with intenser skill
The charm that holds him now, whose bands
May ne'er be loosed by mortal hands.
   And oft they rouse with clamorous chace
The forest, urging wide and far
Through glades and dells the sylvan war.
Satyrs and Fauns would start around,
And through their ferny dingles bound,
To see that nymph, all life and grace
And radiance, like the huntress-queen,
With sandaled feet and vest of green,
In her soft fingers grasp the spear,
Hang on the track of flying deer,
Shout to the dogs as fast they sweep
Tumultuous down the woodland steep,
And hurl, along the tainted air,
The javelin from her streaming hair.
   The bath, the dance, the feast's array,
And sweetest rest, conclude the day.
And 'twere most witching to disclose,

Satyrs and Fauns would start around.

R

The bath concludes the day.

Were there such power in mortal numbers,
How she would charm him to repose,
And gaze upon his troubled slumbers,
With looks of fonder love, than ever
Pale Cynthia on Endymion cast,
While her forsaken chariot passed
O'er Caria's many-winding river.
The love she bore him was a flame
So strong, so total, so intense,
That no desire beside might claim
Dominion in her thought or sense.
The world had nothing to bestow
On her : for wealth and power were hers :
The daemons of the earth (that know
The beds of gems and fountain-springs
Of undiscovered gold, and where,
In subterranean sepulchres
The memory of whose place doth bear
No vestige, long-forgotten kings
Sit gaunt on monumental thrones,
With massy pearls and costly stones
Hanging on their half-mouldered bones)
Were slaves to her.   The fears and cares
Of feebler mortals—Want, and Woe
His daughter, and their mutual child
Remorseless Crime,—keen Wrath, that tears
The breast of Hate unreconciled,—
Ambition's spectral goad,—Revenge,
That finds in consummation food
To nurse anew her hydra brood,—
Shame, Misery's sister,—dread of change,
The bane of wealth and worldly might,—
She knew not : Love alone, like ocean,
Filled up with one unshared emotion
Her soul's capacity : but right
And wrong she recked not of, nor owned
A law beyond her soul's desire ;
And from the hour that first enthroned
Anthemion in her heart, the fire,
That burned within her, like the force
Of floods swept with it in its course

All feelings that might barriers prove
To her illimitable love.
　　Thus, wreathed with ever-varying flowers,
Went by the purple-pinioned hours ;
Till once, returning from the wood
And woodland chace, at evening-fall,
Anthemion and the enchantress stood
Within the many-columned hall,
Alone.　They looked around them.　Where
Are all those youths and maidens fair,
Who followed them but now?　On high
She waves her lyre.　Its murmurs die
Tremulous.　They come not whom she calls.
Why starts she?　Wherefore does she throw
Around the youth her arms of snow,
With passion so intense, and weep?
What mean those murmurs, sad and low,
That like sepulchral echoes creep
Along the marble walls?
Her breath is short and quick ; and, dim
With tears, her eyes are fixed on him :
Her lips are quivering and apart :
He feels the fluttering of her heart :
Her face is pale.　He cannot shun
Her fear's contagion.　Tenderly
He kissed her lips in sympathy,
And said :—' What ails thee, lovely one ? '—
　　Low, trembling, faint, her accents fall :
—' Look round : what seest thou in the hall ? '—
Anthemion looked, and made return :
—' The statues, and the lamps that burn :
No more.'—' Yet look again, where late
The solitary image sate,
The monarch-dwarf.　Dost thou not see
An image there which should not be ? '—
　　Even as she bade he looked again :
From his high throne the dwarf was gone.
Lo ! there, as in the Thespian fane,
Uranian Love !　His bow was bent :
The arrow to its head was drawn :
His frowning brow was fixed intent

And lodged in Rhododaphne's breast.

On Rhododaphne.   Scarce did rest
Upon that form Anthemion's view,
When, sounding shrill, the arrow flew,
And lodged in Rhododaphne's breast.
It was not Love's own shaft, the giver
Of life and joy and tender flame ;
But, borrowed from Apollo's quiver,
The death-directed arrow came.
   Long, slow, distinct in each stern word,
A sweet deep-thrilling voice was heard :
—'With impious spells hast thou profaned
My altars ; and all-ruling Jove,
Though late, yet certain, has unchained
The vengeance of Uranian Love !'—15
   The marble palace burst asunder,
Riven by subterranean thunder.
Sudden clouds around them rolled,
Lucid vapour, fold on fold.
Then Rhododaphne closer prest
Anthemion to her bleeding breast,
As, in his arms upheld, her head
All languid on his neck reclined ;
And in the curls, that overspread
His cheek, her temple-ringlets twined :
Her dim eyes drew, with fading sight,
From his their last reflected light,
And on his lips, as nature failed,
Her lips their last sweet sighs exhaled.
   —'Farewell !'—she said—'another bride
The partner of thy days must be :
But do not hate my memory :
And build a tomb, by Ladon's tide,
To her, who, false in all beside,
Was but too true in loving thee !'—
   The quivering earth beneath them stirred.
In dizzy trance upon her bosom
He fell, as falls a wounded bird
Upon a broken rose's blossom.

   WHAT sounds are in Anthemion's ear ?
It is the lark that carols clear,

And gentle waters murmuring near.
He lifts his head : the new-born day
Is round him, and the sunbeams play
On silver eddies.   Can it be ?
The stream he loved in infancy ?
The hills ? the Aphrodisian grove ?
The fields that knew Calliroë's love ?
And those two sister trees, are they
The cedar and the poplar grey,
That shade old Pheidon's door ?   Alas !
Sad vision now !   Does Phantasy
Play with his troubled sense, made dull
By many griefs ?   He does not dream :
It is his own Arcadian stream,
The fields, the hills : and on the grass,
The dewy grass of Ladon's vale,
Lies Rhododaphne, cold and pale,
But even in death most beautiful ;
And there, in mournful silence by her,
Lies on the ground her golden lyre.

He knelt beside her on the ground :
On her pale face and radiant hair
He fixed his eyes, in sorrow drowned.
That one so gifted and so fair,
All light and music, thus should be
Quenched like a night-star suddenly,
Might move a stranger's tears ; but he
Had known her love ; such love, as yet
Never could heart that knew forget !
He thought not of his wrongs.   Alone
Her love and loveliness possest
His memory, and her fond cares, shewn
In seeking, nature's empire through,
Devices ever rare and new,
To make him calm and blest.
Two maids had loved him ; one, the light
Of his young soul, the morning star
Of life and love ; the other, bright
As are the noon-tide skies, when far
The vertic sun's fierce radiance burns :
The world had been too brief to prove

He fell, as falls a wounded bird.

The measure of each single love :
Yet, from this hour, forlorn, bereft,
Companionless, where'er he turns,
Of all that love on earth is left
No trace but their cinereal urns.
　　But Pheidon's door unfolds ; and who
Comes forth in beauty?　　Oh ! 'tis she,
Herself, his own Calliroë !
And in that burst of blest surprise,
Like Lethe's self upon his brain
Oblivion of all grief and pain
Descends, and tow'rds her path he flies.
The maiden knew
Her love, and flew
To meet him, and her dear arms threw
Around his neck, and wept for bliss,
And on his lips impressed a kiss
He had not dared to give.　　The spell
Was broken now, that gave before
Not death, but magic slumber.　　More
The closing measure needs not tell.
Love, wonder, transport wild and high,
Question that waited not reply,
And answer unrequired, and smiles
Through such sweet tears as bliss beguiles,
Fixed, mutual looks of long delight,
Soft chiding for o'erhasty flight,
And promise never more to roam,
Were theirs.　　Old Pheidon from his home
Came forth, to share their joy, and bless
Their love, and all was happiness.
　　But when the maid Anthemion led
To where her beauteous rival slept
The long last sleep, on earth dispread,
And told her tale, Calliroë wept
Sweet tears for Rhododaphne's doom ;
For in her heart a voice was heard :
—' 'Twas for Anthemion's love she erred ! '—
They built by Ladon's banks a tomb ;
And, when the funeral pyre had burned,
With seemly rites they there inurned

The ashes of the enchantress fair ;
And sad sweet verse they traced, to show
That youth, love, beauty, slept below ;
And bade the votive marble bear
The name of RHODODAPHNE.   There
The laurel-rose luxuriant sprung,
And in its boughs her lyre they hung,
And often, when, at evening hours,
They decked the tomb with mournful flowers,
The lyre upon the twilight breeze
Would pour mysterious symphonies.

And on his lips impressed a kiss.

NOTES

S

NOTES

[1] P. 143, v. 14. Primogenial, or Creative Love, in the Orphic mythology, is the first-born of Night and Chaos, the most ancient of the gods, and the parent of all things. According to Aristophanes, Night produced an egg in the bosom of Erebus, and golden-winged Love burst in due season from the shell. The Egyptians, as Plutarch informs us in his Erotic dialogue, recognised three distinct powers of Love: the Uranian, or Heavenly; the Pandemian, Vulgar or Earthly; and the Sun. That the identity of the Sun and Primogenial Love was recognised also by the Greeks, appears from the community of their epithets in mythological poetry, as in this Orphic line: πρωτόγονος Φαέθων περιμήκεος ἠέρος υἱός. Lactantius observes that Love was called πρωτόγονος, which signifies both first-produced and first-producing, because nothing was born before him, but all things have proceeded from him. Primogenial Love is represented in antiques mounted on the back of a lion, and, being of Egyptian origin, is traced by the modern astronomical interpreters of mythology to the Leo of the Zodiac. Uranian Love, in the mythological philosophy of Plato, is the deity or genius of pure mental passion for the good and the beautiful; and Pandemian Love, of ordinary sexual attachment.

[2] P. 143, v. 20. Lysippus.

[3] P. 143, v. 26. Phryne was the mistress of Praxiteles. She requested him to give her his most beautiful work, which he promised to do, but refused to tell which of his works was in his own estimation the best. One day when he was with Phryne, her servant running in announced to him that his house was on fire. Praxiteles started up in great agitation, declaring that all the fruit of his labour would be lost, if his Love should be injured by the flames. His mistress dispelled his alarm, by telling him that the report of the fire was merely a stratagem, by which she had obtained the information she desired. Phryne thus became possessed of the masterpiece of Praxiteles, and bestowed it on her native Thespia. Strabo names, instead of Phryne, Glycera, who

was also a Thespian; but in addition to the testimony of Pausanias and Athenaeus, Casaubon cites a Greek epigram on Phryne, which mentions her dedication of the Thespian Love.

[4] P. 144, v. 25. Sacrifices were offered at this festival for the appeasing of all public and private dissensions. Autobulus, in the beginning of Plutarch's Erotic dialogue, says that his father and mother, when first married, went to the Thespian festival, to sacrifice to Love, on account of a quarrel between their parents.

[5] P. 158, v. 21. The allusions are to the *Hippolytus* and *Alcestis* of Euripides, and to the *Antigone* of Sophocles.

[6] P. 158, v. 39. Τὰ δὲ ῥόδα ἐκεῖνα οὐκ ἦν ῥόδα ἀληθινά· τὰ δ' ἦν ἐκ τῆς ἀγρίας δάφνης φυόμενα· ῥοδοδάφνην αὐτὴν καλοῦσιν ἄνθρωποι· κακὸν ἄριστον ὄνῳ τοῦτο παντί, καὶ ἵππῳ· φασὶ γὰρ τὸν φαγόντα ἀποθνήσκειν αὐτίκα. Lucianus in *Asino.*—'These roses were not true roses: they were flowers of the wild laurel, which men call rhododaphne, or rose-laurel. It is a bad dinner for either horse or ass, the eating of it being attended by immediate death.' Apuleius has amplified this passage: 'I observed from afar the deep shades of a leafy grove, through whose diversified and abundant verdure shone the snowy colour of refulgent roses. As my perceptions and feelings were not asinine like my shape,[1] I judged it to be a sacred grove of Venus and the Graces, where the celestial splendour of their genial flower glittered through the dark-green shades. I invoked the propitious power of joyful Event, and sprang forward with such velocity, as if I were not indeed an ass, but the horse of an Olympic charioteer. But this splendid effort of energy could not enable me to outrun the cruelty of my fortune. For on approaching the spot, I saw, not those tender and delicate roses, the offspring of auspicious bushes, whose fragrant leaves make nectar of the morning-dew; nor yet the deep wood I had seemed to see from afar; but only a thick line of trees skirting the edge of a river. These trees, clothed with an abundant and laurel-like foliage, from which they stretch forth the cups of their pale and inodorous flowers, are called, among the unlearned rustics, by the far from rustic appellation of laurel-roses: the eating of which is mortal to all quadrupeds. Thus entangled by evil fate, and despairing of safety, I was on the point of swallowing the poison of those fictitious roses, etc.' Pliny says that this plant, though poison to quadrupeds, is an antidote to men against the venom of serpents.

[7] P. 163, v. 24. The plane was sacred to the Genius, as the oak to Jupiter, the olive to Minerva, the palm to the Muses, the myrtle and

---

[1] This is spoken in the character of Lucius, who has been changed to an ass by a Thessalian ointment, and can be restored to his true shape only by the eating of roses.

rose to Venus, the laurel to Apollo, the ash to Mars, the beech to Hercules, the pine to Pan, the fir and ivy to Bacchus, the cypress to Sylvanus, the cedar to the Eumenides, the yew and poppy to Ceres, etc. 'I swear to you,' says Socrates in the *Phaedrus* of Plato, 'by any one of the gods, if you will, by this plane.'

[8] P. 172, v. 23. Ascra derived its name from a nymph, of whom Neptune was enamoured. She bore him a son named Oeoclus, who built Ascra in conjunction with the giants Ophus and Ephialtes, who were also sons of Neptune, by Iphimedia, the wife of Aloeus. Pausanias mentions that nothing but a solitary tower of Ascra was remaining in his time. Strabo describes it as having a lofty and rugged site. It was the birthplace of Hesiod, who gives a dismal picture of it.

[9] P. 173, v. 16. 'The andrachne,' says Pausanias, 'grows abundantly in Helicon, and bears fruit of incomparable sweetness.' Pliny says, 'It is the same plant which is called in Latin *illecebra:* it grows on rocks, and is gathered for food.'

[10] P. 173, v. 26. It was said by the Thracians that those nightingales which had their nests about the tomb of Orpheus sang more sweetly and powerfully than any others. Pausanias, L. IX.

[11] P. 186, v. 11. It was the custom of Pan to repose from the chase at noon. Theocritus, *Id.* I.

[12] P. 199, v. 18. Sophocles, *Oed. Col.* Μὴ φῦναι τὸν ἅπαντα νικᾷ λόγον· Τὸ δ', ἐπεὶ φανῇ, Βῆναι κεῖθεν ὅθεν περ ἥκει, Πολὺ δεύτερον, ὡς τάχιστα. This was a very favourite sentiment among the Greeks. The same thought occurs in Ecclesiastes iv. 2, 3.

[13] P. 206, v. 28. The children of the Sun were known by the splendour of their eyes and hair. Πᾶσα γὰρ ἠελίου γενεὴ ἀρίδηλος ἰδέσθαι Ἦεν· ἐπεὶ βλεφάρων ἀποτηλόθι μαρμαρυγῇσιν Οἷον ἐκ χρυσέων ἀντώπιον ἵεσαν αἴγλην. Apollonius, IV. 727. And in the Orphic Argonautics Circe is thus described : ἐκ δ' ἄρα πάντες Θάμβεον εἰσορόωντες· ἀπὸ κρατὸς γὰρ ἔθειραι Πυρσαῖς ἀκτίνεσσιν ἀλίγκιοι ἠώρηντο· Στίλβε δὲ καλὰ πρόσωπα, φλογὸς δ' ἀπέλαμπεν ἀυτμή.

[14] P. 216, v. 37. 'The dreaded name of Daemogorgon' is familiar to every reader, in Milton's enumeration of the Powers of Chaos. Mythological writers in general afford but little information concerning this terrible Divinity. He is incidentally mentioned in several places by Natalis Comes, who says, in treating of Pan, that Pronapides, in his *Protocosmus*, makes Pan and the three sister Fates the offspring of Daemogorgon. Boccaccio, in a Latin treatise on the Genealogy of the Gods, gives some account of him on the authority of Theodotion and Pronapides. He was the Genius of the Earth, and the Sovereign

Power of the Terrestrial Daemons.   He dwelt originally with Eternity and Chaos, till, becoming weary of inaction, he organised the chaotic elements, and surrounded the earth with the heavens.   In addition to Pan and the Fates, his children were Uranus, Titaea, Pytho, Eris, and Erebus.   This awful Power was so sacred among the Arcadians, that it was held impious to pronounce his name.   The impious, however, who made less scruple about pronouncing it, are said to have found it of great virtue in magical incantations.   He has been supposed to be a philosophical emblem of the principle of vegetable life.   The silence of mythologists concerning him can only be attributed to their veneration for his 'dreaded name'; a proof of genuine piety which must be pleasing to our contemporary Pagans, for some such there are.

[15] P. 249, v. 14.   The late but certain vengeance of the gods occurs in many forms as a sentence among the classical writers, and is the subject of an interesting dialogue, among the moral works of Plutarch, which concludes with the fable of Thespesius, a very remarkable prototype of the *Inferno* of Dante.

THE END

Printed by R. & R. CLARK, LIMITED, *Edinburgh.*

ILLUSTRATED STANDARD NOVELS.

Crown 8vo, cloth, uncut edges.   3s. 6d. each.
"Peacock" Edition, cloth, gilt sides, back, and edges.   5s. each.

BY THE SAME AUTHOR.

MAID MARIAN AND CROTCHET CASTLE. By THOMAS LOVE PEACOCK. Illustrated by F. H. Townsend. With an Introduction by GEORGE SAINTSBURY.

HEADLONG HALL AND NIGHTMARE ABBEY. By THOMAS LOVE PEACOCK. Illustrated by H. R. Millar. With an Introduction by GEORGE SAINTSBURY.

GRYLL GRANGE. By THOMAS LOVE PEACOCK. Illustrated by F. H. Townsend. With an Introduction by GEORGE SAINTSBURY.

MELINCOURT; OR, SIR ORAN HAUT-TON. By THOMAS LOVE PEACOCK. Illustrated by F. H. Townsend. With an Introduction by GEORGE SAINTSBURY.

THE MISFORTUNES OF ELPHIN, AND RHODODAPHNE. By THOMAS LOVE PEACOCK. Illustrated by F. H. Townsend. With an Introduction by GEORGE SAINTSBURY.

'CASTLE RACKRENT' AND 'THE ABSENTEE.' By MARIA EDGEWORTH. Illustrated by Miss Chris Hammond. With an Introduction by ANNE THACKERAY RITCHIE.

JAPHET IN SEARCH OF A FATHER. By Captain MARRYAT. Illustrated by Henry M. Brock. With an Introduction by DAVID HANNAY.

TOM CRINGLE'S LOG. By MICHAEL SCOTT. Illustrated by J. Ayton Symington. With an Introduction by MOWBRAY MORRIS.

THE ANNALS OF THE PARISH AND THE AYRSHIRE LEGATEES. By JOHN GALT. Illustrated by Charles E. Brock. With an Introduction by ALFRED AINGER.

THE ADVENTURES OF HAJJI BABA OF ISPAHAN. By JAMES MORIER. Illustrated by H. R. Millar. With an Introduction by the Hon. GEORGE CURZON, M.P.

ORMOND. By MARIA EDGEWORTH. Illustrated by Carl Schloesser. With an Introduction by ANNE THACKERAY RITCHIE.

JACOB FAITHFUL. By Captain MARRYAT. Illustrated by Henry M. Brock. With an Introduction by DAVID HANNAY.

PETER SIMPLE. By Captain MARRYAT. Illustrated by J. Ayton Symington. With an Introduction by DAVID HANNAY.

PRIDE AND PREJUDICE. By JANE AUSTEN. Illustrated by Charles E. Brock. With an Introduction by AUSTIN DOBSON.

POPULAR TALES. By MARIA EDGEWORTH. Illustrated by Miss Chris Hammond. With an Introduction by ANNE THACKERAY RITCHIE.

SYBIL. By BENJAMIN DISRAELI. Illustrated by Fred Pegram. With an Introduction by H. D. TRAILL.

LAVENGRO. By GEORGE BORROW. Illustrated by E. J. Sullivan. With an Introduction by AUGUSTINE BIRRELL, Q.C., M.P.

HANDY ANDY. By SAMUEL LOVER. Illustrated by H. M. Brock. With an Introduction by CHARLES WHIBLEY.

SENSE AND SENSIBILITY. By JANE AUSTEN. Illustrated by Hugh Thomson. With an Introduction by AUSTIN DOBSON.

MR. MIDSHIPMAN EASY. By Captain MARRYAT. Illustrated by Fred Pegram. With an Introduction by DAVID HANNAY.

HELEN. By MARIA EDGEWORTH. Illustrated by Miss Chris Hammond. With an Introduction by ANNE THACKERAY RITCHIE.

THE KING'S OWN. By Captain MARRYAT. Illustrated by F. H. Townsend. With an Introduction by DAVID HANNAY.

THE PHANTOM SHIP. By Captain MARRYAT. Illustrated by H. R. Millar. With an Introduction by DAVID HANNAY.

EMMA. By JANE AUSTEN. Illustrated by Hugh Thomson. With an Introduction by AUSTIN DOBSON.

BELINDA. By MARIA EDGEWORTH. Illustrated by Miss Chris Hammond. With an Introduction by ANNE THACKERAY RITCHIE.

WESTWARD HO! By CHARLES KINGSLEY. Illustrated by Charles E. Brock.

MACMILLAN AND CO., LTD., LONDON.

BY RUDYARD KIPLING.

SOLDIER TALES. Containing "With the Main Guard," "The Drums of the Fore and Aft," "The Man who was," "Courting of Dinah Shadd," "Incarnation of Krishna Mulvaney," "Taking of Lungtungpen," "The Madness of Private Ortheris." With Head and Tail Pieces, and Twenty-one Page Illustrations by A. S. HARTRICK. Crown 8vo, Cloth gilt. Uniform with *Jungle Book.* 6s.

DAILY NEWS.—"Mr. Kipling's stories of Mulvaney and Co. are as captivating at the tenth reading as at the first—as all stories of first-rate genius are."

THE SECOND JUNGLE BOOK. With Illustrations by J. LOCKWOOD KIPLING. Twenty-second Thousand.

DAILY TELEGRAPH.—"The appearance of *The Second Jungle Book* is a literary event of which no one will mistake the importance. Unlike most sequels, the various stories comprised in the new volume are at least equal to their predecessors."

THE JUNGLE BOOK. With Illustrations by J. L. KIPLING, W. H. DRAKE, and P. FRENZENY. Thirtieth Thousand. Crown 8vo. 6s.

ATHENÆUM.—"We tender our sincere thanks to Mr. Kipling for the hour of pure and unadulterated enjoyment which he has given us, and many another reader, by this inimitable *Jungle Book.*"

PUNCH.—"'Æsop's Fables and dear old Brer Fox and Co.,' observes the Baron sagely, 'may have suggested to the fanciful genius of Rudyard Kipling the delightful idea, carried out in the most fascinating style, of *The Jungle Book.*'"

WEE WILLIE WINKIE and other Stories. Crown 8vo. 6s.

SOLDIERS THREE and other Stories. Crown 8vo. 6s.

ST. JAMES'S GAZETTE.—"In these, as the faithful are aware, is contained some of Mr. Kipling's very finest work."

GLOBE.—"Containing some of the best of his highly vivid work."

PLAIN TALES FROM THE HILLS. Thirty-first Thousand. Crown 8vo. 6s.

SATURDAY REVIEW.—"Mr. Kipling knows and appreciates the English in India, and is a born story-teller and a man of humour into the bargain. . . . It would be hard to find better reading."

GLASGOW HERALD.—"Character, situation, incident, humour, pathos, tragic force, are all in abundance; words alone are at a minimum. Of course these are 'plain' tales—lightning-flash tales. A gleam, and there the whole tragedy or comedy is before you—elaborate it for yourself afterwards."

THE LIGHT THAT FAILED. Rewritten and considerably enlarged. Twentieth Thousand. Crown 8vo. 6s.

ACADEMY.—"Whatever else be true of Mr. Kipling, it is the first truth about him that he has power, real intrinsic power. . . . Mr. Kipling's work has innumerable good qualities."

MANCHESTER COURIER.—"The story is a brilliant one and full of vivid interest."

LIFE'S HANDICAP. Being Stories of Mine Own People. Twenty-third Thousand. Crown 8vo. 6s.

BLACK AND WHITE.—"*Life's Handicap* contains much of the best work hitherto accomplished by the author, and, taken as a whole, is a complete advance upon its predecessors."

OBSERVER.—"The stories are as good as ever, and are quite as well told. . . . *Life's Handicap* is a volume that can be read with pleasure and interest under almost any circumstances."

MANY INVENTIONS. Twentieth Thousand. Crown 8vo. 6s.

PALL MALL GAZETTE.—"The completest book that Mr. Kipling has yet given us in workmanship, the weightiest and most humane in breadth of view. . . . It can only be regarded as a fresh landmark in the progression of his genius."

NATIONAL OBSERVER.—"The book is one for all Mr. Kipling's admirers to rejoice in—some for this, and some for that, and not a few for well-nigh everything it contains."

MACMILLAN AND CO., LTD., LONDON.

A CLASSIFIED
CATALOGUE OF BOOKS
IN GENERAL LITERATURE
PUBLISHED BY
MACMILLAN AND CO., LTD.
BEDFORD STREET, STRAND, LONDON, W.C.

For purely Educational Works see MACMILLAN AND CO.'S *Educational Catalogue.*

AGRICULTURE.

(*See also* BOTANY; GARDENING.)

FRANKLAND (Prof. P. F.).—A HANDBOOK OF AGRICULTURAL CHEMICAL ANALYSIS. Cr. 8vo. 7s. 6d.

KING (F. H.).—THE SOIL, ITS NATURE, ETC. Fcp. 8vo. 3s. net.

LAURIE (A. P.).—PRIMER OF AGRICULTURAL CHEMISTRY, or THE FOOD OF PLANTS. Pott 8vo. 1s.

MUIR (J.).—MANUAL OF DAIRY WORK. Pott 8vo. 1s.

—— AGRICULTURE, PRACTICAL AND SCIENTIFIC. Cr. 8vo. 4s. 6d.

NICHOLLS (H. A. A.).—TEXT BOOK OF TROPICAL AGRICULTURE. Cr. 8vo. 6s.

TANNER (Henry).—ELEMENTARY LESSONS IN THE SCIENCE OF AGRICULTURAL PRACTICE. Fcp. 8vo. 3s. 6d.

—— FIRST PRINCIPLES OF AGRICULTURE. Pott 8vo. 1s.

—— THE PRINCIPLES OF AGRICULTURE. For Use in Elementary Schools. Ext. fcp. 8vo.—THE ALPHABET OF THE PRINCIPLES OF AGRICULTURE. 6d.—FURTHER STEPS IN THE PRINCIPLES OF AGRICULTURE. 1s.—ELEMENTARY SCHOOL READINGS ON THE PRINCIPLES OF AGRICULTURE FOR THE THIRD STAGE. 1s.

—— THE ABBOT'S FARM; or, Practice with Science. Cr. 8vo. 3s. 6d.

ANATOMY, Human. (*See* PHYSIOLOGY.)

ANTHROPOLOGY.

BROWN (J. Allen).—PALÆOLITHIC MAN IN NORTH-WEST MIDDLESEX. 8vo. 7s. 6d.

DAWKINS (Prof. W. Boyd).—EARLY MAN IN BRITAIN AND HIS PLACE IN THE TERTIARY PERIOD. Med. 8vo. 25s.

DE QUATREFAGES (A.)—THE PYGMIES. Translated by F. STARR. Cr. 8vo. 6s. net.

FINCK (Henry T.).—ROMANTIC LOVE AND PERSONAL BEAUTY. 2 vols. Cr. 8vo. 18s.

FISON (L.) and HOWITT (A. W.).—KAMILAROI AND KURNAI GROUP. Group-Marriage and Relationship, and Marriage by Elopement. 8vo. 15s.

FRAZER (J. G.).—THE GOLDEN BOUGH: A Study in Comparative Religion. 2 vols. 8vo. 28s.

GALTON (Francis).—ENGLISH MEN OF SCIENCE: THEIR NATURE AND NURTURE. 8vo. 8s. 6d.

GALTON (Francis).—NATURAL INHERITANCE. 8vo. 9s.

—— INQUIRIES INTO HUMAN FACULTY AND ITS DEVELOPMENT. 8vo. 16s.

—— LIFE-HISTORY ALBUM: Being a Personal Note-book, combining Diary, Photograph Album, a Register of Height, Weight, and other Anthropometrical Observations, and a Record of Illnesses. 4to. 3s. 6d.—Or with Cards of Wool for Testing Colour Vision. 4s. 6d.

—— RECORD OF FAMILY FACULTIES. Consisting of Tabular Forms and Directions for Entering Data. 4to. 2s. 6d.

—— HEREDITARY GENIUS: An Enquiry into its Laws and Consequences. Ext. cr. 8vo. 7s. net.

—— FINGER PRINTS. 8vo. 6s. net.

—— BLURRED FINGER PRINTS. 8vo. 2s. 6d. net

—— FINGER-PRINT DIRECTORIES. 8vo. 5s. net.

HOFFMAN (W. J.).—THE BEGINNINGS OF WRITING. Cr. 8vo. 6s. net.

M'LENNAN (J. F.).—THE PATRIARCHAL THEORY. Edited and completed by DONALD M'LENNAN, M.A. 8vo. 14s.

—— STUDIES IN ANCIENT HISTORY. Comprising "Primitive Marriage." 8vo. 16s.

—— —— Second Series. 8vo. 21s.

MASON (O. T.).—WOMAN'S SHARE IN PRIMITIVE CULTURE. Cr. 8vo. 6s. net.

MONTELIUS—WOODS.—THE CIVILISATION OF SWEDEN IN HEATHEN TIMES. By Prof. OSCAR MONTELIUS. Translated by Rev. F. H. WOODS. Illustr. 8vo. 14s.

ORR (H. B.).—THEORY OF DEVELOPMENT AND HEREDITY. Cr. 8vo. 6s. net.

RATZEL (F.).—HISTORY OF MANKIND. Ed. by E. B. TYLOR. In 30 Monthly Parts. Roy. 8vo. 1s. net each. Vol. I. 12s. net.

SEEBOHM (H. E.).—STRUCTURE OF GREEK TRIBAL SOCIETY. 8vo. 5s. net.

TURNER (Rev. Geo.).—SAMOA, A HUNDRED YEARS AGO AND LONG BEFORE. Cr. 8vo. 9s

TYLOR (E. B.).—ANTHROPOLOGY. With Illustrations. Cr. 8vo. 7s. 6d.

WESTERMARCK (Dr. Edward).—THE HISTORY OF HUMAN MARRIAGE. With Preface by Dr. A. R. WALLACE. 2nd Edit. 8vo. 14s. net.

WILSON (Sir Daniel).—PREHISTORIC ANNALS OF SCOTLAND. Illustrated. 2 vols. 8vo. 36s

—— PREHISTORIC MAN: Researches into the Origin of Civilisation in the Old and New World. Illustrated. 2 vols. 8vo. 36s.

—— THE RIGHT HAND: LEFT-HANDEDNESS. Cr. 8vo. 4s. 6d.

ANTIQUITIES.

(See also ANTHROPOLOGY.*)*

ATKINSON (Rev. J. C.).—FORTY YEARS IN A MOORLAND PARISH. Ext. cr. 8vo. 5*s.* net.—*Illustrated Edition.* 12*s.* net.

—— MEMORIALS OF OLD WHITBY. Illust. Ex. cr. 8vo. 3*s.* 6*d.* net.

BURN (Robert).—ROMAN LITERATURE IN RELATION TO ROMAN ART. With Illustrations. Ext. cr. 8vo. 14*s.*

DILETTANTI SOCIETY'S PUBLICATIONS.
ANTIQUITIES OF IONIA. Vols. I.—III. 2*l.* 2*s.* each, or 5*l.* 5*s.* the set, net.—Vol. IV. Folio, half morocco, 3*l.* 13*s.* 6*d.* net.
AN INVESTIGATION OF THE PRINCIPLES OF ATHENIAN ARCHITECTURE. By F. C. PENROSE. Illustrated. Folio. 7*l.* 7*s.* net.
SPECIMENS OF ANCIENT SCULPTURE: EGYPTIAN, ETRUSCAN, GREEK, AND ROMAN. Vol. II. Folio. 5*l.* 5*s.* net.

DYER (Louis).—STUDIES OF THE GODS IN GREECE AT CERTAIN SANCTUARIES RECENTLY EXCAVATED. Ext. cr. 8vo. 8*s.* 6*d.* net.

ERMAN (A.).—LIFE IN ANCIENT EGYPT. Transl. by H. M. TIRARD. Illust. Super-royal 8vo. 21*s.* net.

EVANS (Lady). CHAPTERS ON GREEK DRESS. Illustrated. 8vo. 5*s.* net.

FOWLER (W. W.).—THE CITY-STATE OF THE GREEKS AND ROMANS. Cr. 8vo. 5*s.*

GARDNER (Ernest).—HANDBOOK OF GREEK SCULPTURE. Illustrated. Ex. cr. 8vo. 5*s.*

GARDNER (Percy).—SAMOS AND SAMIAN COINS: An Essay. 8vo. 7*s.* 6*d.*

GOW (J., Litt.D.).—A COMPANION TO SCHOOL CLASSICS. Illustrated. 3rd Ed. Cr. 8vo. 6*s.*

HARRISON (Miss Jane) and VERRALL (Mrs.).—MYTHOLOGY AND MONUMENTS OF ANCIENT ATHENS. Illustrated. Cr. 8vo. 16*s.*

HELLENIC SOCIETY'S PUBLICATIONS —EXCAVATIONS AT MEGALOPOLIS, 1890–1891. By Messrs. E. A. GARDNER, W. LORING, G. C. RICHARDS, and W. J. WOODHOUSE. With an Architectural Description by R. W. SCHULTZ. 4to. 25*s.*

—— ECCLESIASTICAL SITES IN ISAURIA (CILICIA TRACHEA). By the Rev. A. C. HEADLAM. Imp. 4to. 5*s.*

JONES (H. S.).—SELECT PASSAGES FROM ANCIENT WRITERS, ILLUSTRATIVE OF THE HISTORY OF GREEK SCULPTURE. 8vo. 7*s.* net.

LANCIANI (Prof. R.).—ANCIENT ROME IN THE LIGHT OF RECENT DISCOVERIES. 4to. 24*s.*

—— PAGAN AND CHRISTIAN ROME. 4to. 24*s.*

MAHAFFY (Prof. J. P.).—A PRIMER OF GREEK ANTIQUITIES. Pott 8vo. 1*s.*

—— SOCIAL LIFE IN GREECE FROM HOMER TO MENANDER. 6th Edit. Cr. 8vo. 9*s.*

—— RAMBLES AND STUDIES IN GREECE. Illustrated. 3rd Edit. Cr. 8vo. 10*s.* 6*d.*

(See also HISTORY, p. 13.*)*

NEWTON (Sir C. T.).—ESSAYS ON ART AND ARCHÆOLOGY. 8vo. 12*s.* 6*d.*

SCHUCHHARDT (C.).—DR. SCHLIEMANN'S EXCAVATIONS AT TROY, TIRYNS, MYCENAE, ORCHOMENOS, ITHACA, IN THE LIGHT OF RECENT KNOWLEDGE. Trans. by EUGENIE SELLERS. Preface by WALTER LEAF, Litt.D. Illustrated. 8vo. 18*s.* net.

SCHREIBER (T.).—ATLAS OF CLASSICAL ANTIQUITIES. Edit. by W. C. F. ANDERSON. Oblong 4to. 21*s.* net.

STRANGFORD. *(See* VOYAGES & TRAVELS.*)*

WALDSTEIN (C.).—CATALOGUE OF CASTS IN THE MUSEUM OF CLASSICAL ARCHÆOLOGY, CAMBRIDGE. Crown 8vo. 1*s.* 6*d.*— Large Paper Edition. Small 4to. 5*s.*

WHITE (Gilbert). *(See* NATURAL HISTORY.*)*

WILKINS (Prof. A. S.).—A PRIMER OF ROMAN ANTIQUITIES. Pott 8vo. 1*s.*

ARCHÆOLOGY. *(See* ANTIQUITIES.*)*

ARCHITECTURE.

AVERY ARCHITECTURAL CATALOGUE. Imp. 8vo, half mor. 50*s.* net. £

FREEMAN (Prof. E. A.).—HISTORY OF THE CATHEDRAL CHURCH OF WELLS. Cr. 8vo. 3*s.* 6*d.*

HULL (E.).—A TREATISE ON ORNAMENTAL AND BUILDING STONES OF GREAT BRITAIN AND FOREIGN COUNTRIES. 8vo. 12*s.*

LETHABY (W. R.) and SWAINSON (H.). —THE CHURCH OF ST. SOPHIA AT CONSTANTINOPLE. Illust. Med. 8vo. 21*s.* net.

MOORE (Prof. C. H.).—THE DEVELOPMENT AND CHARACTER OF GOTHIC ARCHITECTURE. Illustrated. Med. 8vo. 18*s.*

PENROSE (F. C.). *(See* ANTIQUITIES.*)*

STEVENSON (J. J.).—HOUSE ARCHITECTURE. With Illustrations. 2 vols. Roy. 8vo. 18*s.* each.—Vol. I. ARCHITECTURE; Vol. II. HOUSE PLANNING.

ART.

(See also MUSIC.*)*

ANDERSON (L.). LINEAR PERSPECTIVE AND MODEL DRAWING. 8vo. 2*s.*

ART AT HOME SERIES. Edited by W. J. LOFTIE, B.A. Cr. 8vo.
THE BEDROOM AND BOUDOIR. By Lady BARKER. 2*s.* 6*d.*
NEEDLEWORK. By ELIZABETH GLAISTER. Illustrated 2*s.* 6*d.*
MUSIC IN THE HOUSE. By JOHN HULLAH. 4th edit. 2*s.* 6*d.*
THE DINING-ROOM. By Mrs. LOFTIE. With Illustrations. 2nd Edit. 2*s.* 6*d.*
AMATEUR THEATRICALS. By WALTER H. POLLOCK and LADY POLLOCK. Illustrated by KATE GREENAWAY. 2*s.* 6*d.*

ATKINSON (J. B.).—AN ART TOUR TO NORTHERN CAPITALS OF EUROPE. 8vo. 12*s.*

BENSON (W. A. S.). HANDICRAFT AND DESIGN. Cr. 8vo. 5*s.* net.

BURN (Robert). *(See* ANTIQUITIES.*)*

CARR (J. C.)—PAPERS ON ART. Cr. 8vo. 8*s.* 6*d.*

COLLIER (Hon. John).—A PRIMER OF ART. Pott 8vo. 1*s.*

COOK (E. T.).—A POPULAR HANDBOOK TO THE NATIONAL GALLERY. Including Notes collected from the Works of Mr. RUSKIN. 4th Edit. Cr. 8vo, half morocco. 14*s.*— Large paper Edition, 250 copies. 2 vols. 8vo.

DELAMOTTE (Prof. P. H.).—A Beginner's Drawing-Book. Cr. 8vo. 3s. 6d.

ELLIS (Tristram).—Sketching from Nature. Illustr. by H. Stacy Marks, R.A., and the Author. 2nd Edit. Cr. 8vo. 3s. 6d.

FLORY (M. A.).—A Book about Fans. Ex. Cr. 8vo. 10s. 6d.

HAMERTON (P. G.).—Thoughts about Art. New Edit. Cr. 8vo. 8s. 6d.

HOOPER (W. H.) and PHILLIPS (W. C.).—A Manual of Marks on Pottery and Porcelain. 2nd Edit. 16mo. 4s. 6d.

HUNT (W.).—Talks about Art. With a Letter from Sir J. E. Millais, Bart., R.A. Cr. 8vo. 3s. 6d.

HUTCHINSON (G. W. C.).—Some Hints on Learning to Draw. Roy. 8vo. 8s. 6d.

LA FARGE (J.)—Considerations on Painting. Cr. 8vo. 6s. net.

LAURIE (A. P.).—Facts about Processes, Pigments, and Vehicles. Cr. 8vo. 3s. net.

LECTURES ON ART. By Regd. Stuart Poole, Professor W. B. Richmond, E. J. Poynter, R.A., J. T. Micklethwaite, and William Morris. Cr. 8vo. 4s. 6d.

NEWTON (Sir C. T.).—(See Antiquities.)

PALGRAVE (Prof. F. T.).—Essays on Art. Ext. fcp. 8vo. 6s.

PATER (W.).—The Renaissance: Studies in Art and Poetry. 5th Edit. Cr. 8vo. 10s. 6d.

PENNELL (Joseph).—Pen Drawing and Pen Draughtsmen. New and Enlarged Edit., with 400 Illust. 4to Buckram. 42s. net.

PROPERT (J. Lumsden).—A History of Miniature Art. Illustrated. Super roy. 4to. 3l. 13s. 6d.—Bound in vellum. 4l. 14s. 6d.

SPANTON (J. H.).—Science and Art Drawing. 8vo. 10s. net.

TAYLOR (E. R.).—Drawing and Design. Ob. cr. 8vo. 2s. 6d.

THOMPSON (E.).—Studies in the Art Anatomy of Animals. Illustrated. 4to.
[In the Press.

TURNER'S LIBER STUDIORUM: A Description and a Catalogue. By W. G. Rawlinson. Med. 8vo. 12s. 6d.

TYRWHITT (Rev. R. St. John).—Our Sketching Club. 5th Edit. Cr. 8vo. 7s. 6d.

WARE (W. R.).—Modern Perspective. With Plates. 5th. Edit. 4to. 21s. net.

WYATT (Sir M. Digby).—Fine Art: A Sketch of its History, Theory, Practice, and Application to Industry. 8vo. 5s.

ASTRONOMY.

AIRY (Sir G. B.).—Popular Astronomy. Illustrated. 7th Edit. Fcp. 8vo. 4s. 6d.

—— Gravitation. An Elementary Explanation of the Principal Perturbations in the Solar System. 2nd Edit. Cr. 8vo. 7s. 6d.

BLAKE (J. F.).—Astronomical Myths. With Illustrations. Cr. 8vo. 9s.

CHEYNE (C. H. H.).—An Elementary Treatise on the Planetary Theory. Cr. 8vo. 7s. 6d.

CLARK (L.) and SADLER (H.).—The Star Guide. Roy. 8vo. 5s.

CROSSLEY (E.), GLEDHILL (J.), and WILSON (J. M.).—A Handbook of Double Stars. 8vo. 21s.
—— Corrections to the Handbook of Double Stars. 8vo. 1s.

GODFRAY (Hugh).—An Elementary Treatise on the Lunar Theory. 2nd Edit. Cr. 8vo. 5s. 6d.
—— A Treatise on Astronomy, for the use of Colleges and Schools. 8vo. 12s. 6d.

GREGORY (R. A.).—The Planet Earth. Gl. 8vo. 2s.

LOCKYER (J. Norman, F.R.S.).—A Primer of Astronomy. Illustrated. Pott 8vo. 1s.
—— Elementary Lessons in Astronomy. Illustr. New Edition. Fcp. 8vo. 5s. 6d.
—— Questions on the same. By J. Forbes Robertson. Fcp. 8vo. 1s. 6d.
—— The Chemistry of the Sun. Illustrated. 8vo. 14s.
—— The Meteoritic Hypothesis of the Origin of Cosmical Systems. Illustrated. 8vo. 17s. net.
—— The Evolution of the Heavens and the Earth. Illustrated. Cr. 8vo.
[In the Press.
—— Star-Gazing Past and Present. Expanded from Notes with the assistance of G. M. Seabroke. Roy. 8vo. 21s.

LODGE (O. J.).—Pioneers of Science. Ex. cr. 8vo. 7s. 6d.

MILLER (R. Kalley).—The Romance of Astronomy. 2nd Edit. Cr. 8vo. 4s. 6d.

NEWCOMB (Prof. Simon).—Popular Astronomy. Engravings and Maps. 8vo. 18s.

ROSCOE—SCHUSTER. (See Chemistry.)

ATLASES.

(See also Geography).

BARTHOLOMEW (J. G.).—Elementary School Atlas. 4to. 1s.
—— Physical and Political School Atlas. 80 maps. 4to. 8s. 6d.; half mor. 10s. 6d.
—— Library Reference Atlas of the World. With Index to 100,000 places. Folio. 52s. 6d. net.—Also in 7 parts, 5s. net each; Geographical Index. 7s. 6d. net.

LABBERTON (R. H.).—New Historical Atlas and General History. 4to. 15s.

BIBLE. (See under Theology, p. 38.)

BIBLIOGRAPHY.

A BIBLIOGRAPHICAL CATALOGUE OF MACMILLAN AND CO.'S PUBLICATIONS, 1843—89. Med. 8vo. 10s. net.

MAYOR (Prof. John E. B.).—A Bibliographical Clue to Latin Literature. Cr. 8vo. 10s. 6d.

RYLAND (F.).—Chronological Outlines of English Literature. Cr. 8vo. 6s.

SMITH (Adam).—Catalogue of Library. Ed. by J. Bonar. 8vo. 7s. 6d. net.

WHITCOMB (L. S.).—Chronological Outlines of American Literature. Introduction by Brander Matthews. Cr. 8vo. 6s. net.

BIOGRAPHY.
(*See also* HISTORY.)

AGASSIZ (Louis): LIFE AND CORRESPONDENCE. Ed. by E. C. AGASSIZ. 2 vols. Cr. 8vo. 18s.
—— LIFE, LETTERS, AND WORKS. By J. MARCOU. 2 vols. 8vo. 17s. net.

ALBEMARLE (Earl of).—FIFTY YEARS OF MY LIFE. 3rd Edit., revised. Cr. 8vo. 7s. 6d.

ALFRED THE GREAT. By THOMAS HUGHES. Cr. 8vo. 6s.

AMIEL (H. F.)-THE JOURNAL INTIME. Trans. Mrs. HUMPHRY WARD. 2nd Ed. Cr. 8vo. 6s.

ANDREWS (Dr. Thomas). (*See* PHYSICS.)

ARNAULD (Angelique). By FRANCES MARTIN. Cr. 8vo. 4s. 6d.

ARTEVELDE. JAMES AND PHILIP VAN ARTEVELDE. By W. J. ASHLEY. Cr. 8vo. 6s.

BACON (Francis): AN ACCOUNT OF HIS LIFE AND WORKS. By E. A. ABBOTT. 8vo. 14s.

BAKER (Sir S. W.).—A MEMOIR. By T. DOUGLAS MURRAY and A. SILVA WHITE. 8vo. 21s.

BARNARD (F. A. P.).—MEMOIRS. By JOHN FULTON. 8vo. 14s. net.

BARNES. LIFE OF WILLIAM BARNES, POET AND PHILOLOGIST. By his Daughter, LUCY BAXTER ("Leader Scott"). Cr. 8vo. 7s. 6d.

BERLIOZ (Hector): AUTOBIOGRAPHY OF. Trns. by R. & E. HOLMES. 2 vols. Cr. 8vo. 21s.

BERNARD (St.). THE LIFE AND TIMES OF ST. BERNARD, ABBOT OF CLAIRVAUX. By J. C. MORISON, M.A. Cr. 8vo. 6s.

BLACKBURNE. LIFE OF THE RIGHT HON. FRANCIS BLACKBURNE, late Lord Chancellor of Ireland, by his Son, EDWARD BLACKBURNE. With Portrait. 8vo. 12s.

BLAKE. LIFE OF WILLIAM BLAKE. With Selections from his Poems, etc. Illustr. from Blake's own Works. By ALEXANDER GILCHRIST. 2 vols. Med. 8vo. 42s.

BOLEYN (Anne): A CHAPTER OF ENGLISH HISTORY, 1527—36. By PAUL FRIEDMANN. 2 vols. 8vo. 28s.

BROOKE (Sir Jas.), THE RAJA OF SARAWAK (Life of). By GERTRUDE L. JACOB. 2 vols. 8vo. 25s.

BURKE. By JOHN MORLEY. Globe 8vo. 5s.

CALLAWAY (Bishop).—HIS LIFE-HISTORY AND WORK. By M. S. BENHAM. Cr. 8vo. 6s.

CALVIN. (*See* SELECT BIOGRAPHY, p. 6.)

CAMPBELL (Sir G.).—MEMOIRS OF MY INDIAN CAREER. Edited by Sir C. E. BERNARD. 2 vols. 8vo. 21s. net.

CARLYLE (Thomas). Edited by CHARLES E. NORTON. Cr. 8vo.
—— REMINISCENCES. 2 vols. 12s.
—— EARLY LETTERS, 1814—26. 2 vols. 18s.
—— LETTERS, 1826—36. 2 vols. 18s.
—— CORRESPONDENCE BETWEEN GOETHE AND CARLYLE. 9s.

CARSTARES (Wm.): A CHARACTER AND CAREER OF THE REVOLUTIONARY EPOCH (1649—1715). By R. H. STORY. 8vo. 12s.

CAVOUR. (*See* SELECT BIOGRAPHY, p. 6.)

CHURCH (R. W.).—LIFE AND LETTERS. 8vo. 7s. 6d.

CHATTERTON: A STORY OF THE YEAR 1770. By Prof. DAVID MASSON. Cr. 8vo. 5s.
—— A BIOGRAPHICAL STUDY. By Sir DANIEL WILSON. Cr. 8vo. 6s. 6d.

CLARK. MEMORIALS FROM JOURNALS AND LETTERS OF SAMUEL CLARK, M.A. Edited by HIS WIFE. Cr. 8vo. 7s. 6d.

CLOUGH (A. H.). (*See* LITERATURE, p. 24.)

COLERIDGE (S. T.): A NARRATIVE OF THE EVENTS OF HIS LIFE. By J. D. CAMPBELL. 8vo. 10s. 6d.

COMBE. LIFE OF GEORGE COMBE. By CHARLES GIBBON. 2 vols. 8vo. 32s.

CROMWELL. (*See* SELECT BIOGRAPHY, p. 6.)

DAMIEN (Father): A JOURNEY FROM CASHMERE TO HIS HOME IN HAWAII. By EDWARD CLIFFORD. Portrait. Cr. 8vo. 2s. 6d.

DANTE: AND OTHER ESSAYS. By Dean CHURCH. Globe 8vo. 5s.

DARWIN (Charles): MEMORIAL NOTICES. By T. H. HUXLEY, G. J. ROMANES, Sir ARCH. GEIKIE, and W. THISELTON DYER. With Portrait. Cr. 8vo. 2s. 6d.

DEAK (Francis): HUNGARIAN STATESMAN. A Memoir. 8vo. 12s. 6d.

DRUMMOND OF HAWTHORNDEN. By Prof. D. MASSON. Cr. 8vo. 10s. 6d.

EADIE. LIFE OF JOHN EADIE, D.D. By JAMES BROWN, D.D. Cr. 8vo. 7s. 6d.

ELLIOTT. LIFE OF H. V. ELLIOTT, OF BRIGHTON. By J. BATEMAN. Cr. 8vo. 6s.

EMERSON. LIFE OF RALPH WALDO EMERSON. By J. L. CABOT. 2 vols. Cr. 8vo. 18s.

ENGLISH MEN OF ACTION. Cr. 8vo. With Portraits. 2s. 6d. each.
CAMPBELL (COLIN). By A. FORBES.
CLIVE. By Colonel Sir CHARLES WILSON.
COOK (CAPTAIN). By WALTER BESANT.
DAMPIER. By W. CLARK RUSSELL.
DRAKE. By JULIAN CORBETT.
DUNDONALD. By Hon. J. W. FORTESCUE.
GORDON (GENERAL). By Col. Sir W. BUTLER.
HASTINGS (WARREN). By Sir A. LYALL.
HAVELOCK (SIR HENRY). By A. FORBES.
HENRY V. By Rev. A. J. CHURCH.
LAWRENCE (LORD). By Sir RICH. TEMPLE.
LIVINGSTONE. By THOMAS HUGHES.
MONK. By JULIAN CORBETT.
MONTROSE. By MOWBRAY MORRIS.
NAPIER (SIR CHAS.). By Sir W. BUTLER.
NELSON. By J. K. LAUGHTON.
PETERBOROUGH. By W. STEBBING.
RODNEY. By DAVID HANNAY.
STRAFFORD. By H. D. TRAILL.
WARWICK, THE KING-MAKER. By C. W. OMAN.
WELLINGTON. By GEORGE HOOPER.
WOLFE. By A. G. BRADLEY.

ENGLISH MEN OF LETTERS. Ed. by JOHN MORLEY. Cr. 8vo. 1s. 6d.; swd. 1s.
ADDISON. By W. J. COURTHOPE.
BACON. By Dean CHURCH.
BENTLEY. By Prof. JEBB.
BUNYAN. By J. A. FROUDE.
BURKE. By JOHN MORLEY.
BURNS. By Principal SHAIRP.
BYRON. By JOHN NICHOL.
CARLYLE. By JOHN NICHOL.
CHAUCER. By Prof. A. W. WARD.
COLERIDGE. By H. D. TRAILL.
COWPER. By GOLDWIN SMITH.

ENGLISH MEN OF LETTERS—*contd.*
DEFOE. By W. MINTO.
DE QUINCEY. By Prof. MASSON.
DICKENS. By A. W. WARD.
DRYDEN. By G. SAINTSBURY.
FIELDING. By AUSTIN DOBSON.
GIBBON. By J. COTTER MORISON.
GOLDSMITH. By WILLIAM BLACK.
GRAY. By EDMUND GOSSE.
HAWTHORNE. By HENRY JAMES.
HUME. By T. H. HUXLEY.
JOHNSON. By LESLIE STEPHEN.
KEATS. By SIDNEY COLVIN.
LAMB. By Rev. ALFRED AINGER.
LANDOR. By SIDNEY COLVIN.
LOCKE. By Prof. FOWLER.
MACAULAY. By J. COTTER MORISON.
MILTON. By MARK PATTISON.
POPE. By LESLIE STEPHEN.
SCOTT. By R. H. HUTTON.
SHELLEY. By J. A. SYMONDS.
SHERIDAN. By Mrs. OLIPHANT.
SIDNEY. By J. A. SYMONDS.
SOUTHEY. By Prof. DOWDEN.
SPENSER. By Dean CHURCH.
STERNE By H. D. TRAILL.
SWIFT. By LESLIE STEPHEN.
THACKERAY. By ANTHONY TROLLOPE.
WORDSWORTH. By F. W. H. MYERS.

ENGLISH MEN OF LETTERS. Reissue in 13 vols. Cr. 8vo. 3s. 6d. each.
Vol. I. CHAUCER, SPENSER, DRYDEN.
Vol. II. MILTON, GOLDSMITH, COWPER.
Vol. III. BYRON, SHELLEY, KEATS.
Vol. IV. WORDSWORTH, SOUTHEY, LANDOR.
Vol. V. LAMB, ADDISON, SWIFT.
Vol. VI. SCOTT, BURNS, COLERIDGE.
Vol. VII. HUME, LOCKE, BURKE.
Vol. VIII. DEFOE, STERNE, HAWTHORNE.
Vol. IX. FIELDING, THACKERAY, DICKENS.
Vol. X. GIBBON, CARLYLE, MACAULAY.
Vol. XI. SIDNEY, DE QUINCEY, SHERIDAN.
Vol. XII. POPE, JOHNSON, GRAY.
Vol. XIII. BACON, BUNYAN, BENTLEY.

ENGLISH STATESMEN, TWELVE. Cr. 8vo. 2s. 6d. each.
WILLIAM THE CONQUEROR. By EDWARD A. FREEMAN, D.C.L., LL.D.
HENRY II. By Mrs. J. R. GREEN.
EDWARD I. By T. F. TOUT, M.A.
HENRY VII. By JAMES GAIRDNER.
CARDINAL WOLSEY. By Bp. CREIGHTON.
ELIZABETH. By E. S. BEESLY.
OLIVER CROMWELL. By F. HARRISON.
WILLIAM III. By H. D. TRAILL.
WALPOLE. By JOHN MORLEY.
CHATHAM. By JOHN MORLEY. [*In Prep.*
PITT. By LORD ROSEBERY.
PEEL. By J. R. THURSFIELD.

FAIRFAX. LIFE OF ROBERT FAIRFAX OF STEETON, Vice-Admiral, Alderman, and Member for York, A.D. 1666-1725. By CLEMENTS R. MARKHAM, C.B. 8vo. 12s. 6d.

FITZGERALD (E.). (*See* LITERATURE p. 25.)

FORBES (Edward): MEMOIR OF. By GEORGE WILSON, M.P., and Sir ARCHIBALD GEIKIE, F.R.S., etc. 8vo. 14s.

FORBES-MITCHELL (W.).—REMINISCENCES OF THE GREAT MUTINY. Cr. 8vo. 3s. 6d.

FOREIGN STATESMEN. Crown 8vo. 2s. 6d. each.
RICHELIEU. By R. LODGE, M.A.
PHILIP AUGUSTUS. By Rev. W. H. HUTTON.

FRANCIS OF ASSISI. By Mrs. OLIPHANT. Cr. 8vo. 6s.

FRASER. JAMES FRASER, SECOND BISHOP OF MANCHESTER: A Memoir. By T. HUGHES. Cr. 8vo. 6s.

FREEMAN (E. A.).—LIFE AND LETTERS. By W. R. W. STEPHENS. 2 vols. 8vo. 17s. net.

GOETHE: LIFE OF. By Prof. HEINRICH DÜNTZER. Translated by T. W. LYSTER. 2 vols. Cr. 8vo. 21s.

GORDON (General): A SKETCH. By REGINALD H. BARNES. Cr. 8vo. 1s.
—— LETTERS OF GENERAL C. G. GORDON TO HIS SISTER, M. A. GORDON. Cr. 8vo. 3s. 6d.

HANDEL: LIFE OF. By W. S. ROCKSTRO. Cr. 8vo. 10s. 6d.

HAUSER, KASPAR: TRUE STORY OF. By the DUCHESS OF CLEVELAND. Cr. 8vo. 4s. 6d.

HIGINBOTHAM (Chief Justice).—LIFE OF. By E. E MORRIS. Ex. cr. 8vo. 9s.

HOBART. (*See* COLLECTED WORKS, p. 26.)

HODGSON. MEMOIR OF REV. FRANCIS HODGSON, B.D. By his Son, Rev. JAMES T. HODGSON, M.A. 2 vols. Cr. 8vo. 18s.

HORT (F. J. A.).—LIFE AND LETTERS. By HIS SON. 2 vols. 8vo. 17s. net.

JEVONS (W. Stanley).—LETTERS AND JOURNAL. Edited by HIS WIFE. 8vo. 14s.

KAVANAGH (Rt. Hon. A. McMurrough): A BIOGRAPHY. From papers chiefly unpublished, compiled by his Cousin, SARAH L. STEELE. With Portrait. 8vo. 14s. net.

KINGSLEY (Chas.): HIS LETTERS, AND MEMORIES OF HIS LIFE. Edit. by HIS WIFE. 2 vols. Cr. 8vo. 12s.—Cheap Edit. 1 vol. 6s.

LAMB. THE LIFE OF CHARLES LAMB. By Rev. ALFRED AINGER, M.A. Globe 8vo. 5s.

LETHBRIDGE (Sir R.).—GOLDEN BOOK OF INDIA. Royal 8vo. 40s.

LIGHTFOOT. BISHOP LIGHTFOOT. Reprinted from *Quarterly Review*. Cr. 8vo. 3s. 6d.

LOUIS (St.). (*See* SELECT BIOGRAPHY, p. 6.)

MACMILLAN (D.). MEMOIR OF DANIEL MACMILLAN. By THOMAS HUGHES, Q.C. With Portrait. Cr. 8vo. 4s. 6d.—Cheap Edition. Cr. 8vo, sewed. 1s.

MALTHUS AND HIS WORK. By JAMES BONAR. 8vo. 12s. 6d.

MANNING (Cardinal): LIFE OF. By E. S. PURCELL. 2 vols. 3rd Edit. 8vo. 30s. net.

MAURICE. LIFE OF FREDERICK DENISON MAURICE. By his Son, F. MAURICE. 2 vols. 8vo. 36s.—Popular Ed. 2 vols. Cr. 8vo. 16s.

MAXWELL. PROFESSOR CLERK MAXWELL, A LIFE OF. By Prof. L. CAMPBELL, M.A., and W. GARNETT, M.A. Cr. 8vo. 7s. 6d.

MAZZINI. (*See* SELECT BIOGRAPHY, p. 6.)

MELBOURNE. MEMOIRS OF VISCOUNT MELBOURNE. By W. M. TORRENS. With Portrait. 2nd Edit. 2 vols. 8vo. 32s.

MILTON. THE LIFE OF JOHN MILTON. By Prof. DAVID MASSON. Vol. I., 21s.; Vol. II., 16s.; Vol. III., 18s.; Vols. IV. and V., 32s.; Vol. VI., with Portrait, 21s.; Index to 6 vols., 16s. (*See also* p. 18.)

MILTON: JOHNSON'S LIFE OF. Introduction and Notes by K. DEIGHTON. Gl. 8vo. 1s. 9d.

BIOGRAPHY—*continued*.

NAPOLEON I. : HISTORY OF. By P. LANFREY. 4 vols. Cr. 8vo. 30s.

NELSON. SOUTHEY'S LIFE OF NELSON. With Introduction and Notes by MICHAEL MACMILLAN, B.A. Globe 8vo. 3s. 6d.

NEWMAN (Cardinal): THE ANGLICAN CAREER OF. By E. A. ABBOTT. 2 vols. 25s. net.

NORTH (M.).—RECOLLECTIONS OF A HAPPY LIFE. Being the Autobiography of MARIANNE NORTH. Ed. by Mrs. J. A SYMONDS. 2nd Edit. 2 vols. Ex. cr. 8vo. 17s. net.
—— SOME FURTHER RECOLLECTIONS OF A HAPPY LIFE. Cr. 8vo. 8s. 6d. net.

OXFORD MOVEMENT, THE, 1833—45. By Dean CHURCH. Gl. 8vo. 5s.

PARKER (W. K.)—A BIOGRAPHICAL SKETCH. By His SON. Cr. 8vo. 4s. net.

PARKES (Sir Harry): LIFE OF. Edited by S. LANE-POOLE and F. V. DICKINS. 2 vols. 8vo. 25s. net.

PATTESON. LIFE AND LETTERS OF JOHN COLERIDGE PATTESON, D.D., MISSIONARY BISHOP. By C. M. YONGE. 2 vols. Cr. 8vo. 12s. (*See also under* AWDRY, p. 48.)

PATTISON (M.).—MEMOIRS. Cr. 8vo. 8s. 6d.

PITT. (*See* SELECT BIOGRAPHY.)

POLLOCK (Sir Frdk., 2nd Bart.).—PERSONAL REMEMBRANCES. 2 vols. Cr. 8vo. 16s.

POOLE, THOS., AND HIS FRIENDS. By Mrs. SANDFORD. 2nd edit. Cr. 8vo. 6s.

RAMSAY (Sir A. C.): LIFE OF. By Sir A. GEIKIE, F.R.S. 8vo. 12s. 6d. net.

RENAN (Ernest): IN MEMORIAM. By Sir M. E. GRANT DUFF. Cr. 8vo. 6s.

ROBINSON (Matthew): AUTOBIOGRAPHY OF. Edited by J. E. B. MAYOR. Fcp. 8vo. 5s.

ROSSETTI (Dante Gabriel): A RECORD AND A STUDY. By W. SHARP. Cr. 8vo. 10s. 6d.

RUMFORD. (*See* COLLECTED WORKS, p. 28.)

SCHILLER, LIFE OF. By Prof. H. DÜNTZER. Transl by P. E. PINKERTON. Cr. 8vo. 10s. 6d.

SELBORNE (Earl of).—FAMILY AND PERSONAL MEMORIALS, 1766—1865. With Portraits. 2 vols. 8vo. [*In the Press.*

SHELBURNE. LIFE OF WILLIAM, EARL OF SHELBURNE. By Lord EDMOND FITZMAURICE. In 3 vols.—Vol. I. 8vo. 12s.—Vol. II. 8vo. 12s.—Vol. III. 8vo. 16s.

SIBSON. (*See* MEDICINE.)

SMETHAM (Jas.): LETTERS OF. Ed. by SARAH SMETHAM and W. DAVIES. Portrait. Globe 8vo. 5s.

SMITH (Adam.): LIFE OF. By J. RAE. 8vo. 12s. 6d. net.

SPINOZA: A STUDY. By Dr. J. MARTINEAU. Cr. 8vo. 6s.

SWIFT: LIFE OF. Edit. by H. CRAIK, C.B. 2 vols. Gl. 8vo. 10s.

TAIT. THE LIFE OF ARCHIBALD CAMPBELL TAIT, ARCHBISHOP OF CANTERBURY. By the BISHOP OF WINCHESTER and Rev. W. BENHAM, B.D. 2 vols. Cr. 8vo. 10s. net.
—— CATHARINE AND CRAWFURD TAIT, WIFE AND SON OF ARCHIBALD CAMPBELL, ARCHBISHOP OF CANTERBURY : A Memoir. Ed. by Rev. W. BENHAM, B.D. Cr. 8vo. 6s.
—Popular Edit., abridged. Cr. 8vo. 2s. 6d.

THRING (Edward): A MEMORY OF. By J. H. SKRINE. Cr. 8vo. 6s.

VICTOR EMMANUEL II., FIRST KING OF ITALY. By G. S. GODKIN. Cr. 8vo. 6s.

WARD. WILLIAM GEORGE WARD AND THE OXFORD MOVEMENT. By his Son, WILFRID WARD. With Portrait. 8vo. 14s.
—— WILLIAM GEORGE WARD AND THE CATHOLIC REVIVAL. By the same. 8vo. 14s.

WATSON. A RECORD OF ELLEN WATSON. By ANNA BUCKLAND. Cr. 8vo. 6s.

WHEWELL. DR. WILLIAM WHEWELL, late Master of Trinity College, Cambridge. An Account of his Writings, with Selections from his Literary and Scientific Correspondence. By I. TODHUNTER, M.A. 2 vols. 8vo. 25s.

WILLIAMS (Montagu).—LEAVES OF A LIFE. Cr. 8vo. 3s. 6d.
—— LATER LEAVES. Being further Reminiscences. With Portrait. Cr. 8vo. 3s. 6d.
—— ROUND LONDON, DOWN EAST AND OF WEST. Cr. 8vo. 3s. 6d.

WILSON. MEMOIR OF PROF. GEORGE WILSON, M.D. By His SISTER. With Portrait. 2nd Edit. Cr. 8vo. 6s.

WORDSWORTH DOVE COTTAGE, WORDSWORTH'S HOME 1800—8. Gl. 8vo, swd. 1s.

Select Biography.

BIOGRAPHIES OF EMINENT PERSONS. 4 vols. Cr. 8vo. 3s. 6d. each.

FARRAR (Archdeacon).—SEEKERS AFTER GOD. Cr. 8vo. 3s. 6d.

FAWCETT (Mrs. H.). — SOME EMINENT WOMEN OF OUR TIMES. Cr. 8vo. 2s. 6d.

GUIZOT.—GREAT CHRISTIANS OF FRANCE: ST. LOUIS AND CALVIN. Cr. 8vo. 6s.

HARRISON (Frederic).—THE NEW CALENDAR OF GREAT MEN. Ex. cr. 8vo. 7s. 6d. net.

LODGE (O. J.).—PIONEERS OF SCIENCE. Cr. 8vo. 7s. 6d.

MARRIOTT (J. A. R.).—THE MAKERS OF MODERN ITALY : MAZZINI, CAVOUR, GARIBALDI. Cr. 8vo. 1s. 6d.

MARTINEAU (Harriet). — BIOGRAPHICAL SKETCHES, 1852—75. Cr. 8vo. 6s.

NEW HOUSE OF COMMONS, JULY, 1895. Reprinted from the *Times*. 16mo. 1s.

RITCHIE (Mrs.).—RECORDS OF TENNYSON, RUSKIN, AND BROWNING. Globe 8vo. 5s.
—— CHAPTERS FROM SOME MEMOIRS. Cr. 8vo. 10s. 6d.

SMALLEY (G. W.).—STUDIES OF MEN. Cr. 8vo. 8s. 6d. net.

SMITH (Goldwin).—THREE ENGLISH STATESMEN : CROMWELL, PYM, PITT. Cr. 8vo. 5s.

STEVENSON (F. S.).—HISTORIC PERSONALITY. Cr. 8vo. 4s. 6d.

THORPE (T. E.).—ESSAYS IN HISTORICAL CHEMISTRY. Cr. 8vo. 8s. 6d. net.

WINKWORTH (Catharine). — CHRISTIAN SINGERS OF GERMANY. Cr. 8vo. 4s. 6d.

YONGE (Charlotte M.).—THE PUPILS OF ST JOHN. Illustrated. Cr. 8vo. 6s.
—— PIONEERS AND FOUNDERS; or, Recent Workers in the Mission Field: Cr. 8vo. 6s.
—— A BOOK OF WORTHIES. Pott 8vo. 2s. 6d. net.
—— A BOOK OF GOLDEN DEEDS. Pott 8vo. 2s. 6d. net.—*Globe Readings Edition.* Globe 8vo. 2s.—*Abridged Edition.* Pott 8vo. 1s.

BIOLOGY.

(*See also* BOTANY; NATURAL HISTORY; PHYSIOLOGY; ZOOLOGY.)

BALFOUR (F. M.).—COMPARATIVE EMBRYOLOGY. Illustrated. 2 vols. 8vo. Vol. I. 18s. Vol. II. 21s.

BALL (W. P.).—ARE THE EFFECTS OF USE AND DISUSE INHERITED? Cr. 8vo. 2s. 6d.

BATESON (W.).—MATERIALS FOR THE STUDY OF VARIATION. Illustr. 8vo. 21s. net.

BERNARD (H. M.).—THE APODIDAE. Cr. 8vo. 7s. 6d.

BIRKS (T. R.).—MODERN PHYSICAL FATALISM, AND THE DOCTRINE OF EVOLUTION. Including an Examination of Mr. Herbert Spencer's "First Principles." Cr. 8vo. 6s.

CALDERWOOD (H.). — EVOLUTION AND MAN'S PLACE IN NATURE. 2nd Edit. 8vo. 10s. net.

DE VARIGNY (H.).—EXPERIMENTAL EVOLUTION. Cr. 8vo. 5s.

EIMER (G. H. T.).—ORGANIC EVOLUTION AS THE RESULT OF THE INHERITANCE OF ACQUIRED CHARACTERS ACCORDING TO THE LAWS OF ORGANIC GROWTH. Translated by J. T. CUNNINGHAM, M.A. 8vo. 12s. 6d.

FISKE (John).—OUTLINES OF COSMIC PHILOSOPHY, BASED ON THE DOCTRINE OF EVOLUTION. 2 vols. 8vo. 25s.
—— MAN'S DESTINY VIEWED IN THE LIGHT OF HIS ORIGIN. Cr. 8vo. 3s. 6d.

FOSTER (Prof. M.) and BALFOUR (F. M.). —THE ELEMENTS OF EMBRYOLOGY. Ed. A. SEDGWICK, and WALTER HEAPE. Illust. 3rd Edit., revised and enlarged. Cr. 8vo. 10s. 6d.

HUXLEY (T. H.) and MARTIN (H. N.).— (*See under* ZOOLOGY, p. 49.)

KLEIN (Dr. E.).—MICRO-ORGANISMS AND DISEASE. 3rd Edit. Cr. 8vo. 6s.

LANKESTER (Prof. E. Ray).—COMPARATIVE LONGEVITY IN MAN AND THE LOWER ANIMALS. Cr. 8vo. 4s. 6d.

LUBBOCK (Sir John, Bart.).—SCIENTIFIC LECTURES. Illustrated. 2nd Edit. 8vo. 8s. 6d.

MURPHY (J. J.).—NATURAL SELECTION. Gl. 8vo. 5s.

ORR (H. B.).—DEVELOPMENT AND HEREDITY. Cr. 8vo. 6s. net.

OSBORN (H. F.).—FROM THE GREEKS TO DARWIN. 8vo. 9s. net.

PARKER (T. Jeffery).—LESSONS IN ELEMENTARY BIOLOGY. Illustr. Cr. 8vo. 10s. 6d.

ROMANES (G. J.).—SCIENTIFIC EVIDENCES OF ORGANIC EVOLUTION. Cr. 8vo. 2s. 6d.

WALLACE (Alfred R.).—DARWINISM: An Exposition of the Theory of Natural Selection. Illustrated. 3rd Edit. Cr. 8vo. 9s.
—— CONTRIBUTIONS TO THE THEORY OF NATURAL SELECTION, AND TROPICAL NATURE: and other Essays. New Ed. Cr. 8vo. 6s.
—— THE GEOGRAPHICAL DISTRIBUTION OF ANIMALS. Illustrated. 2 vols. 8vo. 42s.
—— ISLAND LIFE. Illustr. Ext. Cr. 8vo. 6s.

WILLEY (A.).—AMPHIOXUS, AND THE ANCESTRY OF THE VERTEBRATES. 8vo. 10s. 6d. net.

BIRDS. (*See* ZOOLOGY; ORNITHOLOGY.)

BOOK-KEEPING.

THORNTON (J.).—FIRST LESSONS IN BOOK-KEEPING. New Edition. Cr. 8vo. 2s. 6d.
—— KEY. Oblong 4to. 10s. 6d.
—— EXERCISE BOOKS TO FIRST LESSONS IN BOOKKEEPING.
No. 1. FOR LESSONS I.—IX. 9d.
No. 2. FOR TEST EXERCISES. 9d.
No. 3. FOR TEST EXERCISES. 1s. 6d.
No. 4. FOR LESSONS XIII. and XIV. 1s. 6d.
Case to contain all the above, 6d. Complete set with case, 5s.

No. 5. CONDENSED EDITION FOR WORKING OUT A SELECTION ON ALL THE LESSONS. 2s.
No. 6. JOURNAL. 6d.
EXAMINATION PAPERS IN BOOKKEEPING. 9d.
KEY TO EXAMINATION PAPERS. 2s.
—— PRIMER OF BOOK-KEEPING. Pott 8vo. 1s.
—— KEY. Demy 8vo. 2s. 6d.
—— EXERCISE BOOKS TO PRIMER OF BOOK-KEEPING.
Part I. LEDGER; Part II. JOURNAL. The Set, 1s.
—— EXERCISES IN BOOK-KEEPING. Pott 8vo. 1s.
—— MANUAL OF BOOK-KEEPING. Gl. 8vo. 7s. 6d.

BOTANY.

(*See also* AGRICULTURE; GARDENING.)

ALLEN (Grant). — ON THE COLOURS OF FLOWERS. Illustrated. Cr. 8vo. 3s. 6d.

ATKINSON (G. F.).—BIOLOGY OF FERNS. 8vo. 8s. 6d. net.

BALFOUR (Prof. J. B.) and WARD (Prof. H. M.). — A GENERAL TEXT-BOOK OF BOTANY. 8vo. [*In preparation.*

BETTANY (G. T.).—FIRST LESSONS IN PRACTICAL BOTANY. Pott 8vo. 1s.

BOWER (Prof. F. O.).—A COURSE OF PRACTICAL INSTRUCTION IN BOTANY. Cr. 8vo. 10s. 6d.
—— PRACTICAL BOTANY FOR BEGINNERS. Gl. 8vo. 3s. 6d.

CAMPBELL (Prof. D. H.).—STRUCTURE AND DEVELOPMENT OF MOSSES AND FERNS. Illustrated. 8vo. 14s. net.

GRAY (Prof. Asa).—STRUCTURAL BOTANY; or, Organography on the Basis of Morphology. 8vo. 10s. 6d.
—— THE SCIENTIFIC PAPERS OF ASA GRAY. Selected by C. S. SARGENT. 2 vols. 8vo. 21s.

HANBURY (Daniel). — SCIENCE PAPERS, CHIEFLY PHARMACOLOGICAL AND BOTANICAL. Med. 8vo. 14s.

HARTIG (Dr. Robert).—TEXT-BOOK OF THE DISEASES OF TREES. Transl. by Prof WM. SOMERVILLE, B.Sc. Introduction by Prof. H. MARSHALL WARD. 8vo. 10s. net.

HOOKER (Sir Joseph D.).—THE STUDENT'S FLORA OF THE BRITISH ISLANDS. 3rd Edit. Globe 8vo. 10s. 6d.
—— A PRIMER OF BOTANY. Pott 8vo. 1s.

LASLETT (Thomas).—TIMBER AND TIMBER TREES, NATIVE AND FOREIGN. 2nd Ed. Revised by H. MARSHALL WARD, D.Sc. Cr. 8vo. 8s. 6d.

LUBBOCK (Sir John, Bart.).—ON BRITISH WILD FLOWERS CONSIDERED IN RELATION TO INSECTS. Illustrated. Cr. 8vo. 4s. 6d.
—— FLOWERS, FRUITS, AND LEAVES. With Illustrations. Cr. 8vo. 4s. 6d.

BOTANY—*continued.*

MÜLLER—THOMPSON.—The Fertilisation of Flowers. By Prof. H. Müller. Transl. by D'Arcy W. Thompson. Preface by Charles Darwin, F.R.S. 8vo. 21s.

MURRAY (G.).—Introduction to Study of Seaweeds. Cr. 8vo. 7s. 6d.

NISBET (J.).—British Forest Trees and their Sylvicultural Characteristics and Treatment. Cr. 8vo. 6s. net.

OLIVER (Prof. Daniel).—Lessons in Elementary Botany. Illustr. Fcp. 8vo. 4s. 6d.
— First Book of Indian Botany. Illustrated. Ext. fcp. 8vo. 6s. 6d.

PETTIGREW (J. Bell).—The Physiology of the Circulation in Plants, in the Lower Animals, and in Man. 8vo. 12s

SMITH (J.).—Economic Plants, Dictionary of Popular Names of; Their History, Products, and Uses. 8vo. 14s.

SMITH (W. G.).—Diseases of Field and Garden Crops, chiefly such as are caused by Fungi. Illust. Fcp. 8vo. 4s. 6d.

VINES (S. H.) and KINCH (E.).—Manual of Vegetable Physiology. Illustrated. Crown 8vo. [In preparation

WARD (Prof. H. M.).—Timber and some of its Diseases. Illustrated. Cr. 8vo. 6s.

YONGE (C. M.).—The Herb of the Field. New Edition, revised. Cr. 8vo. 5s.

BREWING.

PASTEUR—FAULKNER.—Studies on Fermentation: The Diseases of Beer, their Causes, and the Means of Preventing them. By L. Pasteur. Translated by Frank Faulkner. 8vo. 21s.

CHEMISTRY.
(*See also* Metallurgy.)

BEHRENS (H.).—Microchemical Analysis. Cr. 8vo. 6s.

BRODIE (Sir Benjamin).—Ideal Chemistry. Cr. 8vo. 2s.

COHEN (J. B.).—The Owens College Course of Practical Organic Chemistry. Fcp. 8vo. 2s. 6d.

COMEY (A. M.).—Dictionary of Chemical Solubilities. 8vo. 15s. net.

COOKE (Prof. J. P., jun.).—Principles of Chemical Philosophy. New Ed. 8vo. 19s.

DOBBIN (L.) and WALKER (Jas.).—Chemical Theory for Beginners. Pott 8vo. 2s. 6d.

FLEISCHER (Emil).—A System of Volumetric Analysis. Transl. with Additions, by M. M. P. Muir, F.R.S.E. Cr. 8vo. 7s. 6d.

FRANKLAND (Prof. P. F.). (*See* Agriculture.)

GLADSTONE (J. H.) and TRIBE (A.).—The Chemistry of the Secondary Batteries of Planté and Faure. Cr. 8vo. 2s. 6d.

HARTLEY (Prof. W. N.).—A Course of Quantitative Analysis for Students. Globe 8vo. 5s.

HEMPEL (Dr. W.).—Methods of Gas Analysis. Translated by L. M. Dennis. Cr. 8vo. 7s. 6d.

HOFMANN (Prof. A. W.).—The Life Work of Liebig in Experimental and Philosophic Chemistry. 8vo. 5s.

JONES (Francis).—The Owens College Junior Course of Practical Chemistry. Illustrated. Fcp. 8vo. 2s. 6d.
— Questions on Chemistry. Fcp. 8vo. 3s.

LANDAUER (J.).—Blowpipe Analysis. Translated by J. Taylor. Gl. 8vo. 4s. 6d.

LASSAR-COHN.—Organic Chemistry. Transl. by A. Smith. Cr. 8vo. 8s. 6d.

LOCKYER (J. Norman, F.R.S.).—The Chemistry of the Sun. Illustr. 8vo. 14s.

LUPTON (S.).—Chemical Arithmetic. With 1200 Problems. Fcp. 8vo. 4s. 6d.

MANSFIELD (C. B.).—A Theory of Salts. Cr. 8vo. 14s.

MELDOLA (Prof. R.).—The Chemistry of Photography. Illustrated. Cr. 8vo. 6s.

MENSCHUTKIN (A.).—Analytical Chemistry. Trsl. by J. Locke. 8vo. 17s. net.

MEYER (E. von).—History of Chemistry from Earliest Times to the Present Day. Transl. G. McGowan. 8vo. 14s. net.

MIXTER (Prof. W. G.).—An Elementary Text-Book of Chemistry. Cr. 8vo. 7s. 6d.

MUIR (M. M. P.).—Practical Chemistry for Medical Students (First M.B. Course). Fcp. 8vo. 1s. 6d.

MUIR (M. M. P.) and WILSON (D. M.).—Elements of Thermal Chemistry. 12s. 6d.

NERNST (Dr.).—Theoretical Chemistry. Translated by C. S. Palmer. 8vo. 15s. net.

OSTWALD (Prof.).—Outlines of General Chemistry. Transl. Dr. J. Walker. 10s. net.
— Manual of Physico-Chemical Measurements. Transl. by Dr. J. Walker. 8vo. 7s. net.
— Analytical Chemistry. Translated by G. McGowan. Cr. 8vo. 5s. net.

RAMSAY (Prof. William).—Experimental Proofs of Chemical Theory for Beginners. Pott 8vo. 2s. 6d.
— Gases of the Atmosphere. Ex. crown 8vo. [In the Press.

REMSEN (Prof. Ira).—The Elements of Chemistry. Fcp. 8vo. 2s. 6d.
— An Introduction to the Study of Chemistry (Inorganic Chemistry). Cr. 8vo. 6s. 6d.
— A Text-Book of Inorganic Chemistry. 8vo. 16s.
— Compounds of Carbon; or, An Introduction to the Study of Organic Chemistry. Cr. 8vo. 6s. 6d.

ROSCOE (Sir Henry E., F.R.S.).—A Primer of Chemistry. Illustrated. Pott 8vo. 1s.
— Lessons in Elementary Chemistry, Inorganic and Organic. Fcp. 8vo. 4s. 6d.

ROSCOE (Sir H. E.) and SCHORLEMMER (Prof. C.).—A Complete Treatise on Inorganic and Organic Chemistry. Illustr. 8vo.—Vols. I. and II. Inorganic Chemistry: Vol. I. The Non-Metallic Elements, New Edit., Revised by Drs. H. G. Colman and A. Harden, 21s. Vol. II. Parts I. and II. Metals, 18s. each.—Vol. III. Organic Chemistry: The Chemistry of the Hydro-Carbons and their Derivatives. Parts I. II. IV. and VI. 21s. each; Parts III. and V. 18s. each.

ROSCOE (Sir H. E.) and HARDEN (A.).—DALTON'S ATOMIC THEORY. 8vo. 6s. net.

ROSCOE (Sir H. E.) and LUNT (J.).—INORGANIC CHEMISTRY FOR BEGINNERS. Gl. 8vo. 2s. 6d.

ROSCOE (Sir H. E.) and SCHUSTER (A.).—SPECTRUM ANALYSIS. By Sir HENRY E. ROSCOE. 4th Edit., revised by the Author and A. SCHUSTER, F.R.S. With Coloured Plates. 8vo. 21s.

SCHORLEMMER (C.).—RISE AND DEVELOPMENT OF ORGANIC CHEMISTRY. Trans. by Prof. SMITHELLS. Cr. 8vo. 5s. net.

SCHULTZ (G.) and JULIUS (P.).—ORGANIC COLOURING MATTERS. Transl. by A. G. GREEN. 8vo. 21s. net.

THORPE (Prof. T. E.) and TATE (W.).—A SERIES OF CHEMICAL PROBLEMS. With KEY. Fcp. 8vo. 2s.

THORPE (Prof. T. E.) and RÜCKER (Prof. A. W.).—A TREATISE ON CHEMICAL PHYSICS. Illustrated 8vo. [In preparation.

TURPIN (G. S.).—LESSONS IN ORGANIC CHEMISTRY. Gl. 8vo. 2s. 6d.

—— PRACTICAL INORGANIC CHEMISTRY. Gl. 8vo. 2s. 6d.

WURTZ (Ad.).—A HISTORY OF CHEMICAL THEORY. Transl. by H. WATTS. Cr. 8vo. 6s.

CHRISTIAN CHURCH, History of the.
(*See under* THEOLOGY, p. 40.)

CHURCH OF ENGLAND, The.
(*See under* THEOLOGY, p. 40.)

COLLECTED WORKS.
(*See under* LITERATURE, p. 24.)

COMPARATIVE ANATOMY.
(*See under* ZOOLOGY, p. 49.)

COOKERY.
(*See under* DOMESTIC ECONOMY, *below*.)

DEVOTIONAL BOOKS.
(*See under* THEOLOGY, p. 41.)

DICTIONARIES AND GLOSSARIES.
AUTENRIETH (Dr. G.).—AN HOMERIC DICTIONARY. Translated from the German, by R. P. KEEP, Ph.D. Cr. 8vo. 6s.

BARTLETT (J.).—FAMILIAR QUOTATIONS. Cr. 8vo. 6s. net.

GROVE (Sir George).—A DICTIONARY OF MUSIC AND MUSICIANS. (*See* MUSIC.)

HOLE (Rev. C.).—A BRIEF BIOGRAPHICAL DICTIONARY. 2nd Edit. Pott 8vo. 4s. 6d.

MASSON (Gustave).—A COMPENDIOUS DICTIONARY OF THE FRENCH LANGUAGE. Cr. 8vo. 3s. 6d.

PALGRAVE (R. H. I.).—A DICTIONARY OF POLITICAL ECONOMY. (*See* POLITICAL ECONOMY.)

WHITNEY (Prof. W. D.).—A COMPENDIOUS GERMAN AND ENGLISH DICTIONARY. Cr. 8vo. 5s.—German-English Part separately. 3s. 6d.

WRIGHT (W. Aldis).—THE BIBLE WORD-BOOK. 2nd Edit. Cr. 8vo. 7s. 6d.

YONGE (Charlotte M.).—HISTORY OF CHRISTIAN NAMES. Cr. 8vo. 7s. 6d.

DOMESTIC ECONOMY.
Cookery—Nursing—Needlework.
Cookery.
BARKER (Lady).—FIRST LESSONS IN THE PRINCIPLES OF COOKING. 3rd Edit. Pott 8vo. 1s.

BARNETT (E. A.) and O'NEILL (H. C.).—PRIMER OF DOMESTIC ECONOMY. Pott 8vo. 1s.

MIDDLE-CLASS COOKERY BOOK, THE. Compiled for the Manchester School of Cookery. Pott 8vo. 1s. 6d.

TEGETMEIER (W. B.).—HOUSEHOLD MANAGEMENT AND COOKERY. Pott 8vo. 1s.

WRIGHT (Miss Guthrie).—THE SCHOOL COOKERY-BOOK. Pott 8vo. 1s.

Nursing.
CRAVEN (Mrs. Dacre).—A GUIDE TO DISTRICT NURSES. Cr. 8vo. 2s. 6d.

FOTHERGILL (Dr. J. M.).—FOOD FOR THE INVALID, THE CONVALESCENT, THE DYSPEPTIC, AND THE GOUTY. Cr. 8vo. 3s. 6d.

JEX-BLAKE (Dr. Sophia).—THE CARE OF INFANTS. Pott 8vo. 1s.

RATHBONE (Wm.).—THE HISTORY AND PROGRESS OF DISTRICT NURSING, FROM 1859 TO THE PRESENT DATE. Cr. 8vo. 2s. 6d.

RECOLLECTIONS OF A NURSE. By E. D. Cr. 8vo. 2s.

STEPHEN (Caroline E.).—THE SERVICE OF THE POOR. Cr. 8vo. 6s. 6d.

Needlework.
GLAISTER (Elizabeth).—NEEDLEWORK. Cr. 8vo. 2s. 6d.

GRAND'HOMME.—CUTTING OUT AND DRESSMAKING. From the French of Mdlle. E. GRAND'HOMME. Pott 8vo. 1s.

GRENFELL (Mrs.)—DRESSMAKING. Pott 8vo. 1s.

ROSEVEAR (E.).—NEEDLEWORK, KNITTING, AND CUTTING OUT. 3rd Edit. Cr. 8vo. 6s.

—— NEEDLEWORK, KNITTING, AND CUTTING-OUT FOR OLDER GIRLS. Standard IV. 6d.; Standard V. 8d.; Standard VI. VII. and Ex-VII. 1s.

—— NEEDLEWORK, KNITTING, AND CUTTING-OUT FOR EVENING CONTINUATION SCHOOLS. Globe 8vo. 2s.

DRAMA, The.
(*See under* LITERATURE, p. 17.)

ELECTRICITY.
See *under* PHYSICS, p. 33.)

EDUCATION.
ARNOLD (Matthew).—HIGHER SCHOOLS AND UNIVERSITIES IN GERMANY. Cr. 8vo. 6s.

—— REPORTS ON ELEMENTARY SCHOOLS, 1852-82. Ed. by Lord SANDFORD. 8vo. 3s. 6d.

—— A FRENCH ETON: OR MIDDLE CLASS EDUCATION AND THE STATE. Cr. 8vo. 6s.

BLAKISTON (J. R.).—THE TEACHER: HINTS ON SCHOOL MANAGEMENT. Cr. 8vo. 2s. 6d.

CALDERWOOD (Prof. H.).—ON TEACHING. 4th Edit. Ext. fcp. 8vo. 2s. 6d.

COMBE (George).—EDUCATION: ITS PRIN-
CIPLES AND PRACTICE AS DEVELOPED BY
GEORGE COMBE. Ed. by W. JOLLY. 8vo. 15*s*.

CRAIK (Henry).—THE STATE IN ITS RELA-
TION TO EDUCATION. Cr. 8vo. 2*s*. 6*d*.
—— STATE EDUCATION: A SPEECH. 8vo.
Sewed. 6*d*. net.

FEARON (D. R.).—SCHOOL INSPECTION.
6th Edit. Cr. 8vo. 2*s*. 6*d*.

FITCH (J. G.).—NOTES ON AMERICAN
SCHOOLS AND TRAINING COLLEGES. Reprinted by permission. Globe 8vo. 2*s*. 6*d*.

GLADSTONE (J. H.).—SPELLING REFORM
FROM AN EDUCATIONAL POINT OF VIEW.
3rd Edit. Cr. 8vo. 1*s*. 6*d*.

HERTEL (Dr.).—OVERPRESSURE IN HIGH
SCHOOLS IN DENMARK. With Introduction
by Sir J. CRICHTON-BROWNE. Cr. 8vo. 3*s*. 6*d*.

KINGSLEY (Charles).—HEALTH AND EDU-
CATION. Cr. 8vo. 6*s*.

LUBBOCK (Sir John, Bart.).—POLITICAL AND
EDUCATIONAL ADDRESSES. 8vo. 8*s*. 6*d*.

MAURICE (F. D.).—LEARNING AND WORK-
ING. Cr. 8vo. 4*s*. 6*d*.

PAULSEN (F.).—THE GERMAN UNIVERSI-
TIES. By E. D. PERRY. Cr. 8vo. 7*s*. net.

RECORD OF TECHNICAL AND SE-
CONDARY EDUCATION. Crown 8vo.
Sewed, 2*s*. 6*d*. No. I. Nov. 1891.

THRING (Rev. Edward).—EDUCATION AND
SCHOOL. 2nd Edit. Cr. 8vo. 6*s*.

ENGINEERING.

ALEXANDER (T.) and THOMSON (A.W.).
—ELEMENTARY APPLIED MECHANICS. Part
II. TRANSVERSE STRESS. Cr. 8vo. 10*s*. 6*d*.

BERG (L. de C.).—SAFE BUILDING. 4th Ed.
2 vols. 4to. 42*s*. net.

CHALMERS (J. B.).—GRAPHICAL DETER-
MINATION OF FORCES IN ENGINEERING
STRUCTURES. Illustrated. 8vo. 24*s*.

CLARK (T. M.).—BUILDING SUPERINTEN-
DENCE. 12th Edit. 4to. 12*s*. net.

COTTERILL (Prof J. H.).—APPLIED ME-
CHANICS: An Elementary General Introduction to the Theory of Structures and Machines. 4th Edit. 8vo. 18*s*.

COTTERILL (Prof. J. H.) and SLADE
(J. H.).—LESSONS IN APPLIED MECHANICS.
Fcp. 8vo. 5*s*. 6*d*.

KENNEDY (Prof. A. B. W.).—THE ME-
CHANICS OF MACHINERY. Cr. 8vo. 8*s*. 6*d*.

LANGMAID (T.) and GAISFORD (H.).—
STEAM MACHINERY. 8vo. 6*s*. net.

PEABODY (Prof. C. H.).—THERMODYNAMICS
OF THE STEAM ENGINE AND OTHER HEAT-
ENGINES. 8vo. 21*s*.

ROBB (R.).—ELECTRIC WIRING. 4to. 10*s*.

SHANN (G.).—AN ELEMENTARY TREATISE
ON HEAT IN RELATION TO STEAM AND THE
STEAM-ENGINE. Illustrated. Cr. 8vo. 4*s*. 6*d*.

VIOLLET-LE-DUC (E. E.).—RATIONAL
BUILDING. Transl. by G. M. HUSS. 8vo.
12*s*. 6*d*. net.

WEISBACH (J.) and HERRMANN (G.).—
MECHANICS OF HOISTING MACHINERY.
Transl. K. P. DAHLSTROM. 8vo. 12*s*. 6*d*. net.

WOODWARD (C. M.).—A HISTORY OF THE
ST. LOUIS BRIDGE. 4to. 2*l*. 2*s*. net.

YOUNG (E. W.).—SIMPLE PRACTICAL ME-
THODS OF CALCULATING STRAINS ON GIR-
DERS, ARCHES, AND TRUSSES. 8vo. 7*s*. 6*d*.

ENGLISH CITIZEN SERIES.
(*See* POLITICS.)

ENGLISH MEN OF ACTION.
(*See* BIOGRAPHY.)

ENGLISH MEN OF LETTERS.
(*See* BIOGRAPHY.)

ENGLISH STATESMEN, Twelve.
(*See* BIOGRAPHY.)

ENGRAVING. (*See* ART.)

ESSAYS. (*See under* LITERATURE, p. 24.)

ETCHING. (*See* ART.)

ETHICS. (*See under* PHILOSOPHY, p. 32.)

FATHERS, The.
(*See under* THEOLOGY, p. 41.)

FICTION, Prose.
(*See under* LITERATURE, p. 21.)

GARDENING.
(*See also* AGRICULTURE; BOTANY.)

AUSTIN (Alfred).—THE GARDEN THAT I
LOVE. Ex. cr. 8vo. 9*s*.
—— IN VERONICA'S GARDEN. Ex. cr. 8vo. 9*s*.

BAILEY (L. H.).—HORTICULTURIST'S RULE
BOOK. Fcp. 8vo. 3*s*. net.
—— PLANT BREEDING. Fcp. 8vo. 4*s*. net.

BLOMFIELD (R.) and THOMAS (F. I.).—
THE FORMAL GARDEN IN ENGLAND. Illustrated. Ex. cr. 8vo. 7*s*. 6*d*. net.

BRIGHT (H. A.).—THE ENGLISH FLOWER
GARDEN. Cr. 8vo. 3*s*. 6*d*.
—— A YEAR IN A LANCASHIRE GARDEN. Cr.
8vo. 3*s*. 6*d*.

COLLINS (C.).—GREENHOUSE AND WINDOW
PLANTS. Ed. by J. WRIGHT. Pott 8vo. 1*s*.

DEAN (A.).—VEGETABLE CULTURE. Ed. by
J. WRIGHT. Pott 8vo. 1*s*.

FOSTER-MELLIAR (A.).—THE BOOK OF
THE ROSE. Illus. Ex. cr. 8vo. 8*s*. 6*d*. net.

FREEMAN-MITFORD (A. B.).—THE BAM-
BOO GARDEN. 8vo. 10*s*. 6*d*.

HOBDAY (E.).—VILLA GARDENING. A
Handbook for Amateur and Practical Gar-
deners. Ext. cr. 8vo. 6*s*.

LODEMAN (E. G.).—SPRAYING OF PLANTS.
Fcp 8vo. 4*s*. net.

WRIGHT (J.).—A PRIMER OF PRACTICAL
HORTICULTURE. Pott 8vo. 1*s*.
—— GARDEN FLOWERS AND PLANTS. Pott
8vo. 1*s*.

GEOGRAPHY.
(*See also* ATLASES.)

BLANFORD (H. F.).—ELEMENTARY GEO-
GRAPHY OF INDIA, BURMA, AND CEYLON.
Globe 8vo. 1*s*. 9*d*.

CLARKE (C. B.).—A GEOGRAPHICAL READER
AND COMPANION TO THE ATLAS. Cr. 8vo. 2*s*.
—— A GEOGRAPHIC READER. With Maps.
Gl. 8vo. 2*s*. 6*d*.
—— READER IN GENERAL GEOGRAPHY. Gl.
8vo swd. 1*s*.
—— A CLASS-BOOK OF GEOGRAPHY. With 18
Coloured Maps. Fcp. 8vo. 2*s*. 6*d*.; swd., 2*s*.
Without Maps, 1*s*. 6*d*.

DAWSON (G. M.) and SUTHERLAND (A.).
ELEMENTARY GEOGRAPHY OF THE BRITISH
COLONIES. Globe 8vo. 2s.

ELDERTON (W. A.).—MAPS AND MAP-
DRAWING. Pott 8vo. 1s.

GEIKIE (Sir Archibald).—THE TEACHING OF
GEOGRAPHY. A Practical Handbook for the
use of Teachers. Globe 8vo. 2s.
—— GEOGRAPHY OF THE BRITISH ISLES.
Pott 8vo. 1s.

GONNER (E. C. K.).—COMMERCIAL GEO-
GRAPHY. Gl. 8vo. 3s.

GREEN (J. R. and A. S.).—A SHORT GEOGRA-
PHY OF THE BRITISH ISLANDS. Fcp. 8vo. 3s. 6d.

GROVE (Sir George).—A PRIMER OF GEO-
GRAPHY. Maps. Pott 8vo. 1s.

KIEPERT (H.).—MANUAL OF ANCIENT
GEOGRAPHY. Cr. 8vo. 5s.

LUBBOCK (Rt. Hon. Sir John, Bart.).—THE
SCENERY OF SWITZERLAND. Illustrated. Cr.
8vo. 6s.

LYDE (L. W.).—MAN AND HIS MARKETS.
Illustrated. Cr. 8vo. [In the Press.

MILL (H. R.).—ELEMENTARY CLASS-BOOK
OF GENERAL GEOGRAPHY. Cr. 8vo. 3s. 6d.

SIME (James).—GEOGRAPHY OF EUROPE.
With Illustrations. Globe 8vo. 2s.

STRACHEY (Lieut.-Gen. R.).—LECTURES ON
GEOGRAPHY. Cr. 8vo. 4s. 6d.

SUTHERLAND (A.).—GEOGRAPHY OF VIC-
TORIA. Pott 8vo. 1s.
—— CLASS BOOK OF GEOGRAPHY. With Maps.
Fcp. 8vo. 2s. 6d.

TOZER (H. F.).—A PRIMER OF CLASSICAL
GEOGRAPHY. Pott 8vo. 1s.

GEOLOGY AND MINERALOGY.

BLANFORD (W. T.). — GEOLOGY AND
ZOOLOGY OF ABYSSINIA. 8vo. 21s.

COAL: ITS HISTORY AND ITS USES. By
Profs. GREEN, MIALL, THORPE, RÜCKER,
and MARSHALL. 8vo. 12s. 6d.

DAWSON (Sir J. W.).—THE GEOLOGY OF
NOVA SCOTIA, NEW BRUNSWICK, AND
PRINCE EDWARD ISLAND; or, Acadian Geo-
logy. 4th Edit. 8vo. 21s.

GEIKIE (Sir Archibald).—A PRIMER OF GEO-
LOGY. Illustrated. Pott 8vo. 1s.
—— CLASS-BOOK OF GEOLOGY. Illustrated.
Cr. 8vo. 4s. 6d.
—— GEOLOGICAL SKETCHES AT HOME AND
ABROAD. Illust. 8vo. 10s. 6d.
—— OUTLINES OF FIELD GEOLOGY. With
numerous Illustrations. Gl. 8vo. 3s. 6d.
—— TEXT-BOOK OF GEOLOGY. Illustrated.
3rd Edit. Med. 8vo. 28s.
—— THE SCENERY OF SCOTLAND. Viewed in
connection with its Physical Geology. 2nd
Edit. Cr. 8vo. 12s. 6d.

HATCH (F. J.) and CHALMERS (J. A.).—
GOLD MINES OF THE RAND. Sup. roy. 8vo.
17s. net.

HULL (E.).—A TREATISE ON ORNAMENTAL
AND BUILDING STONES OF GREAT BRITAIN
AND FOREIGN COUNTRIES. 8vo. 12s.

KELVIN (Lord)—GEOLOGY AND GENERAL
PHYSICS. Cr. 8vo. 7s. 6d.

LOEWENSON-LESSING (F.).—TABLES FOR
DETERMINATION OF ROCK-FORMING MINE-
RALS. Transl. by J. W. GREGORY. 8vo.
4s. 6d. net.

PENNINGTON (Rooke).—NOTES ON THE
BARROWS AND BONE CAVES OF DERBYSHIRE.
8vo. 6s.

PRESTWICH (J.).—PAPERS ON GEOLOGY.
8vo. 10s. net.
—— CERTAIN PHENOMENA BELONGING TO THE
LAST GEOLOGICAL PERIOD. 8vo. 2s. 6d. net.

ROSENBUSCH (H.).—MICROSCOPICAL PHY-
SIOGRAPHY OF THE ROCK-MAKING MINER-
ALS. By H. ROSENBUSCH. Translated by
J. P. IDDINGS. Illust. 8vo. 24s.

TARR (R. S.).—ECONOMIC GEOLOGY OF THE
UNITED STATES. 8vo. 16s. net.

WILLIAMS (G. H.).—ELEMENTS OF CRY-
STALLOGRAPHY. Cr. 8vo. 6s.

GLOBE LIBRARY. (See LITERATURE, p. 25.)

GLOSSARIES. (See DICTIONARIES.)

GOLDEN TREASURY SERIES.
(See LITERATURE, p. 25.)

GRAMMAR. (See PHILOLOGY.)

HEALTH. (See HYGIENE.)

HEAT. (See under PHYSICS, p. 34.)

HISTOLOGY. (See PHYSIOLOGY.)

HISTORY.
(See also BIOGRAPHY.)

ACTON (Lord).—ON THE STUDY OF HISTORY.
Gl. 8vo. 2s. 6d.

AMERICAN HISTORICAL REVIEW.
Quarterly. 8vo. 3s. 6d. net.

ANNALS OF OUR TIME. A Diurnal of
Events, Social and Political, Home and
Foreign. By JOSEPH IRVING. 8vo.—Vol. I.
June 20th, 1837, to Feb. 28th, 1871, 18s.;
Vol. II. Feb. 24th, 1871, to June 24th, 1887,
18s. Also Vol. II. in 3 parts: Part I. Feb.
24th, 1871, to March 19th, 1874, 4s. 6d.; Part
II. March 20th, 1874, to July 22nd, 1878,
4s. 6d.; Part III. July 23rd, 1878, to June
24th, 1887, 9s. Vol. III. By H. H. FYFE.
Part I. June 25th, 1887, to Dec. 30th, 1890.
4s. 6d.; swd. 3s. 6d. Pt. II. 1891, 1s. 6d.; swd. 1s.

ANDREWS (C. M.).—THE OLD ENGLISH
MANOR: A STUDY IN ECONOMIC HISTORY.
Royal 8vo. 6s. net.

ANNUAL SUMMARIES. Reprinted from
the Times. 2 Vols. Cr. 8vo. 3s. 6d. each.

ARNOLD (T.).—THE SECOND PUNIC WAR.
By THOMAS ARNOLD, D.D. Ed. by W. T.
ARNOLD, M.A. With 8 Maps. Cr. 8vo. 5s.

ARNOLD (W. T.).—A HISTORY OF THE
EARLY ROMAN EMPIRE. Cr. 8vo. [In prep.

BEESLY (Mrs.).—STORIES FROM THE HIS-
TORY OF ROME. Fcp. 8vo. 2s. 6d.

BLACKIE (Prof. John Stuart).—WHAT DOES
HISTORY TEACH? Globe 8vo. 2s. 6d.

BRETT (R. B.).—FOOTPRINTS OF STATES-
MEN DURING THE EIGHTEENTH CENTURY
IN ENGLAND. Cr. 8vo. 6s.

BRYCE (James, M.P.).—THE HOLY ROMAN
EMPIRE. 8th Edit. Cr. 8vo. 7s. 6d.—
Library Edition. 8vo. 14s.

BRUCE (P. A.).—ECONOMIC HISTORY OF VIRGINIA. 2 vols. 8vo. 25s. net.

BUCKLEY (Arabella).—HISTORY OF ENGLAND FOR BEGINNERS. Globe 8vo. 3s.
—— PRIMER OF ENGLISH HISTORY. Pott 8vo. 1s.

BURKE (Edmund). (*See* POLITICS.)

BURY (J. B.).—A HISTORY OF THE LATER ROMAN EMPIRE FROM ARCADIUS TO IRENE, A.D. 390—800. 2 vols. 8vo. 32s.

CASSEL (Dr. D.).—MANUAL OF JEWISH HISTORY AND LITERATURE. Translated by Mrs. HENRY LUCAS. Fcp. 8vo. 2s. 6d.

CHURCH (Dean).—THE BEGINNING OF THE MIDDLE AGES. Gl. 8vo. 5s.

COX (G. V.).—RECOLLECTIONS OF OXFORD 2nd Edit. Cr. 8vo. 6s.

DASENT (A. I.).—HISTORY OF ST. JAMES'S SQUARE. 8vo. 12s. net.

ENGLISH STATESMEN, TWELVE. (*See* BIOGRAPHY, p. 5.)

FISKE (John).—THE CRITICAL PERIOD IN AMERICAN HISTORY, 1783—89. Ext. cr. 8vo. 10s. 6d.
—— THE BEGINNINGS OF NEW ENGLAND; or, The Puritan Theocracy in its Relations to Civil and Religious Liberty. Cr. 8vo. 7s. 6d.
—— THE AMERICAN REVOLUTION. 2 vols. Cr. 8vo. 18s.
—— THE DISCOVERY OF AMERICA. 2 vols. Cr. 8vo. 18s.

FRAMJI (Dosabhai). — HISTORY OF THE PARSIS, INCLUDING THEIR MANNERS, CUSTOMS, RELIGION, AND PRESENT POSITION. With Illustrations. 2 vols. Med. 8vo. 36s.

FREEMAN (Prof. E. A.).—HISTORY OF THE CATHEDRAL CHURCH OF WELLS. Cr. 8vo. 3s. 6d.
—— OLD ENGLISH HISTORY. With Coloured Maps. 9th Edit., revised. Ext. fcp. 8vo. 6s.
—— HISTORICAL ESSAYS. First Series. 5th Edit. 8vo. 10s. 6d.
—— —— Second Series. 3rd Edit., with Additional Essays. 8vo. 10s. 6d.
—— —— Third Series. 8vo. 12s.
—— —— Fourth Series. 8vo. 12s. 6d.
—— THE GROWTH OF THE ENGLISH CONSTITUTION FROM THE EARLIEST TIMES. 5th Edit. Cr. 8vo. 5s.
—— COMPARATIVE POLITICS. Lectures at the Royal Institution. To which is added "The Unity of History." 8vo. 14s.
—— SUBJECT AND NEIGHBOUR LANDS OF VENICE. Illustrated. Cr. 8vo. 10s. 6d.
—— ENGLISH TOWNS AND DISTRICTS. A Series of Addresses and Essays. 8vo. 14s.
—— THE OFFICE OF THE HISTORICAL PROFESSOR. Cr. 8vo. 2s.
—— DISESTABLISHMENT AND DISENDOWMENT; WHAT ARE THEY? Cr. 8vo. 2s.
—— GREATER GREECE AND GREATER BRITAIN: GEORGE WASHINGTON THE EXPANDER OF ENGLAND. With an Appendix on IMPERIAL FEDERATION. Cr. 8vo. 3s. 6d.
—— THE METHODS OF HISTORICAL STUDY. Eight Lectures at Oxford. 8vo. 10s. 6d.
—— THE CHIEF PERIODS OF EUROPEAN HISTORY. With Essay on "Greek Cities under Roman Rule." 8vo. 10s. 6d.
—— FOUR OXFORD LECTURES, 1887; FIFTY YEARS OF EUROPEAN HISTORY; TEUTONIC CONQUEST IN GAUL AND BRITAIN 8vo. 5s.

FREEMAN (Prof. E. A.).—HISTORY OF FEDERAL GOVERNMENT IN GREECE AND ITALY. New Edit. by J. B. BURY, M.A. Ex. cr. 8vo. 12s. 6d.
—— WESTERN EUROPE IN THE FIFTH CENTURY. 8vo. [*In the Press*.
—— WESTERN EUROPE IN THE EIGHTH CENTURY. 8vo. [*In the Press*.

FRIEDMANN (Paul). (*See* BIOGRAPHY.)

GIBBINS (H. de B.).—HISTORY OF COMMERCE IN EUROPE. Globe 8vo. 3s. 6d.

GREEN (John Richard).—A SHORT HISTORY OF THE ENGLISH PEOPLE. New Edit., revised. 159th Thousand. Cr. 8vo. 8s. 6d.—Also in Parts, with Analysis. 3s. each.—Part I. 607—1265; II. 1204—1553; III. 1540—1689; IV. 1660—1873.—*Illustrated Edition.* Super roy. 8vo. 4 vols. 12s. each net.
—— HISTORY OF THE ENGLISH PEOPLE. In 4 vols. 8vo. 16s. each.—In 8 vols. Gl. 8vo. 5s. each.
—— THE MAKING OF ENGLAND. 8vo. 16s.
—— THE CONQUEST OF ENGLAND. With Maps and Portrait. 8vo. 18s.
—— READINGS IN ENGLISH HISTORY. In 3 Parts. Fcp. 8vo. 1s. 6d. each.

GREEN (Alice S.).—TOWN LIFE IN THE 15TH CENTURY. 2 vols. 8vo. 32s.

GUEST (Dr. E.).—ORIGINES CELTICÆ. Maps. 2 vols. 8vo. 32s.

GUEST (M. J.).—LECTURES ON THE HISTORY OF ENGLAND. Cr. 8vo. 6s.

HARRISON (F.).—THE MEANING OF HISTORY, AND OTHER HISTORICAL PIECES. Ex. cr. 8vo. 8s. 6d. net.

HASSALL (A.).—HANDBOOK OF EUROPEAN HISTORY. Cr. 8vo. [*In the Press*.

HILL (G. B.).—HARVARD COLLEGE. By AN OXONIAN. Cr. 8vo. 9s.

HISTORY PRIMERS. Edited by JOHN RICHARD GREEN. Pott 8vo. 1s. each.
EUROPE. By E. A. FREEMAN, M.A.
GREECE. By C. A. FYFFE, M.A.
CATALOGUE OF LANTERN SLIDES TO ILLUSTRATE ABOVE. By Rev. T. FIELD, M.A. Pott 8vo. 6d.
ROME. By Bishop CREIGHTON.
FRANCE. By CHARLOTTE M. YONGE.
ENGLISH HISTORY. By A. B. BUCKLEY.

HISTORICAL COURSE FOR SCHOOLS. Ed. by E. A. FREEMAN, D.C.L. Pott 8vo.
GENERAL SKETCH OF EUROPEAN HISTORY. By E. A. FREEMAN. Maps. 3s. 6d.
HISTORY OF ENGLAND. By EDITH THOMPSON. Coloured Maps. 2s. 6d.
HISTORY OF SCOTLAND. By MARGARET MACARTHUR. 2s.
HISTORY OF ITALY. By the Rev. W. HUNT, M.A. With Coloured Maps. 3s. 6d.
HISTORY OF GERMANY. By J. SIME, M.A. 3s.
HISTORY OF AMERICA. By J. A. DOYLE. With Maps. 4s. 6d.
HISTORY OF EUROPEAN COLONIES. By E. J. PAYNE, M.A. Maps. 4s. 6d.
HISTORY OF FRANCE. By CHARLOTTE M. YONGE. Maps. 3s. 6d.

HOLE (Rev. C.).—GENEALOGICAL STEMMA OF THE KINGS OF ENGLAND AND FRANCE. On a Sheet. 1s.

HOLM (A.).—HISTORY OF GREECE FROM ITS COMMENCEMENT TO THE CLOSE OF THE INDEPENDENCE OF THE GREEK NATION. Translated. 4 vols. Vols. I. and II. Cr. 8vo. 6s. net each. [*Vol. III. in Press.*

INGRAM (T. Dunbar).—A HISTORY OF THE LEGISLATIVE UNION OF GREAT BRITAIN AND IRELAND. 8vo. 10s. 6d.
—— TWO CHAPTERS OF IRISH HISTORY: 1. The Irish Parliament of James II.; 2. The Alleged Violation of the Treaty of Limerick. 8vo. 6s.

JEBB (Prof. R. C.).—MODERN GREECE. Two Lectures. Crown 8vo. 5s.

JENNINGS (A. C.).—CHRONOLOGICAL TABLES OF ANCIENT HISTORY. 8vo. 5s.

KEARY (Annie).—THE NATIONS AROUND ISRAEL. Cr. 8vo. 3s. 6d.

KING (G.).—NEW ORLEANS, THE PLACE AND THE PEOPLE. Cr. 8vo. 10s. 6d.

KINGSLEY (Charles).—THE ROMAN AND THE TEUTON. Cr. 8vo. 3s. 6d.
—— HISTORICAL LECTURES AND ESSAYS. Cr. 8vo. 3s. 6d.

LABBERTON (R. H.). (*See* ATLASES.)

LEE-WARNER (W.).—THE PROTECTED PRINCES OF INDIA. 8vo. 10s. 6d.

LEGGE (Alfred O.).—THE GROWTH OF THE TEMPORAL POWER OF THE PAPACY. Cr. 8vo. 8s. 6d.

LETHBRIDGE (Sir Roper).—A SHORT MANUAL OF THE HISTORY OF INDIA. Cr. 8vo. 5s.
—— THE WORLD'S HISTORY. Cr. 8vo, swd. 1s.
—— HISTORY OF INDIA. Cr. 8vo. 2s.; sewed, 1s. 6d.
—— HISTORY OF ENGLAND. Cr. 8vo, swd. 1s. 6d.
—— EASY INTRODUCTION TO THE HISTORY AND GEOGRAPHY OF BENGAL. Cr. 8vo. 1s. 6d.

LIGHTFOOT (J. B.).—HISTORICAL ESSAYS. Gl. 8vo. 5s.

LYTE (H. C. Maxwell).—A HISTORY OF ETON COLLEGE, 1440—1884. Illustrated. 8vo. 21s.
—— A HISTORY OF THE UNIVERSITY OF OXFORD, FROM THE EARLIEST TIMES TO THE YEAR 1530. 8vo. 16s.

MAHAFFY (Prof. J. P.).—SOCIAL LIFE IN GREECE, FROM HOMER TO MENANDER. 6th Edit. Cr. 8vo. 9s.
—— GREEK LIFE AND THOUGHT, FROM THE AGE OF ALEXANDER TO THE ROMAN CONQUEST. Cr 8vo. 12s. 6d.
—— THE GREEK WORLD UNDER ROMAN SWAY, FROM POLYBIUS TO PLUTARCH. Cr. 8vo. 10s. 6d.
—— PROBLEMS IN GREEK HISTORY. Crown 8vo. 7s. 6d.
—— HISTORY OF THE PTOLEMIES. Cr. 8vo. 12s. 6d.

MARRIOTT (J. A. R.). (*See* SELECT BIOGRAPHY, p. 6.)

MATHEW (E. J.).—FIRST SKETCH OF ENGLISH HISTORY. Part II. Gl. 8vo. 2s.

MICHELET (M.).—A SUMMARY OF MODERN HISTORY. Translated by M. C. M. SIMPSON. Globe 8vo. 4s. 6d.

MULLINGER (J. B.).—CAMBRIDGE CHARACTERISTICS IN THE SEVENTEENTH CENTURY. Cr. 8vo. 4s. 6d.

NORGATE (Kate).—ENGLAND UNDER THE ANGEVIN KINGS. In 2 vols. 8vo. 32s.

OLIPHANT (Mrs. M. O. W.).—THE MAKERS OF FLORENCE: DANTE, GIOTTO, SAVONAROLA, AND THEIR CITY. Illustr. Cr. 8vo. 10s. 6d.—*Edition de Luxe.* 8vo. 21s. net.
—— THE MAKERS OF VENICE: DOGES, CONQUERORS, PAINTERS, AND MEN OF LETTERS. Illustrated. Cr. 8vo. 10s 6d.
—— ROYAL EDINBURGH: HER SAINTS, KINGS, PROPHETS, AND POETS. Illustrated by Sir G. REID, R.S.A. Cr. 8vo. 10s. 6d.
—— JERUSALEM, ITS HISTORY AND HOPE. Illust. Cr. 8vo. 10s. 6d.—Large Paper Edit. 50s. net.
—— THE REIGN OF QUEEN ANNE. Illust. Ex. cr. 8vo. 8s. 6d. net.
—— THE MAKERS OF MODERN ROME. With Illustrations. 8vo. 21s.

OTTE (E. C.).—SCANDINAVIAN HISTORY. With Maps. Globe 8vo. 6s.

PALGRAVE (Sir F.).—HISTORY OF NORMANDY AND OF ENGLAND. 4 vols. 8vo. 4l. 4s.

PARKIN (G. R.).—THE GREAT DOMINION. Crown 8vo. 6s.

PARKMAN (Francis). — MONTCALM AND WOLFE. Library Edition. Illustrated with Portraits and Maps. 2 vols. 8vo. 12s. 6d. each.
—— THE COLLECTED WORKS OF FRANCIS PARKMAN. Popular Edition. In 12 vols. Cr. 8vo. 7s. 6d. each.—PIONEERS OF FRANCE IN THE NEW WORLD, 1 vol.; THE JESUITS IN NORTH AMERICA, 1 vol.; LA SALLE AND THE DISCOVERY OF THE GREAT WEST, 1 vol.; THE OREGON TRAIL, 1 vol.; THE OLD RÉGIME IN CANADA UNDER LOUIS XIV., 1 vol.; COUNT FRONTENAC AND NEW FRANCE UNDER LOUIS XIV., 1 vol.; MONTCALM AND WOLFE, 2 vols.; THE CONSPIRACY OF PONTIAC, 2 vols.; A HALF CENTURY OF CONFLICT 2 vols.
—— THE OREGON TRAIL. Illustrated. Med. 8vo. 21s.

PERKINS (J. B.).—FRANCE UNDER THE REGENCY. Cr. 8vo. 8s. 6d.

PIKE (L. O.).—CONSTITUTIONAL HISTORY OF THE HOUSE OF LORDS. 8vo. 12s. 6d. net.

POOLE (R. L.).—A HISTORY OF THE HUGUENOTS OF THE DISPERSION AT THE RECALL OF THE EDICT OF NANTES. Cr. 8vo. 6s.

PROWSE (D. W.).—HISTORY OF NEWFOUNDLAND. 8vo. 21s. net.

RHODES (J. F.).—HISTORY OF THE UNITED STATES FROM THE COMPROMISE OF 1850 TO 1880. Vols. I. II. 24s. Vol. III. 8vo. 12s.

ROGERS (Prof. J. E. Thorold).—HISTORICAL GLEANINGS. Cr. 8vo.—1st Series. 4s. 6d.—2nd Series. 6s.

ROTHSCHILD (F.).—PERSONAL CHARACTERISTICS FROM FRENCH HISTORY. 8vo. 10s. 6d. net.

SAYCE (Prof. A. H.).—THE ANCIENT EMPIRES OF THE EAST. Cr. 8vo. 6s.

SEELEY (Sir J. R.). — LECTURES AND ESSAYS. Globe 8vo. 5s.
—— THE EXPANSION OF ENGLAND. Two Courses of Lectures. Globe 8vo. 5s.
—— OUR COLONIAL EXPANSION. Extracts from the above. Cr. 8vo. 1s.

SEWELL (E. M.) and YONGE (C. M.).—EUROPEAN HISTORY: A SERIES OF HISTORICAL SELECTIONS FROM THE BEST AUTHORITIES. 2 vols. 3rd Edit. Cr. 8vo. 6s.

HISTORY—*contd.*

SHAW (Miss).—AUSTRALIA.   [*In the Press.*

SHUCKBURGH (E. S.).—A HISTORY OF ROME TO THE BATTLE OF ACTIUM. Cr. 8vo. 8s. 6d.

SMITH (Goldwin).—OXFORD AND HER COLLEGES. Pott 8vo. 3s.—Illustrated Edition. 6s. (*See also under* POLITICS, p. 37.)

STEPHEN (Sir J. Fitzjames).—THE STORY OF NUNCOMAR AND THE IMPEACHMENT OF SIR ELIJAH IMPEY. 2 vols. Cr. 8vo. 15s.

TAIT (C. W. A.).—ANALYSIS OF ENGLISH HISTORY, BASED ON GREEN'S "SHORT HISTORY OF THE ENGLISH PEOPLE." Cr. 8vo. 3s. 6d.

TOUT (T. F.).—ANALYSIS OF ENGLISH HISTORY. Pott 8vo. 1s.

TREVELYAN (Sir Geo. Otto).—CAWNPORE. Cr. 8vo. 6s.

TUCKWELL (W.).—THE ANCIENT WAYS: WINCHESTER FIFTY YEARS AGO. Globe 8vo. 4s. 6d.

WHEELER (J. Talboys).—PRIMER OF INDIAN HISTORY, ASIATIC AND EUROPEAN. Pott 8vo. 1s.
—— COLLEGE HISTORY OF INDIA, ASIATIC AND EUROPEAN. Cr. 8vo. 2s. 6d.; swd. 2s.
—— A SHORT HISTORY OF INDIA. With Maps. Cr. 8vo. 12s.
—— INDIA UNDER BRITISH RULE. 8vo. 12s. 5d.

WILLIAMS (H.).—BRITAIN'S NAVAL POWER. Cr. 8vo. 4s. 6d. net.

WOOD (Rev. E. G.).—THE REGAL POWER OF THE CHURCH. 8vo. 4s. 6d.

YONGE (Charlotte).—CAMEOS FROM ENGLISH HISTORY. Ext. fcp. 8vo. 5s. each.—Vol. 1. FROM ROLLO TO EDWARD II.; Vol. 2. THE WARS IN FRANCE; Vol. 3. THE WARS OF THE ROSES; Vol. 4. REFORMATION TIMES; Vol. 5. ENGLAND AND SPAIN; Vol. 6. FORTY YEARS OF STEWART RULE (1603—43); Vol. 7. THE REBELLION AND RESTORATION (1642—1678).
—— THE VICTORIAN HALF-CENTURY. Cr. 8vo. 1s. 6d.; sewed, 1s.
—— THE STORY OF THE CHRISTIANS AND MOORS IN SPAIN. Pott 8vo. 2s. 6d. net.

HORSE BREEDING.

PEASE (A. E.).—HORSE BREEDING FOR FARMERS. Cr. 8vo. 2s. 6d.

HORTICULTURE. (*See* GARDENING.)

HYGIENE.

BERNERS (J.).—FIRST LESSONS ON HEALTH. Pott 8vo. 1s.

BLYTH (A. Wynter).—A MANUAL OF PUBLIC HEALTH. 8vo. 17s. net.
—— LECTURES ON SANITARY LAW. 8vo. 8s. 6d. net.

BROWNE (J. H. Balfour).—WATER SUPPLY. Cr. 8vo. 2s. 6d.

CLIMATES AND BATHS OF GREAT BRITAIN. 8vo. 21s. net.

CORFIELD (Dr. W. H.).—THE TREATMENT AND UTILISATION OF SEWAGE. 3rd Edit. Revised by the Author, and by LOUIS C. PARKES, M.D. 8vo. 16s.

FAYRER (Sir J.).—ON PRESERVATION OF HEALTH IN INDIA. Pott 8vo. 1s.

GOODFELLOW (J.).—THE DIETETIC VALUE OF BREAD. Cr. 8vo. 6s.

KINGSLEY (Charles).—SANITARY AND SOCIAL LECTURES. Cr. 8vo. 3s. 6d.
—— HEALTH AND EDUCATION. Cr. 8vo. 6s.

MIERS (H. A.) and CROSSKEY (R.).—THE SOIL IN RELATION TO HEALTH. Cr. 8vo. 3s. 6d.

REYNOLDS (E. S.).—PRIMER OF HYGIENE. Pott 8vo. 1s.

REYNOLDS (Prof. Osborne).—SEWER GAS, AND HOW TO KEEP IT OUT OF HOUSES. 3rd Edit. Cr. 8vo. 1s. 6d.

RICHARDSON (Dr. Sir B. W.).—HYGEIA: A CITY OF HEALTH. Cr. 8vo. 1s.
—— THE FUTURE OF SANITARY SCIENCE. Cr. 8vo. 1s.
—— ON ALCOHOL. Cr. 8vo. 1s.

WILLOUGHBY (E. F.).—PUBLIC HEALTH AND DEMOGRAPHY. Fcp. 8vo. 4s. 6d.

HYMNOLOGY.
(*See under* THEOLOGY, p. 42.)

ILLUSTRATED BOOKS.

ÆSOP'S FABLES. Selected by J. JACOBS. With 300 Illustrations by R. HEIGHWAY. Cr. 8vo. 6s.—Also with uncut edges, paper label, 6s.

BALCH (Elizabeth).—GLIMPSES OF OLD ENGLISH HOMES. Gl. 4to. 14s.

BARLOW (J.).—THE END OF ELFINTOWN. Illust. by L. HOUSMAN. Cr. 8vo. 5s.

BLAKE. (*See* BIOGRAPHY, p. 4.)

BOUGHTON (G. H.) and ABBEY (E. A.). (*See* VOYAGES AND TRAVELS.)

CHRISTMAS CAROL (A). Printed in Colours, with Illuminated Borders. 4to. 21s.

CORIDON'S SONG, AND OTHER VERSES. Preface by AUSTIN DOBSON. Illustrations by HUGH THOMSON. Cr. 8vo. 6s.—Also with uncut edges, paper label, 6s.

CRAWFORD (F. M.).—CONSTANTINOPLE. Illustrated by E. L. WEEKS. Sm. 4to. 6s. 6d.

DAYS WITH SIR ROGER DE COVERLEY. From the *Spectator.* Illustrated by HUGH THOMSON. Cr. 8vo. 6s.—Also with uncut edges, paper label. 6s.

DELL (E. C.).—PICTURES FROM SHELLEY. Engraved by J. D. COOPER. Folio. 21s. net.

FIELDE (A. M.).—A CORNER OF CATHAY. Illustrated. Fcap. 4to. 8s. 6d. net.

GASKELL (Mrs.).—CRANFORD. Illustrated by HUGH THOMSON. Cr. 8vo. 6s.—Also with uncut edges, paper label. 6s.

GOETHE.—REYNARD THE FOX. Edited by J. JACOBS. Illustrated by F. CALDERON. Cr. 8vo. 6s. Also with uncut edges, paper label. 6s.

GOLDSMITH (Oliver).—THE VICAR OF WAKEFIELD. New Edition, with 182 Illustrations by HUGH THOMSON. Preface by AUSTIN DOBSON. Cr. 8vo. 6s.—Also with Uncut Edges, paper label. 6s.

GREEN (John Richard).—ILLUSTRATED EDITION OF THE SHORT HISTORY OF THE ENGLISH PEOPLE. 4 vols. Sup. roy. 8vo. 12s. each net.

GRIMM. (*See* BOOKS FOR THE YOUNG, p. 48.)

HALLWARD (R. F.).—FLOWERS OF PARADISE. Music, Verse, Design, Illustration. 6s

HAMERTON (P. G.).—Man in Art With Etchings and Photogravures. 3*l.* 13*s.* 6*d.* net. —Large Paper Edition. 10*l.* 10*s.* net.

HARRISON (F.).—Annals of an Old Manor House, Sutton Place, Guildford. 4to. 42*s.* net.

HENLEY (W. E.).—A London Garland. Selected from Five Centuries of English Verse. Illustrated. 4to. 21*s.* net.

HOOD (Thomas).—Humorous Poems. Illustrated by C. E. Brock. Cr. 8vo. 6*s.*—Also with uncut edges, paper label. 6*s.*

IRVING (Washington).—Old Christmas. From the Sketch Book. Illustr. by Randolph Caldecott. Cr. 8vo. 6*s.*—Also with uncut edges, paper label. 6*s.*—Large Paper Edition. 30*s.* net.
—— Bracebridge Hall. Illustr. by Randolph Caldecott. Cr. 8vo. 6*s.*—Also with uncut edges, paper label. 6*s.*
—— Old Christmas and Bracebridge Hall. *Edition de Luxe.* Roy. 8vo. 21*s.*
—— Rip Van Winkle and the Legend of Sleepy Hollow. Illustr. by G. H. Boughton. Cr. 8vo. 6*s.*—Also with uncut edges, paper label. 6*s.*—*Edition de Luxe.* Roy. 8vo. 30*s.* net.

KINGSLEY (Charles).—The Water Babies. (*See* Books for the Young, p. 48.)
—— The Heroes. (*See* Books for the Young.)
—— Glaucus. (*See* Natural History.)

KIPLING (Rudyard). (*See* Books for the Young.)

LANG (Andrew).—The Library. With a Chapter on Modern English Illustrated Books, by Austin Dobson. Cr. 8vo. 4*s.* 6*d.* —Large Paper Edition. 21*s.* net.

LYTE (H. C. Maxwell). (*See* History.)

MAHAFFY (Rev. Prof. J. P.) and ROGERS (J. E.). (*See* Voyages and Travels.)

MEREDITH (L. A.).—Bush Friends in Tasmania. Native Flowers, Fruits, and Insects, with Prose and Verse Descriptions. Folio. 52*s.* 6*d.* net.

MITFORD (M. R.).—Our Village. Illustrated by Hugh Thomson. Cr. 8vo. 6*s.*— Also with uncut edges, paper label. 6*s.*

OLD SONGS. With Drawings by E. A. Abbey and A. Parsons. 4to, mor. gilt. 31*s.* 6*d.*

OLIPHANT (Mrs.). (*See* History.)

PENNELL (Jos.). (*See* Art.)

PROPERT (J. L.). (*See* Art.)

STEEL (F. A.).—Tales of the Punjab. Illustr. by J. L. Kipling. Cr. 8vo. 6*s.*— Also with uncut edges, paper label, 6*s.*

STUART, RELICS OF THE ROYAL HOUSE OF. Illustrated by 40 Plates in Colours drawn from Relics of the Stuarts by William Gibb. With an Introduction by John Skelton, C.B., LL.D., and Descriptive Notes by W. St. John Hope. Folio, half morocco, gilt edges. 10*l.* 10*s.* net.

SWIFT.—Gulliver's Travels. Illustrated by C. E. Brock. Preface by H. Craik, C.B. Cr. 8vo. 6*s.*—Also with uncut edges, paper label, 6*s.*

TENNYSON (Hallam Lord).—Jack and the Bean-Stalk. English Hexameters. Illustrated by R. Caldecott. Fcp. 4to. 3*s.* 6*d.*

TRISTRAM (W. O.).—Coaching Days and Coaching Ways. Illust. H. Railton and Hugh Thomson. Cr. 8vo. 6*s.*—Also with uncut edges, paper label, 6*s.*—Large Paper Edition, 30*s.* net.

TURNER'S LIBER STUDIORUM: A Description and a Catalogue. By W. G. Rawlinson. Med. 8vo. 12*s.* 6*d.*

WALTON and COTTON—LOWELL.—The Complete Angler. With Introduction by Jas. Russell Lowell. 2 vols. Ext. cr. 8vo. 52*s.* 6*d.* net.

WHITE (G.).—Natural History of Selborne. Introduction by J. Burroughs. Illustrations by C. Johnson. 2 vols. Cr. 8vo. 10*s.* 6*d.*

WINTER (W.).—Shakespeare's England. 80 Illustrations. Cr. 8vo. 6*s.*

LANGUAGE. (*See* Philology.)

LAW.

BALL (W. W. R.).—The Student's Guide to the Bar. 6th Ed. Cr. 8vo. 2*s.* 6*d.* net.

BERNARD (M.).—Four Lectures on Subjects connected with Diplomacy. 8vo. 9*s.*

BIGELOW (M. M.).—History of Procedure in England from the Norman Conquest, 1066-1204. 8vo. 16*s.*

BIRRELL (A.).—Duties and Liabilities of Trustees. Cr. 8vo. 3*s.* 6*d.*

BORGEAUD (C.). — Constitutions in Europe and America. Transl. by C. D. Hazen. Cr. 8vo. 8*s.* 6*d.* net.

BOUTMY (E.). — Studies in Constitutional Law. Transl. by Mrs. Dicey. Preface by Prof. A. V. Dicey. Cr. 8vo. 6*s.*
—— The English Constitution. Transl. by Mrs. Eaden. Introduction by Sir F. Pollock, Bart. Cr. 8vo. 6*s.*

CHERRY (R. R.). — Lectures on the Growth of Criminal Law in Ancient Communities. 8vo. 5*s.* net.

DICEY (Prof. A. V.).—Introduction to the Study of the Law of the Constitution. 4th Edit. 8vo. 2*s.* 6*d.*

ENGLISH CITIZEN SERIES, THE. (*See* Politics.)

GOODNOW (F. J.).—Municipal Home Rule. Cr. 8vo. 6*s.* 6*d.* net.

HOLLAND (Prof. T. E.).—The Treaty Relations of Russia and Turkey, from 1774 to 1853. Cr. 8vo. 2*s.*

HOLMES (O. W., jun.). — The Common Law. 8vo. 12*s.*

HOWELL (G.).—Handy Book of the Labour Laws. 3rd Ed. Cr. 8vo. 3*s.* 6*d.* net.

LAWRENCE (T. J.).—International Law. 8vo. 12*s.* 6*d.* net.

LIGHTWOOD (J. M.).—The Nature of Positive Law. 8vo. 12*s.* 6*d.*

MAITLAND (F. W.).—Pleas of the Crown for the County of Gloucester, A.D. 1221. 8vo. 7*s.* 6*d.*
—— Justice and Police. Cr. 8vo. 2*s.* 6*d.*

MONAHAN (James H.).—The Method of Law. Cr. 8vo. 6*s.*

MUNRO (J. E. C.).—Commercial Law. Globe 8vo. 3*s.* 6*d.*

LAW—continued.

PATERSON (James).—COMMENTARIES ON THE LIBERTY OF THE SUBJECT, AND THE LAWS OF ENGLAND RELATING TO THE SECURITY OF THE PERSON. 2 vols. Cr. 8vo. 21s.
—— THE LIBERTY OF THE PRESS, SPEECH, AND PUBLIC WORSHIP. Cr. 8vo. 12s.

PHILLIMORE (John G.).—PRIVATE LAW AMONG THE ROMANS. 8vo. 6s.

POLLOCK (Sir F., Bart.).—ESSAYS IN JORISPRUDENCE AND ETHICS. 8vo. 10s. 6d.
—— THE LAND LAWS. Cr. 8vo. 2s. 6d.
—— LEADING CASES DONE INTO ENGLISH. Cr. 8vo. 3s. 6d.
—— A FIRST BOOK OF JURISPRUDENCE. Cr. 8vo.   [In the Press.

RICHEY (Alex. G.).—THE IRISH LAND LAWS. Cr. 8vo. 3s. 6d.

STEPHEN (Sir J. F., Bart.).—A DIGEST OF THE LAW OF EVIDENCE. 6th Ed. Cr. 8vo. 6s.
—— A DIGEST OF THE CRIMINAL LAW: CRIMES AND PUNISHMENTS. 5th Ed. 8vo. 16s.
—— A DIGEST OF THE LAW OF CRIMINAL PROCEDURE IN INDICTABLE OFFENCES. By Sir J. F., Bart., and HERBERT STEPHEN, LL.M. 8vo. 12s. 6d.
—— A HISTORY OF THE CRIMINAL LAW OF ENGLAND. 3 vols. 8vo. 48s.
—— A GENERAL VIEW OF THE CRIMINAL LAW OF ENGLAND. 2nd Edit. 8vo. 14s.

STEPHEN (J. K.).—INTERNATIONAL LAW AND INTERNATIONAL RELATIONS. Cr. 8vo. 6s.

STEVENS (C. E.).—SOURCES OF THE CONSTITUTION OF THE UNITED STATES, CONSIDERED IN RELATION TO COLONIAL AND ENGLISH HISTORY. Cr. 8vo. 6s. 6d. net.

WILLIAMS (S. E.).—FORENSIC FACTS AND FALLACIES. Globe 8vo. 4s. 6d.

LETTERS. (See under LITERATURE, p. 24.)

LIFE-BOAT.

GILMORE (Rev. John).—STORM WARRIORS; or, Life-Boat Work on the Goodwin Sands. Cr. 8vo. 3s. 6d.

LEWIS (Richard).—HISTORY OF THE LIFE-BOAT AND ITS WORK. Cr. 8vo. 5s.

LIGHT. (See under PHYSICS, p. 34.)

LITERATURE.

History and Criticism of—Commentaries, etc.—Poetry and the Drama—Poetical Collections and Selections—Prose Fiction—Collected Works, Essays, Lectures, Letters, Miscellaneous Works.

History and Criticism of.
(See also ESSAYS, p. 24.)

ARNOLD (M.). (See ESSAYS. p. 24.)

EROOKE (Stopford A.).—A PRIMER OF ENGLISH LITERATURE. Pott 8vo. 1s.—Large Paper Edition. 8vo. 7s. 6d.
—— A HISTORY OF EARLY ENGLISH LITERATURE. 2 vols. 8vo. 20s. net.

CLASSICAL WRITERS. Edited by JOHN RICHARD GREEN. Fcp. 8vo. 1s. 6d. each.
DEMOSTHENES. By Prof. BUTCHER, M.A.
EURIPIDES. By Prof. MAHAFFY.
LIVY. By the Rev. W. W. CAPES, M.A.
MILTON. By STOPFORD A. BROOKE.
SOPHOCLES. By Prof. L. CAMPBELL, M.A.
TACITUS. By Messrs. CHURCH and BRODRIBB.
VERGIL. By Prof. NETTLESHIP, M.A.

COURTHOPE (W. J.).—HISTORY OF ENGLISH POETRY. Vol. I. 8vo. 10s. net.

ENGLISH MEN OF LETTERS. (See BIOGRAPHY, p. 4.)

HISTORY OF ENGLISH LITERATURE. In 4 vols. Cr. 8vo.
EARLY ENGLISH LITERATURE. By STOPFORD BROOKE, M.A. [In preparation.
ELIZABETHAN LITERATURE (1560—1665). By GEORGE SAINTSBURY. 7s. 6d.
EIGHTEENTH CENTURY LITERATURE (1660—1780). By EDMUND GOSSE, M.A. 7s. 6d.
NINETEENTH CENTURY LITERATURE. By G. SAINTSBURY. 7s. 6d.

JEBB (Prof. R. C.).—A PRIMER OF GREEK LITERATURE. Pott 8vo. 1s.
—— THE ATTIC ORATORS, FROM ANTIPHON TO ISAEOS. 2nd Edit. 2 vols 8vo. 25s.
—— RISE AND DEVELOPMENT OF GREEK POETRY. Cr. 8vo. 7s. net.

JOHNSON'S LIVES OF THE POETS. MILTON, DRYDEN, POPE, ADDISON, SWIFT, AND GRAY With Macaulay's "Life of Johnson" Ed. by M. ARNOLD. Cr. 8vo. 4s. 6d.

JONES (H. A.).—RENASCENCE OF THE ENGLISH DRAMA. Cr. 8vo. 6s.

KINGSLEY (Charles). — LITERARY AND GENERAL LECTURES. Cr. 8vo. 3s. 6d.

MAHAFFY (Prof. J. P.).—A HISTORY OF CLASSICAL GREEK LITERATURE. 2 vols. Cr. 8vo.—Vol. 1. THE POETS. With an Appendix on Homer by Prof. SAYCE. In 2 Parts.—Vol. 2. THE PROSE WRITERS. In 2 Parts. 4s. 6d. each.

MORLEY (John). (See COLLECTED WORKS, p. 27.)

OLIPHANT (Mrs. M. O. W.).—THE LITERARY HISTORY OF ENGLAND IN THE END OF THE 18TH AND BEGINNING OF THE 19TH CENTURY. 3 vols. 8vo. 21s.

PATER (W.).—GREEK STUDIES. Ex. cr. 8vo. 10s. 6d.
—— PLATO AND PLATONISM. Ex. cr. 8vo. 8s. 6d.

RYLAND (F.).—CHRONOLOGICAL OUTLINES OF ENGLISH LITERATURE. Cr. 8vo. 6s.

SAINTSBURY (G.).—A SHORT HISTORY OF ENGLISH LITERATURE. Gl. 8vo. [In prep.

TYRRELL (Prof. R. Y.).—LATIN POETRY. Cr. 8vo. 7s. net

WARD (Prof. A. W.).—A HISTORY OF ENGLISH DRAMATIC LITERATURE, TO THE DEATH OF QUEEN ANNE. 2 vols. 8vo. 32s.

WHITCOMB (L. S.).—CHRONOLOGICAL OUTLINES OF AMERICAN LITERATURE. Cr. 8vo. 6s. net.

WILKINS (Prof. A. S.).—A PRIMER OF ROMAN LITERATURE. Pott 8vo. 1s.

WULKER. — ANGLO SAXON LITERATURE. Transl. by A. W. DEERING and C. F. MC CLUMPHA. [In the Press.

Commentaries, etc.

BROWNING.
A PRIMER OF BROWNING. By MARY WILSON. Cr. 8vo. 2s. 6d.

CHAUCER.
A PRIMER OF CHAUCER. By A. W. POLLARD. Pott 8vo. 1s.

DANTE.

READINGS ON THE PURGATORIO OF DANTE. Chiefly based on the Commentary of Benvenuto da Imola. By the Hon. W. W. VERNON, M.A. With an Introduction by Dean CHURCH. 2 vols. Cr. 8vo. 24s.

READINGS ON THE INFERNO OF DANTE. By the Hon. W. W. VERNON, M.A. With an Introduction by Rev. E. MOORE, D.D. 2 vols. Cr. 8vo. 30s.

COMPANION TO DANTE. From G. A. SCARTAZZINI. By A. J. BUTLER. Cr. 8vo. 10s. 6d.

HOMER.

HOMERIC DICTIONARY. (See DICTIONARIES.)

THE PROBLEM OF THE HOMERIC POEMS. By Prof. W. D. GEDDES. 8vo. 14s.

HOMERIC SYNCHRONISM. An Inquiry Into the Time and Place of Homer. By the Rt. Hon. W. E. GLADSTONE. Cr. 8vo. 6s.

PRIMER OF HOMER. By the Rt. Hon. W. E. GLADSTONE. Pott 8vo. 1s.

LANDMARKS OF HOMERIC STUDY, TOGETHER WITH AN ESSAY ON THE POINTS OF CONTACT BETWEEN THE ASSYRIAN TABLETS AND THE HOMERIC TEXT. By the same. Cr. 8vo. 2s. 6d.

COMPANION TO THE ILIAD FOR ENGLISH READERS. By W. LEAF. Cr. 8vo. 7s. 6d.

HORACE.

STUDIES, LITERARY AND HISTORICAL, IN THE ODES OF HORACE. By A. W. VERRALL, Litt.D. 8vo. 8s. 6d.

SHAKESPEARE.

A PRIMER OF SHAKSPERE. By Prof. DOWDEN. Pott 8vo. 1s.

A SHAKESPEARIAN GRAMMAR. By Rev. E. A. ABBOTT. Ext. fcp. 8vo. 6s.

A SHAKESPEARE CONCORDANCE. By J. BARTLETT. 4to. 42s. net. ; half mor., 45s. net.

SHAKESPEAREANA GENEALOGICA. By G. R. FRENCH. 8vo. 15s.

A SELECTION FROM THE LIVES IN NORTH'S PLUTARCH WHICH ILLUSTRATE SHAKESPEARE'S PLAYS. Edited by Rev. W. W. SKEAT, M.A. Cr. 8vo. 6s.

SHORT STUDIES OF SHAKESPEARE'S PLOTS. By Prof. CYRIL RANSOME. Cr. 8vo. 3s. 6d. —Also separately : HAMLET, 9d. ; MACBETH, 9d. ; TEMPEST, 9d.

CALIBAN : A Critique on "The Tempest" and "A Midsummer Night's Dream." By Sir DANIEL WILSON. 8vo. 10s. 6d.

TENNYSON.

A COMPANION TO "IN MEMORIAM." By ELIZABETH R. CHAPMAN. Globe 8vo. 2s.

"IN MEMORIAM"—ITS PURPOSE AND STRUCTURE : A STUDY. By J. F. GENUNG. Cr. 8vo. 5s.

ESSAYS ON THE IDYLLS OF THE KING. By H. LITTLEDALE, M.A. Cr. 8vo. 4s. 6d.

A STUDY OF THE WORKS OF ALFRED LORD TENNYSON. By E. C. TAINSH. New Ed. Cr. 8vo. 6s.

THACKERAY.

THACKERAY : A Study. By A. A. JACK. Cr. 8vo. 3s. 6d.

WORDSWORTH.

WORDSWORTHIANA : A Selection of Papers read to the Wordsworth Society. Edited by W. KNIGHT. Cr. 8vo. 7s. 6d.

Poetry and the Drama.

ALDRICH (T. Bailey).—THE SISTERS' TRAGEDY : with other Poems, Lyrical and Dramatic. Fcp. 8vo. 3s. 6d. net.

ALEXANDER (C. F.).—POEMS. Gl. 8vo. 7s. 6d.

AN ANCIENT CITY : AND OTHER POEMS. Ext. fcp. 8vo. 6s.

ANDERSON (A.).—BALLADS AND SONNETS. Cr. 8vo. 5s.

ARNOLD (Matthew). — THE COMPLETE POETICAL WORKS. New Edition. 3 vols. Cr. 8vo. 7s. 6d. each ; Globe 8vo. 5s. each.
Vol. 1. EARLY POEMS, NARRATIVE POEMS AND SONNETS.
Vol. 2. LYRIC AND ELEGIAC POEMS.
Vol. 3. DRAMATIC AND LATER POEMS.

—— COMPLETE POETICAL WORKS. 1 vol. Cr. 8vo. 7s. 6d.

—— SELECTED POEMS. Pott 8vo. 2s. 6d. net.

AUSTIN (Alfred).—POETICAL WORKS. New Collected Edition. 7 vols. Cr. 8vo. 5s. each.
Vol. 1. THE TOWER OF BABEL.
Vol. 2. SAVONAROLA, etc.
Vol. 3. PRINCE LUCIFER.
Vol. 4. THE HUMAN TRAGEDY.
Vol. 5. LYRICAL POEMS.
Vol. 6. NARRATIVE POEMS.
Vol. 7. FORTUNATUS THE PESSIMIST.

—— SOLILOQUIES IN SONG. Cr. 8vo. 6s.

—— AT THE GATE OF THE CONVENT : and other Poems. Cr. 8vo. 6s.

—— MADONNA'S CHILD. Fcp. 8vo. 2s. 6d. net.

—— ROME OR DEATH. Cr. 4to. 9s.

—— THE GOLDEN AGE. Cr. 8vo. 5s.

—— THE SEASON. Cr. 8vo. 5s.

—— LOVE'S WIDOWHOOD. Cr. 8vo. 6s.

—— ENGLISH LYRICS. Cr. 8vo. 3s. 6d.

—— ENGLAND'S DARLING. Cr. 8vo. 6s.

BETSY LEE : A Fo'c's'le Yarn. Ext. fcp. 8vo. 3s. 6d.

BLACKIE (J. S.).—MESSIS VITAE : Gleanings of Song from a Happy Life. Cr. 8vo. 4s. 6d.

—— THE WISE MEN OF GREECE. In a Series of Dramatic Dialogues. Cr. 8vo. 9s.

—— GOETHE'S FAUST. Translated into English Verse. 2nd Edit. Cr. 8vo. 9s.

BLAKE. (See BIOGRAPHY, p. 4.)

BROOKE (Stopford A.).—RIQUET OF THE TUFT : A Love Drama. Ext. cr. 8vo. 6s.

—— POEMS. Globe 8vo. 6s.

BROWN (T. E.).—THE MANX WITCH : and other Poems. Cr. 8vo. 6s.

—— OLD JOHN, AND OTHER POEMS. Cr. 8vo. 6s.

BURGON (Dean).—POEMS. Ex. fcp. 8vo. 4s. 6d.

BURNS. THE POETICAL WORKS. With a Biographical Memoir by A. SMITH. In 2 vols. Fcp. 8vo. 10s. (See also GLOBE LIBRARY, p. 25.)

BUTLER (Samuel).—HUDIBRAS. Edit. by ALFRED MILNES. Fcp. 8vo.—Part I. 3s. 6d. ; Parts II. and III. 4s. 6d.

BYRON. (See GOLDEN TREASURY SERIES, p. 25)

CALDERON.—SELECT PLAYS. Edited by NORMAN MACCOLL. Cr. 8vo. 14s.

CARR (J. Comyns).—KING ARTHUR. A Drama, as performed at the Lyceum. 8vo 2s. net ; sewed, 1s. net.

CAUTLEY (G. S.).—A CENTURY OF EMBLEMS. With Illustrations by Lady MARION ALFORD. Small 4to. 10s. 6d.

CHAUCER.—CANTERBURY TALES. Edit. by A. W. POLLARD. 2 vols. Gl. 8vo. 10s.

—— THE RICHES OF CHAUCER. With Notes by C. COWDEN CLARKE. Cr. 8vo. 7s. 6d.

CLOUGH (A. H.).—POEMS. Cr. 8vo. 7s. 6d.

—— SELECTIONS FROM THE POEMS. Pott 8vo. 2s. 6d. net.

Poetry and the Drama—*continued*.

COLERIDGE: POETICAL AND DRAMATIC WORKS. 4 vols. Fcp. 8vo. 31s. 6d.—Also an Edition on Large Paper, 2l. 12s. 6d.
—— COMPLETE POETICAL WORKS. With Introduction by J. D. CAMPBELL, and Portrait. Cr. 8vo. 7s. 6d.

COLQUHOUN.—RHYMES AND CHIMES. By F. S. Colquhoun (*née* F. S. FULLER MAITLAND). Ext. fcp. 8vo. 2s. 6d.

COWPER.—THE TASK, BOOK IV. With Introduction and Notes by W. T. WEBB, M.A. Sewed, 1s.—BOOK V. With Notes. Gl. 8vo. 6d. (*See* GLOBE LIBRARY, p. 25 | GOLDEN TREASURY SERIES, p. 25.)
—— SHORTER POEMS. By W. T. WEBB, M.A. Globe 8vo. 2s. 6d.

CRAIK (Mrs.).—POEMS. Ext. fcp. 8vo. 6s.

DABBS (G. H. R.)—RIGHTON (E.).— DANTE: A DRAMATIC POEM. Fcp. 8vo. 2s. 6d.

DAWSON (W. J.).—POEMS AND LYRICS. Fcp. 8vo. 4s. 6d.

DE VERE (A.).—POETICAL WORKS. 7 vols. Cr. 8vo. 5s. each.
—— SELECTIONS FROM POETICAL WORKS OF. By G. E. WOODBERRY. Globe 8vo. 5s.

DOYLE (Sir F. H.).—THE RETURN OF THE GUARDS: and other Poems. Cr. 8vo. 7s. 6d.

DRYDEN. (*See* COLLECTED WORKS *and* GLOBE LIBRARY, pp. 24, 25.)

EMERSON. (*See* COLLECTED WORKS, p. 24.)

EVANS (Sebastian). — BROTHER FABIAN'S MANUSCRIPT : and other Poems. Fcp. 8vo. 6s.
—— IN THE STUDIO: A Decade of Poems. Ext. fcp. 8vo. 5s.

FITZ GERALD (Caroline).—VENETIA VICTRIX : and other Poems. Ext. fcp. 8vo. 3s. 6d.

FITZGERALD (Edward).—THE RUBÁIYÁT OF OMAR KHÁYYÁM. Ext. cr. 8vo. 10s. 6d.

FO'C'SLE YARNS, including " Betsy Lee," and other Poems. Cr. 8vo. 6s.

FRASER-TYTLER. — SONGS IN MINOR KEYS. By C. C. FRASER-TYTLER (Mrs. EDWARD LIDDELL). 2nd Edit. Pott 8vo. 6s.

FURNIVALL (F. J.).—LE MORTE ARTHUR. Edited from the Harleian MSS. 2252, in the British Museum. Fcp. 8vo. 7s. 6d.

GARNETT (R.).—IDYLLS AND EPIGRAMS. Chiefly from the Greek Anthology. Fcp. 8vo. 2s. 6d.

GOETHE.—FAUST. (*See* BLACKIE.)
—— REYNARD THE FOX. Transl. into English Verse by A. D. AINSLIE. Cr. 8vo. 7s. 6d.

GOLDSMITH.—THE TRAVELLER AND THE DESERTED VILLAGE. With Introduction and Notes, by ARTHUR BARRETT, B.A. 1s. 9d.; sewed, 1s. 6d.; (separately), sewed, 1s. each. —By J. W. HALES. Cr. 8vo. 6d (*See also* GLOBE LIBRARY, p. 25.)

GRAHAM (David).—KING JAMES I. An Historical Tragedy. Globe 8vo. 7s.

GRAY.—POEMS. With Introduction and Notes, by J. BRADSHAW, LL.D. Gl. 8vo. 1s. 9d.; sewed, 1s. 6d. (*See also* COLLECTED WORKS, p. 26.)
—— SELECT ODES. With Notes. Gl. 8vo, sewed. 6d.

HALLWARD. (*See* ILLUSTRATED BOOKS.)

HAYES (A.).—THE MARCH OF MAN: and other Poems. Fcp. 8vo. 3s. 6d. net.

HERRICK. (*See* GOLDEN TREASURY SERIES, p. 25.)

HOPKINS (Ellice).—AUTUMN SWALLOWS: A Book of Lyrics. Ext. fcp. 8vo. 6s.

HOSKEN (J. D.).—PHAON AND SAPPHO, AND NIMROD. Fcp. 8vo. 5s.

JEWETT (S.).—THE PILGRIM, AND OTHER POEMS. Fcp. 8vo. 5s.

JONES (H. A.).—SAINTS AND SINNERS. Ext. fcp. 8vo. 3s. 6d.
—— THE CRUSADERS. Fcp. 8vo. 2s. 6d.
—— JUDAH. Fcp. 8vo. 2s. 6d.

KEATS. (*See* GOLDEN TREASURY SERIES, p. 25.)

KINGSLEY (Charles).—POEMS. Cr. 8vo. 3s. 6d.—*Pocket Edition.* Pott 8vo. 1s. 6d.— *Eversley Edition.* 2 vols. Cr. 8vo. 10s.

LAMB. (*See* COLLECTED WORKS, p. 27.)

LANDOR. (*See* GOLDEN TREASURY SERIES, p. 25.)

LONGFELLOW. (*See* GOLDEN TREASURY SERIES, p. 25.)

LOWELL (Jas. Russell).—COMPLETE POETICAL WORKS. Pott 8vo. 4s. 6d.
—— With Introduction by THOMAS HUGHES, and Portrait. Cr. 8vo. 7s. 6d.
—— HEARTSEASE AND RUE. Cr. 8vo. 5s.
—— OLD ENGLISH DRAMATISTS. Cr. 8vo. 5s. (*See also* COLLECTED WORKS, p. 27.)

LUCAS (F.).—SKETCHES OF RURAL LIFE. Poems. Globe 8vo. 5s.

MEREDITH (George). — A READING OF EARTH. Ext. fcp. 8vo. 5s.
—— POEMS AND LYRICS OF THE JOY OF EARTH. 3rd Edit. Ext. fcp. 8vo. 6s.
—— BALLADS AND POEMS OF TRAGIC LIFE. 2nd Edit. Ext. fcp. 8vo. 6s.
—— MODERN LOVE. Ex. fcap. 8vo. 5s.
—— THE EMPTY PURSE. Fcp. 8vo. 5s.

MILTON.—POETICAL WORKS. Edited, with Introductions and Notes, by Prof. DAVID MASSON, M.A. 3 vols. 8vo. 2l. 2s.—[Uniform with the Cambridge Shakespeare.]
—— —— Edited by Prof. MASSON. 3 vols. Globe 8vo. 15s.
—— —— *Globe Edition.* Edited by Prof. MASSON. Crown 8vo. 3s. 6d.
—— PARADISE LOST, BOOKS 1 and 2. Edited by MICHAEL MACMILLAN, B.A. 1s. 9d.; —BOOKS 1 to 4 (separately), 1s. 3d. each; sewed, 1s. each.
—— L'ALLEGRO, IL PENSEROSO, LYCIDAS, ARCADES, SONNETS, ETC. Edited by WM. BELL, M.A. 1s. 9d.
—— COMUS. By the same. 1s. 3d.; swd. 1s.
—— SAMSON AGONISTES. Edited by H. M. PERCIVAL, M.A. 2s.

MOULTON (Louise Chandler). — IN THE GARDEN OF DREAMS: Lyrics and Sonnets. Cr. 8vo. 6s.
—— SWALLOW FLIGHTS. Cr. 8vo. 6s.

MUDIE (C. E.).—STRAY LEAVES: Poems. 4th Edit. Ext. fcp. 8vo. 3s. 6d.

MYERS (E.).—THE PURITANS: A Poem. Ext. fcp. 8vo. 2s. 6d.
—— POEMS. Ext. fcp. 8vo. 4s. 6d.
—— THE DEFENCE OF ROME: and other Poems. Ext. fcp. 8vo. 5s.
—— THE JUDGMENT OF PROMETHEUS: and other Poems. Ext. fcp. 8vo. 3s. 6d.

MYERS (F. W. H.).—The Renewal of Youth: and other Poems. Cr. 8vo. 7s. 6d.
—— St. Paul: A Poem. Ext. fcp. 8vo. 2s.6d.
NORTON (Hon. Mrs.).—The Lady of La Garaye. 9th Edit. Fcp. 8vo. 4s. 6d.
PALGRAVE (Prof. F. T.).—Original Hymns. 3rd Edit. Pott 8vo. 1s. 6d.
—— Lyrical Poems. Ext. fcp. 8vo. 6s.
—— Visions of England. Cr. 8vo. 7s. 6d.
—— Amenophis. Pott 8vo. 4s. 6d.
PALGRAVE (W. G.).—A Vision of Life: Semblance and Reality. Cr. 8vo. 7s. net.
PATERSON (A. B.).—Man from Snowy River. Cr. 8vo. 6s.
PEEL (Edmund).—Echoes from Horeb: and other Poems. Cr. 8vo. 3s. 6d
POPE. (See Globe Library, p. 25.)
RAWNSLEY (H. D.).—Poems, Ballads, and Bucolics. Fcp. 8vo. 5s.
ROSCOE (W. C.).—Poems. Edit. by E. M. Roscoe. Cr. 8vo. 7s. net.
ROSSETTI (Christina).—Poems. New Collected Edition. Globe 8vo. 7s. 6d.
—— New Poems. Hitherto unpublished or uncollected. Edited by W. M. Rossetti. Gl. 8vo. 7s. 6d.
—— Sing-Song: A Nursery Rhyme Book. Small 4to. Illustrated. 4s. 6d.
—— Goblin Market. Illust. Fcp. 8vo. 5s.
—— Rossetti Birthday Book. Edited by O. Rossetti. 16mo. 2s. 6d.
SCOTT.—The Lay of the Last Minstrel, and The Lady of the Lake. Edited by Prof. F. T. Palgrave. 1s.
—— The Lay of the Last Minstrel. By G. H. Stuart, M.A., and E. H. Elliot, B.A. Globe 8vo. 2s.—Canto I. 9d.—Cantos I.—III. and IV.—VI. 1s. 3d. each; sewed, 1s. each.
—— Marmion. Edited by Michael Macmillan, B A. 3s.; sewed, 2s. 6d.
—— Marmion, and The Lord of the Isles. By Prof. F. T. Palgrave. 1s.
—— The Lady of the Lake. By G. H. Stuart, M.A. Gl. 8vo. 2s. 6d.; swd. 2s.—Canto I., sewed, 9d.
—— Rokeby. By Michael Macmillan, B.A. 3s.; sewed, 2s. 6d.
(See also Globe Library, p. 25.)
SHAIRP (John Campbell).—Glen Desseray: and other Poems, Lyrical and Elegiac. Ed. by F. T. Palgrave. Cr. 8vo. 6s.
SHAKESPEARE.—The Works of William Shakespeare. *Cambridge Edition.* New and Revised Edition, by W. Aldis Wright, M.A. 9 vols. 8vo. 10s. 6d. each.—*Edition de Luxe.* 40 vols. Sup. roy. 8vo. 6s. each net.
—— *Victoria Edition.* In 3 vols.—Comedies; Histories; Tragedies. Cr. 8vo. 6s. each.
—— The Tempest. With Introduction and Notes, by K. Deighton.. Gl. 8vo. 1s. 9d.
—— Much Ado about Nothing. 2s.
—— A Midsummer Night's Dream. 1s. 9d.
—— The Merchant of Venice. 1s. 9d.
—— As You Like It. 1s. 9d.
—— Twelfth Night. 1s. 9d.
—— The Winter's Tale. 2s.
—— King John. 1s. 9d.
—— Richard II. 1s. 9d.
—— Henry IV. Part I. 2s. 6d.; sewed, 2s.
—— Henry IV. Part II. 2s. 6d.; sewed, 2s.

SHAKESPEARE.—Coriolanus. By K. Deighton. 2s. 6d; sewed, 2s.
—— Henry V. 1s. 9d.
—— Richard III. By C. H. Tawney, M.A. 2s. 6d.; sewed, 2s.
—— Henry VIII. By K. Deighton. 1s. 9d.
—— Romeo and Juliet. 2s. 6d.; sewed, 2s.
—— Julius Cæsar. 1s. 9d.
—— Macbeth. 1s. 9d.
—— Hamlet. 2s. 6d.; sewed, 2s.
—— King Lear. 1s. 9d.
—— Othello. 2s.
—— Antony and Cleopatra. 2s.6d.; swd. 2s.
—— Cymbeline. 2s. 6d.; sewed, 2s.
(See also Globe Library, p. 25; Golden Treasury Series, p. 26.)
SHELLEY.—Complete Poetical Works. Edited by Prof. Dowden. Portrait. Cr. 8vo. 7s.6d. (See Golden Treasury Series, p. 26.)
SKRINE (J. H.).—Joan the Maid. Ex. cr. 8vo. 6s. 6d.
SMITH (C. Barnard).—Poems. Fcp. 8vo. 5s.
SMITH (Horace).—Poems. Globe 8vo. 5s.
—— Interludes. Cr. 8vo. 5s.
—— Interludes. Second Series. Cr. 8vo. 5s.
SPENSER.—Fairie Queene. Book I. By H. M. Percival, M.A. Gl. 8vo. 3s.; swd., 2s. 6d.
—— Shepheard's Calendar. By C. H. Herford, Litt.D. Gl. 8vo. 2s. 6d.
(See also Globe Library, p. 25.)
STEPHENS (J. B.).—Convict Once: and other Poems. Cr. 8vo. 7s. 6d.
STRETTELL (Alma).—Spanish and Italian Folk Songs. Illustr. Roy.16mo. 12s.6d.
SYMONS (Arthur).—Days and Nights. Globe 8vo. 6s.
TENNYSON (Lord).—Complete Works. New and Enlarged Edition, with Portrait. Cr. 8vo. 7s. 6d.—*School Edition.* In Four Parts. Cr. 8vo. 2s. 6d. each.
—— Poetical Works. *Pocket Edition.* Pott 8vo, morocco, gilt edges. 7s. 6d. net.
—— Works. *Library Edition.* In 9 vols. Globe 8vo. 5s. each. [Each volume may be had separately.]—Poems, 2 vols.—Idylls of the King.—The Princess, and Maud.—Enoch Arden, and In Memoriam.—Ballads, and other Poems.—Queen Mary, and Harold.—Becket, and other Plays.—Demeter, and other Poems.
—— Works. *Ext. fcp. 8vo. Edition*, on Handmade Paper. In 10 vols. (supplied in sets only). 5l. 5s. 0d.—Early Poems.—Lucretius, and other Poems.—Idylls of the King.—The Princess, and Maud.—Enoch Arden, and In Memoriam.—Queen Mary, and Harold.—Ballads, and other Poems. —Becket, The Cup.—The Foresters, The Falcon, The Promise of May.—Tiresias, and other Poems.
—— Works. *Miniature Edition*, In 16 vols., viz. The Poetical Works. 12 vols. In a box. 25s.—The Dramatic Works. 4 vols. In a box. 10s. 6d.
—— *The Original Editions.* Fcp. 8vo. Poems. 6s.
Maud: and other Poems. 3s. 6d.
The Princess. 3s. 6d.
The Holy Grail: and other Poems. 4s.6d.
Ballads: and other Poems. 5s.
Harold: A Drama. 6s.
Queen Mary: A Drama. 6s.

LITERATURE.

Poetry and the Drama—*continued.*

TENNYSON (Lord)—*continued.*

The Original Editions. Fcp. 8vo.
THE CUP, and THE FALCON. 5s.
BECKET. 6s.
TIRESIAS: and other Poems. 6s.
LOCKSLEY HALL SIXTY YEARS AFTER, etc. 6s.
DEMETER: and other Poems. 6s.
THE FORESTERS: ROBIN HOOD AND MAID
  MARIAN. 6s.
THE DEATH OF OENONE, AKBAR'S DREAM,
  AND OTHER POEMS. 6s.
—— *The People's Edition.* In 23 volumes,
demy 16mo., cloth, 1s. net; leather, 1s. 6d.
net per volume. Two volumes monthly from
November, 1895.—JUVENILIA.—THE LADY
OF SHALOTT, and other Poems.—A DREAM
OF FAIR WOMEN, and other Poems.—LOCK-
SLEY HALL, and other Poems.—WILL WATER-
PROOF, and other Poems.—THE PRINCESS,
I.—III.—THE PRINCESS IV. to end.—ENOCH
ARDEN, AYLMER'S FIELD, and LUCRETIUS.
—IN MEMORIAM.—MAUD, THE WINDOW,
and other Poems.—THE BROOK, and other
Poems.—IDYLLS OF THE KING: THE COMING
OF ARTHUR, GARETH AND LYNETTE.—
IDYLLS OF THE KING: THE MARRIAGE OF
GERAINT, GERAINT AND ENID.—IDYLLS OF
THE KING: BALIN AND BALAN, MERLIN
AND VIVIEN.—IDYLLS OF THE KING: LANCE-
LOT AND ELAINE, THE HOLY GRAIL.—IDYLLS
OF THE KING: PELLEAS AND ETTARRE, THE
LAST TOURNAMENT.—IDYLLS OF THE KING:
GUINEVERE, THE PASSING OF ARTHUR, TO
THE QUEEN.—THE LOVER'S TALE, and other
Poems.—RIZPAH, and other Poems.—THE
VOYAGE OF MAELDUNE, and other Poems.—
THE SPINSTER'S SWEET ARTS, and other
Poems.—DEMETER, and other Poems.—THE
DEATH OF ŒNONE, and other Poems.
—— POEMS BY TWO BROTHERS. Fcp. 8vo. 6s.
—— MAUD. *Kelmscott Edition.* Small 4to,
vellum. 42s. net.
—— POEMS. Reprint of 1857 Edition. Ori-
ginal Illustrations. 4to. 21s.—*Edition de
Luxe.* Roy. 8vo. 42s. net.
—— *The Royal Edition.* 1 vol. 8vo. 16s.
—— THE TENNYSON BIRTHDAY BOOK. Edit.
by EMILY SHAKESPEAR. Pott 8vo. 2s. 6d.
—— SONGS FROM TENNYSON'S WRITINGS.
Square 8vo. 2s. 6d.
—— SELECTIONS FROM TENNYSON. With In-
troduction and Notes, by F. J. ROWE, M.A.,
and W. T. WEBB, M.A. Globe 8vo. 3s. 6d.
Or Part I. 2s. 6d.; Part II. 2s. 6d.
—— MORTE D'ARTHUR. By F. J. ROWE,
M.A., and W. T. WEBB, M.A. Swd., 1s.
—— GERAINT AND ENID: AND THE MARRIAGE
OF GERAINT. By G. C. MACAULAY, M.A.
Globe 8vo. 2s. 6d.
—— ENOCH ARDEN. By W. T. WEBB, M.A.
Globe 8vo. 2s. 6d.
—— AYLMER'S FIELD. By W. T. WEBB, M.A.
Globe 8vo. 2s. 6d.
—— THE COMING OF ARTHUR, and THE PASS-
ING OF ARTHUR. By F. J. ROWE. Gl. 8vo. 2s. 6d.
—— THE PRINCESS. By P. M. WALLACE, M.A.
Globe 8vo. 3s. 6d.
—— GARETH AND LYNETTE. By G. C.
MACAULAY, M.A. Globe 8vo. 2s. 6d.
—— THE HOLY GRAIL. By G. C. MACAULAY,
M.A. Globe 8vo. 2s. 6d.

TENNYSON (Lord).—GUINEVERE. By G. C.
MACAULAY, M.A. 2s. 6d.
—— LANCELOT AND ELAINE. By F. J. ROWE,
M.A. 2s. 6d.
—— TENNYSON FOR THE YOUNG. By Canon
AINGER. Pott 8vo. 1s. net.—Large Paper,
uncut, 3s. 6d.; gilt edges, 4s. 6d.
—— BECKET. As arranged for the Stage by H.
IRVING. 8vo. swd. 2s. net
—— THE BROOK. With 20 Illustrations by A.
WOODRUFF. 32mo. 2s. 6d.
TENNYSON (Frederick).—THE ISLES OF
GREECE: SAPPHO AND ALCAEUS. Cr. 8vo.
7s. 6d.
—— DAPHNE: and other Poems. Cr. 8vo. 7s. 6d.
TENNYSON (Hallam, Lord). (*See* ILLUS-
TRATED BOOKS.)
TREVOR (G. H.).—RHYMES OF RAJPUTANA.
Cr. 8vo. 7s. 6d.
TRUMAN (Jos.).—AFTER-THOUGHTS: Poems.
Cr. 8vo. 3s. 6d.
TURNER (Charles Tennyson).—COLLECTED
SONNETS, OLD AND NEW. Ext. fcp. 8vo. 7s. 6d.
TYRWHITT (R. St. John).—FREE FIELD.
Lyrics, chiefly Descriptive. Gl. 8vo. 3s. 6d.
—— BATTLE AND AFTER, CONCERNING SER-
GEANT THOMAS ATKINS, GRENADIER
GUARDS: and other Verses. Gl. 8vo. 3s. 6d.
WARD (Samuel).—LYRICAL RECREATIONS.
Fcp. 8vo. 6s.
WATSON (W.).—POEMS. Fcap. 8vo. 5s.
—— LACHRYMAE MUSARUM. Fcp. 8vo. 4s. 6d.
(*See also* GOLDEN TREASURY SERIES, p. 25.)
WEBSTER (A.).—PORTRAITS. Fcp. 8vo. 5s.
—— SELECTIONS FROM VERSE. Fp. 8vo. 4s. 6d.
—— DISGUISES: A Drama. Fcp. 8vo. 5s.
—— IN A DAY: A Drama. Fcp. 8vo. 2s. 6d.
—— THE SENTENCE. Fcp. 8vo. 3s. 6d.
—— SONNETS. Fcp. 8vo. 2s. 6d. net.
—— MOTHER AND DAUGHTER. Fcp. 8vo.
2s. 6d. net.
WHITTIER.—COMPLETE POETICAL WORKS
OF JOHN GREENLEAF WHITTIER. With
Portrait. Pott 8vo. 4s. 6d. (*See also* GOL-
DEN TREASURY SERIES, p. 26; COLLECTED
WORKS, p. 28.)
WILLS (W. G.).—MELCHIOR. Cr. 8vo. 9s.
WOOD (Andrew Goldie).—THE ISLES OF THE
BLEST: and other Poems. Globe 8vo. 5s.
WOOLNER (Thomas). — MY BEAUTIFUL
LADY. 3rd Edit. Fcp. 8vo. 5s.
—— PYGMALION. Cr. 8vo. 7s. 6d.
—— SILENUS. Cr. 8vo. 6s.
WORDSWORTH. — COMPLETE POETICAL
WORKS. Copyright Edition. With an Intro-
duction by JOHN MORLEY, and Portrait.
Cr. 8vo. 7s. 6d.
—— THE RECLUSE. Fcp. 8vo. 2s. 6d.—Large
Paper Edition. 8vo. 10s. 6d.
(*See also* GOLDEN TREASURY SERIES, p. 26;
COLLECTED WORKS, p. 28.)

Poetical Collections and Selections.
(*See also* GOLDEN TREASURY SERIES, p. 25;
BOOKS FOR THE YOUNG, p. 48.)
ELLIS (A.).—CHOSEN ENGLISH. Selections
from Wordsworth, Byron, Shelley, Lamb,
Scott. Globe 8vo. 2s. 6d.
**GEORGE (H. B.)—SIDGWICK (A.)—POEMS
OF ENGLAND. With Notes. Gl. 8vo. 2s. 6d.

HALES (Prof. J. W.).—LONGER ENGLISH POEMS. With Notes, Philological and Explanatory, and an Introduction on the Teaching of English. Ext. fcp. 8vo. 4s. 6d.

MACDONALD (George).—ENGLAND'S ANTIPHON. Cr. 8vo. 4s. 6d.

MARTIN (F.). (See BOOKS FOR THE YOUNG, p. 48.)

MASSON (R. O. and D.).—THREE CENTURIES OF ENGLISH POETRY. Being Selections from Chaucer to Herrick. Globe 8vo. 3s. 6d.

PALGRAVE (Prof. F. T.).—THE GOLDEN TREASURY OF THE BEST SONGS AND LYRICAL POEMS IN THE ENGLISH LANGUAGE. Large Type. Cr. 8vo. 10s. 6d. (See also GOLDEN TREASURY SERIES, p. 25; BOOKS FOR THE YOUNG, p. 49.)

SMITH (Goldwin).—BAY LEAVES. Translations from Latin Poets. Globe 8vo. 5s.

WARD (T. H.).—ENGLISH POETS. Selections, with Critical Introductions by various Writers, and a General Introduction by MATTHEW ARNOLD. Edited by T. H. WARD, M.A. 4 vols. 2nd Edit. Cr. 8vo.—Vol. I. CHAUCER TO DONNE, 7s. 6d.; II. BEN JONSON TO DRYDEN, 7s. 6d.; III. ADDISON TO BLAKE, 7s. 6d. IV. WORDSWORTH TO TENNYSON, 8s. 6d.
—— Appendix to Vol. IV. containing BROWNING, ARNOLD, and TENNYSON. Cr. 8vo. 2s.

WOODS (M. A.).—A FIRST POETRY BOOK. Fcp. 8vo. 2s. 6d.
—— A SECOND POETRY BOOK. 2 Parts. Fcp. 8vo. 2s. 6d. each.—Complete, 4s. 6d.
—— A THIRD POETRY BOOK. Fcp. 8vo. 4s. 6d.

WORDS FROM THE POETS. With a Vignette and Frontispiece. 12th Edit. Pott 8vo. 1s

Prose Fiction.

AUSTEN (Jane).—PRIDE AND PREJUDICE. Illustrated. Cr. 8vo. 3s. 6d.
—— SENSE AND SENSIBILITY, Illustrated. Cr. 8vo. 3s. 6d.

BIKELAS (D.).—LOUKIS LARAS; or, The Reminiscences of a Chiote Merchant during the Greek War of Independence. Translated by J. GENNADIUS. Cr. 8vo. 7s. 6d.

BJÖRNSON (B.).—SYNNÖVE SOLBAKKEN. Translated by JULIE SUTTER. Cr. 8vo. 6s.

BOLDREWOOD (Rolf).—Uniform Edition. Cr. 8vo. 3s. 6d. each.
ROBBERY UNDER ARMS.
THE MINER'S RIGHT.
THE SQUATTER'S DREAM.
A SYDNEY-SIDE SAXON.
A COLONIAL REFORMER.
NEVERMORE. | A MODERN BUCCANEER.
—— THE CROOKED STICK. Cr. 8vo. 6s.
—— OLD MELBOURNE MEMORIES. Cr. 8vo. 6s.
—— THE SPHINX OF EAGLEHAWK. Fcp. 8vo. 2s.

BORROW (G.).—LAVENGRO. Illustrated. Cr. 8vo. 3s. 6d.

BURNETT (F. H.).—HAWORTH'S. Gl. 8vo. 2s.
—— LOUISIANA, and THAT LASS o' LOWRIE'S. Illustrated. Cr. 8vo. 3s. 6d.

CALMIRE. 2 vols. Cr. 8vo. 21s.

CARMARTHEN (Marchioness of).—A LOVER OF THE BEAUTIFUL. Cr. 8vo. 6s.

CONWAY (Hugh).—A FAMILY AFFAIR. Cr. 8vo. 3s. 6d.
—— LIVING OR DEAD. Cr. 8vo. 3s. 6d.

COOPER (E. H.).—RICHARD ESCOTT. Cr. 8vo. 6s.

CORBETT (Julian).—THE FALL OF ASGARD: A Tale of St. Olaf's Day. 2 vols. Gl. 8vo. 12s.
—— FOR GOD AND GOLD. Cr. 8vo. 6s.
—— KOPHETUA THE THIRTEENTH. 2 vols. Globe 8vo. 12s.

COTES (E.).—THE STORY OF SONNY SAHIB. Fcp. 8vo. 2s. (See also under DUNCAN.)

CRAIK (Mrs.).—Uniform Edition. Cr. 8vo. 3s. 6d. each.
OLIVE.
THE OGILVIES. Also Globe 8vo, 2s.
AGATHA'S HUSBAND. Also Globe 8vo, 2s.
THE HEAD OF THE FAMILY.
TWO MARRIAGES. Also Globe 8vo, 2s.
THE LAUREL BUSH. | MY MOTHER AND I.
MISS TOMMY: A Mediæval Romance.
KING ARTHUR: Not a Love Story.

CRAWFORD (F. Marion).—Uniform Edition. Cr. 8vo. 3s. 6d. each.
MR. ISAACS: A Tale of Modern India.
DR. CLAUDIUS.
A ROMAN SINGER. | ZOROASTER.
A TALE OF A LONELY PARISH.
MARZIO'S CRUCIFIX. | PAUL PATOFF.
WITH THE IMMORTALS.
GREIFENSTEIN. | SANT' ILARIO.
A CIGARETTE MAKER'S ROMANCE.
KHALED: A Tale of Arabia.
THE WITCH OF PRAGUE.
THE THREE FATES. | DON ORSINO.
CHILDREN OF THE KING.
PIETRO GHISLERI. | MARION DARCHE.
KATHARINE LAUDERDALE.
—— THE RALSTONS. Cr. 8vo. 6s.
—— CASA BRACCIO. 2 vols. Gl. 8vo. 12s.
—— LOVE IN IDLENESS. Fcp. 8vo. 2s.
—— ADAM JOHNSTONE'S SON. Cr. 8vo. 6s.

CUNNINGHAM (Sir H. S.).—THE CŒRULEANS: A Vacation Idyll. Cr. 8vo. 3s. 6d.
—— THE HERIOTS. Cr. 8vo. 3s. 6d.
—— WHEAT AND TARES. Cr. 8vo. 3s. 6d.
—— SIBYLLA. 2 vols. Gl. 8vo. 12s.

CURTIN (J.).—HERO TALES OF IRELAND. Ex. cr. 8vo. 8s. 6d. net.

DAHN (Felix).—FELICITAS. Translated by M. A. C. E. Cr. 8vo. 4s. 6d.

DAVIS (R. H.).—THE PRINCESS ALINE. Fcp. 8vo. 1s. 6d.

DAY (Rev. Lal Behari).—BENGAL PEASANT LIFE. Cr. 8vo. 6s.
—— FOLK TALES OF BENGAL. Cr. 8vo. 4s. 6d.

DEFOE (D.). (See GLOBE LIBRARY, p. 25; GOLDEN TREASURY SERIES, p. 25.)

DEMOCRACY: AN AMERICAN NOVEL. Cr. 8vo. 4s. 6d.

DICKENS (Charles).—Uniform Edition. Cr. 8vo. 2s. 6d. each.
THE PICKWICK PAPERS.
OLIVER TWIST. | NICHOLAS NICKLEBY.
MARTIN CHUZZLEWIT.
THE OLD CURIOSITY SHOP.
BARNABY RUDGE. | DOMBEY AND SON.
CHRISTMAS BOOKS. | SKETCHES BY BOZ.
DAVID COPPERFIELD.
AMERICAN NOTES, AND PICTURES FROM ITALY.
BLEAK HOUSE.
—— THE POSTHUMOUS PAPERS OF THE PICKWICK CLUB. Illust. Edit. by C. DICKENS, Jun. 2 vols. Ext. cr. 8vo. 21s.

LITERATURE.
Prose Fiction—*continued.*

DICKENS (M. A.).—A MERE CYPHER. Cr. 8vo. 3s. 6d.
—— A VALIANT IGNORANCE. Cr. 8vo. 3s. 6d.

DILLWYN (E. A.).—JILL. Cr. 8vo. 6s.
—— JILL AND JACK. 2 vols. Globe 8vo. 12s.

DISRAELI (B.).—SYBIL. Illustrated. Cr. 8vo. 3s. 6d.

DOUGLAS (Theo.).—A BRIDE ELECT. Cr. 8vo, sewed. 1s.

DUNCAN (S. J.).—HIS HONOR AND A LADY. Illustrated. Cr. 8vo. 6s.

DUNSMUIR (Amy).—VIDA: Study of a Girl. 3rd Edit. Cr. 8vo. 6s.

DURAND (Sir M.).—HELEN TREVERVAN. Cr. 8vo. 3s. 6d.

EBERS (Dr. George).—THE BURGOMASTER'S WIFE. Transl. by C. BELL. Cr. 8vo. 4s. 6d.
—— ONLY A WORD. Translated by CLARA BELL. Cr. 8vo. 4s. 6d.

EDGEWORTH (M.).—CASTLE RACKRENT. Illustrated. Cr. 8vo. 3s. 6d.
—— ORMOND. Illustrated. Cr. 8vo. 3s. 6d.
—— POPULAR TALES. Illust. Cr. 8vo. 3s. 6d.

"ESTELLE RUSSELL" (The Author of).—HARMONIA. 3 vols. Cr. 8vo. 31s. 6d.

FALCONER (Lanoe).—CECILIA DE NOEL. Cr. 8vo. 3s. 6d.

FIELD (Mrs. E. M.).—DENIS. Cr. 8vo. 6s.

FLEMING (G.).—A NILE NOVEL. Gl. 8vo. 2s.
—— MIRAGE: A Novel. Globe 8vo. 2s.
—— THE HEAD OF MEDUSA. Globe 8vo. 2s
—— VESTIGIA. Globe 8vo. 2s.

FRANCIS (Francis)—WILD ROSE. Cr. 8vo. 6s.

FRATERNITY: A Romance. 2 vols. Cr 8vo. 21s.

"FRIENDS IN COUNCIL" (The Author of).—REALMAH. Cr. 8vo. 6s.

GALT (J.).—ANNALS OF THE PARISH AND THE AYRSHIRE LEGATEES. Illustrated. Cr. 8vo. 3s. 6d.

GRAHAM (John W.).—NEÆRA: A Tale of Ancient Rome. Cr. 8vo. 6s.

GRANT (C.).—TALES OF NAPLES AND THE CAMORRA. [*In the Press.*

HARBOUR BAR, THE. Cr. 8vo. 6s.

HARDY (Arthur Sherburne).—BUT YET A WOMAN: A Novel. Cr. 8vo. 4s. 6d.
—— THE WIND OF DESTINY. 2 vols. Gl. 8vo. 12s.

HARTE (Bret).—CRESSY. Cr. 8vo. 3s. 6d.
—— THE HERITAGE OF DEDLOW MARSH: and other Tales. Cr. 8vo. 3s. 6d.
—— A FIRST FAMILY OF TASAJARA. Cr. 8vo. 3s. 6d.

"HOGAN, M.P." (The Author of).—HOGAN, M.P. Cr. 8vo. 3s. 6d.
—— THE HON. MISS FERRARD. Gl. 8vo. 2s.
—— FLITTERS, TATTERS, AND THE COUNSELLOR, ETC. Cr 8vo. 3s. 6d
—— CHRISTY CAREW. Globe 8vo. 2s.
—— ISMAY'S CHILDREN. Globe 8vo. 2s.

HOPPUS (Mary).—A GREAT TREASON: A Story of the War of Independence. 2 vols. Cr. 8vo. 9s.

HUGHES (Thomas).—TOM BROWN AT OXFORD. Cr. 8vo. 3s. 6d.
—— THE SCOURING OF THE WHITE HORSE, and THE ASHEN FAGGOT. Cr. 8vo. 3s. 6d.

HUGHES (Thomas).—TOM BROWN'S SCHOOL DAYS. By AN OLD BOY.—Golden Treasury Edition. 2s. 6d. net.—Uniform Edit. 3s. 6d. —People's Edition. 2s.—People's Sixpenny Edition. Illustr. Med. 4to. 6d.—Uniform with Sixpenny Kingsley. Med. 8vo. 6d.

IRVING (Washington). (*See* ILLUSTRATED BOOKS, p. 15.)

JACKSON (Helen).—RAMONA. Gl. 8vo. 2s.

JAMES (Henry).—THE EUROPEANS: A Novel. Cr. 8vo. 6s.; Pott 8vo, 2s.
—— DAISY MILLER: and other Stories. Cr. 8vo. 6s.; Globe 8vo, 2s.
—— THE AMERICAN. Cr. 8vo. 6s.—Pott 8vo. 2 vols. 4s.
—— RODERICK HUDSON. Cr. 8vo. 6s.; Gl. 8vo, 2s.; Pott 8vo, 2 vols. 4s.
—— THE MADONNA OF THE FUTURE: and other Tales. Cr. 8vo. 6s.; Globe 8vo, 2s.
—— WASHINGTON SQUARE, THE PENSION BEAUREPAS. Globe 8vo. 2s.
—— THE PORTRAIT OF A LADY. Cr. 8vo. 6s. Pott 8vo, 3 vols. 6s.
—— STORIES REVIVED. In Two Series. Cr. 8vo. 6s. each.
—— THE BOSTONIANS. Cr. 8vo. 6s.
—— NOVELS AND TALES. Pocket Edition. Pott 8vo. 2s. each volume.
  CONFIDENCE. 1 vol.
  THE SIEGE OF LONDON; MADAME DE MAUVES. 1 vol.
  AN INTERNATIONAL EPISODE; THE PENSION BEAUREPAS; THE POINT OF VIEW. 1 vol.
  DAISY MILLER, a Study; FOUR MEETINGS; LONGSTAFF'S MARRIAGE; BENVOLIO. 1 vol.
  THE MADONNA OF THE FUTURE; A BUNDLE OF LETTERS; THE DIARY OF A MAN OF FIFTY; EUGENE PICKERING. 1 vol.
—— TALES OF THREE CITIES. Cr. 8vo. 4s. 6d.
—— THE PRINCESS CASAMASSIMA. Cr. 8vo. 6s.; Globe 8vo, 2s.
—— THE REVERBERATOR. Cr. 8vo. 6s.
—— THE ASPERN PAPERS; LOUISA PALLANT; THE MODERN WARNING. Cr. 8vo. 3s. 6d.
—— A LONDON LIFE. Cr. 8vo. 3s. 6d.
—— THE TRAGIC MUSE. Cr. 8vo. 3s. 6d.
—— THE LESSON OF THE MASTER, AND OTHER STORIES. Cr. 8vo. 6s.
—— THE REAL THING, AND OTHER TALES. Cr. 8vo. 6s.

KEARY (Annie).—JANET'S HOME. Cr. 8vo. 3s. 6d.
—— CLEMENCY FRANKLYN. Globe 8vo. 2s.
—— OLDBURY. Cr. 8vo. 3s. 6d.
—— A YORK AND A LANCASTER ROSE. Cr. 8vo. 3s. 6d.
—— CASTLE DALY. Cr. 8vo. 3s. 6d.
—— A DOUBTING HEART. Cr. 8vo. 3s. 6d

KENNEDY (P.).—LEGENDARY FICTIONS OF THE IRISH CELTS. Cr. 8vo. 3s. 6d.

KINGSLEY (Charles).—*Eversley Edition.* 13 vols. Globe 8vo. 5s. each.—WESTWARD HO! 2 vols.—TWO YEARS AGO. 2 vols.—HYPATIA. 2 vols.—YEAST. 1 vol.—ALTON LOCKE. 2 vols.—HEREWARD THE WAKE. 2 vols.
—— *Sixpenny Edition.* Med. 8vo. 6d. each. — WESTWARD HO! — HYPATIA. — YEAST.—ALTON LOCKE.—TWO YEARS AGO. —HEREWARD THE WAKE.

KINGSLEY (C.).—*Complete Edition.* Cr. 8vo. 3*s.* 6*d.* each —WESTWARD HO! With a Portrait. — HYPATIA. — YEAST. — ALTON LOCKE. — TWO YEARS AGO. — HEREWARD THE WAKE.
—— *Pocket Edition.* Pott 8vo. 1*s.* 6*d.* each. HYPATIA. — ALTON LOCKE. — WESTWARD HO! 2 vols.—HEREWARD THE WAKE.—TWO YEARS AGO. 2 vols.—YEAST.

KIPLING (Rudyard).—PLAIN TALES FROM THE HILLS. Cr. 8vo. 6*s.*
—— THE LIGHT THAT FAILED. Cr. 8vo. 6*s.*
—— LIFE'S HANDICAP : Being Stories of mine own People. Cr. 8vo. 6*s.*
—— MANY INVENTIONS. Cr. 8vo. 6*s.*
—— SOLDIERS THREE, ETC. Cr. 8vo. 6*s.*
—— WEE WILLIE WINKIE, ETC. Cr. 8vo. 6*s.*

LAFARGUE (Philip).—THE NEW JUDGMENT OF PARIS. 2 vols. Globe 8vo. 12*s.*

LEE (Margaret).—FAITHFUL AND UNFAITHFUL. Cr. 8vo 3*s.* 6*d.*

LEVY (A.).—REUBEN SACHS. Cr. 8vo. 3*s.*6*d.*

LITTLE PILGRIM IN THE UNSEEN, A. 24th Thousand. Cr. 8vo. 2*s.* 6*d.*

"LITTLE PILGRIM IN THE UNSEEN, A" (Author of).—THE LAND OF DARKNESS. Cr. 8vo. 5*s.*

LOVER (S.).—HANDY ANDY. Illustrated. Cr. 8vo. 3*s.* 6*d.*

LYSAGHT (S. R.).—THE MARPLOT. Cr. 8vo. 3*s.* 6*d.*

LYTTON (Earl of).—THE RING OF AMASIS : A Romance. Cr. 8vo. 3*s.* 6*d.*

McLENNAN (Malcolm).—MUCKLE JOCK : and other Stories of Peasant Life in the North. Cr. 8vo. 3*s.* 6*d.*

MACMILLAN (M. K.).—DAGONET THE JESTER. Cr. 8vo. 3*s.* 6*d.*

MACQUOID (K. S.).—PATTY. Gl. 8vo. 2*s.*

MADOC (Fayr).—THE STORY OF MELICENT. Cr. 8vo. 4*s.* 6*d.*

MALET (Lucas).—MRS. LORIMER : A Sketch in Black and White. Cr. 8vo. 3*s.* 6*d.*

MALORY (Sir Thos.). (*See* GLOBE LIBRARY, p. 25.)

MARRYAT (Capt.).—JAPHET IN SEARCH OF A FATHER. Illustrated. Cr. 8vo. 3*s.* 6*d.*
—— JACOB FAITHFUL. Illust. Cr. 8vo. 3*s.* 6*d.*
—— PETER SIMPLE. Illust. Cr. 8vo. 3*s.* 6*d.*
—— MIDSHIPMAN EASY. Illust. Cr. 8vo.
[*In the Press.*
—— THE PHANTOM SHIP. Illust. Cr. 8vo.
[*In the Press.*
—— THE KING'S OWN. Illust. Cr. 8vo.
[*In the Press.*
—— POOR JACK. Illust. Cr. 8vo. [*In Press.*
—— THE DOG-FIEND. Illust. Cr. 8vo. [*In Press.*

MASON (A. E. W.).—THE COURTSHIP OF MORRICE BUCKLER. Cr. 8vo. 6*s.*

MINTO (W.).—THE MEDIATION OF RALPH HARDELOT. 3 vols. Cr. 8vo. 31*s.* 6*d.*

MITFORD (A. B.).—TALES OF OLD JAPAN. With Illustrations. Cr. 8vo. 3*s.* 6*d.*

MIZ MAZE, THE ; OR, THE WINKWORTH PUZZLE. A Story in Letters by Nine Authors. Cr. 8vo. 4*s.* 6*d.*

MORIER (J.).—HAJJI BABA OF ISPAHAN. Illustrated. Cr. 8vo. 3*s.* 6*d.*

MURRAY (D. Christie). — AUNT RACHEL. Cr. 8vo. 3*s.* 6*d.*
—— SCHWARTZ. Cr. 8vo. 3*s.* 6*d.*
—— THE WEAKER VESSEL. Cr. 8vo. 3*s.* 6*d.*
—— JOHN VALE'S GUARDIAN. Cr. 8vo. 3*s.* 6*d.*

MURRAY (D. Christie) and HERMAN (H.). —HE FELL AMONG THIEVES. Cr. 8vo. 3*s.* 6*d.*

NEW ANTIGONE, THE : A ROMANCE. Cr. 8vo. 3*s.* 6*d.*

NOEL (Lady Augusta).—HITHERSEA MERE. 3 vols. Cr. 8vo. 31*s.* 6*d.*

NORRIS (W. E.).—MY FRIEND JIM. Globe 8vo. 2*s.*
—— CHRIS. Globe 8vo. 2*s.*

NORTON (Hon. Mrs.).—OLD SIR DOUGLAS. Cr. 8vo. 6*s.*

OLIPHANT (Mrs. M. O. W.).—*Uniform Edition.* Cr. 8vo. 3*s.* 6*d.* each.
A SON OF THE SOIL.
THE CURATE IN CHARGE.
YOUNG MUSGRAVE. | SIR TOM.
HE THAT WILL NOT WHEN HE MAY.
THE WIZARD'S SON. | HESTER.
A COUNTRY GENTLEMAN AND HIS FAMILY.
THE SECOND SON.
THE MARRIAGE OF ELINOR.
NEIGHBOURS ON THE GREEN. | JOYCE.
A BELEAGUERED CITY. | KIRSTEEN.
THE RAILWAY MAN AND HIS CHILDREN.
THE HEIR-PRESUMPTIVE AND THE HEIR-APPARENT.
LADY WILLIAM.

PALMER (Lady Sophia).—MRS. PENICOTT'S LODGER : and other Stories. Cr. 8vo. 2*s.* 6*d.*

PARRY (Gambier).—THE STORY OF DICK. Cr. 8vo. 3*s.* 6*d.*

PATER (Walter).—MARIUS THE EPICUREAN : His SENSATIONS AND IDEAS. 3rd Edit. 2 vols. 8vo. 15*s.*

PATERSON (A.).—A SON OF THE PLAINS. Cr. 8vo. 6*s.*

PEACOCK (T. L.).—MAID MARIAN, ETC. Illustrated. Cr. 8vo. 3*s.* 6*d.*
—— HEADLONG HALL AND NIGHTMARE ABBEY. Illust. Cr. 8vo. 3*s.* 6*d.*
—— GRYLL GRANGE. Illust. Cr. 8vo. 3*s.* 6*d.*
—— MELINCOURT. Illustr. Cr. 8vo. 3*s.* 6*d.*

PHILLIPS (F. E.). — THE EDUCATION OF ANTONIA. Cr. 8vo. 6*s.*

PRICE (E. C.).—IN THE LION'S MOUTH. Cr. 8vo. 3*s.* 6*d.*

RHOADES (J.).—THE STORY OF JOHN TREVENNICK. Cr. 8vo. 3*s.* 6*d.*

ROSS (Percy).—A MISGUIDIT LASSIE. Cr. 8vo. 4*s.* 6*d.*

ROY (Neil).—THE HORSEMAN'S WORD. Cr. 8vo. 6*s.*

RUSSELL (W. Clark).—MAROONED. Cr. 8vo. 3*s.* 6*d.*
—— A STRANGE ELOPEMENT. Cr. 8vo. 3*s.* 6*d.*

ST. JOHNSTON (A.). — A SOUTH SEA LOVER : A Romance. Cr. 8vo. 6*s.*

SCOTT (M.).—TOM CRINGLE'S LOG. Illustrated. Cr. 8vo. 3*s.* 6*d.*

SHIPTON (Helen). — THE HERONS. Cr. 8vo. 6*s.*

SHORTHOUSE (J. Henry).—*Uniform Edition.* Cr. 8vo. 3*s.* 6*d.* each.
JOHN INGLESANT : A Romance.
BLANCHE, LADY FALAISE.

LITERATURE.
Prose Fiction—*continued*.

SHORTHOUSE (J. Henry).—*Uniform Edition*. Cr. 8vo. 3s. 6d. each.
SIR PERCIVAL: A Story of the Past and of the Present.
THE LITTLE SCHOOLMASTER MARK: A Spiritual Romance.
THE COUNTESS EVE.
A TEACHER OF THE VIOLIN: and other Tales.

SLIP IN THE FENS, A. Globe 8vo. 2s.

SMITH (F. H.).—TOM GROGAN. Illustrated. Cr. 8vo. 6s.
—— A GENTLEMAN VAGABOND. Cr. 8vo, sd. 1s.

SMITH (Garnet).—THE MELANCHOLY OF STEPHEN ALLARD. Cr. 8vo. 7s. 6d. net.

SMITH (L. P.).—THE YOUTH OF PARNASSUS. Cr. 8vo. 6s.

STEEL (Mrs. F. A.).—MISS STUART'S LEGACY. Cr. 8vo. 3s. 6d.
—— THE FLOWER OF FORGIVENESS. Crown 8vo. 3s. 6d.
—— RED ROWANS. Cr. 8vo. 6s.
—— TALES OF THE PUNJAB. Illust. Cr. 8vo. 6s.

THEODOLI (Marchesa)—UNDER PRESSURE. Cr. 8vo. 3s. 6d.

TIM. Cr. 8vo. 3s. 6d.

TOURGÉNIEF.—VIRGIN SOIL. Translated by ASHTON W. DILKE. Cr. 8vo. 6s.

VELEY (Margaret).—A GARDEN OF MEMORIES; MRS. AUSTIN; LIZZIE'S BARGAIN. Three Stories. 2 vols. Globe 8vo. 12s.

VICTOR (H.).—MARIAM: OR TWENTY-ONE DAYS. Cr. 8vo. 6s.

VOICES CRYING IN THE WILDERNESS: A NOVEL. Cr. 8vo. 7s. 6d.

WARD (Mrs. T. Humphry).—MISS BRETHERTON. Cr. 8vo. 3s. 6d.

WEST (M.).—A BORN PLAYER. Cr. 8vo. 6s.

WORTHEY (Mrs.).—THE NEW CONTINENT! A Novel. 2 vols. Globe 8vo. 12s.

YONGE (C. M.).—THE LONG VACATION. Cr. 8vo. 6s.
—— THE RELEASE. Cr. 8vo. 6s.
—— THE RUBIES OF ST. LO. Fcp. 8vo. 2s.
(See also p. 28.)

YONGE (C. M.) and COLERIDGE (C. R.).—STROLLING PLAYERS. Cr. 8vo. 6s.

Collected Works; Essays; Lectures; Letters; Miscellaneous Works.

ADDISON.—SELECTIONS FROM THE "SPECTATOR." With Introduction and Notes by K. DEIGHTON. Globe 8vo. 2s. 6d.

AN AUTHOR'S LOVE. Being the Unpublished Letters of PROSPER MÉRIMÉE'S "Inconnue." 2 vols. Ext. cr. 8vo. 12s.

ARNOLD (Matthew).—LETTERS. Edited by G. W. E. RUSSELL, M.P. 2 vols. Cr. 8vo. 15s. net.
—— ESSAYS IN CRITICISM 6th Ed. Cr. 8vo 9s. Gl. 8vo. 5s.
—— ESSAYS IN CRITICISM. Second Series. Cr. 8vo. 7s. 6d. Gl. 8vo. 5s.
—— DISCOURSES IN AMERICA. Cr. 8vo. 4s. 6d. Gl. 8vo. 5s.

ASPECTS OF MODERN STUDY. Cr. 8vo. 2s. 6d. net.

AUSTIN (A.).—THE GARDEN THAT I LOVE. 3rd Edit. Ex. cr. 8vo. 9s.
—— IN VERONICA'S GARDEN. Ex. cr. 8vo. 9s.

BACON.—ESSAYS. Introduction and Notes, by F. G. SELBY, M.A. Gl. 8vo. 3s.; swd., 2s. 6d.
—— ADVANCEMENT OF LEARNING. By the same. Gl. 8vo. Book I. 2s. Book II. 4s. 6d. (*See also* GOLDEN TREASURY SERIES, p. 25.)

BATES (K. L.).—ENGLISH RELIGIOUS DRAMA. Cr. 8vo. 6s. 6d. net.

BLACKIE (J. S.).—LAY SERMONS. Cr. 8vo. 6s.

BRADFORD (G.).—TYPES OF AMERICAN CHARACTER. Pott 8vo. 3s.

BRIDGES (John A.).—IDYLLS OF A LOST VILLAGE. Cr. 8vo. 7s. 6d.

BRIMLEY (George).—ESSAYS. Globe 8vo. 5s.

BUNYAN (John).—THE PILGRIM'S PROGRESS FROM THIS WORLD TO THAT WHICH IS TO COME. Pott 8vo. 2s. 6d. net.

BUTCHER (Prof. S. H.)—SOME ASPECTS OF THE GREEK GENIUS. Cr. 8vo. 7s. net.

CARLYLE (Thomas). (*See* BIOGRAPHY.)

CHURCH (Dean).—MISCELLANEOUS WRITINGS. Collected Edition. 7 vols. Globe 8vo. 5s. each.—Vol. I. MISCELLANEOUS ESSAYS.—II. DANTE: AND OTHER ESSAYS.—III. ST. ANSELM.—IV. SPENSER.—V. BACON.—VI. THE OXFORD MOVEMENT, 1833—45.—VII. THE BEGINNING OF THE MIDDLE AGES.

CLIFFORD (Prof. W. K.). LECTURES AND ESSAYS. Edited by LESLIE STEPHEN and Sir F. POLLOCK. Cr. 8vo. 8s. 6d.

CLOUGH (A. H.).—PROSE REMAINS. With a Selection from his Letters, and a Memoir by HIS WIFE. Cr. 8vo. 7s. 6d.

COLLINS (J. Churton).—THE STUDY OF ENGLISH LITERATURE. Cr. 8vo. 4s. 6d.
—— ESSAYS AND STUDIES. 8vo. 9s. net.

CORSON (Hiram).—THE AIMS OF LITERARY STUDY. Pott 8vo. 3s.
—— THE VOICE AND SPIRITUAL EDUCATION. Pott 8vo. 3s.

COURTHOPE (W. J.).—LIBERTY AND AUTHORITY IN MATTERS OF TASTE. 8vo. 1s. net.

COWPER.—LETTERS. Ed. by W. T. WEBB, M.A. Globe 8vo. 2s. 6d.

CRAIK (H.).—ENGLISH PROSE SELECTIONS. With Critical Introductions by various writers, and General Introductions to each Period. Edited by H. CRAIK, C.B. Vols. I. II. III. and IV. Cr. 8vo. 7s. 6d. each. [*V. in Press.*

CRAIK (Mrs.).—CONCERNING MEN: and other Papers. Cr. 8vo. 3s. 6d.
—— ABOUT MONEY: and other Things. Cr. 8vo. 3s. 6d.
—— SERMONS OUT OF CHURCH. Cr. 8vo. 3s. 6d.

CRAWFORD (F. M.).—THE NOVEL: WHAT IT IS. Pott 8vo. 3s.

CRAWSHAW (W. H.).—THE INTERPRETATION OF LITERATURE. Gl. 8vo. 3s. 6d. net.

CUNLIFFE (J. W.).—THE INFLUENCE OF SENECA ON ELIZABETHAN TRAGEDY. 4s. net.

DE VERE (Aubrey).—ESSAYS CHIEFLY ON POETRY. 2 vols. Globe 8vo. 12s.
—— ESSAYS, CHIEFLY LITERARY AND ETHICAL. Globe 8vo. 6s.

DICKENS.—LETTERS OF CHARLES DICKENS. Edited by his Sister-in-Law and MARY DICKENS. Cr. 8vo. 3s. 6d.

DRYDEN, ESSAYS OF. Edited by Prof. C. D. YONGE. Fcp. 8vo. 2s. 6d. (*See also* GLOBE LIBRARY, p. 25.)
—— THE SATIRES. Edited by J. CHURTON COLLINS. Gl. 8vo. 1s. 9d.

DUFF (Rt. Hon. Sir M. E. Grant).—MISCELLANIES, Political and Literary. 8vo. 10s. 6d.

ELLIS (A.).—CHOSEN ENGLISH. Selections from Wordsworth, Byron, Shelley, Lamb, Scott. Globe 8vo. 2s. 6d.

EMERSON (Ralph Waldo).—THE COLLECTED WORKS. 6 vols. Globe 8vo. 5s. each.—I. MISCELLANIES. With an Introductory Essay by JOHN MORLEY.—II. ESSAYS.—III. POEMS.—IV. ENGLISH TRAITS; REPRESENTATIVE MEN.—V. CONDUCT OF LIFE; SOCIETY AND SOLITUDE.—VI. LETTERS; SOCIAL AIMS ETC.

FASNACHT (G. E.).—SELECT SPECIMENS OF THE GREAT FRENCH WRITERS IN THE SEVENTEENTH, EIGHTEENTH, AND NINETEENTH CENTURIES. With Literary Appreciations by the most eminent French Critics, and a Historical Sketch of French Literature. Edit. by G. E. FASNACHT. Cr. 8vo. 7s. 6d.

FITZGERALD (Edward): LETTERS AND LITERARY REMAINS OF. Ed. by W. ALDIS WRIGHT, M.A. 3 vols. Cr. 8vo. 31s. 6d.
—— LETTERS. Edited by W. A. WRIGHT. 2 vols. Globe 8vo. 10s.

FOWLER (W. W.).—SUMMER STUDIES OF BIRDS AND BOOKS. Ex. cr. 8vo. 6s.

GLOBE LIBRARY. Cr. 8vo. 3s. 6d. each:
BOSWELL'S LIFE OF JOHNSON. Introduction by MOWBRAY MORRIS.
BURNS.—COMPLETE POETICAL WORKS AND LETTERS. Edited, with Life and Glossarial Index, by ALEXANDER SMITH.
COWPER.—POETICAL WORKS. Edited by the Rev. W. BENHAM, B.D.
DEFOE.—THE ADVENTURES OF ROBINSON CRUSOE. Introduction by H. KINGSLEY.
DRYDEN.—POETICAL WORKS. A Revised Text and Notes. By W. D. CHRISTIE, M.A.
FROISSART'S CHRONICLES. Transl. by Lord BERNERS. Ed. by G. C. MACAULAY, M.A.
GOLDSMITH. — MISCELLANEOUS WORKS. Edited by Prof. MASSON.
HORACE.—WORKS. Rendered into English Prose by JAMES LONSDALE and S. LEE.
MALORY.—LE MORTE D'ARTHUR. Sir Thos. Malory's Book of King Arthur and of his Noble Knights of the Round Table. The Edition of Caxton, revised for modern use. By Sir E. STRACHEY, Bart.
MILTON.—POETICAL WORKS. Edited, with Introductions, by Prof. MASSON.
POPE.—POETICAL WORKS. Edited, with Memoir and Notes, by Prof. WARD.
SCOTT.—POETICAL WORKS. With Essay by Prof. PALGRAVE.
SHAKESPEARE.—COMPLETE WORKS. Edit. by W. G. CLARK and W. ALDIS WRIGHT. *India Paper Edition.* Cr. 8vo, cloth extra, gilt edges. 10s. 6d. net.
SPENSER.—COMPLETE WORKS Edited by R. MORRIS. Memoir by J. W. HALES, M.A.
VIRGIL.—WORKS. Rendered into English Prose by JAMES LONSDALE and S. LEE.

GOETHE. — MAXIMS AND REFLECTIONS. Trans. by T. B. SAUNDERS. Gl. 8vo. 5s.
—— NATURE APHORISMS. Transl. by T. B. SAUNDERS. Pott 8vo 6d. net.

GOLDEN TREASURY SERIES.—Uniformly printed in Pott 8vo, with Vignette Titles by Sir J. E. MILLAIS, Sir NOEL PATON, T. WOOLNER W. HOLMAN HUNT, ARTHUR HUGHES, etc. 2s. 6d. net each.
GOLDEN TREASURY OF THE BEST SONGS AND LYRICAL POEMS IN THE ENGLISH LANGUAGE, THE. Selected and arranged, with Notes, by Prof. F T. PALGRAVE.—Large Type. Cr. 8vo. 10s. 6d.—Large Paper Edition. 8vo. 10s. 6d. net
LYRIC LOVE: An Anthology. Edited by W. WATSON.
CHILDREN'S GARLAND FROM THE BEST POETS, THE. Selected by COVENTRY PATMORE.
CHILDREN'S TREASURY OF LYRICAL POETRY. By F. T. PALGRAVE.
THE JEST BOOK. The Choicest Anecdotes and Sayings. Arranged by MARK LEMON.
FAIRY BOOK, THE: the BEST POPULAR FAIRY STORIES. Selected by Mrs. CRAIK, Author of "John Halifax, Gentleman."
BOOK OF GOLDEN THOUGHTS, A. By HENRY ATTWELL.
SUNDAY BOOK OF POETRY FOR THE YOUNG, THE. Selected by C. F. ALEXANDER.
GOLDEN TREASURY PSALTER. By Four Friends.
BOOK OF PRAISE, THE. From the Best English Hymn Writers. Selected by ROUNDELL, EARL OF SELBORNE.
THEOLOGIA GERMANICA. By S. WINKWORTH.
THE BALLAD BOOK. A Selection of the Choicest British Ballads. Edited by WILLIAM ALLINGHAM.
SONG BOOK, THE. Words and Tunes selected and arranged by JOHN HULLAH.
SCOTTISH SONG. Compiled by MARY CARLYLE AITKEN.
LA LYRE FRANÇAISE Selected and arranged, with Notes, by G. MASSON.
BALLADEN UND ROMANZEN. Being a Selection of the best German Ballads and Romances. Edited, with Introduction and Notes, by Dr. BUCHHEIM.
DEUTSCHE LYRIK. The Golden Treasury of the best German Lyrical Poems. Selected by Dr. BUCHHEIM.
MATTHEW ARNOLD.—SELECTED POEMS.
ADDISON.—ESSAYS. Chosen and Edited by JOHN RICHARD GREEN
BACON.—ESSAYS, and COLOURS OF GOOD AND EVIL. With Notes and Glossarial Index by W. ALDIS WRIGHT, M.A.—Large Paper Edition. 8vo. 10s. 6d net.
BROWNE, SIR THOMAS.—RELIGIO MEDICI, LETTER TO A FRIEND, &c., AND CHRISTIAN MORALS. Ed. by W. A. GREENHILL.
— HYDRIOTAPHIA AND THE GARDEN OF CYRUS. Ed. by W. A. GREENHILL.
BUNYAN.—THE PILGRIM'S PROGRESS FROM THIS WORLD TO THAT WHICH IS TO COME. —Large Paper Edition. 8vo. 10s. 6d. net.
BYRON.—POETRY. Chosen and arranged by M. ARNOLD.—Large Paper Edit. 9s.
CLOUGH.—SELECTIONS FROM THE POEMS.
COWPER.—LETTERS. Edited, with Introduction. by Rev. W. BENHAM.
— SELECTIONS FROM POEMS. With an Introduction by Mrs. OLIPHANT.
DEFOE.—THE ADVENTURES OF ROBINSON CRUSOE. Edited by J. W. CLARK, M.A.
GRACIAN (BALTHASAR).—ART OF WORLDLY WISDOM. Translated by J. JACOBS.

LITERATURE.
Collected Works; Essays; Lectures; Letters; Miscellaneous Works—*contd.*

GOLDEN TREASURY SERIES—*contd.*

HERRICK.—CHRYSOMELA. Edited by Prof. F. T. PALGRAVE.

HUGHES.—TOM BROWN'S SCHOOL DAYS.

KEATS.—THE POETICAL WORKS. Edited by Prof. F. T. PALGRAVE.

KEBLE.—THE CHRISTIAN YEAR. Edit. by C. M. YONGE.

LAMB.—TALES FROM SHAKSPEARE. Edited by Rev. ALFRED AINGER, M.A.

LANDOR.—SELECTIONS. Ed. by S. COLVIN.

LONGFELLOW. — BALLADS, LYRICS, AND SONNETS.

MOHAMMAD.—SPEECHES AND TABLE-TALK. Translated by STANLEY LANE-POOLE.

NEWCASTLE.—THE CAVALIER AND HIS LADY. Selections from the Works of the First Duke and Duchess of Newcastle. With Introductory Essay by E. JENKINS.

PLATO.—THE REPUBLIC. Translated by J. LL. DAVIES, M.A., and D. J. VAUGHAN. —Large Paper Edition. 8vo. 10s. 6d. net.

— THE TRIAL AND DEATH OF SOCRATES. Being the Euthyphron, Apology, Crito and Phaedo of Plato. Trans. by F. J. CHURCH.

— THE PHAEDRUS, LYSIS, AND PROTAGORAS. Translated by J. WRIGHT.

SHAKESPEARE.—SONGS AND SONNETS. Ed. with Notes, by Prof. F. T. PALGRAVE.

SHELLEY.—POEMS. Edited by STOPFORD A. BROOKE.—Large Paper Edit. 12s. 6d.

SOUTHEY.—POEMS. Chosen and Arranged by E. DOWDEN.

THEOCRITUS, BION, AND MOSCHUS. Rendered into English Prose by ANDREW LANG.—Large Paper Edition. 9s.

WHITTIER.—POEMS, RELIGIOUS AND DEVOTIONAL.

WORDSWORTH.—POEMS. Chosen and Edited by M. ARNOLD.—Large Paper Edition. 10s. 6d. net.

YONGE.—A BOOK OF GOLDEN DEEDS.

— A BOOK OF WORTHIES.

— THE STORY OF THE CHRISTIANS AND MOORS IN SPAIN.

HARE.—GUESSES AT TRUTH. By Two Brothers. 4s. 6d.

LONGFELLOW.—POEMS OF PLACES: ENGLAND AND WALES. Edited by H. W. LONGFELLOW. 2 vols. 9s.

TENNYSON.—LYRICAL POEMS. Selected and Annotated by Prof. F. T. PALGRAVE. 4s. 6d. —Large Paper Edition. 9s.

— IN MEMORIAM. 4s. 6d.—Large Paper Edition. 9s.

GOLDSMITH, ESSAYS OF. Edited by C. D. YONGE, M.A. Fcp. 8vo. 2s. 6d. (*See also* GLOBE LIBRARY, p. 25; ILLUSTRATED BOOKS, p. 14.)

GRAY (Asa).—LETTERS. Edited by J. L. GRAY. 2 vols. Cr. 8vo. 15s. net.

GRAY (Thomas).—WORKS. Edited by EDMUND GOSSE. In 4 vols. Gl. 8vo. 5s. each.— Vol. I. POEMS, JOURNALS, AND ESSAYS.— II. LETTERS.—III. LETTERS.—IV. NOTES ON ARISTOPHANES AND PLATO.

GREEN (J. R.).—STRAY STUDIES FROM ENGLAND AND ITALY. Globe 8vo. 5s.

GREENWOOD (F.).—THE LOVER'S LEXICON. Cr. 8vo. 6s.

HAMERTON (P. G.).—THE INTELLECTUAL LIFE. Cr. 8vo. 10s. 6d.

— HUMAN INTERCOURSE. Cr. 8vo. 8s. 6d.

— FRENCH AND ENGLISH: A Comparison. Cr. 8vo. 10s. 6d.

HARRISON (Frederic).—THE CHOICE OF BOOKS. Gl. 8vo. 6s.—Large Paper Ed. 15s.

HELPS (Sir Arthur).—ESSAYS WRITTEN IN THE INTERVALS OF BUSINESS. With Introduction and Notes, by F. J. ROWE, M.A., and W. T. WEBB, M.A. 1s. 9d.; swd. 1s. 6d.

HOBART (Lord).—ESSAYS AND MISCELLANEOUS WRITINGS. With Biographical Sketch. Ed. Lady HOBART. 2 vols. 8vo. 25s.

HUTTON (R. H.).—ESSAYS ON SOME OF THE MODERN GUIDES OF ENGLISH THOUGHT IN MATTERS OF FAITH. Globe 8vo. 5s.

— ESSAYS. 2 vols. Gl. 8vo 5s. each.—Vol. I. LITERARY; II. THEOLOGICAL.

— CRITICISMS ON CONTEMPORARY THOUGHT AND THINKERS. 2 vols. Gl. 8vo. 10s.

HUXLEY (Prof. T. H.).—COLLECTED ESSAYS. Gl. 8vo. 5s. each.—I. METHOD AND RESULTS.—II. DARWINIANA.—III. SCIENCE AND EDUCATION.—IV. SCIENCE AND HEBREW TRADITION.—V. SCIENCE AND CHRISTIAN TRADITION.—VI. HUME.—VII. MAN'S PLACE IN NATURE.—VIII. DISCOURSES, BIOLOGICAL AND GEOLOGICAL.—IX. EVOLUTION AND ETHICS, ETC.

— LAY SERMONS, ADDRESSES, AND REVIEWS. 8vo. 7s. 6d.

— CRITIQUES AND ADDRESSES. 8vo. 10s. 6d.

— AMERICAN ADDRESSES, WITH A LECTURE ON THE STUDY OF BIOLOGY. 8vo. 6s. 6d.

— SCIENCE AND CULTURE, AND OTHER ESSAYS. 8vo. 10s. 6d.

— INTRODUCTORY SCIENCE PRIMER. Pott 8vo. 1s.

— ESSAYS UPON SOME CONTROVERTED QUESTIONS. 8vo. 14s.

IRELAND (A.).—THE BOOK-LOVER'S ENCHIRIDION. Fcp. 8vo. 7s.; vellum, 10s. 6d.

JAMES (Henry).—FRENCH POETS AND NOVELISTS. New Edition. Gl. 8vo. 5s.

— PORTRAITS OF PLACES. Cr. 8vo. 7s. 6d.

— PARTIAL PORTRAITS. Gl. 8vo. 5s.

JEBB (R. C.).—GROWTH AND INFLUENCE OF CLASSICAL GREEK POETRY. Cr. 8vo. 7s. net.

JOCELINE (E.). THE MOTHER'S LEGACIE TO HER UNBORN CHILD. Cr. 16mo. 4s. 6d.

JONES (H. A.).—THE RENASCENCE OF THE ENGLISH DRAMA. Cr. 8vo. 6s.

KEATS.—LETTERS. Edited by SIDNEY COLVIN. Globe 8vo. 5s.

KINGSLEY (Charles).—COMPLETE EDITION OF THE WORKS OF CHARLES KINGSLEY. Cr. 8vo. 3s. 6d. each.

WESTWARD HO! With a Portrait.

HYPATIA. | YEAST.

ALTON LOCKE. | TWO YEARS AGO.

HEREWARD THE WAKE.

POEMS.

THE HEROES; or, Greek Fairy Tales for my Children.

THE WATER BABIES: A Fairy Tale for a Land Baby.

KINGSLEY (C.). — COMPLETE EDITION—*continued*.
MADAM HOW AND LADY WHY; or, First Lesson in Earth-Lore for Children.
AT LAST: A Christmas in the West Indies.
PROSE IDYLLS.
PLAYS AND PURITANS.
THE ROMAN AND THE TEUTON. With Preface by Professor MAX MÜLLER.
SANITARY AND SOCIAL LECTURES.
HISTORICAL LECTURES AND ESSAYS.
SCIENTIFIC LECTURES AND ESSAYS.
LITERARY AND GENERAL LECTURES.
THE HERMITS
GLAUCUS; or, The Wonders of the Sea-Shore. With Coloured Illustrations.
VILLAGE AND TOWN AND COUNTRY SERMONS.
THE WATER OF LIFE, AND OTHER SERMONS.
SERMONS ON NATIONAL SUBJECTS: AND THE KING OF THE EARTH.
SERMONS FOR THE TIMES.
GOOD NEWS OF GOD.
THE GOSPEL OF THE PENTATEUCH: AND DAVID.
DISCIPLINE, AND OTHER SERMONS.
WESTMINSTER SERMONS.
ALL SAINTS' DAY, AND OTHER SERMONS.
—— *Pocket Edition.* Pott 8vo. 1s. 6d. each.
—HYPATIA.—ALTON LOCKE.—WESTWARD HO! 2 vols.—HEREWARD THE WAKE.—TWO YEARS AGO. 2 vols.—YEAST.—WATER BABIES.—HEROES.

KIPLING (Rudyard).—A BIRTHDAY BOOK. Selections from Writings. Illust. 16mo. 2s. 6d.

LAMB (Charles).—COLLECTED WORKS. Ed., with Introduction and Notes, by the Rev. ALFRED AINGER, M.A. Globe 8vo. 5s. each volume.—I. ESSAYS OF ELIA.—II. PLAYS, POEMS, AND MISCELLANEOUS ESSAYS.—III. MRS. LEICESTER'S SCHOOL; THE ADVENTURES OF ULYSSES; AND OTHER ESSAYS.—IV. TALES FROM SHAKESPEARE.—V. and VI. LETTERS. Newly arranged, with additions.
—— TALES FROM SHAKESPEARE. Pott 8vo. 2s. 6d. net.
—— ESSAYS OF ELIA. Edit. by N. L. HALLWARD, M.A. and S. C. HILL, B.A. Gl. 8vo. 3s.; sewed, 2s. 6d.

LANKESTER (Prof. E. Ray).—THE ADVANCEMENT OF SCIENCE. Occasional Essays and Addresses. 8vo. 10s. 6d.

LAWTON (W. C.).—ART AND HUMANITY IN HOMER. Pott 8vo. 3s.

LESLIE (G. D.).—LETTERS TO MARCO. Ex. cr. 8vo. 7s. 6d.
—— RIVERSIDE LETTERS. Ex. cr. 8vo. 7s. 6d.

LETTERS FROM SOUTH AFRICA. Reprinted from the *Times.* Cr. 8vo. 2s. 6d.

LETTERS FROM QUEENSLAND. Reprinted from the *Times.* Cr. 8vo. 2s. 6d.

LODGE (Prof. Oliver).—THE PIONEERS OF SCIENCE. Illustrated. Ext. cr. 8vo. 7s. 6d.

LOWELL (Jas. Russell).—COMPLETE WORKS. 10 vols. Cr. 8vo. 6s. each.—Vols. I.—IV. LITERARY ESSAYS.—V. POLITICAL ESSAYS.—VI. LITERARY AND POLITICAL ADDRESSES. VII.—X. POETICAL WORKS.
—— POLITICAL ESSAYS. Ext. cr. 8vo. 7s. 6d.
—— LATEST LITERARY ESSAYS. Cr. 8vo. 6s.

LUBBOCK (Rt. Hon. Sir John, Bart.).—SCIENTIFIC LECTURES. Illustrated. 2nd Edit. revised. 8vo. 8s. 6d.

LUBBOCK (Rt. Hon. Sir John, Bart.).—POLITICAL AND EDUCATIONAL ADDRESSES. 8vo. 8s. 6d.
—— FIFTY YEARS OF SCIENCE: Address to the British Association, 1881. Cr. 8vo. 2s. 6d.
—— THE PLEASURES OF LIFE. New Edit. Gl. 8vo. Part I. 1s. 6d.; swd. 1s.— Part II. 1s. 6d.; sewed, 1s.—Complete in 1 vol. 2s. 6d.
—— THE BEAUTIES OF NATURE. Cr. 8vo. 6s.
—— —— Without Illustrations. Cr. 8vo. 1s. 6d.; sewed, 1s.
—— THE USE OF LIFE. Globe 8vo. 3s. 6d.; Cheap Edition, 1s. 6d.; sewed, 1s.

LYTTELTON (E.).—MOTHERS AND SONS. Cr. 8vo. 2s. 6d.

MACAULAY.—ESSAY ON WARREN HASTINGS. Ed. by K. DEIGHTON. Gl. 8vo. 2s. 6d.
—— ESSAY ON LORD CLIVE. By the same. 2s.
—— ESSAY ON ADDISON. Edited by J. W. HALES. Globe 8vo. [*In the Press.*
—— BOSWELL'S LIFE OF JOHNSON. Edit. by R. F. WINCH. Gl. 8vo. 2s. 6d.

MACMILLAN (Rev. Hugh).—ROMAN MOSAICS, or, Studies in Rome and its Neighbourhood. Globe 8vo. 6s.

MAHAFFY (Prof. J. P.).—THE PRINCIPLES OF THE ART OF CONVERSATION. Cr. 8vo. 4s. 6d.

MAURICE (F. D.).—THE FRIENDSHIP OF BOOKS: and other Lectures. Cr. 8vo. 3s. 6d.

MILTON.—TRACTATE OF EDUCATION. Ed. by E. E. MORRIS. Gl. 8vo. 1s. 9d.

MORLEY (John).—WORKS. Collected Edit. In 11 vols. Globe 8vo. 5s. each.—VOLTAIRE. 1 vol.—ROUSSEAU. 2 vols.—DIDEROT AND THE ENCYCLOPÆDISTS. 2 vols.—ON COMPROMISE. 1 vol.—MISCELLANIES. 3 vols.—BURKE. 1 vol.—STUDIES IN LITERATURE. 1 vol.

MYERS (F. W. H.).—ESSAYS. 2 vols. Cr. 8vo. 4s. 6d. each.—I. CLASSICAL; II. MODERN.
—— SCIENCE AND A FUTURE LIFE. Gl. 8vo. 5s.

NADAL (E. S.).—ESSAYS AT HOME AND ELSEWHERE. Cr. 8vo. 6s.

OLIPHANT (T. L. Kington).—THE DUKE AND THE SCHOLAR: and other Essays. 8vo. 7s. 6d.

OWENS COLLEGE ESSAYS AND ADDRESSES. By Professors and Lecturers of the College. 8vo. 14s.

PATER (W.).—THE RENAISSANCE; Studies in Art and Poetry. 4th Ed. Cr. 8vo. 10s. 6d.
—— IMAGINARY PORTRAITS. Cr. 8vo. 6s.
—— APPRECIATIONS. With an Essay on "Style." 2nd Edit. Cr. 8vo. 8s. 6d.
—— MARIUS THE EPICUREAN. 2 vols. Cr. 8vo. 15s.
—— PLATO AND PLATONISM. Ex. cr. 8vo. 8s. 6d.
—— GREEK STUDIES. Ex. cr. 8vo. 10s. 6d.
—— MISCELLANEOUS STUDIES. Ex. cr. 8vo. 9s.

PICTON (J. A.).—THE MYSTERY OF MATTER: and other Essays. Cr. 8vo. 6s.

POLLOCK (Sir F., Bart.).—OXFORD LECTURES: and other Discourses. 8vo. 9s.

POOLE (M. E.).—PICTURES OF COTTAGE LIFE IN THE WEST OF ENGLAND. 2nd Ed. Cr. 8vo. 3s. 6d.

POPE.—ESSAY ON MAN, I.—IV. Edited by E. E. MORRIS, M.A. 1s. 9d.
—— ESSAY ON MAN. Epistle I. Gl. 8vo. 6d.

POTTER (Louisa).—LANCASHIRE MEMORIES. Cr. 8vo. 6s.

LITERATURE.
Collected Works; Essays; Lectures; Letters; Miscellaneous Works—*contd.*

POTTS (W.) — FROM A NEW ENGLAND HILLSIDE. Pott 8vo. 3s.

PRICKARD (A. O.).—ARISTOTLE ON THE ART OF POETRY. Cr. 8vo. 3s. 6d.

RUMFORD.—COMPLETE WORKS OF COUNT RUMFORD. Memoir by G. ELLIS. Portrait. 5 vols. 8vo. 4l. 14s. 6d.

SCAIFE (W. B.).—FLORENTINE LIFE DURING THE RENAISSANCE. 8vo. 6s. net.

SCIENCE LECTURES AT SOUTH KENSINGTON. Illustr. 2 vols. Cr. 8vo. 6s. each.

SMALLEY (George W.).—LONDON LETTERS AND SOME OTHERS. 2 vols. 8vo. 32s.

—— STUDIES OF MEN. Cr. 8vo. 8s. 6d. net.

SMITH (Goldwin).—ESSAYS ON QUESTIONS OF THE DAY. 2nd Ed. revised. Ex. cr. 8vo. 9s.

STEPHEN (Sir James F., Bart.).—HORAE SABBATICAE. Three Series. Gl. 8vo. 5s each.

THOREAU.—SELECTIONS FROM WRITINGS. Edited by H. S. SALT. Gl. 8vo. 5s.

THRING (Edward).—THOUGHTS ON LIFE SCIENCE. 2nd Edit. Cr. 8vo. 7s. 6d.

TREVELYAN (G. O.).—THE COMPETITION WALLAH. Cr. 8vo. 6s.

TYRRELL (R. Y.).—LATIN POETRY. Cr. 8vo. 7s net.

VAUGHAN (D. J.).—QUESTIONS OF THE DAY. Cr. 8vo. 5s.

WARD (W.).—WITNESSES TO THE UNSEEN. 8vo. 10s. 6d.

WESTCOTT (Bishop). (*See* THEOLOGY, p 45.)

WHITE (A. D.).—THE WARFARE OF SCIENCE WITH THEOLOGY IN CHRISTENDOM. 2 vols. 8vo. 21s. net.

WHITTIER (John Greenleaf). THE COMPLETE WORKS. 7 vols. Cr. 8vo. 6s. each.— Vol. I. NARRATIVE AND LEGENDARY POEMS. —II. POEMS OF NATURE; POEMS SUBJECTIVE AND REMINISCENT; RELIGIOUS POEMS. —III. ANTI-SLAVERY POEMS; SONGS OF LABOUR AND REFORM.—IV. PERSONAL POEMS; OCCASIONAL POEMS; THE TENT ON THE BEACH; with the Poems of ELIZABETH H. WHITTIER, and an Appendix containing Early and Uncollected Verses.—V. MARGARET SMITH'S JOURNAL; TALES AND SKETCHES.—VI. OLD PORTRAITS AND MODERN SKETCHES; PERSONAL SKETCHES AND TRIBUTES; HISTORICAL PAPERS.—VII. THE CONFLICT WITH SLAVERY, POLITICS, AND REFORM; THE INNER LIFE, CRITICISM.

WILSON (Dr. George).—RELIGIO CHEMICI. Cr. 8vo. 8s. 6d.

—— THE FIVE GATEWAYS OF KNOWLEDGE. 9th Edit. Ext. fcp. 8vo. 2s. 6d.

WORDSWORTH. —THE WORKS OF WILLIAM AND DOROTHY WORDSWORTH. Edited by W. KNIGHT. 16 vols. Gl. 8vo. 5s. each.

[Monthly from April, 1896.

WRIGHT (M. O.).—THE FRIENDSHIP OF NATURE. 16mo. 3s.

YONGE (Charlotte M.).—*Uniform Edition* Cr. 8vo. 3s. 6d. each.

THE HEIR OF REDCLYFFE.

HEARTSEASE. | HOPES AND FEARS

DYNEVOR TERRACE. | THE DAISY CHAIN.

THE TRIAL · More Links of the Daisy Chain.

PILLARS OF THE HOUSE. 2 vols.

THE YOUNG STEPMOTHER.

CLEVER WOMAN OF THE FAMILY.

THE THREE BRIDES.

YONGE (C. M.)—*continued.*

MY YOUNG ALCIDES. | THE CAGED LION.

THE DOVE IN THE EAGLE'S NEST.

THE CHAPLET OF PEARLS.

LADY HESTER, and THE DANVERS PAPERS.

MAGNUM BONUM. | LOVE AND LIFE.

UNKNOWN TO HISTORY. | STRAY PEARLS.

THE ARMOURER'S PRENTICES.

THE TWO SIDES OF THE SHIELD.

NUTTIE'S FATHER. | CHANTRY HOUSE.

SCENES AND CHARACTERS.

A MODERN TELEMACHUS. | BYE WORDS.

BEECHCROFT AT ROCKSTONE.

MORE BYWORDS. | A REPUTED CHANGELING.

THE LITTLE DUKE, RICHARD THE FEARLESS.

THE LANCES OF LYNWOOD.

THE PRINCE AND THE PAGE.

P's AND Q's: LITTLE LUCY'S WONDERFUL GLOBE.

THE TWO PENNILESS PRINCESSES.

AN OLD WOMAN'S OUTLOOK.

THAT STICK. | GRISLY GRISELL.

LOGIC. (*See under* PHILOSOPHY, p. 32.)

MAGAZINES. (*See* PERIODICALS, p. 31).

MAGNETISM. (*See under* PHYSICS, p. 33.)

MATHEMATICS, History of.

BALL (W. W. R.).—A SHORT ACCOUNT OF THE HISTORY OF MATHEMATICS. 2nd Ed. Cr. 8vo. 10s. net.

—— MATHEMATICAL RECREATIONS AND PROBLEMS. Cr. 8vo. 7s. net.

—— PRIMER OF HISTORY OF MATHEMATICS. Gl. 8vo. 2s. net.

—— AN ESSAY ON NEWTON'S PRINCIPIA. Cr. 8vo. 6s. net.

CAJORI (F.).—HISTORY OF MATHEMATICS. Ext. cr. 8vo. 14s. net.

KLEIN (F.).—LECTURES ON MATHEMATICS. 8vo. 6s. 6d. net.

MEDICINE.
(*See also* DOMESTIC ECONOMY; NURSING; HYGIENE; PHYSIOLOGY.)

ALLBUTT (Dr. T. Clifford).—ON THE USE OF THE OPHTHALMOSCOPE. 8vo. 15s.

—— SYSTEM OF MEDICINE. Vol. I. 8vo. 25s. net.

ALLBUTT (T. C.) and PLAYFAIR (W. S.)— SYSTEM OF GYNAECOLOGY. 8vo. [*In Press.*

ANDERSON (Dr. McCall).—LECTURES ON CLINICAL MEDICINE. Illustr. 8vo. 10s. 6d.

BALLANCE (C. A.) and EDMUNDS (Dr. W.). LIGATION IN CONTINUITY. Illustr. Roy. 8vo. 10s. net.

BARWELL (Richard, F.R.C.S.). — THE CAUSES AND TREATMENT OF LATERAL CURVATURE OF THE SPINE. Cr. 8vo. 6s.

—— ON ANEURISM, ESPECIALLY OF THE THORAX AND ROOT OF THE NECK. 3s. 6d.

BICKERTON (T. H.).—ON COLOUR BLINDNESS. Cr. 8vo.

BRAIN: A JOURNAL OF NEUROLOGY. Edited for the Neurological Society of London, by A. DE WATTEVILLE, Quarterly. 8vo. 3s. 6d. (Part I. in Jan. 1878.) Vols. 15s. each. [Cloth covers for binding, 1s. each.]

BRUNTON (Dr. T. Lauder). — A TEXT-BOOK OF PHARMACOLOGY, THERAPEUTICS, AND MATERIA MEDICA. 3rd Edit. Med. 8vo. 21s.—Or in 2 vols. 22s. 6d.

—— DISORDERS OF DIGESTION: THEIR CONSEQUENCES AND TREATMENT. 8vo. 10s. 6d.

—— PHARMACOLOGY AND THERAPEUTICS; or, Medicine Past and Present. Cr. 8vo. 6s.

BRUNTON (Dr. T. L.).—TABLES OF MATERIA MEDICA: A Companion to the Materia Medica Museum. 4to. 5s.
—— AN INTRODUCTION TO MODERN THERAPEUTICS. Croonian Lectures on the Relationship between Chemical Structure and Physiological Action. 8vo. 3s. 6d. net.
—— MODERN DEVELOPMENTS OF HARVEY'S WORK. 8vo. 2s.

BUCKNILL (Dr.).—THE CARE OF THE INSANE. Cr. 8vo. 3s. 6d.

CARTER (R. Brudenell, F.C.S.).—A PRACTICAL TREATISE ON DISEASES OF THE EYE. 8vo. 16s.
—— EYESIGHT, GOOD AND BAD. Cr. 8vo. 6s.
—— MODERN OPERATIONS FOR CATARACT. 8vo. 6s.

COWELL (George).—LECTURES ON CATARACT: ITS CAUSES, VARIETIES, AND TREATMENT. Cr. 8vo. 4s. 6d.

ECCLES (A. S.).—SCIATICA. 8vo. 3s. 6d.
—— PRACTICE OF MASSAGE. Ex. cr. 8vo. 7s. 6d. net.

FLÜCKIGER (F. A.) and HANBURY (D.).—PHARMACOGRAPHIA. A History of the Principal Drugs of Vegetable Origin met with in Great Britain and India. 8vo. 21s.

FOTHERGILL (Dr. J. Milner).—THE PRACTITIONER'S HANDBOOK OF TREATMENT; or, The Principles of Therapeutics. 8vo. 16s.
—— THE ANTAGONISM OF THERAPEUTIC AGENTS, AND WHAT IT TEACHES. Cr. 8vo. 6s.
—— FOOD FOR THE INVALID, THE CONVALESCENT, THE DYSPEPTIC, AND THE GOUTY. 2nd Edit. Cr. 8vo. 3s. 6d.

FOX (Dr. Wilson). — ON THE ARTIFICIAL PRODUCTION OF TUBERCLE IN THE LOWER ANIMALS. With Plates. 4to. 5s. 6d.
—— ON THE TREATMENT OF HYPERPYREXIA, AS ILLUSTRATED IN ACUTE ARTICULAR RHEUMATISM BY MEANS OF THE EXTERNAL APPLICATION OF COLD. 8vo. 2s. 6d.

GILLIES (H. C.).—COUNTER-IRRITATION. 8vo. 6s. net.

GRIFFITHS (W. H.).—LESSONS ON PRESCRIPTIONS AND THE ART OF PRESCRIBING. New Edition. Pott 8vo. 3s. 6d.

HAMILTON (Prof. D. J.).—ON THE PATHOLOGY OF BRONCHITIS, CATARRHAL PNEUMONIA, TUBERCLE, AND ALLIED LESIONS OF THE HUMAN LUNG. 8vo. 8s. 6d.
—— A TEXT-BOOK OF PATHOLOGY, SYSTEMATIC AND PRACTICAL. Illustrated. 8vo. Vol. I. 21s. net. Vol. II. in 2 parts. 15s. each net.

HANBURY (Daniel). — SCIENCE PAPERS, CHIEFLY PHARMACOLOGICAL AND BOTANICAL. Med. 8vo. 14s.

HAWKINS (H. P.).—DISEASES OF THE VERMIFORM APPENDIX. 8vo. 7s. net.

KAHLDEN (C.).—METHODS OF PATHOLOGICAL HISTOLOGY. Transl. by H. M. FLETCHER. 8vo. 6s.

KANTHACK (A. A.) and DRYSDALE (J. H.).—ELEMENTARY PRACTICAL BACTERIOLOGY. Cr. 8vo. 4s. 6d.

KLEIN (Dr. E.).—MICRO-ORGANISMS AND DISEASE. An Introduction into the Study of Specific Micro-Organisms. Cr. 8vo. 6s.
—— THE BACTERIA IN ASIATIC CHOLERA. Cr. 8vo. 5s.

LEPROSY INVESTIGATION COMMITTEE, JOURNAL OF THE. Edited by P. S. ABRAHAM, M.A. Nos. 2—4. 8vo. 2s. 6d. each net.
—— PRIZE ESSAYS. By E. S. EHLERS and S. P. IMPEY. 8vo. 3s. 6d. net.

LINDSAY (Dr. J. A.). — THE CLIMATIC TREATMENT OF CONSUMPTION. Cr. 8vo. 5s.

MACDONALD (G.).—DISEASES OF THE NOSE. 2nd Edit. Cr. 8vo. 10s. 6d. net.

MACLAGAN (Dr. T.).—THE GERM THEORY. 8vo. 10s. 6d.

MACLEAN (Surgeon-General W. C.).—DISEASES OF TROPICAL CLIMATES. Cr. 8vo. 10s. 6d.

MERCIER (Dr. C.).—THE NERVOUS SYSTEM AND THE MIND. 8vo. 12s. 6d.

NEWMAN (G.).—DECLINE AND EXTINCTION OF LEPROSY. 8vo. 2s. 6d. net.

PIFFARD (H. G.).—AN ELEMENTARY TREATISE ON DISEASES OF THE SKIN. 8vo. 16s.

PRACTITIONER, THE: INDEX TO VOLS. I.-L. 8vo. 10s. 6d.

REYNOLDS (Sir J. R.)—A SYSTEM OF MEDICINE. Edited by Sir J. RUSSELL REYNOLDS, Bart., M.D., In 5 vols. Vols. I.—III. and V. 8vo. 25s. each.—Vol. IV. 21s.

RICHARDSON (Dr. B. W.).—DISEASES OF MODERN LIFE. Cr. 8vo.
—— THE FIELD OF DISEASE. A Book of Preventive Medicine. 8vo. 25s.

SEATON (Dr. Edward C.).—A HANDBOOK OF VACCINATION. Ext. fcp. 8vo. 8s. 6d.

SEILER (Dr. Carl). — MICRO-PHOTOGRAPHS IN HISTOLOGY, NORMAL AND PATHOLOGICAL. 4to. 31s. 6d.

SIBSON (Dr. Francis).—COLLECTED WORKS. Edited by W. M. ORD, M.D. Illustrated. 4 vols. 8vo. 3l. 3s.

SPENDER (J. Kent).—THERAPEUTIC MEANS FOR THE RELIEF OF PAIN. 8vo. 8s. 6d.

SURGERY (THE INTERNATIONAL ENCYCLOPAEDIA OF). A Systematic Treatise on the Theory and Practice of Surgery by Authors of various Nations. Edited by JOHN ASHHURST, jun., M.D. 7 vols. Roy. 8vo. 31s. 6d. each.

THORNE (Dr. Thorne).—DIPHTHERIA. Cr. 8vo. 8s. 6d.

WHITE (Dr. W. Hale).—A TEXT-BOOK OF GENERAL THERAPEUTICS. Cr. 8vo. 8s. 6d.

WILLIAMS (C. T.).—AERO-THERAPEUTICS. 8vo. 6s. net.

ZIEGLER (Ernst).—A TEXT-BOOK OF PATHOLOGICAL ANATOMY AND PATHOGENESIS. Translated and Edited by DONALD MACALISTER, M.A., M.D. Illustrated. 8vo.—Part I. GENERAL PATHOLOGICAL ANATOMY. 12s. 6d.—Part II. SPECIAL PATHOLOGICAL ANATOMY. Sections I.—VIII. and IX.—XII. 8vo. 12s. 6d. each.

METALLURGY.
(See also CHEMISTRY.)

HIORNS (Arthur H.).—A TEXT-BOOK OF ELEMENTARY METALLURGY. 2nd Edition. Gl. 8vo. 3s.
—— PRACTICAL METALLURGY AND ASSAYING. Illustrated. 2nd Edit. Globe 8vo. 6s.

METALLURGY—*continued.*

HIORNS (A. H.).—MIXED METALS OR ME-
TALLIC ALLOYS Globe 8vo. 6s.
—— IRON AND STEEL MANUFACTURE. Illus-
trated. Globe 8vo. 3s. 6d.
—— METAL COLOURING AND BRONZING.
Globe 8vo. 5s.
—— PRINCIPLES OF METALLURGY. Gl. 8vo. 6s.
—— QUESTIONS ON METALLURGY. Gl. 8vo,
sewed. 1s.

PHILLIPS (J. A.).—A TREATISE ON ORE
DEPOSITS. Illustrated.
[*New edition in preparation.*

METAPHYSICS.

(*See under* PHILOSOPHY, p. 32.)

MILITARY ART AND HISTORY.

AITKEN (Sir W.).—THE GROWTH OF THE
RECRUIT AND YOUNG SOLDIER. Cr.8vo. 8s.6d.

CUNYNGHAME (Gen. Sir A. T.).—MY
COMMAND IN SOUTH AFRICA, 1874—78.
8vo. 12s. 6d.

DILKE (Sir C) and WILKINSON (S.).—IM-
PERIAL DEFENCE. Cr. 8vo. 3s. 6d.

FORTESCUE (J. W.). — HISTORY OF THE
17TH LANCERS. Roy. 8vo. 25s. net.

HOZIER (Lieut.-Col. H. M.).—THE SEVEN
WEEKS' WAR. 2rd Edit. Cr. 8vo. 6s.
—— THE INVASIONS OF ENGLAND. 2 vols.
8vo. 28s.

MARTEL (Chas.).—MILITARY ITALY. With
Map. 8vo. 12s. 6d.

MAURICE (Maj.-Gen.).—WAR. 8vo. 5s. net.
—— THE NATIONAL DEFENCES. Cr. 8vo.

MERCUR (Prof. J.).—ELEMENTS OF THE
ART OF WAR. 8vo. 17s.

MOLYNEUX (W. C. F.).—CAMPAIGNING IN
SOUTH AFRICA AND EGYPT. 8vo. 10s. net.

SCRATCHLEY — KINLOCH COOKE. —
AUSTRALIAN DEFENCES AND NEW GUINEA.
Compiled from the Papers of the late Major-
General Sir PETER SCRATCHLEY, R.E., by
C. KINLOCH COOKE. 8vo. 14s.

THROUGH THE RANKS TO A COM-
MISSION. New Edition. Cr. 8vo. 2s. 6d.

WINGATE (Major F. R.).—MAHDIISM AND
THE EGYPTIAN SUDAN. An Account of the
Rise and Progress of Mahdiism, and of Sub-
sequent Events in the Sudan to the Present
Time. With 17 Maps. 8vo. 30s. net.

WOLSELEY (General Viscount).—THE SOL-
DIER'S POCKET-BOOK FOR FIELD SERVICE.
5th Edit. 16mo, roan. 5s.
—— FIELD POCKET-BOOK FOR THE AUXILIARY
FORCES. 16mo. 1s. 6d.

YOUNGHUSBAND (G. J. and F. E.).—
RELIEF OF CHITRAL. 8vo. 8s. 6d. net.

MINERALOGY. (*See* GEOLOGY.)

MISCELLANEOUS WORKS.

(*See under* LITERATURE, p. 24.)

MUSIC.

CHAPPELL (W.).—OLD ENGLISH POPULAR
MUSIC. 2 vols. 4to. 42s. net.—*Edition de
Luxe.* 4to. 84s. net.

FAY (Amy).—MUSIC-STUDY IN GERMANY.
Preface by Sir GEO. GROVE. Cr.8vo. 4s.6d.

GROVE (Sir George).—A DICTIONARY OF
MUSIC AND MUSICIANS, A.D. 1450—1889.
Edited by Sir GEORGE GROVE, D.C.L. In
4 vols. 8vo. 21s. each. With Illustrations in
Music Type and Woodcut.—Also published
in Parts. Parts I.—XIV., XIX.—XXII
3s. 6d. each; XV. XVI. 7s.; XVII. XVIII.
7s.; XXIII.—XXV. Appendix, Edited by
J. A. FULLER MAITLAND, M.A. 9s. [Cloth
cases for binding the volumes, 1s. each.]
—— A COMPLETE INDEX TO THE ABOVE. By
Mrs. E. WODEHOUSE. 8vo. 7s. 6d.

HULLAH (John).—MUSIC IN THE HOUSE.
4th Edit. Cr. 8vo. 2s. 6d.

TAYLOR (Franklin).—A PRIMER OF PIANO-
FORTE PLAYING. Pott 8vo. 1s.

TAYLOR (Sedley).—SOUND AND MUSIC. 3rd
Edit. Ext. cr. 8vo. 8s. 6d.
—— A SYSTEM OF SIGHT-SINGING FROM THE
ESTABLISHED MUSICAL NOTATION. 8vo.
5s. net.
—— RECORD OF THE CAMBRIDGE CENTENARY
OF W. A. MOZART. Cr. 8vo. 2s. 6d. net.

NATURAL HISTORY.

ATKINSON (J. C.) (*See* ANTIQUITIES, p. 1.)

BADENOCH (L. N.).—ROMANCE OF INSECT
WORLD. Cr. 8vo. 6s.

BAKER (Sir Samuel W.) (*See* SPORT, p. 37.)

BLANFORD (W. T.). — GEOLOGY AND
ZOOLOGY OF ABYSSINIA. 8vo. 21s.

CAMBRIDGE NATURAL HISTORY,
THE. Edit. by J. W. CLARK, S. F. HAR-
MER, and A. E. SHIPLEY. 8vo. Vol. III.
MOLLUSCS AND BRACHIOPODS. By Rev.
A. H. COOKE. 17s. net. Vol. V. PERIPATUS,
MYRIAPODS, INSECTS. By A. SEDGWICK,
F. G. SINCLAIR, and D. SHARP. 17s. net.

FOWLER (W. W.).—TALES OF THE BIRDS.
Illustrated. Cr. 8vo. 3s. 6d.
—— A YEAR WITH THE BIRDS. Illustrated.
Cr. 8vo. 3s. 6d.
—— SUMMER STUDIES OF BIRDS AND BOOKS.
Cr. 8vo. 6s.

HEADLEY (F. W)—STRUCTURE AND LIFE
OF BIRDS. Cr. 8vo. 7s. 6d.

KINGSLEY (Charles).—MADAM HOW AND
LADY WHY; or, First Lessons in Earth-Lore
for Children. Cr. 8vo. 3s. 6d.
—— GLAUCUS; or, The Wonders of the Sea-
Shore. With Coloured Illustrations. Cr.
8vo. 3s. 6d.—*Presentation Edition.* Cr.
8vo, extra cloth. 7s. 6d.

KLEIN (E.).—ETIOLOGY AND PATHOLOGY
OF GROUSE DISEASE. 8vo. 7s. net.

MEYRICK (E.). — HANDBOOK OF BRITISH
LEPIDOPTERA. Ex. cr. 8vo. 10s. 6d. net.

MIALL (L. C.).—NATURAL HISTORY OF
AQUATIC INSECTS. Cr. 8vo. 6s.

WALLACE (Alfred Russel).—THE MALAY
ARCHIPELAGO: The Land of the Orang
Utang and the Bird of Paradise. Maps and
Illustr. Ext. cr. 8vo. 6s. (*See also* BIOLOGY.)

WATERTON (Charles).—WANDERINGS IN
SOUTH AMERICA, THE NORTH-WEST OF
THE UNITED STATES, AND THE ANTILLES.
Edited by Rev. J. G. WOOD. Illustrated.
Cr. 8vo. 6s.—*People's Edition.* 4to. 6d.

WHITE (Gilbert).—NATURAL HISTORY AND ANTIQUITIES OF SELBORNE. Ed. by FRANK BUCKLAND. With a Chapter on Antiquities by the EARL OF SELBORNE. Cr. 8vo. 6s.
—— Edited by J. BURROUGHS. 2 vols. Cr. 8vo. 10s. 6d

WRIGHT (M. O.).—BIRDCRAFT. Ex. cr. 8vo. 12s. 6d. net.

NATURAL PHILOSOPHY. (See PHYSICS.)

NAVAL SCIENCE AND HISTORY.

DELBOS (L.).—LECTURES MARITIMES. Cr. 8vo. 2s. net.
—— SEA STORIES FOR FRENCH COMPOSITION. Fcp. 8vo. 2s. net.

FLAGG (A. T.).—PRIMER OF NAVIGATION. Pott 8vo. 1s.

GOW (W.).—MARINE INSURANCE. Globe 8vo. 4s. 6d.

KELVIN (Lord).—POPULAR LECTURES AND ADDRESSES.—Vol. III. NAVIGATION. Cr. 8vo. 7s. 6d.

NORWAY (A. H.).—HISTORY OF THE POST OFFICE PACKET SERVICE, 1793—1815. Illustrated. Cr. 8vo. 8s. 6d. net.

ROBINSON (Rev. J. L.).—ELEMENTS OF MARINE SURVEYING. For Junior Naval Officers. Illustrated. 2nd Edit. Cr. 8vo. 7s. 6d.

SHORTLAND (Admiral).—NAUTICAL SURVEYING. 8vo. 21s.

WILLIAMS (H.)—BRITAIN'S NAVAL POWER. Cr. 8vo. 4s. 6d. net.

NOVELS. (See PROSE FICTION, p. 21.)

NURSING.

(See under DOMESTIC ECONOMY, p. 9.)

OPTICS (or LIGHT). (See PHYSICS, p. 34.)

PAINTING. (See ART, p. 2.)

PATHOLOGY. (See MEDICINE, p. 28.)

PERIODICALS.

AMERICAN HISTORICAL REVIEW. (See HISTORY.)

AMERICAN JOURNAL OF PHILOLOGY, THE. (See PHILOLOGY.)

BRAIN. (See MEDICINE.)

CANTERBURY DIOCESAN GAZETTE. Monthly. 8vo. 2d.

CENTURY MAGAZINE. Monthly. 8vo. 1s. 4d

ECONOMIC JOURNAL, THE. (See POLITICAL ECONOMY.)

ECONOMICS, THE QUARTERLY JOURNAL OF. (See POLITICAL ECONOMY.)

HELLENIC STUDIES, THE JOURNAL OF. Published Half-Yearly from 1880. 8vo. 30s.; or Quarterly Parts, 15s. net.
The Journal will be sold at a reduced price to Libraries wishing to subscribe, but official application must in each case be made to the Council. Information on this point, and upon the conditions of Membership, may be obtained on application to the Hon. Sec., Mr. George Macmillan, 29, Bedford Street, Covent Garden.

JEWISH QUARTERLY REVIEW. Edited by I. ABRAHAMS and C. G. MONTEFIORE. 8vo. 3s. 6d.

LEPROSY INVESTIGATION COMMITTEE, JOURNAL OF. (See MEDICINE.)

MACMILLAN'S MAGAZINE. Published Monthly. 1s.—Half-Yearly Vols. 7s. 6d. each. [Cloth covers for binding, 1s. each.]

MATHEMATICAL GAZETTE, THE. (See MATHEMATICS.)

NATURE: A WEEKLY ILLUSTRATED JOURNAL OF SCIENCE. Published every Thursday. Price 6d. Monthly Parts, 2s. and 2s. 6d.; Current Half-yearly vols., 15s. each. [Cases for binding vols. 1s. 6d. each.]

PHILOLOGY, THE JOURNAL OF. (See PHILOLOGY.)

PHYSICAL REVIEW, THE. (See PHYSICS.)

PSYCHOLOGICAL REVIEW, THE. (See PSYCHOLOGY.)

RECORD OF TECHNICAL AND SECONDARY EDUCATION. (See EDUCATION, p. 10.)

ST. NICHOLAS MAGAZINE. Monthly. 8vo. 1s.

PHILOLOGY.

AMERICAN JOURNAL OF PHILOLOGY, THE. Edited by Prof. BASIL L. GILDERSLEEVE. 4s. 6d. each No. (quarterly).

CORNELL UNIVERSITY STUDIES IN CLASSICAL PHILOLOGY. Edited by I. FLAGG, W. G. HALE, and B. I. WHEELER. I. THE C U M-CONSTRUCTIONS: their History and Functions. Part I. Critical. 1s. 8d. oet Part II. Constructive By W. G. HALE. 2s. 4d. net.—II. ANALOGY AND THE SCOPE OF ITS APPLICATION IN LANGUAGE. By B. I. WHEELER 1s. 3d. net.

EMERSON (O. F.).—HISTORY OF THE ENGLISH LANGUAGE. Cr. 8vo. 6s. net.

GILES (P.).—A MANUAL OF COMPARATIVE PHILOLOGY FOR CLASSICAL STUDENTS. Cr. 8vo. 10s. 6d.

JOURNAL OF SACRED AND CLASSICAL PHILOLOGY. 4 vols. 8vo. 12s. 6d. each.

JOURNAL OF PHILOLOGY. New Series. Edited by W. A. WRIGHT M.A., I. BYWATER, M.A., and H. JACKSON, M.A. 4s. 6d. each No. (half-yearly).

KELLNER (Dr. L.). — HISTORICAL OUTLINES IN ENGLISH SYNTAX. Revised by L. KELLNER and H. BRADLEY. Globe 8vo. 6s.

MACLEAN (G. E.).—AN OLD AND MIDDLE ENGLISH READER. Cr. 8vo. 8s. net.

MORRIS (Rev. Richard, LL.D.).—PRIMER OF ENGLISH GRAMMAR. Pott 8vo. 1s.
—— ELEMENTARY LESSONS IN HISTORICAL ENGLISH GRAMMAR. Pott 8vo. 2s. 6d.
—— HISTORICAL OUTLINES OF ENGLISH ACCIDENCE. Revised by L. KELLNER and H. BRADLEY. Gl 8vo. 6s.

MORRIS (R.) and BOWEN (H. C.).—ENGLISH GRAMMAR EXERCISES. Pott 8vo. 1s.

OLIPHANT (T. L. Kington). — THE OLD AND MIDDLE ENGLISH. Globe 8vo. 9s.
—— THE NEW ENGLISH. 2 vols. Cr. 8vo. 21s.

PEILE (John). — A PRIMER OF PHILOLOGY. Pott 8vo. 1s.

PELLISSIER (E.).—FRENCH ROOTS AND THEIR FAMILIES. Globe 8vo. 6s.

TAYLOR (Isaac).—WORDS AND PLACES. 9th Edit. Maps. Globe 8vo. 6s.

—— ETRUSCAN RESEARCHES. 8vo. 14s.

—— GREEKS AND GOTHS: A Study of the Runes. 8vo. 9s.

WETHERELL (J.).—EXERCISES ON MOR-RIS'S PRIMER OF ENGLISH GRAMMAR. Pott 8vo. 1s.

YONGE (C. M.).—HISTORY OF CHRISTIAN NAMES. New Edit., revised. Cr. 8vo. 7s. 6d.

PHILOSOPHY.
Ethics and Metaphysics—Logic—Psychology.

Ethics and Metaphysics.

BIRKS (Thomas Rawson).—FIRST PRINCIPLES OF MORAL SCIENCE. Cr. 8vo. 8s. 6d.

—— MODERN UTILITARIANISM; or, The Systems of Paley, Bentham, and Mill Examined and Compared. Cr. 8vo. 6s. 6d.

—— MODERN PHYSICAL FATALISM, AND THE DOCTRINE OF EVOLUTION. Including an Examination of Mr. Herbert Spencer's "First Principles." Cr. 8vo. 6s.

CALDERWOOD (Prof. H.).—A HANDBOOK OF MORAL PHILOSOPHY. Cr. 8vo. 6s.

D'ARCY (C. F.).—SHORT STUDY OF ETHICS. Cr. 8vo. 5s. net.

DEUSSEN (P.)—ELEMENTS OF METAPHY-SICS. Cr. 8vo. 6s.

FISKE (John).—OUTLINES OF COSMIC PHILO-SOPHY, BASED ON THE DOCTRINE OF EVOLU-TION. 2 vols. 8vo. 25s.

FOWLER (Rev. Thomas). — PROGRESSIVE MORALITY: An Essay in Ethics. 2nd Edit. Cr. 8vo. 3s net.

HILL (D. J.).—GENETIC PHILOSOPHY. Cr. 8vo. 7s. net.

HUXLEY (Prof. T. H.).—EVOLUTION AND ETHICS. 8vo. 2s. net.

KANT.—KANT'S CRITICAL PHILOSOPHY FOR ENGLISH READERS. By J. P. MAHAFFY, D.D., and J. H. BERNARD, B.D. 2 vols. Cr. 8vo.—Vol. I. THE KRITIK OF PURE REASON EXPLAINED AND DEFENDED. 7s. 6d. —Vol. II. THE PROLEGOMENA. Translated, with Notes and Appendices. 6s.

—— KRITIK OF JUDGMENT. Translated by J. H. BERNARD, D.D. 8vo. 10s. net.

KANT—MAX MÜLLER. — CRITIQUE OF PURE REASON BY IMMANUEL KANT. Trans-lated by F. MAX MÜLLER. With Intro-duction by LUDWIG NOIRÉ. 2 vols. 8vo. 16s. each (sold separately).—Vol. I. HIS-TORICAL INTRODUCTION, by LUDWIG NOIRÉ, etc.—Vol. II. CRITIQUE OF PURE REASON.

KNIGHT (W. A.).—ASPECTS OF THEISM. 8vo. 8s. 6d.

MARSHALL (H. R.). — PAIN, PLEASURE, AND AESTHETICS. 8vo. 8s. 6d. net.

—— AESTHETIC PRINCIPLES. Cr. 8vo. 5s. net.

MAURICE (F. D.).—MORAL AND META-PHYSICAL PHILOSOPHY. 2 vols. 8vo. 16s.

McCOSH (Rev. Dr. James).—THE METHOD OF THE DIVINE GOVERNMENT, PHYSICAL AND MORAL. 8vo. 10s. 6d.

—— THE SUPERNATURAL IN RELATION TO THE NATURAL. Cr. 8vo. 7s. 6d.

—— INTUITIONS OF THE MIND. 8vo. 10s. 6d.

—— AN EXAMINATION OF MR. J. S. MILL'S PHILOSOPHY. 8vo. 10s. 6d.

—— CHRISTIANITY AND POSITIVISM. Lec-tures on Natural Theology and Apologetics. Cr 8vo. 7s. 6d.

—— THE SCOTTISH PHILOSOPHY FROM HUT-CHESON TO HAMILTON, BIOGRAPHICAL, EX-POSITORY, CRITICAL. Roy. 8vo. 16s.

—— REALISTIC PHILOSOPHY DEFENDED IN A PHILOSOPHIC SERIES. 2 vols. — Vol. I. EXPOSITORY. Vol. II. HISTORICAL AND CRITICAL. Cr. 8vo. 14s.

—— FIRST AND FUNDAMENTAL TRUTHS. Being a Treatise on Metaphysics. 8vo. 9s.

—— THE PREVAILING TYPES OF PHILOSOPHY: CAN THEY LOGICALLY REACH REALITY? 8vo. 3s. 6d.

—— OUR MORAL NATURE. Cr. 8vo. 2s. 6d.

MASSON (Prof. David).—RECENT BRITISH PHILOSOPHY. 3rd Edit. Cr. 8vo. 6s.

SHELDON (W. L.).—AN ETHICAL MOVE-MENT. Cr. 8vo. 5s. net.

SIDGWICK (Prof. Henry).—THE METHODS OF ETHICS. 5th Edit., revised. 8vo. 14s.

—— A SUPPLEMENT TO THE SECOND EDITION. Containing all the important Additions and Alterations in the Fourth Edition. 8vo. 6s.

—— OUTLINES OF THE HISTORY OF ETHICS FOR ENGLISH READERS. Cr. 8vo. 3s. 6d.

THORNTON (W. T.). — OLD-FASHIONED ETHICS AND COMMON-SENSE METAPHYSICS. 8vo. 10s. 6d.

WILLIAMS (C. M.).—A REVIEW OF THE SYS-TEMS OF ETHICS FOUNDED ON THE THEORY OF EVOLUTION. Cr. 8vo. 12s. net.

WINDELBAND (W.).—HISTORY OF PHILO-SOPHY. Transl. by J. H. TUFTS. 8vo. 21s. net.

Logic.

BOOLE (George). — THE MATHEMATICAL ANALYSIS OF LOGIC. 8vo. sewed. 5s.

BOSANQUET (B.).—ESSENTIALS OF LOGIC. Cr. 8vo. 3s. net.

CARROLL (Lewis).—THE GAME OF LOGIC. Cr. 8vo. 3s. net.

—— SYMBOLIC LOGIC. I. ELEMENTARY. Gl. 8vo. 2s. net.

JEVONS (W. Stanley).—A PRIMER OF LOGIC. Pott 8vo. 1s.

—— ELEMENTARY LESSONS IN LOGIC, DE-DUCTIVE AND INDUCTIVE. Pott 8vo. 3s. 6d.

—— STUDIES IN DEDUCTIVE LOGIC. 2nd Edit. Cr. 8vo. 6s.

—— THE PRINCIPLES OF SCIENCE: Treatise on Logic and Scientific Method. Cr. 8vo. 12s. 6d.

—— PURE LOGIC: and other Minor Works. Edited by R. ADAMSON, M.A., and HAR-RIET A. JEVONS. 8vo. 10s. 6d.

KEYNES (J. N.).—STUDIES AND EXERCISES IN FORMAL LOGIC. 3rd Edit. 8vo. 12s.

McCOSH (Rev. Dr.).—THE LAWS OF DIS-CURSIVE THOUGHT. A Text-Book of Formal Logic. Cr. 8vo. 5s.

RAY (Prof. P. K.).—A TEXT-BOOK OF DE-DUCTIVE LOGIC. 4th Edit. Globe 8vo. 4s. 6d.

VENN (Rev. John).—The Logic of Chance. 2nd Edit. Cr. 8vo. 10s. 6d.
—— Symbolic Logic. 2nd Ed. Cr. 8vo. 10s.6d.
—— The Principles of Empirical or Inductive Logic. 8vo. 18s.

Psychology.

BALDWIN (Prof. J. M.).—Handbook of Psychology: Senses and Intellect. 8vo. 8s. 6d. net.
—— Feeling and Will. 8vo. 8s. 6d. net.
—— Elements of Psychology. Cr.8vo. 7s.6d.
—— Mental Development in the Child and the Race. 8vo. 10s. net.

CALDERWOOD (Prof. H.). — The Relations of Mind and Brain. 3rd Ed. 8vo. 8s.

CATTELL (J. McK.). — Experimental Psychology. [In the Press.

CLIFFORD (W. K.).—Seeing and Thinking. Cr. 8vo. 3s. 6d.

HÖFFDING (Prof. H.).—Outlines of Psychology. Translated by M. E. Lowndes. Cr. 8vo. 6s.

JAMES (Prof. William).—The Principles of Psychology. 2 vols. Demy 8vo. 25s. net.
—— Text-Book of Psychology. Cr. 8vo. 7s. net.

JARDINE (Rev. Robert).—The Elements of the Psychology of Cognition. 3rd Edit. Cr. 8vo. 6s. 6d.

McCOSH (Rev. Dr.).—Psychology. Cr. 8vo. I. The Cognitive Powers. 6s. 6d.—II. The Motive Powers. 6s. 6d.
—— The Emotions. 8vo. 9s.

MAUDSLEY (Dr. Henry).—The Physiology of Mind. Cr. 8vo. 10s. 6d.
—— The Pathology of Mind. 8vo. 15s. net.
—— Body and Mind. Cr. 8vo. 6s. 6d.

MURPHY (J. J.).—Habit and Intelligence. 2nd Edit. Illustrated. 8vo. 16s.

PSYCHOLOGICAL REVIEW, THE. Ed. by J. M. Cattell and J. M. Baldwin. 8vo. 3s. net. Annual Subscription, 16s. 6d. net.

PHOTOGRAPHY.

MELDOLA (Prof. R.).—The Chemistry of Photography. Cr. 8vo. 6s.

PHYSICS OR NATURAL PHILOSOPHY.
General—Electricity and Magnetism— Heat, Light, and Sound.

General.

ANDREWS (Dr. Thomas): The Scientific Papers of the late. With a Memoir by Profs. Tait and Crum Brown. 8vo. 18s.

BARKER (G. F.).—Physics: Advanced Course. 8vo. 21s.

DANIELL (A.).—A Text-Book of the Principles of Physics. Illustrated. 3rd Edit. Med. 8vo. 21s.
—— Physics for Students of Medicine. Fcp. 8vo. 4s. 6d.

EARL (A.).—Practical Lessons in Physical Measurement. Cr. 8vo. 5s.

EVERETT (Prof. J. D.).—The C. G. S. System of Units, with Tables of Physical Constants. New Edit. Globe 8vo. 5s.

FESSENDEN (C.).—Elements of Physics. Fcp. 8vo. 3s.

FISHER (Rev. Osmond).—Physics of the Earth's Crust. 2nd Edit. 8vo. 12s.

GEE (W.). — Short Studies in Nature Knowledge. Globe 8vo. 3s. 6d.

GORDON (H.)—Practical Science. Part I. Pott 8vo. 1s. [Part II. in the Press.

GREGORY (R. A.).—Elementary Practical Physics. 4to. 2s. 6d.

GUILLEMIN (Amédée).—The Forces of Nature. A Popular Introduction to the Study of Physical Phenomena. 455 Woodcuts. Rcy. 8vo. 21s.

HUXLEY (T. H.).—Introductory Primer of Science. Pott 8vo. 1s.

KELVIN (Lord).—Popular Lectures and Addresses.—Vol. I. Constitution of Matter. Cr. 8vo. 7s. 6d.

KEMPE (A. B.).—How to draw a Straight Line. Cr. 8vo. 1s. 6d.

LOEWY (B.).—Questions and Examples in Experimental Physics, Sound, Light, Heat, Electricity, and Magnetism. Fcp. 8vo. 2s.
—— A Graduated Course of Natural Science. Part I. Gl. 8vo. 2s.—Part II. 2s.6d.

LOUDON (W. J.) and McLENNAN (J. C.).—Laboratory Course in Experimental Physics. 8vo. 8s. 6d. net.

MOLLOY (Rev. G.).—Gleanings in Science: A Series of Popular Lectures on Scientific Subjects. 8vo. 7s. 6d.

NICHOLS (E. L.).—Laboratory Manual of Physics and Applied Electricity. Vol. I. Junior Course in General Physics. With Tables. 8vo. 12s. 6d. net.—Vol. II. Senior Courses. 12s. 6d. net.

NICHOLS (E. L.) and FRANKLIN (W. S.). Elements of Physics. Vol. I. Mechanics and Heat. 8vo. 6s. net.

PHYSICAL REVIEW, THE. Edited by E. L. Nichols and E. Merritt. Bi-Monthly. 8vo. 3s. net.

SCHUSTER (A.) and LEES (C. H.).—Intermediate Class Book in Physics. Gl. 8vo. [In the Press.

STEWART (Prof. Balfour). — A Primer of Physics. Illustrated. Pott 8vo. 1s.
—— Lessons in Elementary Physics. Illustrated. Fcp. 8vo. 4s. 6d.
—— Questions on the Same. By T. H. Core. Pott 8vo. 2s.

STEWART (Prof. Balfour) and GEE (W. W. Haldane).—Lessons in Elementary Practical Physics. Illustrated.—General Physical Processes. Cr. 8vo. 6s.

TAIT (Prof. P. G.).—Lectures on some Recent Advances in Physical Science. 3rd Edit. Cr. 8vo. 9s.

Electricity and Magnetism.

CUMMING (Linnæus).—An Introduction to Electricity. 4th Ed. Cr. 8vo. 8s. 6d.

DAY (R. E.).—Electric Light Arithmetic. Pott 8vo. 2s.

Electricity—*continued.*

GRAY (Prof. Andrew).—THE THEORY AND PRACTICE OF ABSOLUTE MEASUREMENTS IN ELECTRICITY AND MAGNETISM. 2 vols. Cr. 8vo. Vol. I. 12s. 6d.—Vol. II. 2 parts. 25s.
—— ABSOLUTE MEASUREMENTS IN ELECTRICITY AND MAGNETISM. Fcp. 8vo. 5s. 6d.
—— MAGNETISM AND ELECTRICITY. 8vo.
[In the Press.

GUILLEMIN (A.).—ELECTRICITY AND MAGNETISM. A Popular Treatise. Translated and Edited by Prof. SILVANUS P. THOMPSON. Super Roy. 8vo. 31s. 6d.

HEAVISIDE (O.)—ELECTRICAL PAPERS. 2 vols. 8vo. 30s. net.

HERTZ (H.).—ELECTRIC WAVES. Transl. by D. E. JONES, B.Sc. 8vo. 10s. net.
—— MISCELLANEOUS PAPERS. Translated by JONES and SCHOTT. 8vo. 10s. net.

JACKSON (D. C.).—TEXT-BOOK ON ELECTRO-MAGNETISM. Vol. I. Cr. 8vo. 9s. net.

KELVIN (Lord). — PAPERS ON ELECTROSTATICS AND MAGNETISM. 8vo. 18s.

LODGE (Prof. Oliver).—MODERN VIEWS OF ELECTRICITY. Illust. Cr. 8vo. 6s. 6d.

MENDENHALL (T. C.).—A CENTURY OF ELECTRICITY. Cr. 8vo. 4s. 6d.

STEWART (Prof. Balfour) and GEE (W. W. Haldane).—LESSONS IN ELEMENTARY PRACTICAL PHYSICS. Cr. 8vo. Illustrated.—ELECTRICITY AND MAGNETISM. 7s. 6d.
—— PRACTICAL PHYSICS FOR SCHOOLS. Gl. 8vo.—ELECTRICITY AND MAGNETISM. 2s. 6d.

THOMPSON (Prof. Silvanus P.). — ELEMENTARY LESSONS IN ELECTRICITY AND MAGNETISM. New Edition. Illustrated. Fcp. 8vo. 4s. 6d.

TURNER (H. H.).—EXAMPLES ON HEAT AND ELECTRICITY. Cr. 8vo. 2s. 6d.

Heat, Light, and Sound.

AIRY (Sir G. B.).—ON SOUND AND ATMOSPHERIC VIBRATIONS. Cr. 8vo. 9s.

CARNOT—THURSTON.—REFLECTIONS ON THE MOTIVE POWER OF HEAT, AND ON MACHINES FITTED TO DEVELOP THAT POWER. From the French of N. L. S. CARNOT. Edited by R. H. THURSTON, LL.D. Cr. 8vo. 7s. 6d.

JOHNSON (A.).—SUNSHINE. Illust. Cr. 8vo. 6s.

JONES (Prof. D. E.).—HEAT, LIGHT, AND SOUND. Globe 8vo. 2s. 6d.
—— LESSONS IN HEAT AND LIGHT. Globe 8vo. 3s. 6d.

MARTINEAU (C. A.).—EASY LESSONS IN HEAT. Gl. 8vo. 2s. 6d.

MAYER (Prof. A. M.).—SOUND. A Series of Simple Experiments. Illustr. Cr. 8vo. 3s. 6d.

MAYER (Prof. A. M.) and BARNARD (C.)—LIGHT. A Series of Simple Experiments. Illustrated. Cr. 8vo. 2s. 6d.

PARKINSON (S.).—A TREATISE ON OPTICS. 4th Edit., revised. Cr. 8vo. 10s. 6d.

PEABODY (Prof. C. H.).—THERMODYNAMICS OF THE STEAM ENGINE AND OTHER HEAT-ENGINES. 8vo. 21s.

PRESTON T.).—THE THEORY OF LIGHT. Illustrated. 8vo. 15s. net.
—— THE THEORY OF HEAT. 8vo. 17s. net.

RAYLEIGH (Lord).—THEORY OF SOUND. 2 vols. 8vo. 12s. net each.

SHANN (G.).—AN ELEMENTARY TREATISE ON HEAT IN RELATION TO STEAM AND THE STEAM-ENGINE. Illustr. Cr. 8vo. 4s. 6d.

SPOTTISWOODE (W.).—POLARISATION OF LIGHT. Illustrated. Cr. 8vo. 3s. 6d.

STEWART (Prof. Balfour) and GEE (W. W. Haldane).—LESSONS IN ELEMENTARY PRACTICAL PHYSICS. Cr. 8vo. Illustrated.—OPTICS, HEAT, AND SOUND. *[In the Press.*
—— PRACTICAL PHYSICS FOR SCHOOLS. Gl. 8vo.—HEAT, LIGHT, AND SOUND.

STOKES (Sir George G.).—ON LIGHT. The Burnett Lectures. Cr. 8vo. 7s. 6d.

STONE (W. H.).—ELEMENTARY LESSONS ON SOUND. Illustrated. Fcp. 8vo. 3s. 6d.

TAIT (Prof. P. G.).—HEAT. With Illustrations. Cr. 8vo. 6s.

TAYLOR (Sedley).—SOUND AND MUSIC. 2nd Edit. Ext. cr. 8vo. 8s. 6d.

TURNER (H. H.). (*See* ELECTRICITY.)

WRIGHT (Lewis).—LIGHT. A Course of Experimental Optics. Illust. Cr. 8vo. 7s. 6d.

YEO (J.).—STEAM AND THE MARINE STEAM ENGINE. 8vo. 7s. 6d. net.

PHYSIOGRAPHY and METEOROLOGY.

ARATUS.—THE SKIES AND WEATHER FORECASTS OF ARATUS. Translated by E. POSTE, M.A. Cr. 8vo. 3s. 6d.

BLANFORD (H. F.).—THE RUDIMENTS OF PHYSICAL GEOGRAPHY FOR THE USE OF INDIAN SCHOOLS. Illustr. Cr. 8vo. 2s. 6d.
—— A PRACTICAL GUIDE TO THE CLIMATES AND WEATHER OF INDIA, CEYLON AND BURMAH, AND THE STORMS OF INDIAN SEAS. 8vo. 12s. 6d.

FERREL (Prof. W.).—A POPULAR TREATISE ON THE WINDS. 2nd Ed. 8vo. 17s. net.

GEIKIE (Sir Archibald).—A PRIMER OF PHYSICAL GEOGRAPHY. Illustr. Pott 8vo. 1s.
—— ELEMENTARY LESSONS IN PHYSICAL GEOGRAPHY. Illustrated. Fcp. 8vo. 4s. 6d.
—— QUESTIONS ON THE SAME. 1s. 6d.

HUXLEY (Prof. T. H.).—PHYSIOGRAPHY. Illustrated. Cr. 8vo. 6s.

LOCKYER (J. Norman).—OUTLINES OF PHYSIOGRAPHY: THE MOVEMENTS OF THE EARTH. Illustrated. Cr. 8vo, swd. 1s. 6d.

MARR (J. E.) and HARKER (A.).—PHYSIOGRAPHY FOR BEGINNERS. Gl. 8vo. *In Press.*

MELDOLA (Prof. R.) and WHITE (Wm.)—REPORT ON THE EAST ANGLIAN EARTHQUAKE OF APRIL 22ND, 1884. 8vo. 3s. 6d.

RUSSELL (T.)—METEOROLOGY. 8vo. 16s. net.

TARR (R. S.).—ELEMENTARY PHYSICAL GEOGRAPHY. Cr. 8vo. 7s. 6d. net.

PHYSIOLOGY.

FEARNLEY (W.).—A MANUAL OF ELEMENTARY PRACTICAL HISTOLOGY. Cr. 8vo. 7s. 6d.

FOSTER (Prof. M.) and LANGLEY (J. N.).—A COURSE OF ELEMENTARY PRACTICAL PHYSIOLOGY AND HISTOLOGY. Cr. 8vo. 7s. 6d.

FOSTER (Prof. M.) and SHORE (L. E.).—PHYSIOLOGY FOR BEGINNERS. Gl. 8vo. 2s. 6d.

FOSTER (Prof. Michael).—A Text-Book of Physiology. Illustrated. 6th Edit. 8vo.—Part I. Book I. Blood: the Tissues of Movement, the Vascular Mechanism. 10s. 6d.—Part II. Book II. The Tissues of Chemical Action, with their Respective Mechanisms: Nutrition. 10s. 6d.—Part III. Book III. The Central Nervous System. 7s. 6d.—Part IV. Book III. The Senses, and some Special Muscular Mechanisms.—Book IV. The Tissues and Mechanisms of Reproduction. 10s. 6d.—Appendix, by A. S. Lea. 7s. 6d.

—— A Primer of Physiology. Pott 8vo. 1s.

GAMGEE (Arthur).—A Text-Book of the Physiological Chemistry of the Animal Body. 8vo. Vol. I. 18s. Vol. II. 18s.

HUMPHRY (Prof. Sir G. M.).—The Human Foot and the Human Hand. Illustrated. Fcp. 8vo. 4s. 6d.

HUXLEY (Prof. Thos. H.).—Lessons in Elementary Physiology. Fcp. 8vo. 4s. 6d.
—— Questions. By T. Alcock. Pott 8vo. 1s. 6d.

KIMBER (D. C.).—Anatomy and Physiology for Nurses. 8vo. 10s. net.

MIVART (St. George).—Lessons in Elementary Anatomy. Fcp. 8vo. 6s. 6d.

PETTIGREW (J. Bell).—The Physiology of the Circulation in Plants in the Lower Animals and in Man. 8vo. 12s.

SEILER (Dr. Carl).—Micro-Photographs in Histology, Normal and Pathological. 4to. 31s. 6d.

WIEDERSHEIM (R.).—The Structure of Man. Translated by H. M. Bernard. Revised by G. B. Howes. 8vo. 8s. net.

POETRY. (See under Literature, p. 17.)

POLITICAL ECONOMY.

BASTABLE (Prof. C. F.).—Public Finance. 2nd Ed. 8vo. 12s. 6d. net.

BÖHM-BAWERK (Prof.).—Capital and Interest. Transl. by W. Smart. 8vo. 12s. net.
—— The Positive Theory of Capital. By the same Translator. 8vo. 12s. net.

BONAR (James).—Malthus and his Work. 8vo. 12s. 6d.
—— Catalogue of the Library of Adam Smith. 8vo. 7s. 6d. net.

BRUCE (P. A.).. (See under History.)

CAIRNES (J. E.).—Some Leading Principles of Political Economy newly Expounded. 8vo. 14s.
—— The Character and Logical Method of Political Economy. Cr. 8vo. 6s.

CANTILLON.—Essai sur le Commerce. 12mo. 7s. net.

CLARE (G.).—A B C of the Foreign Exchanges. Cr. 8vo. 3s. net.

CLARKE (C. B.). — Speculations from Political Economy. Cr. 8vo. 3s. 6d.

COLUMBIA COLLEGE. Studies in History, Economics, and Public Laws. 4 vols. 8vo. 18s. net. each.

COMMONS (J. R.)—Distribution of Wealth. Cr. 8vo 7s. net.

COSSA (L.).—Introduction to the Study of Political Economy. Translated by L. Dyer. Cr. 8vo. 8s. 6d. net.

DE ROUSIERS (P.).—Labour Question in Britain. Translated. 8vo. 12s. net.

DICTIONARY OF POLITICAL ECONOMY, A. By various Writers. Ed. R. H. I. Palgrave. Parts I. to VI. 3s. 6d. each net.—Vol. I. Med. 8vo. 21s. net.

ECONOMIC CLASSICS. Edited by W. J. Ashley Globe 8vo. 3s. net. each.
 Select Chapters from the "Wealth of Nations" of Adam Smith.
 First Six Chapters of "Principles of Political Economy" of David Ricardo.
 Parallel Chapters from First and Second Editions of "Principle of Population." By T. R. Malthus.
 England's Treasure by Forraign Trade. By T. Mun.
 Peasant Rents. By Richard Jones.
 Mercantile System. By G. Schmoller.

ECONOMIC JOURNAL, THE. — The Journal of the British Economic Association. Edit. by Prof. F. Y. Edgeworth. Published Quarterly. 8vo. 5s. net. (Part I. April, 1891.) Vols. I.-IV. 21s. net each. [Cloth Covers for binding Volumes, 1s. 6d. net each.]

ECONOMICS: The Quarterly Journal of. Vol. II. Parts II. III. IV. 2s. 6d. net each.—Vol. III. 4 parts. 2s. 6d. net each.—Vol. IV. 4 parts. 2s. 6d. net each.—Vol. V. 4 parts. 2s. 6d. net each.—Vol. VI. 4 parts. 2s. 6d. net each.—Vol. VII. 4 parts. 2s. 6d. net each.—Vol. VIII. 4 parts. 2s. 6d. net each.—Vol. IX. 4 parts. 2s. 6d net each.—Vol. X. Part I. 2s. 6d. net.

FAWCETT (Henry).—Manual of Political Economy. 7th Edit. Cr. 8vo. 12s.
—— An Explanatory Digest of the above. By C. A. Waters. Cr. 8vo. 2s. 6d.
—— Free Trade and Protection. 6th Edit. Cr. 8vo. 3s. 6d.

FAWCETT (Mrs. H.).—Political Economy for Beginners, with Questions. 7th Edit. Pott 8vo. 2s. 6d.

FIRST LESSONS IN BUSINESS MATTERS. By A Banker's Daughter. 2nd Edit. Pott 8vo. 1s.

FONDA (A. J.) —Honest Money. Cr. 8vo. 3s. 6d. net.

GILMAN (N. P.). — Profit-Sharing between Employer and Employee. Cr. 8vo. 7s. 6d.

GOSCHEN (Rt. Hon. George J.).—Reports and Speeches on Local Taxation. 8vo. 5s.

GUIDE TO THE UNPROTECTED: In Every-day Matters relating to Property and Income. Ext. fcp. 8vo. 3s. 6d.

GUNTON (George).—Wealth and Progress. Cr. 8vo. 6s.

HALLE (E. von).—Trusts or Industrial Combinations and Coalitions in the United States. Cr. 8vo. 5s. net.

HELM (E.).—The Joint Standard. Cr. 8vo. 3s. 6d. net.

HORTON (Hon. S. Dana).—The Silver Pound and England's Monetary Policy since the Restoration. 8vo. 14s.

HOWELL (George).—The Conflicts of Capital and Labour. Cr. 8vo. 7s. 6d.
—— A Handy Book of the Labour Laws. 3rd Edit. Cr. 8vo. 3s. 6d. net.

JEVONS (W. Stanley).—A Primer of Political Economy. Pott 8vo. 1s.

POLITICAL ECONOMY—*continued.*

JEVONS (W. S.).—The Theory of Political Economy. 3rd Ed. 8vo. 10s. 6d.

—— Investigations in Currency and Finance. Edit. by H. S. Foxwell. 8vo. 21s

KEYNES (J. N.).—The Scope and Method of Political Economy. Cr. 8vo. 7s. net.

LEIBNITZ.—Nouveaux Essais. Transl. by A. G. Langley. *[In the Press.*

MARSHALL (Prof. Alfred).—Principles of Economics. 3rd Ed. 8vo. Vol. 1. 12s. 6d. net.

—— Elements of Economics of Industry. Crown 8vo. 3s. 6d.

MARTIN (Frederick).—The History of Lloyds, and of Marine Insurance in Great Britain. 8vo. 14s.

MENGER (C.).—The Right to the whole Produce of Labour. Transl. by M. E. Tanner. *[In the Press.*

PRICE (L. L. F. R).—Industrial Peace: its Advantages, Methods, and Difficulties. Med. 8vo. 6s.

QUESNAY (F.).—Tableau Oeconomique. 4to. 2s. 6d. net.

RABBENO (U.).—American Commercial Policy. 8vo. 12s. net.

RAE (J.).—Eight Hours for Work. Cr. 8vo. 4s. 6d. net.

RICARDO.—Chapters I.—VI. of "The Principles of Political Economy and Taxation." Globe 8vo. 3s. net.

SELIGMAN (E. R. A.).—Essays in Taxation. 8vo. 12s. 6d. net.

SIDGWICK (Prof. Henry).—The Principles of Political Economy. *[New Ed. in Press.*

SMART (W.).—An Introduction to the Theory of Value. Cr. 8vo. 3s. net.

—— Studies in Economics. Ex. cr. 8vo. 8s. 6d. net.

SMITH (Adam).—Select Chapters from "The Wealth of Nations." Gl. 8vo. 3s. net.

THOMPSON (H. M.).—The Theory of Wages and its Application to the Eight Hours Question. Cr. 8vo. 3s. 6d.

WALKER (Francis A.).—First Lessons in Political Economy. Cr. 8vo. 5s.

—— A Brief Text-Book of Political Economy. Cr. 8vo. 6s. 6d.

—— Political Economy. 8vo. 12s. 6d.

—— The Wages Question. Ext. cr. 8vo. 8s. 6d. net.

—— Money. New Edit. Ext. cr. 8vo. 8s. 6d. net.

—— Money in its Relation to Trade and Industry. Cr. 8vo. 7s. 6d.

——Land and its Rent. Fcp. 8vo. 3s. 6d.

WALLACE (A. R.).—Bad Times: An Essay. Cr. 8vo. 2s. 6d.

WICKSTEED (Ph. H.).—The Alphabet of Economic Science.—I. Elements of the Theory of Value or Worth. Gl. 8vo. 2s. 6d.

WIESER (F. von).—Natural Value. Edit. by W. Smart, M.A. 8vo. 10s. net.

WILLOUGHBY (W. W.).—Nature of the State. 8vo. 12s. 6d.

POLITICS.
(*See also* History, p. 11.)

ADAMS (Sir F. O.) and CUNNINGHAM (C.).—The Swiss Confederation. 8vo. 14s

BAKER (Sir Samuel W.).—The Egyptian Question. 8vo, sewed. 2s.

BATH (Marquis of).—Observations on Bulgarian Affairs. Cr. 8vo. 3s. 6d.

BRIGHT (John).—Speeches on Questions of Public Policy. Edit. by J. E. Thorold Rogers. With Portrait. 2 vols. 8vo. 25s.
—*Popular Edition.* Ext. fcp. 8vo. 3s. 6d.

—— Public Addresses. Edited by J. E. T. Rogers. 8vo. 14s.

BRYCE (Jas., M.P.).—The American Commonwealth. 3rd Edit. Ext. cr. 8vo. 2 vols. 12s. 6d. each.

BUCKLAND (Anna).—Our National Institutions. Pott 8vo. 1s.

BURKE (Edmund).—Letters, Tracts, and Speeches on Irish Affairs. Edited by Matthew Arnold, with Preface. Cr. 8vo. 6s.

—— Reflections on the French Revolution. Ed. by F. G. Selby. Globe 8vo. 5s.

—— Speech on American Taxation, Speech on Conciliation with America, Letter to the Sheriffs of Bristol. Edited by F. G. Selby. Globe 8vo. 3s. 6d.

CAIRNES (J. E.).—Political Essays. 8vo. 10s. 6d.

—— The Slave Power. 8vo. 10s. 6d

CHIROL (V.).—The Far Eastern Question. 8vo. 8s. 6d. net.

COBDEN (Richard).—Speeches on Questions of Public Policy. Ed. by J. Bright and J. E. Thorold Rogers. Gl. 8vo. 3s. 6d.

DICEY (Prof. A. V.).—Letters on Unionist Delusions. Cr. 8vo. 2s. 6d.

DILKE (Rt. Hon. Sir Charles W.).—Greater Britain. 9th Edit. Cr. 8vo. 6s.

—— Problems of Greater Britain. Maps. 3rd Edit. Ext. cr. 8vo. 12s. 6d.

DONISTHORPE (Wordsworth).—Individualism: A System of Politics. 8vo. 14s.

—— Law in a Free State. Cr. 8vo. 5s. net.

DUFF (Rt. Hon. Sir M. E. Grant).—Miscellanies, Political and Literary. 8vo. 10s. 6d.

ENGLISH CITIZEN, THE.—His Rights and Responsibilities. Ed. by Henry Craik, C.B. New Edit. Cr. 8vo. 2s. 6d. each.
Central Government. By H. D. Traill.
The Electorate and the Legislature. By Spencer Walpole.
The Land Laws. By Sir F. Pollock, Bart. 2nd Edit.
The Punishment and Prevention of Crime. By Col. Sir Edmund du Cane.
Local Government. By M. D. Chalmers.
Colonies and Dependencies: Part I. India. By J. S Cotton, M.A.—II. The Colonies. By E. J. Payne.
The State in its Relation to Education. By Henry Craik, C.B.
The State and the Church. By Hon. Arthur Elliott, M.P.
The State in its Relation to Trade. By Sir T. H. Farrer, Bart.
The Poor Law. By the Rev. T. W. Fowle.
The State in Relation to Labour. By W. Stanley Jevons. 3rd. Edit. By M. Cababé.
Justice and Police. By F. W. Maitland.
The National Defences. By Major-Gen. Maurice, R.A. *[In the Press.*
Foreign Relations. By S. Walpole.
The National Budget; National Debt; Taxes and Rates. By A. J. Wilson.

FAWCETT (Henry).—SPEECHES ON SOME CURRENT POLITICAL QUESTIONS. 8vo. 10s. 6d.
—— FREE TRADE AND PROTECTION. 6th Edit. Cr. 8vo. 3s. 6d.

FAWCETT (Henry and Mrs. H.).—ESSAYS AND LECTURES ON POLITICAL AND SOCIAL SUBJECTS. 8vo. 10s. 6d.

FISKE (John).—AMERICAN POLITICAL IDEAS VIEWED FROM THE STAND-POINT OF UNIVERSAL HISTORY. Cr. 8vo. 4s.
—— CIVIL GOVERNMENT IN THE UNITED STATES CONSIDERED WITH SOME REFERENCE TO ITS ORIGIN. Cr. 8vo. 6s. 6d.

FREEMAN (E. A.).—DISESTABLISHMENT AND DISENDOWMENT. WHAT ARE THEY? 4th Edit. Cr. 8vo. 1s.
—— THE GROWTH OF THE ENGLISH CONSTITUTION. 5th Edit. Cr. 8vo. 5s.

HILL (Florence D.).—CHILDREN OF THE STATE. Edited by FANNY FOWKE. Crown 8vo. 3s. 6d.

HILL (Octavia).—OUR COMMON LAND, AND OTHER ESSAYS. Ext. fcp. 8vo. 3s. 6d.

HOLLAND (Prof. T. E.).—THE TREATY RELATIONS OF RUSSIA AND TURKEY, FROM 1774 TO 1853. Cr. 8vo. 2s.

JENKS (Prof. Edward).—THE GOVERNMENT OF VICTORIA (AUSTRALIA). 8vo. 14s.

JEPHSON (H.).—THE PLATFORM: ITS RISE AND PROGRESS. 2 vols. 8vo. 21s.

LOWELL (J. R.). (See COLLECTED WORKS.)

LUBBOCK (Sir J.). (See COLLECTED WORKS.)

MACKNIGHT (J.).—ULSTER AS IT IS. 2 vols. 8vo. 21s. net.

MATHEW (E. J.).—REPRESENTATIVE GOVERNMENT. Gl. 8vo. 1s. 6d.

PALGRAVE (W. Gifford).—ESSAYS ON EASTERN QUESTIONS. 8vo. 10s. 6d.

PARKIN (G. R.).—IMPERIAL FEDERATION. Cr. 8vo. 4s. 6d.
—— THE GREAT DOMINION, STUDIES IN CANADA. Cr. 8vo. 6s.

POLLOCK (Sir F., Bart.).—INTRODUCTION TO THE HISTORY OF THE SCIENCE OF POLITICS. Cr. 8vo. 2s. 6d.
—— LEADING CASES DONE INTO ENGLISH. Crown 8vo. 3s. 6d.

PRACTICAL POLITICS. 8vo. 6s.

ROGERS (Prof. J. E. T.).—COBDEN AND POLITICAL OPINION. 8vo. 10s. 6d.

ROUTLEDGE (Jas.).—POPULAR PROGRESS IN ENGLAND. 8vo. 16s.

RUSSELL (Sir Charles).—NEW VIEWS ON IRELAND. Cr. 8vo. 2s. 6d.
—— THE PARNELL COMMISSION: THE OPENING SPEECH FOR THE DEFENCE. 8vo. 10s. 6d.
—Popular Edition. Sewed. 2s.

SEELEY (Sir J. R.).—INTRODUCTION TO POLITICAL SCIENCE. Gl. 8vo. 5s.

SIDGWICK (Prof. Henry).—THE ELEMENTS OF POLITICS. 8vo. 14s. net.

SMITH (Goldwin).—CANADA AND THE CANADIAN QUESTION. 8vo. 8s. net.
—— THE UNITED STATES, 1492—1871. Cr. 8vo. 8s. 6d.

STATESMAN'S YEAR-BOOK, THE. (See under STATISTICS.)

STATHAM (R.).—BLACKS, BOERS, AND BRITISH. Cr. 8vo. 6s.

STRACHEY (J. St. L.).—THE EMPIRE. Gl. 8vo. 1s. 6d.

THORNTON (W. T.).—A PLEA FOR PEASANT PROPRIETORS. New Edit. Cr. 8vo. 7s. 6d.
—— INDIAN PUBLIC WORKS, AND COGNATE INDIAN TOPICS. Cr. 8vo. 8s. 6d.

TRENCH (Capt. F.).—THE RUSSO-INDIAN QUESTION. Cr. 8vo. 7s. 6d.

WALLACE (Sir Donald M.).—EGYPT AND THE EGYPTIAN QUESTION. 8vo. 14s.

PSYCHOLOGY.
(See under PHILOSOPHY, p. 33.)

SCULPTURE. (See ART.)

SOCIAL ECONOMY.

BARNETT (E. A.).—TRAINING OF GIRLS FOR WORK. Gl. 8vo. 2s. 6d.

BOOTH (C.).—A PICTURE OF PAUPERISM. Cr. 8vo. 5s.—Cheap Edit. 8vo. Swd., 6d.
—— LIFE AND LABOUR OF THE PEOPLE OF LONDON. Vols. I.-IV. Cr. 8vo. 3s. 6d. each.—Vols. V. VI. and VII., 7s. 6d. net each vol.—Maps to illustrate the above. 5s.
—— THE AGED POOR IN ENGLAND AND WALES—CONDITION. Ext. crown 8vo. 8s. 6d. net.

BOSANQUET (B.).—ASPECTS OF THE SOCIAL PROBLEM. By VARIOUS WRITERS. Ed. by B. BOSANQUET. Cr. 8vo. 2s. 6d. net.

DRAGE (G.).—THE UNEMPLOYED. Cr. 8vo. 3s. 6d. net.

DYER (H.).—THE EVOLUTION OF INDUSTRY. 8vo. 10s. net.

FAWCETT (H. and Mrs. H.). (See POLITICS.)

GIDDINGS (F. H.).—PRINCIPLES OF SOCIOLOGY. 8vo. 12s. 6d. net.

GILMAN (N. P.).—SOCIALISM AND THE AMERICAN SPIRIT. Cr. 8vo. 6s. 6d.

GOLDIE (J.).—THE POOR AND THEIR HAPPINESS Cr. 8vo. 3s. 6d. net.

HILL (Octavia).—HOMES OF THE LONDON POOR. Cr. 8vo, sewed. 1s.

HUXLEY (Prof. T. H.).—SOCIAL DISEASES AND WORSE REMEDIES: Letters to the "Times." Cr. 8vo. sewed. 1s. net.

JEVONS (W. Stanley).—METHODS OF SOCIAL REFORM. 8vo. 10s. 6d.

KIDD (B.).—SOCIAL EVOLUTION. Cr. 8vo. 5s. net.

MAVO-SMITH (R.).—STATISTICS AND SOCIOLOGY. 8vo. 12s. 6d. net.

PEARSON (C. H.).—NATIONAL LIFE AND CHARACTER: A FORECAST. Cr. 8vo. 5s. net.

STANLEY (Hon. Maude).—CLUBS FOR WORKING GIRLS. Cr. 8vo. 3s. 6d.

SOUND. (See under PHYSICS, p. 34.)

SPORT.

BAKER (Sir Samuel W.).—WILD BEASTS AND THEIR WAYS: REMINISCENCES OF EUROPE, ASIA, AFRICA, AMERICA, FROM 1845—88. Illustrated. Ext. cr. 8vo. 12s. 6d.

CHASSERESSE (D.).—SPORTING SKETCHES. Illustrated. Cr. 8vo. 3s. 6d.

CLARK (R.).—GOLF: A Royal and Ancient Game. Small 4to. 8s. 6d. net.

EDWARDS-MOSS (Sir J. E., Bart).—A SEASON IN SUTHERLAND. Cr. 8vo. 1s. 6d.

KINGSLEY (G.).—SKETCHES IN SPORT AND NATURAL HISTORY. Ex. cr. 8vo. [In Press.

LOCKYER (J. N.) and RUTHERFORD (W). RULES OF GOLF. 32mo. 1s. 6d.; roan, 2s.

STATISTICS.

STATESMAN'S YEAR-BOOK, THE. Statistical and Historical Annual of the States of the World for the Year 1896. Revised after Official Returns. Ed. by J. SCOTT KELTIE and I. P. A. RENWICK. Cr. 8vo. 10s. 6d.

SURGERY. (See MEDICINE.)

SWIMMING.

LEAHY (Sergeant).—THE ART OF SWIMMING IN THE ETON STYLE. Cr. 8vo. 2s.

TECHNOLOGY.

BENEDIKT (R.) and LEWKOWITSCH (J.)—CHEMICAL ANALYSIS OF OILS, FATS, WAXES, AND THEIR COMMERCIAL PRODUCTS 8vo. 21s. net.

BENSON (W. A. S.).—HANDICRAFT AND DESIGN. Cr. 8vo. 5s. net.

BURDETT (C. W. B.).—BOOT AND SHOE MANUFACTURE Cr. 8vo. [In the Press.

DEGERDON (W. E.).—THE GRAMMAR OF WOODWORK. 4to. 3s.; sewed, 2s.

FOX (T. W.).—THE MECHANISM OF WEAVING. Cr. 8vo. 7s. 6d. net.

LETHABY (W. R.).—LEAD WORK. Cr. 8vo. 4s. 6d. net.

LOUIS (H.).—HANDBOOK OF GOLD-MILLING. Cr. 8vo. 10s. net.

TAGGART (W. S.).—COTTON SPINNING. Cr. 8vo. 4s. net.

VICKERMAN (C.).—WOOLLEN SPINNING. Cr. 8vo. 6s. net.

WALKER (Louisa).—VARIED OCCUPATIONS IN WEAVING AND CANE AND STRAW WORK. Globe 8vo. 3s. 6d.

—— VARIED OCCUPATIONS IN STRING WORK. By the same. Gl. 8vo. 3s. 6d.

THEOLOGY.

The Bible—History of the Christian Church— The Church of England—Devotional Books —The Fathers—Hymnology—Sermons, Lectures, Addresses, and Theological Essays.

The Bible.

History of the Bible—

THE ENGLISH BIBLE; An External and Critical History of the various English Translations of Scripture. By Prof. JOHN EADIE. 2 vols. 8vo. 28s.

THE BIBLE IN THE CHURCH. By Right Rev. Bp. WESTCOTT. 10th edit. Pott 8vo. 4s. 6d.

Biblical History—

THE BIBLE FOR HOME READING. By C. G. MONTEFIORE. Part I. Cr. 8vo. 6s. net.

THE MODERN READER'S BIBLE. A Series of Books from the Sacred Scriptures presented in Modern Literary Form. Ed. by R. G. MOULTON, M.A.

PROVERBS. A Miscellany of Sayings and Poems embodying isolated Observations of Life. 2s. 6d.

ECCLESIASTICUS. A Miscellany including longer compositions, still embodying only isolated Observations of Life. 2s. 6d.

Biblical History—

ECCLESIASTES—WISDOM OF SOLOMON. Each is a Series of Connected Writings embodying, from different standpoints, a Solution of the whole Mystery of Life. 2s. 6d.

THE BOOK OF JOB. A Dramatic Poem in which are embodied Varying Solutions of the Mystery of Life. 2s. 6d.

BIBLE LESSONS. By Rev. E. A. ABBOTT. Cr. 8vo. 4s 6d.

SIDE-LIGHTS UPON BIBLE HISTORY. By Mrs. SYDNEY BUXTON. Cr. 8vo. 5s.

STORIES FROM THE BIBLE. By Rev. A. J. CHURCH. Illust. Cr. 8vo. 2 parts. 3s. 6d. each.

BIBLE READINGS SELECTED FROM THE PENTATEUCH AND THE BOOK OF JOSHUA. By Rev. J. A. CROSS. Gl. 8vo. 2s. 6d.

A CLASS-BOOK OF OLD TESTAMENT HISTORY. By Rev. Dr. MACLEAR. Pott 8vo. 4s. 6d.

A CLASS-BOOK OF NEW TESTAMENT HISTORY. By the same. Pott 8vo. 5s. 6d.

A SHILLING BOOK OF OLD TESTAMENT HISTORY. By the same. Pott 8vo. 1s.

A SHILLING BOOK OF NEW TESTAMENT HISTORY. By the same. Pott 8vo. 1s.

THE CHILDREN'S TREASURY OF BIBLE STORIES. By Mrs. H. GASKOIN. Pott 8vo. 1s. each.—Part I. Old Testament; II. New Testament; III. Three Apostles.

THE NATIONS AROUND ISRAEL. By A. KEARY. Cr. 8vo. 3s. 6d.

The Old Testament—

SCRIPTURE READINGS FOR SCHOOLS AND FAMILIES. By C. M. YONGE. Globe 8vo. 1s. 6d. each: also with comments, 3s. 6d. each. — GENESIS TO DEUTERONOMY. — JOSHUA TO SOLOMON.—KINGS AND THE PROPHETS.—THE GOSPEL TIMES.—APOSTOLIC TIMES.

THE DIVINE LIBRARY OF THE OLD TESTAMENT. By Prof. KIRKPATRICK. Cr. 8vo. 3s. net.

DOCTRINE OF THE PROPHETS. By Prof. KIRKPATRICK. Cr. 8vo. 6s.

THE PATRIARCHS AND LAWGIVERS OF THE OLD TESTAMENT. By F. D. MAURICE. Cr. 8vo. 3s. 6d.

THE PROPHETS AND KINGS OF THE OLD TESTAMENT. By same. Cr. 8vo. 3s. 6d.

THE CANON OF THE OLD TESTAMENT. By Prof. H. E. RYLE. 2nd Ed. Cr. 8vo. 6s.

PHILO AND HOLY SCRIPTURE. By Prof. H. E. RYLE. Cr. 8vo. 10s. net.

The Pentateuch—

AN HISTORICO-CRITICAL INQUIRY INTO THE ORIGIN AND COMPOSITION OF THE HEXATEUCH (PENTATEUCH AND BOOK OF JOSHUA). By Prof. A. KUENEN. Trans. by P. H. WICKSTEED, M.A. 8vo. 14s.

The Psalms—

THE PSALMS CHRONOLOGICALLY ARRANGED. By FOUR FRIENDS. Cr. 8vo. 5s. net.

GOLDEN TREASURY PSALTER. Student's Edition of the above. Pott 8vo. 2s. 6d. net.

THE PSALMS. With Introduction and Notes. By A. C. JENNINGS, M.A., and W. H. LOWE, M.A. 2 vols. Cr. 8vo. 10s. 6d. each.

INTRODUCTION TO THE STUDY AND USE OF THE PSALMS. By Rev. J. F. THRUPP. 2nd Edit. 2 vols. 8vo. 21s.

Isaiah—

ISAIAH XL.—LXVI. With the Shorter Prophecies allied to it. Edited by MATTHEW ARNOLD. Cr. 8vo. 5s.

Isaiah—
ISAIAH OF JERUSALEM. In the Authorised
English Version, with Introduction and
Notes. By M. ARNOLD. Cr. 8vo. 4s. 6d.
A BIBLE-READING FOR SCHOOLS. The Great
Prophecy of Israel's Restoration (Isaiah
xl.—lxvi.). Arranged and Edited for Young
Learners. By the same. Pott 8vo. 1s.
COMMENTARY ON THE BOOK OF ISAIAH:
Critical, Historical, and Prophetical; in-
cluding a Revised English Translation.
By T. R. BIRKS. 2nd Edit. 8vo. 12s. 6d.
THE BOOK OF ISAIAH CHRONOLOGICALLY
ARRANGED. By T. K. CHEYNE. Cr.
8vo. 7s. 6d.

Zechariah—
THE HEBREW STUDENT'S COMMENTARY ON
ZECHARIAH, Hebrew and LXX. By W. H.
LOWE, M.A. 8vo. 10s. 6d.

The New Testament—
THE NEW TESTAMENT. Essay on the Right
Estimation of MS. Evidence in the Text
of the New Testament. By T. R. BIRKS.
Cr. 8vo. 3s. 6d.
THE MESSAGES OF THE BOOKS. Discourses
and Notes on the Books of the New Testa-
ment. By Archd. FARRAR. 8vo. 14s.
THE CLASSICAL ELEMENT IN THE NEW
TESTAMENT. Considered as a Proof of its
Genuineness, with an Appendix on the
Oldest Authorities used in the Formation
of the Canon. By C. H. HOOLE. 8vo. 10s. 6d.
ON A FRESH REVISION OF THE ENGLISH
NEW TESTAMENT. With an Appendix on
the last Petition of the Lord's Prayer. By
Bishop LIGHTFOOT. Cr. 8vo. 7s. 6d.
THE UNITY OF THE NEW TESTAMENT. By
F. D. MAURICE. 2 vols. Cr. 8vo. 12s.
THE SYNOPTIC PROBLEM FOR ENGLISH
READERS. By A. J. JOLLEY. Cr. 8vo. 3s. net.
A GENERAL SURVEY OF THE HISTORY OF
THE CANON OF THE NEW TESTAMENT
DURING THE FIRST FOUR CENTURIES. By
Bishop WESTCOTT. Cr. 8vo. 10s. 6d
GREEK-ENGLISH LEXICON TO THE NEW
TESTAMENT. By W. J. HICKIE, M.A.
Pott 8vo. 3s.
THE NEW TESTAMENT IN THE ORIGINAL
GREEK. The Text revised by Bishop
WESTCOTT, D.D., and Prof. F. J. A.
HORT, D.D. 2 vols. Cr. 8vo. 10s. 6d.
each.—Vol. I. Text.—Vol. II. Introduc-
tion and Appendix.
SCHOOL EDITION OF THE ABOVE. Pott 8vo,
4s. 6d.; Pott 8vo, roan, 5s. 6d.; morocco,
gilt edges, 6s. 6d.—Library Edition. 8vo.
10s. net.
ESSENTIALS OF NEW TESTAMENT GREEK.
By J. H. HUDDILSTON. Pott 8vo. 3s. net.

The Gospels—
THE COMMON TRADITION OF THE SYNOPTIC
GOSPELS. In the Text of the Revised
Version. By Rev. E. A. ABBOTT and
W. G. RUSHBROOKE. Cr. 8vo. 3s. 6d.
SYNOPTICON: An Exposition of the Common
Matter of the Synoptic Gospels. By W. G.
RUSHBROOKE. Printed in Colours. 4to. 35s.
INTRODUCTION TO THE STUDY OF THE FOUR
GOSPELS. By Bp. WESTCOTT. Cr. 8vo. 10s. 6d.
THE COMPOSITION OF THE FOUR GOSPELS.
By Rev. ARTHUR WRIGHT. Cr. 8vo. 5s.

The Gospels—
SYNOPSIS OF THE GOSPELS IN GREEK. By
Rev. A. WRIGHT. 4to. 6s. net.
SYRO-LATIN TEXT OF THE GOSPELS. By
F. H. CHASE. 7s. 6d. net.
THE AKHMIM FRAGMENT OF THE APOCRY-
PHAL GOSPEL OF ST. PETER. By H. B.
SWETE. 8vo. 5s. net.

Gospel of St. Matthew—
THE GREEK TEXT, with Introduction and
Notes by Rev. A. SLOMAN. Fcp. 8vo. 2s. 6d.
CHOICE NOTES ON ST. MATTHEW. Drawn
from Old and New Sources. Cr. 8vo. 4s. 6d.
(St. Matthew and St. Mark in 1 vol. 9s.)

Gospel of St. Mark—
SCHOOL READINGS IN THE GREEK TESTA-
MENT. Being the Outlines of the Life of
our Lord as given by St. Mark, with addi-
tions from the Text of the other Evange-
lists. Edited, with Notes and Vocabulary,
by Rev. A. CALVERT, M.A. Fcp. 8vo. 2s. 6d.
CHOICE NOTES ON ST. MARK. Drawn from
Old and New SOURCES. Cr. 8vo. 4s. 6d.
(St. Matthew and St. Mark in 1 vol. 9s.)

Gospel of St. Luke—
GREEK TEXT, with Introduction and Notes
by Rev. J. BOND, M.A. Fcp. 8vo. 2s. 6d.
CHOICE NOTES ON ST. LUKE. Drawn from
Old and New Sources. Cr. 8vo. 4s. 6d.
THE GOSPEL OF THE KINGDOM OF HEAVEN.
A Course of Lectures on the Gospel of St.
Luke. By F. D. MAURICE. Cr. 8vo. 3s 6d.

Gospel of St. John—
THE GOSPEL OF ST. JOHN. By F. D.
MAURICE. Cr. 8vo. 3s. 6d.
CHOICE NOTES ON ST. JOHN. Drawn from
Old and New Sources. Cr. 8vo. 4s. 6d.

The Acts of the Apostles—
THE OLD SYRIAC ELEMENT IN THE TEXT
OF THE CODEX BEZÆ. By F. H. CHASE.
8vo. 7s. 6d. net.
THE ACTS OF THE APOSTLES. By F. D.
MAURICE. Cr. 8vo. 3s. 6d.
ENGLISH VERSION. By T. E. PAGE, M.A.,
and Rev. A. S. WALPOLE, M.A. Pott 8vo
2s. 6d.
GREEK TEXT, with Notes by T. E. PAGE,
M.A. Fcp. 8vo. 3s. 6d.
THE CHURCH OF THE FIRST DAYS: THE
CHURCH OF JERUSALEM, THE CHURCH OF
THE GENTILES, THE CHURCH OF THE
WORLD. Lectures on the Acts of the
Apostles. By Very Rev. C. J. VAUGHAN.
Cr. 8vo. 10s. 6d.

The Epistles of St. Paul—
NOTES ON EPISTLES OF ST. PAUL FROM
UNPUBLISHED COMMENTARIES. By Bishop
LIGHTFOOT. 8vo. 12s.
THE EPISTLE TO THE ROMANS. The
Greek Text, with English Notes. By the
Very Rev. C. J. VAUGHAN. 7th Edit.
Cr. 8vo. 7s. 6d.
PROLEGOMENA TO THE ROMANS AND THE
EPHESIANS. By F. J. A. HORT, D.D.
Cr. 8vo. 6s.
THE EPISTLES TO THE CORINTHIANS. Greek
Text, with Commentary. By Rev. W.
KAY. 8vo. 9s.
THE EPISTLE TO THE GALATIANS. A
Revised Text, with Introduction, Notes,
and Dissertations. By Bishop LIGHTFOOT.
10th Edit. 8vo. 12s.

THEOLOGY.
The Bible—*continued.*

The Epistles of St. Paul—
THE EPISTLE TO THE PHILIPPIANS. A Revised Text, with Introduction, Notes, and Dissertations. By Bishop LIGHTFOOT. 8vo. 12s.

THE EPISTLE TO THE PHILIPPIANS. With Translation, Paraphrase, and Notes for English Readers. By the Very Rev. C. J. VAUGHAN. Cr. 8vo. 5s.

THE EPISTLES TO THE COLOSSIANS AND TO PHILEMON. A Revised Text, with Introductions, etc. By Bishop LIGHTFOOT. 9th Edit. 8vo. 12s.

THE EPISTLES TO THE EPHESIANS, THE COLOSSIANS, AND PHILEMON. With Introduction and Notes. By Rev. J. Ll. DAVIES. 2nd Edit. 8vo. 7s. 6d.

THE FIRST EPISTLE TO THE THESSALONIANS. By Very Rev. C. J. VAUGHAN. 8vo, sewed. 1s. 6d.

THE EPISTLES TO THE THESSALONIANS. Commentary on the Greek Text. By Prof. JOHN EADIE. 8vo. 12s.

The Epistle of St. James—
THE GREEK TEXT, with Introduction and Notes. By Rev. JOSEPH B. MAYOR. 8vo. 14s.

The Epistles of St. John—
THE EPISTLES OF ST. JOHN. By F. D. MAURICE. Cr. 8vo. 3s. 6d.

— The Greek Text, with Notes, by Bishop WESTCOTT. 3rd Edit. 8vo. 12s. 6d.

The Epistle to the Hebrews—
GREEK AND ENGLISH. Edited by Rev. FREDERIC RENDALL. Cr. 8vo. 6s.

ENGLISH TEXT, with Commentary. By the same. Cr. 8vo 7s. 6d.

THE GREEK TEXT, with Notes, by Very Rev C. J. VAUGHAN. Cr. 8vo. 7s. 6d.

THE GREEK TEXT, with Notes and Essays, by Bishop WESTCOTT. 8vo. 14s.

Revelation—
LECTURES ON THE APOCALYPSE. By F. D. MAURICE. Cr. 8vo. 3s. 6d.

THE REVELATION OF ST. JOHN. By Rev. Prof. W. MILLIGAN. Cr. 8vo. 7s. 6d.

LECTURES ON THE APOCALYPSE. By the same. Crown 8vo. 5s.

DISCUSSIONS ON THE APOCALYPSE. By the same. Cr. 8vo. 5s.

LECTURES ON THE REVELATION OF ST. JOHN. By Very Rev. C. J. VAUGHAN. 5th Edit. Cr. 8vo. 10s. 6d.

THE BIBLE WORD-BOOK. By W. ALDIS WRIGHT. 2nd Edit. Cr. 8vo. 7s. 6d.

History of the Christian Church.

CHEETHAM (Archdeacon).—HISTORY OF THE CHRISTIAN CHURCH DURING THE FIRST SIX CENTURIES. Cr. 8vo. 10s. 6d.

CUNNINGHAM (Rev. John).—THE GROWTH OF THE CHURCH IN ITS ORGANISATION AND INSTITUTIONS. 8vo. 9s.

CUNNINGHAM (Rev. William). — THE CHURCHES OF ASIA: A Methodical Sketch of the Second Century. Cr. 8vo. 6s.

DALE (A. W. W.).—THE SYNOD OF ELVIRA, AND CHRISTIAN LIFE IN THE FOURTH CENTURY. Cr. 8vo. 10s. 6d.

GEE (H.) and HARDY (W. J.).—DOCUMENTS ILLUSTRATIVE OF ENGLISH CHURCH HISTORY. Cr. 8vo. 10s. 6d.

GWATKIN (H. M.).—SELECTIONS FROM EARLY WRITERS ILLUSTRATIVE OF CHURCH HISTORY TO THE TIME OF CONSTANTINE. Cr. 8vo. 4s. net.

HARDWICK (Archdeacon).—A HISTORY OF THE CHRISTIAN CHURCH: MIDDLE AGE. Edited by Bp. STUBBS. Cr. 8vo. 10s. 6d.

—— A HISTORY OF THE CHRISTIAN CHURCH DURING THE REFORMATION. 9th Edit., revised by Bishop STUBBS. Cr. 8vo. 10s. 6d.

HORT (Dr. F. J. A.).—TWO DISSERTATIONS. I. On MONOΓENHΣ ΘEOΣ in SCRIPTURE AND TRADITION. II. On the "CONSTANTINOPOLITAN" CREED AND OTHER EASTERN CREEDS OF THE FOURTH CENTURY. 8vo. 7s. 6d.

—— JUDAISTIC CHRISTIANITY. Cr. 8vo. 6s.

SIMPSON (Rev. W.).—AN EPITOME OF THE HISTORY OF THE CHRISTIAN CHURCH. 7th Edit. Fcp. 8vo 3s. 6d.

SOHM (R.).—OUTLINES OF CHURCH HISTORY. Transl. by Miss SINCLAIR. Ed. by Prof. GWATKIN. Cr. 8vo. 3s. 6d.

VAUGHAN (Very Rev. C. J.).—THE CHURCH OF THE FIRST DAYS: THE CHURCH OF JERUSALEM, THE CHURCH OF THE GENTILES, THE CHURCH OF THE WORLD. Cr. 8vo. 10s. 6d.

The Church of England.

Catechism of—
CATECHISM AND CONFIRMATION. By Rev. J. C. P. ALDOUS. Pott 8vo. 1s. net.

A CLASS-BOOK OF THE CATECHISM OF THE CHURCH OF ENGLAND. By Rev. Canon MACLEAR. Pott 8vo. 1s. 6d.

A FIRST CLASS-BOOK OF THE CATECHISM OF THE CHURCH OF ENGLAND. By the same. Pott 8vo. 6d.

THE ORDER OF CONFIRMATION. With Prayers and Devotions. By the same. 32mo. 6d.

Collects—
COLLECTS OF THE CHURCH OF ENGLAND. With a Coloured Floral Design to each Collect. Cr. 8vo. 12s.

Disestablishment—
DISESTABLISHMENT AND DISENDOWMENT. WHAT ARE THEY? By Prof. E. A. FREEMAN. 4th Edit. Cr. 8vo. 1s.

HAND BOOK ON WELSH CHURCH DEFENCE. By the BISHOP OF ST. ASAPH. Fcap. 8vo, sewed. 6d.

A DEFENCE OF THE CHURCH OF ENGLAND AGAINST DISESTABLISHMENT. By ROUNDELL, EARL OF SELBORNE. Cr. 8vo. 2s. 6d.

ANCIENT FACTS AND FICTIONS CONCERNING CHURCHES AND TITHES. By the same. 2nd Edit. Cr. 8vo. 7s. 6d.

Dissent in its Relation to—
DISSENT IN ITS RELATION TO THE CHURCH OF ENGLAND. By Rev. G. H. CURTEIS. Bampton Lectures for 1871. Cr. 8vo. 7s. 6d.

Holy Communion—

THOSE HOLY MYSTERIES. By Rev. J. C. P. ALDOUS. 16mo. 1s. net.

THE COMMUNION SERVICE FROM THE BOOK OF COMMON PRAYER. With Select Readings from the Writings of the Rev. F. D. MAURICE. Edited by Bishop COLENSO. 6th Edit. 16mo. 2s. 6d.

BEFORE THE TABLE: An Inquiry, Historical and Theological, into the Meaning of the Consecration Rubric in the Communion Service of the Church of England. By Very Rev. J. S. HOWSON. 8vo. 7s. 6d.

FIRST COMMUNION. With Prayers and Devotions for the newly Confirmed. By Rev. Canon MACLEAR. 32mo. 6d.

A MANUAL OF INSTRUCTION FOR CONFIRMATION AND FIRST COMMUNION. With Prayers and Devotions. By the same. 32mo. 2s.

Liturgy—

AN INTRODUCTION TO THE CREEDS. By Rev. Canon MACLEAR. Pott 8vo. 3s. 6d.

AN INTRODUCTION TO THE ARTICLES OF THE CHURCH OF ENGLAND. By Rev. G. F. MACLEAR and Rev. W. W. WILLIAMS. Cr. 8vo. 10s. 6d.

A HISTORY OF THE BOOK OF COMMON PRAYER. By Rev F. PROCTER. 18th Edit. Cr. 8vo. 10s. 6d.

AN ELEMENTAY INTRODUCTION TO THE BOOK OF COMMON PRAYER. By Rev. F. PROCTER and Rev. Canon MACLEAR. Pott 8vo. 2s. 6d.

TWELVE DISCOURSES ON SUBJECTS CONNECTED WITH THE LITURGY AND WORSHIP OF THE CHURCH OF ENGLAND. By Very Rev. C. J. VAUGHAN. Fcp. 8vo. 6s.

A COMPANION TO THE LECTIONARY. By Rev. W. BENHAM, B.D. Cr. 8vo. 4s. 6d.

READ AND OTHERS v. THE LORD BISHOP OF LINCOLN. JUDGMENT, Nov. 21, 1890. 2nd Edit. 8vo. 2s. net.

Historical and Biographical—,

THE OXFORD MOVEMENT, 1833—45. By DEAN CHURCH. Gl. 8vo. 5s.

THE LIFE AND LETTERS OF R. W. CHURCH, late Dean of St. Paul's. 8vo. 7s. 6d.

JAMES FRASER, Second Bishop of Manchester. A Memoir. 1818—1885. By THOMAS HUGHES, Q.C. 2nd Edit. Cr. 8vo. 6s.

THE LIFE OF FREDERICK DENISON MAURICE. Chiefly told in his own letters. Ed. by his Son, FREDERICK MAURICE. With Portraits. In 2 vols. 2nd Edit. 8vo. 36s. Cheap Edit. 2 vols. Cr. 8vo. 16s.

LIFE OF ARCHIBALD CAMPBELL TAIT, Archbishop of Canterbury. By the BISHOP OF WINCHESTER and W. BENHAM, B.D. With Portraits. 3rd Ed. 2 vols. Cr. 8vo. 10s.net.

WILLIAM GEORGE WARD AND THE OXFORD MOVEMENT. By W. WARD. Portrait. 8vo. 14s.

WILLIAM GEORGE WARD AND THE CATHOLIC REVIVAL. By the Same. 8vo. 14s.

———

CANTERBURY DIOCESAN GAZETTE. Monthly. 8vo. 2d.

JEWISH QUARTERLY REVIEW. Edited by I. ABRAHAMS and C. G. MONTEFIORE. Demy 8vo. 3s. 6d.

Devotional Books.

EASTLAKE (Lady).—FELLOWSHIP: LETTERS ADDRESSED TO MY SISTER-MOURNERS. Cr. 8vo. 2s. 6d.

IMITATIO CHRISTI. Libri IV. Printed in Borders after Holbein, Dürer, and other old Masters, containing Dances of Death, Acts of Mercy, Emblems, etc. Cr. 8vo. 7s. 6d.

KINGSLEY (Charles).—OUT OF THE DEEP: WORDS FOR THE SORROWFUL. From the Writings of CHARLES KINGSLEY. Ext. fcp. 8vo. 3s. 6d.

—— DAILY THOUGHTS. Selected from the Writings of CHARLES KINGSLEY. By HIS WIFE. Cr. 8vo. 6s.

—— FROM DEATH TO LIFE. Fragments of Teaching to a Village Congregation. Edit. by HIS WIFE. Fcp. 8vo. 2s. 6d.

MACLEAR (Rev. Canon).—A MANUAL OF INSTRUCTION FOR CONFIRMATION AND FIRST COMMUNION, WITH PRAYERS AND DEVOTIONS. 32mo. 2s.

—— THE HOUR OF SORROW; or, The Office for the Burial of the Dead. 32mo. 2s.

MAURICE (F. D.).—LESSONS OF HOPE. Readings from the Works of F. D. MAURICE. Selected by Rev. J. LL. DAVIES, M.A. Cr. 8vo. 5s.

RAYS OF SUNLIGHT FOR DARK DAYS. With a Preface by Very Rev. C. J. VAUGHAN. D.D. New Edition. Pott 8vo. 3s. 6d.

SERVICE (Rev. J.).—PRAYERS FOR PUBLIC WORSHIP. Cr. 8vo. 4s. 6d.

THE WORSHIP OF GOD, AND FELLOWSHIP AMONG MEN. By Prof. MAURICE and others. Fcp. 8vo. 3s. 6d.

WELBY-GREGORY (Hon. Lady).—LINKS AND CLUES. 2nd Edit. Cr. 8vo. 6s.

WESTCOTT (Rt. Rev. Bishop).—THOUGHTS ON REVELATION AND LIFE. Selections from the Writings of Bishop WESTCOTT. Edited by Rev. S. PHILLIPS. Cr. 8vo. 6s.

WILBRAHAM (Francis M.).—IN THE SERE AND YELLOW LEAF: THOUGHTS AND RECOLLECTIONS FOR OLD AND YOUNG. Globe 8vo. 3s. 6d.

The Fathers.

DONALDSON (Prof. James).—THE APOSTOLIC FATHERS. A Critical Account of their Genuine Writings, and of their Doctrines. 2nd Edit. Cr. 8vo. 7s. 6d.

Works of the Greek and Latin Fathers:

THE APOSTOLIC FATHERS. Revised Texts, with Introductions, Notes, Dissertations, and Translations. By Bishop LIGHTFOOT. —Part I. ST. CLEMENT OF ROME. 2 vols. 8vo. 32s.—Part II. ST. IGNATIUS TO ST. POLYCARP. 3 vols. 2nd Edit. 8vo. 48s.

THE APOSTOLIC FATHERS. Abridged Edit. With Short Introductions, Greek Text, and English Translation. By same. 8vo. 16s.

INDEX OF NOTEWORTHY WORDS AND PHRASES FOUND IN THE CLEMENTINE WRITINGS. 8vo. 5s.

SIX LECTURES ON THE ANTE-NICENE FATHERS. By F. J. A. HORT. Cr. 8vo. 3s. 6d.

THE EPISTLE OF ST. BARNABAS. Its Date and Authorship. With Greek Text, Latin Version, Translation and Commentary. By Rev. W. CUNNINGHAM. Cr. 8vo. 7s. 6d.

THEOLOGY.
Hymnology.

BROOKE (S. A.).—CHRISTIAN HYMNS. Gl. 8vo. 2s.6d. net.—CHRISTIAN HYMNS AND SERVICE BOOK OF BEDFORD CHAPEL, BLOOMSBURY. Gl. 8vo. 3s. 6d. net.—SERVICE BOOK. Gl. 8vo. 1s. net.

PALGRAVE (Prof. F. T.). — ORIGINAL HYMNS. 3rd Edit. Pott 8vo. 1s. 6d.

SELBORNE (Roundell, Earl of).—THE BOOK OF PRAISE. Pott 8vo. 2s. 6d. net.
—— A HYMNAL. Chiefly from "The Book of Praise."—A. Royal 32mo, limp. 6d.—B. Pott 8vo, larger type. 1s.—C. Fine paper. 1s.6d.—With Music, Selected, Harmonised, and Composed by JOHN HULLAH. Pott 8vo. 3s. 6d.

WOODS (Miss M. A.).—HYMNS FOR SCHOOL WORSHIP. Pott 8vo. 1s. 6d.

Sermons, Lectures, Addresses, and Theological Essays.

ABBOT (F. E.).—SCIENTIFIC THEISM. Cr 8vo. 7s. 6d.
—— THE WAY OUT OF AGNOSTICISM ; or, The Philosophy of Free Religion. Cr. 8vo. 4s. 6d

ABBOTT (Rev. E. A.).—CAMBRIDGE SERMONS. 8vo. 6s.
—— OXFORD SERMONS. 8vo. 7s. 6d.
—— PHILOMYTHUS. A discussion of Cardinal Newman's Essay on Ecclesiastical Miracles. Cr. 8vo. 3s. 6d.
—— NEWMANIANISM. Cr. 8vo. 1s. net.

ABRAHAMS(I.)and MONTEFIORE(C. G.) —ASPECTS OF JUDAISM. 2nd Edit. Fcp. 8vo. 3s. 6d. net.

AINGER (Canon).—SERMONS PREACHED IN THE TEMPLE CHURCH. Ext. fcp. 8vo. 6s.

ALEXANDER (Archbishop).—THE LEADING IDEAS OF THE GOSPELS. New Edit. Cr. 8vo. 6s.

BAINES (Rev. Edward).—SERMONS. Preface and Memoir by Bishop BARRY. Cr. 8vo. 6s.

BARRY (A.).—ECCLESIASTICAL EXPANSION OF ENGLAND. Cr. 8vo. 6s.

BATHER (Archdeacon).—ON SOME MINISTERIAL DUTIES, CATECHISING, PREACHING, Etc. Edited, with a Preface, by Very Rev. C. J. VAUGHAN, D.D. Fcp. 8vo. 4s. 6d.

BERNARD (Canon). —THE CENTRAL TEACHING OF CHRIST. Cr. 8vo. 7s. 6d.
—— SONGS OF THE HOLY NATIVITY. Cr. 8vo. 5s.

BINNIE (Rev. W.).—SERMONS. Cr. 8vo. 6s.

BIRKS (Thomas Rawson).—THE DIFFICULTIES OF BELIEF IN CONNECTION WITH THE CREATION AND THE FALL, REDEMPTION, AND JUDGMENT. 2nd Edit. Cr. 8vo. 5s.
—— JUSTIFICATION AND IMPUTED RIGHTEOUSNESS. A Review. Cr. 8vo. 6s.
—— SUPERNATURAL REVELATION ; or, First Principles of Moral Theology. 8vo. 8s.

BRADFORD (A. H.).—HEREDITY AND CHRISTIAN PROBLEMS. Cr. 8vo. 5s. net.

BROOKE (S. A.).—SHORT SERMONS. Crown 8vo. 6s.

BROOKS (Bishop Phillips).—THE CANDLE OF THE LORD : and other Sermons. Cr. 8vo. 6s.
—— SERMONS PREACHED IN ENGLISH CHURCHES. Cr. 8vo. 6s.
—— TWENTY SERMONS. Cr. 8vo. 6s.
—— TOLERANCE. Cr. 8vo. 2s. 6d.
—— THE LIGHT OF THE WORLD. Cr. 8vo. 3s. 6d.
—— THE MYSTERY OF INIQUITY. Cr. 8vo. 6s.
—— ESSAYS AND ADDRESSES. Cr. 8vo. 8s.6d. net.

BRUNTON (T. Lauder).—THE BIBLE AND SCIENCE. Illustrated. Cr. 8vo. 10s. 6d.

BUTLER (Archer).—SERMONS, DOCTRINAL AND PRACTICAL. 11th Edit. 8vo. 8s.
—— SECOND SERIES OF SERMONS. 8vo. 7s.
—— LETTERS ON ROMANISM. 8vo. 10s. 6d.

BUTLER (Rev. Geo.).—SERMONS PREACHED IN CHELTENHAM COLLEGE CHAPEL. 8vo. 7s. 6d.

CAMPBELL (Dr. John M'Leod).—THE NATURE OF THE ATONEMENT. Cr. 8vo. 6s.
—— REMINISCENCES AND REFLECTIONS. Edited by his Son, DONALD CAMPBELL, M.A. Cr. 8vo. 7s. 6d.
—— THOUGHTS ON REVELATION. Cr. 8vo. 5s.
—— RESPONSIBILITY FOR THE GIFT OF ETERNAL LIFE. Compiled from Sermons preached 1829—31. Cr. 8vo. 5s.

CANTERBURY (Edward White, Archbishop of).—BOY-LIFE : ITS TRIAL, ITS STRENGTH, ITS FULNESS. Sundays in Wellington College, 1859—73. Cr. 8vo. 6s.
—— THE SEVEN GIFTS. Primary Visitation Address. Cr. 8vo. 6s.
—— CHRIST AND HIS TIMES. Second Visitation Address. Cr. 8vo. 6s.
—— A PASTORAL LETTER TO THE DIOCESE OF CANTERBURY, 1890. 8vo, sewed. 1d.
—— FISHERS OF MEN. Third Visitation Address. Cr. 8vo. 6s.

CARPENTER (W. Boyd, Bishop of Ripon).— TRUTH IN TALE. Addresses, chiefly to Children. Cr. 8vo. 4s. 6d.
—— TWILIGHT DREAMS. Cr. 8vo. 4s. 6d.
—— THE PERMANENT ELEMENTS OF RELIGION. 2nd Edit. Cr. 8vo. 6s.
—— LECTURES ON PREACHING. Cr. 8vo. 3s. 6d. net.
—— THOUGHTS ON CHRISTIAN REUNION. Cr. 8vo. 3s. 6d. net.

CAZENOVE (J. Gibson).—CONCERNING THE BEING AND ATTRIBUTES OF GOD. 8vo. 5s

CHURCH (Dean).—HUMAN LIFE AND ITS CONDITIONS. Cr. 8vo. 6s.
—— THE GIFTS OF CIVILISATION : and other Sermons and Letters. Cr. 8vo. 7s. 6d.
—— DISCIPLINE OF THE CHRISTIAN CHARACTER ; and other Sermons. Cr. 8vo. 4s. 6d.
—— ADVENT SERMONS, 1885. Cr. 8vo. 4s. 6d.
—— VILLAGE SERMONS. Cr. 8vo. 6s.
—— VILLAGE SERMONS. 2nd Series. Cr. 8vo. 6s.
—— CATHEDRAL AND UNIVERSITY SERMONS. Cr. 8vo. 6s.
—— PASCAL, AND OTHER SERMONS. Cr. 8vo. 6s.

CLERGYMAN'S SELF-EXAMINATION CONCERNING THE APOSTLES' CREED. Ext. fcp. 8vo. 1s. 6d.

CONFESSION OF FAITH (A). Fcp. 8vo. 3s. 6d.

CONGREVE (Rev. John). — HIGH HOPES AND PLEADINGS FOR A REASONABLE FAITH, NOBLER THOUGHTS, AND LARGER CHARITY. Cr. 8vo. 5s.

COOKE (Josiah P., jun.).—RELIGION AND CHEMISTRY. Cr. 8vo. 7s. 6d.
—— THE CREDENTIALS OF SCIENCE, THE WARRANT OF FAITH. 8vo. 8s. 6d. net.

CORNISH (F.).—WEEK BY WEEK. Fcap. 8vo. 3s. 6d.

COTTON (Bishop).—SERMONS PREACHED TO ENGLISH CONGREGATIONS IN INDIA. Cr 8vo. 7s. 6d.

CUNNINGHAM (Rev. W.). — CHRISTIAN CIVILISATION, WITH SPECIAL REFERENCE TO INDIA. Cr. 8vo. 5s.

CURTEIS (Rev. G. H.).—THE SCIENTIFIC OBSTACLES TO CHRISTIAN BELIEF. The Boyle Lectures, 1884. Cr. 8vo. 6s.

DAVIES (Rev. J. Llewelyn).—THE GOSPEL AND MODERN LIFE. Ext. fcp. 8vo. 6s.
—— SOCIAL QUESTIONS FROM THE POINT OF VIEW OF CHRISTIAN THEOLOGY. Cr. 8vo. 6s.
—— WARNINGS AGAINST SUPERSTITION. Ext. fcp. 8vo. 2s. 6d.
—— THE CHRISTIAN CALLING. Ext. fp. 8vo. 6s.
—— ORDER AND GROWTH AS INVOLVED IN THE SPIRITUAL CONSTITUTION OF HUMAN SOCIETY. Cr. 8vo. 3s. 6d.
—— BAPTISM, CONFIRMATION, AND THE LORD'S SUPPER. Addresses. Pott 8vo. 1s.

DAVIDSON (Bp.).—CHARGE DELIVERED TO THE CLERGY OF THE DIOCESE OF ROCHESTER, 1894. 8vo, sewed. 2s. net.

DAVIES (W.).—THE PILGRIM OF THE INFINITE. Fcp. 8vo. 3s. 6d.

DIGGLE (Rev. J. W.).—GODLINESS AND MANLINESS. Cr. 8vo. 6s.

DRUMMOND (Prof. Jas.).—INTRODUCTION TO THE STUDY OF THEOLOGY. Cr. 8vo. 5s.

DU BOSE (W. P.).—THE SOTERIOLOGY OF THE NEW TESTAMENT. Cr. 8vo. 7s. 6d.

ELLERTON (Rev. John).—THE HOLIEST MANHOOD, AND ITS LESSONS FOR BUSY LIVES. Cr. 8vo. 6s.

FAITH AND CONDUCT: AN ESSAY ON VERIFIABLE RELIGION. Cr. 8vo. 7s. 6d.

FARRAR (Ven. Archdeacon).—WORKS. Uniform Edition. Cr. 8vo. 3s. 6d. each
SEEKERS AFTER GOD.
ETERNAL HOPE. Westminster Abbey Sermons.
THE FALL OF MAN: and other Sermons.
THE WITNESS OF HISTORY TO CHRIST Hulsean Lectures, 1870.
THE SILENCE AND VOICES OF GOD. Sermons.
IN THE DAYS OF THY YOUTH. Marlborough College Sermons
SAINTLY WORKERS. Five Lenten Lectures.
EPHPHATHA; or, The Amelioration of the World.
MERCY AND JUDGMENT.
SERMONS AND ADDRESSES DELIVERED IN AMERICA.
—— THE HISTORY OF INTERPRETATION. Bampton Lectures, 1885. 8vo. 16s.

FISKE (John).—MAN'S DESTINY VIEWED IN THE LIGHT OF HIS ORIGIN. Cr. 8vo. 3s. 6d.

FORBES (Rev. Granville).—THE VOICE OF GOD IN THE PSALMS. Cr. 8vo. 6s. 6d.

FOWLE (Rev. T. W.).—A NEW ANALOGY BETWEEN REVEALED RELIGION AND THE COURSE AND CONSTITUTION OF NATURE. Cr. 8vo. 6s.

FOXELL (W. J.).—GOD'S GARDEN, SUNDAY TALKS WITH BOYS. Gl. 8vo. 3s. 6d.

FRASER (Bishop).—SERMONS. Edited by JOHN W. DIGGLE. 2 vols. Cr. 8vo. 6s. each.

GLOVER (E.). — MEMORIALS OF. By G. GLOVER. Cr. 8vo. 3s. net.

GRANE (W. L.).—THE WORD AND THE WAY. Cr. 8vo. 6s.

HARE (Julius Charles).—THE MISSION OF THE COMFORTER. New Edition. Edited by Dean PLUMPTRE. Cr. 8vo. 7s. 6d.

HAMILTON (John).—ON TRUTH AND ERROR. Cr. 8vo. 5s.
—— ARTHUR'S SEAT; or, The Church of the Banned. Cr. 8vo. 6s
—— ABOVE AND AROUND: Thoughts on God and Man. 12mo. 2s. 6d.

HARDWICK (Archdeacon).—CHRIST AND OTHER MASTERS. 6th Edit. Cr. 8vo. 10s. 6d.

HARRIS (Rev. G. C.).—SERMONS. With a Memoir by C. M. YONGE. Ext. fcp. 8vo. 6s.

HORT (F. J. A.).—THE WAY, THE TRUTH, THE LIFE. Cr. 8vo. 6s.
—— JUDAISTIC CHRISTIANITY. Cr. 8vo. 6s.

HUGHES (T.).—MANLINESS OF CHRIST. 2nd Edit. Fcp. 8vo. 3s. 6d.

HUTTON (R. H.). (See p. 26.)

HYDE (W. de W.).—OUTLINES OF SOCIAL THEOLOGY. Cr. 8vo. 6s.

ILLINGWORTH (Rev. J. R.).—SERMONS PREACHED IN A COLLEGE CHAPEL. Cr. 8vo. 5s.
—— UNIVERSITY AND CATHEDRAL SERMONS. Crown 8vo. 5s.
—— PERSONALITY, HUMAN, AND DIVINE. Crown 8vo. 6s.

JACOB (Rev. J. A.).—BUILDING IN SILENCE: and other Sermons. Ext. fcp. 8vo. 6s.

JAMES (Rev. Herbert). — THE COUNTRY CLERGYMAN AND HIS WORK. Cr. 8vo. 6s.

JEANS (Rev. G. E.).—HAILEYBURY CHAPEL: and other Sermons. Fcp. 8vo. 3s. 6d.

JELLETT (Rev. Dr.).—THE ELDER SON: and other Sermons. Cr. 8vo. 6s.
—— THE EFFICACY OF PRAYER. Cr. 8vo. 5s.

KELLOGG (Rev. S. H.).—THE LIGHT OF ASIA AND THE LIGHT OF THE WORLD. Cr. 8vo. 7s. 6d.
—— GENESIS AND GROWTH OF RELIGION. Cr. 8vo. 6s.

KELLY (E). — EVOLUTION AND EFFORT. Cr. 8vo. 4s. 6d. net.

KINGSLEY (Charles). (See COLLECTED WORKS, p. 26.)

KIRKPATRICK (Prof.).—THE DIVINE LIBRARY OF THE OLD TESTAMENT. Cr. 8vo. 3s. net.
—— DOCTRINE OF THE PROPHETS. Cr. 8vo. 6s.

KYNASTON (Rev. Herbert, D.D.).—CHELTENHAM COLLEGE SERMONS. Cr. 8vo. 6s.

LEGGE (A. O.).—THE GROWTH OF THE TEMPORAL POWER OF THE PAPACY. Cr. 8vo. 8s. 6d

LIGHTFOOT (Bishop).—LEADERS IN THE NORTHERN CHURCH: Sermons. Cr. 8vo. 6s
—— ORDINATION ADDRESSES AND COUNSELS TO CLERGY. Cr. 8vo. 6s.
—— CAMBRIDGE SERMONS. Cr. 8vo. 6s.
—— SERMONS PREACHED IN ST. PAUL'S CATHEDRAL. Cr. 8vo. 6s.
—— SERMONS ON SPECIAL OCCASIONS. 8vo. 6s.
—— A CHARGE DELIVERED TO THE CLERGY OF THE DIOCESE OF DURHAM, 1886. 8vo. 2s.

THEOLOGY.
Sermons, Lectures, Addresses, and Theological Essays—*continued.*

LIGHTFOOT (Bp.).—ESSAYS ON THE WORK ENTITLED "SUPERNATURAL RELIGION." 2nd Edit. 8vo. 10s. 6d

—— ON A FRESH REVISION OF THE ENGLISH NEW TESTAMENT. Cr. 8vo. 7s. 6d.

—— DISSERTATIONS ON THE APOSTOLIC AGE. 8vo. 14s.

—— BIBLICAL ESSAYS. 8vo. 12s.

—— HISTORICAL ESSAYS. Gl. 8vo. 5s.

LYTTELTON (A. T.). SERMONS. Cr. 8vo. 6s.

MACLAREN (Rev. A.).—SERMONS PREACHED AT MANCHESTER. 11th Ed. Fcp. 8vo. 4s. 6d.

—— SECOND SERIES 7th Ed. Fcp. 8vo 4s. 6d.

—— THIRD SERIES. 6th Ed. Fcp. 8vo. 4s. 6d

—— WEEK-DAY EVENING ADDRESSES. 4th Edit. Fcp. 8vo. 2s. 6d.

—— THE SECRET OF POWER : and other Sermons. Fcp. 8vo. 4s. 6d,

MACMILLAN (Rev. Hugh).—BIBLE TEACHINGS IN NATURE. 15th Edit. Globe 8vo. 6s.

—— THE TRUE VINE; or, The Analogies of our Lord's Allegory. 5th Edit. Gl. 8vo. 6s.

—— THE MINISTRY OF NATURE. 8th Edit. Globe 8vo. 6s.

—— THE SABBATH OF THE FIELDS. 6th Edit. Globe 8vo. 6s.

—— THE MARRIAGE IN CANA. Gl. 8vo. 6s.

—— TWO WORLDS ARE OURS. Gl. 8vo. 6s.

—— THE OLIVE LEAF. Globe 8vo. 6s.

—— THE GATE BEAUTIFUL : and other Bible Teachings for the Young. Cr. 8vo. 3s. 6d.

MAHAFFY (Prof. J. P.).—THE DECAY OF MODERN PREACHING. Cr. 8vo. 3s. 6d.

MATURIN (Rev. W.).—THE BLESSEDNESS OF THE DEAD IN CHRIST. Cr. 8vo. 7s. 6d.

MAURICE (Frederick Denison).—THE KINGDOM OF CHRIST. 3rd Ed. 2 vols. Cr. 8vo 12s.

—— DIALOGUES ON FAMILY WORSHIP. Cr. 8vo. 4s. 6d.

—— EXPOSITORY SERMONS ON THE PRAYER-BOOK, AND THE LORD'S PRAYER. Cr. 8vo. 6s.

—— SERMONS PREACHED IN COUNTRY CHURCHES. 2nd Edit. Cr. 8vo. 6s.

—— THE CONSCIENCE : Lectures on Casuistry. 3rd Edit. Cr. 8vo. 4s. 6d.

—— THE DOCTRINE OF SACRIFICE DEDUCED FROM THE SCRIPTURES. 2nd Edit. Cr. 8vo. 6s.

—— THE RELIGIONS OF THE WORLD. 6th Edit. Cr. 8vo. 4s. 6d

—— ON THE SABBATH DAY; THE CHARACTER OF THE WARRIOR; AND ON THE INTERPRETATION OF HISTORY. Fcp. 8vo. 2s. 6d.

—— LEARNING AND WORKING. Cr. 8vo. 4s. 6d.

—— THE LORD'S PRAYER, THE CREED, AND THE COMMANDMENTS. Pott 8vo. 1s.

—— SERMONS PREACHED IN LINCOLN'S INN CHAPEL. 6 vols. Cr. 8vo. 3s. 6d. each.

—— COLLECTED WORKS. Cr. 8vo. 3s. 6d. each.
CHRISTMAS DAY AND OTHER SERMONS.
THEOLOGICAL ESSAYS.
PROPHETS AND KINGS.
PATRIARCHS AND LAWGIVERS.
THE GOSPEL OF THE KINGDOM OF HEAVEN.
GOSPEL OF ST. JOHN.
EPISTLE OF ST. JOHN.
LECTURES ON THE APOCALYPSE.
FRIENDSHIP OF BOOKS.
SOCIAL MORALITY.
PRAYER BOOK AND LORD'S PRAYER.
THE DOCTRINE OF SACRIFICE.
THE ACTS OF THE APOSTLES.

McCURDY (J. F.).—HISTORY, PROPHECY, AND THE MONUMENTS. 2 vols. Vol. I., 14s. net

MILLIGAN (Rev. Prof. W.).—THE RESURRECTION OF OUR LORD. 4th Edit. Cr. 8vo. 5s.

—— THE ASCENSION AND HEAVENLY PRIESTHOOD OF OUR LORD. Cr. 8vo. 7s. 6d.

MOORHOUSE (J., Bishop of Manchester).—JACOB : Three Sermons. Ext. fcp. 8vo. 3s 6d.

—— THE TEACHING OF CHRIST : its Conditions, Secret, and Results. Cr. 8vo. 3s. net.

—— CHURCH WORK : ITS MEANS AND METHODS. Cr. 8vo. 3s. net.

MURPHY (J. J.).—NATURAL SELECTION AND SPIRITUAL FREEDOM. Gl. 8vo. 5s.

MYLNE (L. G., Bishop of Bombay).—SERMONS PREACHED IN ST. THOMAS'S CATHEDRAL, BOMBAY. Cr. 8vo. 6s.

PATTISON (Mark).—SERMONS. Cr. 8vo. 6s.

PAUL OF TARSUS. 8vo. 10s. 6d.

PHILOCHRISTUS : MEMOIRS OF A DISCIPLE OF THE LORD. 3rd. Edit. 8vo. 12s.

PLUMPTRE (Dean).—MOVEMENTS IN RELIGIOUS THOUGHT. Fcp. 8vo. 3s. 6d.

POTTER (R.).—THE RELATION OF ETHICS TO RELIGION. Cr. 8vo. 2s. 6d.

REASONABLE FAITH : A SHORT ESSAY By "Three Friends." Cr. 8vo. 1s.

REICHEL (C. P., Bishop of Meath).—THE LORD'S PRAYER. Cr. 8vo. 7s. 6d.

—— CATHEDRAL AND UNIVERSITY SERMONS. Cr. 8vo. 6s.

RENDALL (Rev. F.).—THE THEOLOGY OF THE HEBREW CHRISTIANS. Cr. 8vo. 5s.

REYNOLDS (H. R.).—NOTES OF THE CHRISTIAN LIFE. Cr. 8vo. 7s. 6d.

ROBINSON (Prebendary H. G.).—MAN IN THE IMAGE OF GOD : and other Sermons. Cr. 8vo. 7s. 6d.

RUSSELL (Dean).—THE LIGHT THAT LIGHTETH EVERY MAN : Sermons. With an Introduction by Dean PLUMPTRE, D.D. Cr. 8vo. 6s.

RYLE (Rev. Prof. H.).—THE EARLY NARRATIVES OF GENESIS. Cr. 8vo. 3s. net.

SALMON (Rev. George, D.D.).—NON-MIRACULOUS CHRISTIANITY : and other Sermons. 2nd Edit. Cr. 8vo. 6s.

—— GNOSTICISM AND AGNOSTICISM : and other Sermons. Cr. 8vo. 7s. 6d.

SANDFORD (Rt. Rev. C. W., Bishop of Gibraltar).—COUNSEL TO ENGLISH CHURCHMEN ABROAD. Cr. 8vo. 6s.

SCOTCH SERMONS, 1880. By Principal CAIRD and others. 3rd Edit. 8vo. 10s. 6d.

SEELEY (J. R.).—ECCE HOMO. Gl. 8vo. 5s.

—— NATURAL RELIGION. Gl. 8vo. 5s.

SERVICE (Rev. J.).—SERMONS. Cr. 8vo. 6s.

SHIRLEY (W. N.).—ELIJAH : Four University Sermons. Fcp. 8vo. 2s. 6d.

SMITH (Rev. Travers).—MAN'S KNOWLEDGE OF MAN AND OF GOD. Cr. 8vo. 6s.

STANLEY (Dean).—THE NATIONAL THANKSGIVING. Sermons Preached in Westminster Abbey. 2nd Edit. Cr. 8vo. 2s. 6d.

—— ADDRESSES AND SERMONS delivered in America, 1878. Cr. 8vo. 6s.

STEWART (Prof. Balfour) and TAIT (Prof. P. G.).—THE UNSEEN UNIVERSE, OR PHYSICAL SPECULATIONS ON A FUTURE STATE. 15th Edit. Cr. 8vo. 6s.

—— PARADOXICAL PHILOSOPHY: A Sequel to the above. Cr. 8vo. 7s. 6d.

STUBBS (Dean).—FOR CHRIST AND CITY. Sermons and Addresses. Cr. 8vo. 6s.

—— "CHRISTUS IMPERATOR!" A Series of Lecture-Sermons. Cr. 8vo. 6s.

TAIT (Archbp.).—THE PRESENT CONDITION OF THE CHURCH OF ENGLAND. Primary Visitation Charge. 3rd Edit. 8vo. 3s. 6d.

—— DUTIES OF THE CHURCH OF ENGLAND. Second Visitation Addresses. 8vo. 4s. 6d.

—— THE CHURCH OF THE FUTURE. Quadrennial Visitation Charges. Cr. 8vo. 3s. 6d.

TAYLOR (Isaac).—THE RESTORATION OF BELIEF. Cr. 8vo. 8s. 6d.

TEMPLE (Frederick, Bishop of London).—SERMONS PREACHED IN THE CHAPEL OF RUGBY SCHOOL. Second Series. Ex. fcp. 8vo. 6s. Third Series 4th Edit. Ext. fcp. 8vo. 6s.

—— THE RELATIONS BETWEEN RELIGION AND SCIENCE. Bampton Lectures, 1884. 7th and Cheaper Edition. Cr. 8vo. 6s.

TRENCH (Archbishop). — THE HULSEAN LECTURES FOR 1845—6. 8vo. 7s. 6d.

TULLOCH (Principal).—THE CHRIST OF THE GOSPELS AND THE CHRIST OF MODERN CRITICISM. Ext. fcp. 8vo. 4s. 6d.

VAUGHAN (C. J., Dean of Landaff).—MEMORIALS OF HARROW SUNDAYS. 8vo. 10s. 6d.

—— EPIPHANY, LENT, AND EASTER. 8vo. 10s. 6d.

—— HEROES OF FAITH. 2nd Edit. Cr. 8vo. 6s.

—— LIFE'S WORK AND GOD'S DISCIPLINE. Ext. fcp. 8vo. 2s. 6d.

—— THE WHOLESOME WORDS OF JESUS CHRIST. 2nd Edit. Fcp. 8vo. 3s. 6d.

—— FOES OF FAITH. 2nd Edit. Fcp. 8vo. 3s. 6d.

—— CHRIST SATISFYING THE INSTINCTS OF HUMANITY. 2nd Edit. Ext. fcp. 8vo. 3s. 6d.

—— COUNSELS FOR YOUNG STUDENTS. Fcp. 8vo. 2s. 6d.

—— THE TWO GREAT TEMPTATIONS. 2nd Edit. Fcp. 8vo. 3s. 6d.

—— ADDRESSES FOR YOUNG CLERGYMEN. Ext. fcp. 8vo. 4s. 6d.

—— "MY SON GIVE ME THINE HEART." Ext. fcp. 8vo. 5s.

—— REST AWHILE. Addresses to Toilers in the Ministry. Ext. fcp. 8vo. 5s.

—— TEMPLE SERMONS. Cr. 8vo. 10s. 6d.

—— AUTHORISED OR REVISED? Sermons. Cr. 8vo 7s. 6d.

—— LESSONS OF THE CROSS AND PASSION; WORDS FROM THE CROSS; THE REIGN OF SIN; THE LORD'S PRAYER. Four Courses of Lent Lectures. Cr. 8vo. 10s. 6d.

—— UNIVERSITY SERMONS, NEW AND OLD. Cr. 8vo. 10s. 6d.

—— THE PRAYERS OF JESUS CHRIST. Globe 8vo. 3s. 6d.

—— DONCASTER SERMONS; LESSONS OF LIFE AND GODLINESS; WORDS FROM THE GOSPELS. Cr. 8vo. 10s. 6d.

—— NOTES FOR LECTURES ON CONFIRMATION. 14th Edit. Fcp. 8vo. 1s. 6d.

—— RESTFUL THOUGHTS IN RESTLESS TIMES. Crown 8vo. 5s.

—— LAST WORDS IN THE TEMPLE CHURCH. Gl. 8vo. 5s.

VAUGHAN (Rev. D. J.).—THE PRESENT TRIAL OF FAITH. Cr. 8vo. 5s. (See p. 26.)

VAUGHAN (Rev. E. T.)—SOME REASONS OF OUR CHRISTIAN HOPE. Hulsean Lectures for 1875. Cr. 8vo. 6s. 6d.

VAUGHAN (Rev. Robert).—STONES FROM THE QUARRY. Sermons. Cr. 8vo. 5s.

VENN (Rev. John).—ON SOME CHARACTERISTICS OF BELIEF, SCIENTIFIC, AND RELIGIOUS. Hulsean Lectures, 1869. 8vo. 6s. 6d.

WELLDON (Rev. J. E. C.).—THE SPIRITUAL LIFE: and other Sermons. Cr. 8vo. 6s.

WESTCOTT (Rt. Rev. B. F., Bishop of Durham).—ON THE RELIGIOUS OFFICE OF THE UNIVERSITIES. Sermons. Cr. 8vo. 4s. 6d.

—— GIFTS FOR MINISTRY. Addresses to Candidates for Ordination. Cr. 8vo. 1s. 6d.

—— THE VICTORY OF THE CROSS. Sermons Preached in 1888. Cr. 8vo. 3s. 6d.

—— FROM STRENGTH TO STRENGTH. Three Sermons (In Memoriam J. B. D.). Cr. 8vo. 2s.

—— THE REVELATION OF THE RISEN LORD. 4th Edit. Cr. 8vo. 6s.

—— THE HISTORIC FAITH. Cr. 8vo. 6s.

—— THE GOSPEL OF THE RESURRECTION. 6th Edit. Cr. 8vo. 6s.

—— THE REVELATION OF THE FATHER. Cr. 8vo. 6s.

—— CHRISTUS CONSUMMATOR. Cr. 8vo. 6s.

—— SOME THOUGHTS FROM THE ORDINAL. Cr. 8vo. 1s. 6d.

—— SOCIAL ASPECTS OF CHRISTIANITY. Cr. 8vo. 6s.

—— THE GOSPEL OF LIFE. Cr. 8vo. 6s.

—— ESSAYS IN THE HISTORY OF RELIGIOUS THOUGHT IN THE WEST. Globe 8vo. 5s.

—— INCARNATION AND COMMON LIFE. Cr. 8vo. 9s.

WHITTUCK (C. A.).—CHURCH OF ENGLAND AND RECENT RELIGIOUS THOUGHT. Cr. 8vo. 7s. 6d.

WICKHAM (Rev. E. C.).—WELLINGTON COLLEGE SERMONS. Cr. 8vo. 6s.

WILKINS (Prof. A. S.).—THE LIGHT OF THE WORLD: An Essay. 2nd Ed. Cr. 8vo. 3s. 6d.

WILLIAMSON (M. B).—TRUTH AND THE WITNESS Cr. 8vo. 4s. 6d.

WILLINK (A.).—THE WORLD OF THE UNSEEN. Cr. 8vo. 3s. 6d.

WILSON (J. M., Archdeacon of Manchester).—SERMONS PREACHED IN CLIFTON COLLEGE CHAPEL. 2nd Series, 1888—90. Cr. 8vo. 6s.

—— ESSAYS AND ADDRESSES. Crown 8vo. 2s. 6d net.

—— SOME CONTRIBUTIONS TO THE RELIGIOUS THOUGHT OF OUR TIME. Cr. 8vo. 6s.

WOOD (C. J.).—SURVIVALS IN CHRISTIANITY. Crown 8vo. 6s.

WOOD (Rev. E. G.).—THE REGAL POWER OF THE CHURCH. 8vo. 4s. 6d.

THERAPEUTICS. (See MEDICINE, p. 28.)

TRANSLATIONS.

From the Greek—From the Italian—From the Latin—Into Latin and Greek Verse.

From the Greek.

SPECIMENS OF GREEK TRAGEDY. Transl. by GOLDWIN SMITH, D.C.L. 2 vols. Gl. 8vo. 10s.

TRANSLATIONS—*continued.*

AESCHYLUS.—The Supplices. With Translation, by T. G. Tucker, Litt.D. 8vo. 10s. 6d.

—— The Seven against Thebes. With Translation, by A. W. Verrall, Litt.D. 8vo. 7s. 6d.

—— The Choephori. With Translation. By the same. 8vo. 12s.

—— Eumenides. With Verse Translation, by Bernard Drake, M.A. 8vo. 5s.

ARATUS. (*See* Physiography, p. 34.)

ARISTOPHANES.—The Birds. Trans. into English Verse, by B. H. Kennedy. 8vo. 6s.

—— Scholia Aristophanica. Transl. by W. G. Rutherford, LL.D. Vols. I. and II. 8vo. 50s. net.

ARISTOTLE ON FALLACIES; or, The Sophistici Elenchi. With Translation, by E. Poste M.A. 8vo. 8s. 6d.

ARISTOTLE.—The First Book of the Metaphysics of Aristotle. By a Cambridge Graduate. 8vo. 5s.

—— The Politics. By J. E. C. Welldon, M.A. Cr. 8vo. 10s. 6d.

—— The Rhetoric. By same. Cr. 8vo. 7s. 6d.

—— The Nicomachean Ethics. By same. Cr. 8vo. 7s. 6d.

—— On the Constitution of Athens. By E. Poste. 2nd Edit. Cr. 8vo. 3s. 6d.

—— The Poetics. By S. H. Butcher, Litt.D. 8vo. 10s. net.—Text and Translation. 3s. net.

BION. (*See* Theocritus.)

EURIPIDES.—The Tragedies in English Verse. By A. S. Way, M.A. 3 vols. Cr. 8vo. 6s. net each.

—— Alcestis, Hecuba, Medea. Separately, sewed. 1s. 6d. each.

HERODOTUS.—The History. By G. C. Macaulay, M.A. 2 vols. Cr. 8vo. 18s.

HOMER.—The Odyssey done into English Prose, by S. H. Butcher, M.A., and A. Lang, M.A. Cr. 8vo. 6s.

—— The Odyssey. Books I.—XII. Transl. into English Verse by Earl of Carnarvon. Cr. 8vo. 7s. 6d.

—— The Iliad done into English Prose, by Andrew Lang, Walter Leaf, and Ernest Myers. Cr. 8vo. 12s. 6d.

—— The Iliad done into English Verse. By A. S. Way, M.A. 2 vols. 4to. 10s. 6d. net.

MOSCHUS. (*See* Theocritus).

PINDAR.—The Extant Odes. By Ernest Myers. Cr. 8vo. 5s.

PLATO.—Timæus. With Translation, by R. D. Archer-Hind, M.A. 8vo. 16s. (*See also* Golden Treasury Series, p. 26.)

POLYBIUS.—The Histories. By E. S. Shuckburgh. Cr. 8vo. 24s.

SOPHOCLES.—Œdipus the King. Translated into English Verse by E. D. A. Morshead, M.A. Fcp. 8vo. 3s. 6d.

THEOCRITUS, BION, and MOSCHUS. By A. Lang, M.A. Pott 8vo. 2s 6d. net.—Large Paper Edition. 8vo. 9s.

XENOPHON.—The Complete Works. By H. G. Dakyns, M.A. Cr. 8vo.—Vols. I and II. 10s. 6d. each.

From the Italian.

DANTE.—The Purgatory. With Transl. and Notes, by A. J. Butler. Cr. 8vo. 12s. 6d.

DANTE.—The Paradise. By A. J. Butler. 2nd Edit. Cr. 8vo. 12s. 6d.

—— The Hell. By the same. Cr. 8vo. 12s. 6d.

—— De Monarchia. By F. J. Church. 8vo. 4s. 6d.

—— The Divine Comedy. By C. E. Norton. I. Hell. II. Purgatory. III. Paradise. Cr. 8vo. 6s. each.

—— New Life of Dante. Transl. by C. E. Norton. 5s.

—— The Purgatory. Transl. by C. L. Shadwell. Ext. cr. 8vo. 10s. net

From the Latin.

CICERO.—The Life and Letters of Marcus Tullius Cicero. By the Rev. G. E. Jeans, M.A. 2nd Edit. Cr. 8vo. 10s. 6d.

—— The Academics. By J. S. Reid. 8vo. 5s. 6d.

—— In Defence of Cluentius. By W. Peterson, M.A. Cr. 8vo. 5s.

HORACE: The Works of. By J. Lonsdale, M.A., and S. Lee, M.A. Gl. 8vo. 3s. 6d.

—— The Odes in a Metrical Paraphrase. By R. M. Hovenden, B.A. Ext. fcp. 8vo. 4s. 6d.

—— Life and Character: an Epitome of his Satires and Epistles. By R. M. Hovenden, B.A. Ext. fcp. 8vo. 4s. 6d.

—— Word for Word from Horace: The Odes Literally Versified. By W. T. Thornton, C.B. Cr. 8vo. 7s. 6d.

JUVENAL.—Thirteen Satires. By Alex. Leeper, LL.D. New Ed. Cr. 8vo. 3s. 6d.

LIVY.—Books XXI.—XXV. The Second Punic War. By A. J. Church, M.A., and W. J. Brodribb, M.A. Cr. 8vo. 7s. 6d.—Book XXI separately, 2s.

MARCUS AURELIUS ANTONINUS.—Book IV. of the Meditations. With Translation and Commentary, by H. Crossley, M.A. 8vo. 6s.

SALLUST.—The Conspiracy of Catiline and the Jugurthine War. By A. W. Pollard. Cr. 8vo. 6s.—Catiline. 3s.

TACITUS, The Works of. By A. J. Church, M.A., and W. J Brodribb, M.A. The History. 4th Edit. Cr. 8vo. 6s. The Agricola and Germania. With the Dialogue on Oratory. Cr. 8vo. 4s. 6d. The Annals. 5th Edit. Cr. 8vo. 7s. 6d.

VIRGIL: The Works of. By J. Lonsdale, M.A., and S. Lee, M.A. Globe 8vo. 3s. 6d.

—— The Æneid. By J. W. Mackail, M.A. Cr. 8vo. 7s. 6d.

Into Latin and Greek Verse.

CHURCH (Rev. A. J.).—Latin Version of Selections from Tennyson. By Prof. Conington, Prof Seeley, Dr. Hessey, T. E. Kebbel, &c. Edited by A. J. Church, M.A. Ext. fcp. 8vo. 6s.

GEDDES (Prof. W. D.).—Flosculi Græci Boreales. Cr. 8vo. 6s.

KYNASTON (Herbert D.D.).—Exemplaria Cheltoniensia. Ext. fcp. 8vo. 5s.

VOYAGES AND TRAVELS.

(*See also* History, p. 11; Sport, p. 37.)

APPLETON (T. G.).—A Nile Journal. Illustrated by Eugene Benson. Cr. 8vo. 6s.

'BACCHANTE.' The Cruise of H.M.S. "Bacchante," 1879—1882. Compiled from the Private Journals, Letters and Note-books of Prince Albert Victor and Prince George of Wales. By the Rev. Canon Dalton. 2 vols. Med. 8vo. 52s. 6d.

BAKER (Sir Samuel W.).—ISMAILIA. A Narrative of the Expedition to Central Africa for the Suppression of the Slave Trade, organised by ISMAIL, Khedive of Egypt. Cr. 8vo. 6s.
—— THE NILE TRIBUTARIES OF ABYSSINIA, AND THE SWORD HUNTERS OF THE HAMRAN ARABS. Cr. 8vo. 6s.
—— THE ALBERT N'VANZA GREAT BASIN OF THE NILE AND EXPLORATION OF THE NILE SOURCES. Cr. 8vo. 6s.
—— CYPRUS AS I SAW IT IN 1879. 8vo. 12s. 6d.

BARKER (Lady).—A YEAR'S HOUSEKEEPING IN SOUTH AFRICA. Illustr. Cr. 8vo. 3s. 6d.
—— STATION LIFE IN NEW ZEALAND. Cr. 8vo. 3s. 6d.
—— LETTERS TO GUY. Cr. 8vo. 5s.

BLENNERHASSETT (R.) and SLEEMAN (L.)—ADVENTURES IN MASHONALAND. Cr. 8vo. 3s. 6d.

BOUGHTON (G. H.) and ABBEY (E. A.).—SKETCHING RAMBLES IN HOLLAND. With Illustrations. Fcp. 4to. 21s.

BROOKS (Bishop P.).—LETTERS OF TRAVEL. Ext. cr. 8vo. 8s. 6d. net.

CAMERON (V. L.).—OUR FUTURE HIGHWAY TO INDIA. 2 vols. Cr. 8vo. 21s.

CAMPBELL (J. F.).—MY CIRCULAR NOTES. Cr. 8vo. 6s.

CARLES (W. R.).—LIFE IN COREA. 8vo. 12s. 6d.

CAUCASUS: NOTES ON THE. By "WANDERER." 8vo. 9s.

CHANLER (W. A.).—THROUGH JUNGLE AND DESERT. Roy. 8vo. 21s. net.

COLE (G. A. G.).—THE GYPSY ROAD: A JOURNEY FROM KRAKOW TO COBLENTZ. Cr. 8vo. 6s.

CRAIK (Mrs.).—AN UNKNOWN COUNTRY. Illustr. by F. NOEL PATON. Roy. 8vo. 7s 6d.
—— AN UNSENTIMENTAL JOURNEY THROUGH CORNWALL. Illustrated. 4to. 12s. 6d.

DILKE (Sir Charles). (See pp. 30, 36.)

DORR (J. C. R.).—THE FLOWER OF ENGLAND'S FACE. Pott 8vo. 3s.

DUFF (Right Hon. Sir M. E. Grant).—NOTES OF AN INDIAN JOURNEY. 8vo. 10s. 6d

FORBES (Archibald).—SOUVENIRS OF SOME CONTINENTS. Cr. 8vo. 3s. 6d.
—— BARRACKS, BIVOUACS, AND BATTLES. Cr. 8vo. 3s. 6d

FORBES-MITCHELL (W.)—REMINISCENCES OF THE GREAT MUTINY. Cr. 8vo. 3s. 6d.

FULLERTON (W. M.).—IN CAIRO. Fcp. 8vo. 3s. 6d.

GONE TO TEXAS: LETTERS FROM OUR BOYS. Ed. by THOS. HUGHES. Cr. 8vo. 4s. 6d.

GORDON (Lady Duff). — LAST LETTERS FROM EGYPT, TO WHICH ARE ADDED LETTERS FROM THE CAPE. 2nd Edit. Cr. 8vo. 9s.

GREEN (W. S.).—AMONG THE SELKIRK GLACIERS. Cr. 8vo. 7s. 6d.

HOOKER (Sir Joseph D.) and BALL (J.).—JOURNAL OF A TOUR IN MAROCCO AND THE GREAT ATLAS. 8vo. 21s.

HÜBNER (Baron von).—A RAMBLE ROUND THE WORLD. Cr. 8vo. 6s.

HUGHES (Thos.).—RUGBY, TENNESSEE. Cr. 8vo. 4s. 6d.
—— VACATION RAMBLES. Cr. 8vo. 6s.

JACKSON (F. G.).—THE GREAT FROZEN LAND. Ed. by A. MONTEFIORE. 8vo. 15s. net.

KALM (P.).—ACCOUNT OF HIS VISIT TO ENGLAND. Trans. J. LUCAS. Illus. 8vo. 12s. net.

KINGSLEY (Charles).—AT LAST: A Christmas in the West Indies. Cr. 8vo. 3s. 6d.

KINGSLEY (Henry). — TALES OF OLD TRAVEL. Cr. 8vo. 3s. 6d.

KIPLING (J. L.).—BEAST AND MAN IN INDIA. Illustrated. Ext. cr. 8vo. 7s. 6d.

MAHAFFY (Prof. J. P.).—RAMBLES AND STUDIES IN GREECE. Illust. Cr. 8vo. 10s. 6d.

MAHAFFY (Prof. J. P.) and ROGERS (J. E.).—SKETCHES FROM A TOUR THROUGH HOLLAND AND GERMANY. Illustrated by J. E. ROGERS. Ext. cr. 8vo. 10s. 6d.

NORDENSKIÖLD. — VOYAGE OF THE "VEGA" ROUND ASIA AND EUROPE. By Baron A. E. VON NORDENSKIÖLD. Trans. by ALEX. LESLIE. 400 Illustrations, Maps, etc. 2 vols. 8vo. 45s.—Popular Edit. Cr. 8vo. 6s.

OLIPHANT (Mrs.). (See HISTORY, p. 13.)

OLIVER (Capt. S. P.).—MADAGASCAR: AN HISTORICAL AND DESCRIPTIVE ACCOUNT OF THE ISLAND. 2 vols. Med. 8vo. 52s. 6d.

PALGRAVE (W. Gifford).—A NARRATIVE OF A YEAR'S JOURNEY THROUGH CENTRAL AND EASTERN ARABIA, 1862-63. Cr. 8vo. 6s.
—— DUTCH GUIANA. 8vo. 9s.
—— ULYSSES; or, Scenes and Studies in many Lands. 8vo. 12s. 6d.

PARKMAN (F.). — THE OREGON TRAIL. Illustrated. Med. 8vo. 21s.

PERSIA, EASTERN. AN ACCOUNT OF THE JOURNEYS OF THE PERSIAN BOUNDARY COMMISSION, 1870-71-72. 2 vols. 8vo. 42s.

PIKE (W.)—THE BARREN GROUND OF NORTHERN CANADA. 8vo. 10s. 6d.

ST. JOHNSTON (A.).—CAMPING AMONG CANNIBALS. Cr. 8vo. 4s. 6d.

SANDYS (J. E.).—AN EASTER VACATION IN GREECE. Cr. 8vo. 3s. 6d.

SMITH (Goldwin)—A TRIP TO ENGLAND. Pott 8vo. 3s.
—— OXFORD AND HER COLLEGES. Pott 8vo. 3s. Illustrated Edition. 6s.

STRANGFORD (Viscountess). — EGYPTIAN SEPULCHRES AND SYRIAN SHRINES. New Edition. Cr. 8vo. 7s. 6d.

TAVERNIER (Baron): TRAVELS IN INDIA OF JEAN BAPTISTE TAVERNIER. Transl. by V. BALL, LL.D. 2 vols. 8vo. 42s.

TRISTRAM (O.). (See ILLUSTRATED BOOKS.)

TURNER (Rev. G.). (See ANTHROPOLOGY.)

WALLACE (A. R.). (See NATURAL HISTORY.)

WATERTON (Charles).—WANDERINGS IN SOUTH AMERICA, THE NORTH-WEST OF THE UNITED STATES, AND THE ANTILLES. Edited by Rev. J. G. WOOD. Illustr. Cr. 8vo. 6s.—People's Edition. 4to. 6d.

WATSON (R. Spence).—A VISIT TO WAZAN, THE SACRED CITY OF MOROCCO. 8vo. 10s. 6d.

YOE (Shway).—THE BURMAN. 2nd Edition. 8vo. 12s. 6d.

YOUNG, Books for the.
(*See also* BIBLICAL HISTORY, p. 38.)

ÆSOP—CALDECOTT —SOME OF ÆSOP'S FABLES, with Modern Instances, shown in Designs by RANDOLPH CALDECOTT. 4to. 5s.
—— ÆSOP'S FABLES. Selected by J. JACOBS. Illustrated by R. HEIGHWAY. Gilt or uncut. Cr. 8vo. 6s.

ARIOSTO.—PALADIN AND SARACEN. Stories from Ariosto. By H. C. HOLLWAY-CAL-THROP. Illustrated. Cr. 8vo. 6s.

ATKINSON (Rev. J. C.).—THE LAST OF THE GIANT KILLERS. Globe 8vo. 3s. 6d.
—— WALKS, TALKS, TRAVELS, AND EXPLOITS OF TWO SCHOOLBOYS. Cr. 8vo. 3s. 6d.
—— PLAYHOURS AND HALF-HOLIDAYS, OR FURTHER EXPERIENCES OF TWO SCHOOL-BOYS. Cr. 8vo. 3s 6d.
—— SCENES IN FAIRYLAND. Cr. 8vo. 4s. 6d.

AWDRY (Frances).—THE STORY OF A FEL-LOW SOLDIER. (A Life of Bishop Patteson for the Young.) Globe 8vo. 2s. 6d.

BAKER (Sir S. W.).—TRUE TALES FOR MY GRANDSONS. Illustrated. Cr. 8vo. 3s. 6d.
—— CAST OF BY THE SEA: OR, THE ADVEN-TURES OF NED GRAY. Illust. Cr. 8vo. 6s.

BARKER (Lady).—THE WHITE RAT. Gl. 8vo. 2s. 6d.

BARLOW (Jane).—THE END OF ELFINTOWN. Illust. by L. HOUSMAN. Cr. 8vo. 5s.—*Edition de Luxe.* Roy. 8vo. 21s. net.

CARROLL (Lewis).—ALICE'S ADVENTURES IN WONDERLAND. With 42 Illustrations by TENNIEL. Cr. 8vo. 6s. net.
People's Edition. With all the original Illustrations. Cr. 8vo. 2s. 6d. net.
A GERMAN TRANSLATION OF THE SAME. Cr. 8vo. 6s. net. —A FRENCH TRANSLA-TION OF THE SAME. Cr. 8vo. 6s. net. AN ITALIAN TRANSLATION OF THE SAME. Cr. 8vo. 6s. net.
—— ALICE'S ADVENTURES UNDER-GROUND. Being a Fascimile of the Original MS. Book, afterwards developed in to "Alice's Adven-tures in Wonderland." With 27 Illustra-tions by the Author. Cr. 8vo. 4s net.
—— THROUGH THE LOOKING-GLASS AND WHAT ALICE FOUND THERE. With 50 Illus-trations by TENNIEL. Cr. 8vo. 6s. net.
People's Edition. With all the original Illustrations. Cr. 8vo. 2s. 6d. net.
People's Edition of "Alice's Adventures in Wooderland," and "Through the Looking-Glass." 1 vol. Cr 8vo. 4s. 6d. net.
—— RHYME? AND REASON With 65 Illus-trations by ARTHUR B. FROST, and 9 by HENRY HOLIDAY. Cr. 8vo. 6s. net.
—— A TANGLED TALE. With 6 Illustrations by ARTHUR B. FROST. Cr. 8vo. 4s. 6d. net.
—— SYLVIE AND BRUNO. With 46 Illustra-tions by HARRY FURNISS. Cr. 8vo. 7s. 6d. net.
—— —— CONCLUDED. With Illustrations by HARRY FURNISS. Cr. 8vo. 7s. 6d. net.
—— THE NURSERY "ALICE." Twenty Coloured Enlargements from TENNIEL'S Illustrations to "Alice's Adventures in Wonderland," with Text adapted to Nursery Readers. 4to. 4s. net.
—— THE HUNTING OF THE SNARK, AN AGONY IN EIGHT FITS. With 9 Illustrations by HENRY HOLIDAY. Cr. 8vo. 4s. 6d. net.

CLIFFORD (Mrs. W. K.).—ANYHOW STORIES. With Illustrations by DOROTHY TENNANT. Cr. 8vo. 1s. 6d. ; paper covers, 1s.

CORBETT (Julian).—FOR GOD AND GOLD. Cr. 8vo. 6s.

CRAIK (Mrs.).—ALICE LEARMONT : A FAIRY TALE. Illustrated. Globe 8vo. 2s. 6d.
—— THE ADVENTURES OF A BROWNIE. Illus-trated by Mrs. ALLINGHAM. Gl. 8vo. 2s. 6d.
—— THE LITTLE LAME PRINCE AND HIS TRAVELLING CLOAK. Illustrated by J. McL. RALSTON. Globe 8vo. 2s. 6d.
—— OUR YEAR : A CHILD'S BOOK IN PROSE AND VERSE. Illustrated. Gl. 8vo. 2s. 6d.
—— LITTLE SUNSHINE'S HOLIDAY. Globe 8vo. 2s. 6d.
—— THE FAIRY BOOK : THE BEST POPULAR FAIRY STORIES. Pott 8vo. 2s. 6d. net.
—— CHILDREN'S POETRY. Ex. fcp. 8vo. 4s. 6d.
—— SONGS OF OUR YOUTH. Small 4to. 6s.

DE MORGAN (Mary).—THE NECKLACE OF PRINCESS FIORIMONDE, AND OTHER STORIES. Illustrated by WALTER CRANE. Ext. fcp. 8vo. 3s. 6d.—Large Paper Ed., with Illus-trations on India Paper. 100 copies printed.

FOWLER (W. W.). (*See* NATURAL HISTORY.)

FRASER (Mrs.).—THE BROWN AMBASSADOR. Cr. 8vo. 3s. 6d.

GRIMM'S FAIRY TALES. Translated by LUCY CRANE, and Illustrated by WALTER CRANE. Cr. 8vo. 6s.

GREENWOOD (Jessy E.). — THE MOON MAIDEN: AND OTHER STORIES. Cr. 8vo. 3s. 6d.

JERSEY (Countess of).—MAURICE : OR, THE RED JAR. Illustrated by ROSIE M. M. PITMAN. Gl. 8vo. 2s. 6d.
—— ERIC, PRINCE OF LORLONIA. Illustrated by A. R. WOODWARD. Cr. 8vo. 6s.

KEARY (A. and E.). — THE HEROES OF ASGARD. Tales from Scandinavian My-thology. Globe 8vo. 2s. 6d

KEARY (E.).—THE MAGIC VALLEY. Illustr. by "E. V. B." Globe 8vo. 2s. 6d.

KINGSLEY (Charles).—THE HEROES ; or, Greek Fairy Tales for my Children. Cr. 8vo. 3s. 6d.—*Presentation Ed.,* gilt edges. 7s. 6d.
—— MADAM HOW AND LADY WHY ; or, First Lessons in Earth-Lore. Cr. 8vo. 3s. 6d.
—— THE WATER-BABIES : A Fairy Tale for a Land Baby. Cr. 8vo. 3s. 6d.—New Edit. Illus. by L. SAMBOURNE. Fcp. 4to. 12s. 6d.

KIPLING (Rudyard).—THE JUNGLE BOOK. Illustrated. Cr. 8vo. 6s.
—— THE SECOND JUNGLE BOOK. Illustrated Cr. 8vo. 6s.

MACLAREN (Arch.).—THE FAIRY FAMILY. A Series of Ballads and Metrical Tales. Cr. 8vo. 5s.

MACMILLAN (Rev. Hugh). (*See* p. 44.)

MADAME TABBY'S ESTABLISHMENT. By KARI. Illust. by L. WAIN. Cr. 8vo. 4s. 6d.

MAGUIRE (J. F.).—YOUNG PRINCE MARI-GOLD. Illustrated. Globe 8vo. 4s. 6d.

MARTIN (Frances).—THE POET'S HOUR. Poetry selected for Children. Pott 8vo. 2s. 6d.
—— SPRING-TIME WITH THE POETS. Pott 8vo. 3s. 6d.

MAZINI (Linda).—IN THE GOLDEN SHELL. With Illustrations. Globe 8vo. 4s. 6d.

MOLESWORTH (Mrs.).—WORKS. Illustr. Globe 8vo. 2s. 6d. each.
"CARROTS," JUST A LITTLE BOY.
A CHRISTMAS CHILD.
CHRISTMAS-TREE LAND.
THE CUCKOO CLOCK.
FOUR WINDS FARM.
GRANDMOTHER DEAR.
HERR BABY.
LITTLE MISS PEGGY.
THE RECTORY CHILDREN.
ROSY.
THE TAPESTRY ROOM.
TELL ME A STORY.
TWO LITTLE WAIFS.
"US": An Old-Fashioned Story.
CHILDREN OF THE CASTLE.
A CHRISTMAS POSY.
NURSE HEATHERDALE'S STORY.
THE GIRLS AND I.
MY NEW HOME.
MARY.
—— FOUR GHOST STORIES. Cr. 8vo. 6s.
—— SHEILA'S MYSTERY. Illustrated. Cr. 8vo. 3s. 6d.
—— THE CARVED LIONS. Illust. Cr. 8vo. 3s. 6d.

OLIPHANT (Mrs.). — AGNES HOPETOUN'S SCHOOLS AND HOLIDAYS. Illust. Gl. 8vo. 2s. 6d.

PALGRAVE (Francis Turner).—THE FIVE DAYS' ENTERTAINMENTS AT WENTWORTH GRANGE. Small 4to. 6s.
—— THE CHILDREN'S TREASURY OF LYRICAL POETRY. Pott 8vo. 2s. 6d.—Or in 2 parts, 1s. each.

PATMORE (C.).—THE CHILDREN'S GARLAND FROM THE BEST POETS. Pott 8vo. 2s. 6d. net.

ROSSETTI (Christina). — SPEAKING LIKENESSES. Illust. by A. HUGHES. Cr. 8vo. 4s. 6d.
—— SING-SONG: A Nursery Rhyme-Book. Small 4to. 4s. 6d.

RUTH AND HER FRIENDS: A STORY FOR GIRLS. Illustrated. Globe 8vo. 2s. 6d.

ST. JOHNSTON (A.). — CAMPING AMONG CANNIBALS. Cr. 8vo. 4s. 6d.
—— CHARLIE ASGARDE: THE STORY OF A FRIENDSHIP. Illustrated by HUGH THOMSON. Cr. 8vo. 5s.

"ST. OLAVE'S" (Author of). Illustrated. Globe 8vo.
WHEN I WAS A LITTLE GIRL. 2s. 6d.
NINE YEARS OLD. 2s. 6d.
WHEN PAPA COMES HOME. 4s. 6d.
PANSIE'S FLOUR BIN. 2s. 6d.

STEEL (F. A.).—TALES OF THE PUNJAB. (See under ILLUSTRATED BOOKS, p. 15.)

STEWART (Aubrey).—THE TALE OF TROY, Done into English. Globe 8vo. 3s. 6d.

SWIFT.—GULLIVER'S TRAVELS. (See under ILLUSTRATED BOOKS, p. 15.)

TENNYSON (Lord H.).—JACK AND THE BEAN-STALK. English Hexameters. Illust. by R. CALDECOTT. Fcp. 4to. 3s. 6d.

"WANDERING WILLIE" (Author of).— CONRAD THE SQUIRREL. Globe 8vo. 2s. 6d.

WARD (Mrs. T. Humphry).—MILLY AND OLLY. With Illustrations by Mrs. ALMA TADEMA. Globe 8vo. 2s. 6d.

WEBSTER (Augusta).—DAFFODIL AND THE CROÄXAXICANS. Cr. 8vo. 6s.

WILLOUGHBY (F.).—FAIRY GUARDIANS. Illustr. by TOWNLEY GREEN. Cr. 8vo. 5s.

WOODS (M. A.). (See COLLECTIONS, p. 21.)

YONGE (Charlotte M.).—THE PRINCE AND THE PAGE. Cr. 8vo. 3s. 6d.
—— A BOOK OF GOLDEN DEEDS. Pott 8vo. 2s. 6d. net. Globe 8vo. 2s.—Abridged Edition. 1s.
—— LANCES OF LYNWOOD. Cr. 8vo. 3s. 6d. —Abridged Edition. 1s. 6d.
—— P's AND Q's; and LITTLE LUCY'S WONDERFUL GLOBE. Illustrated. Cr. 8vo. 3s. 6d.
—— A STOREHOUSE OF STORIES. 2 vols. Globe 8vo. 2s. 6d. each.
—— THE POPULATION OF AN OLD PEARTREE; or, Stories of Insect Life. From E. VAN BRUYSSEL. Illustr. Gl. 8vo. 2s. 6d.

ZOOLOGY.

Comparative Anatomy—Practical Zoology— Entomology—Ornithology.

(See also BIOLOGY; NATURAL HISTORY; PHYSIOLOGY.)

Comparative Anatomy.

FLOWER (Sir W. H.).—AN INTRODUCTION TO THE OSTEOLOGY OF THE MAMMALIA. Illustrated. 3rd Edit., revised with the assistance of HANS GADOW, Ph.D. Cr. 8vo. 10s. 6d.

HUMPHRY (Prof. Sir G. M.).—OBSERVATIONS IN MYOLOGY. 8vo. 6s.

LANG (Prof. Arnold).—TEXT-BOOK OF COMPARATIVE ANATOMY. Transl. by H. M. and M. BERNARD. Preface by Prof. E. HAECKEL. Illustr. 2 vols. 8vo. 17s. net each.

PARKER (T. Jeffery).—A COURSE OF INSTRUCTION IN ZOOTOMY (VERTEBRATA). Illustrated. Cr. 8vo. 8s. 6d.

PETTIGREW (J. Bell).—THE PHYSIOLOGY OF THE CIRCULATION IN PLANTS, IN THE LOWER ANIMALS, AND IN MAN. 8vo. 12s.

SHUFELDT (R. W.).—THE MYOLOGY OF THE RAVEN (*Corvus corax Sinuatus*). A Guide to the Study of the Muscular System In Birds. Illustrated. 8vo. 13s. net.

WIEDERSHEIM (Prof. R.).—ELEMENTS OF THE COMPARATIVE ANATOMY OF VERTEBRATES. Adapted by W. NEWTON PARKER. With Additions. Illustrated. 8vo. 12s. 6d.

Practical Zoology.

CALDERWOOD (W. L.)—MUSSEL CULTURE AND THE BAIT SUPPLY. Cr. 8vo. 2s. 6d.

DEAN (B.).—FISHES, LIVING AND FOSSIL. 8vo. 10s. 6d. net.

HOWES (Prof. G. B.).—AN ATLAS OF PRACTICAL ELEMENTARY BIOLOGY. With a Preface by Prof. HUXLEY. 4to. 14s.

HUXLEY (T. H.) and MARTIN (H. N.).— A COURSE OF ELEMENTARY INSTRUCTION IN PRACTICAL BIOLOGY. Revised and extended by Prof. G. B. HOWES and D. H. SCOTT, Ph.D. Cr. 8vo. 10s. 6d.

THOMSON (Sir C. Wyville).—THE VOYAGE OF THE "CHALLENGER": THE ATLANTIC. With Illustrations, Coloured Maps, Charts, etc. 2 vols. 8vo. 45*s*.
—— THE DEPTHS OF THE SEA. An Account of the Results of the Dredging Cruises of H.M.SS. "Lightning" and "Porcupine," 1868-69-70. With Illustrations, Maps, and Plans. 8vo. 31*s*. 6*d*.

WILSON (E. B.) and LEAMING (E.).—ATLAS OF THE KARYOKINESIS OF THE OVUM. 4to. 17*s*. net.

Entomology.

BADENOCH (L. N.).—ROMANCE OF THE INSECT WORLD. Cr. 8vo. 6*s*.

BUCKTON (G. B.).—MONOGRAPH OF THE BRITISH CICADÆ, OR TETTIGIDÆ. 2 vols. 42*s*. net; or in 8 Parts. 8*s*. each net.
—— NATURAL HISTORY OF ERISTALIS TENAX. 8vo. 8*s*. net.

LUBBOCK (Sir John).—THE ORIGIN AND METAMORPHOSES OF INSECTS. Illustrated. Cr. 8vo. 3*s*. 6*d*.

MEYRICK (E.).—HANDBOOK OF BRITISH LEPIDOPTERA. Ex. cr. 8vo. 10*s*. 6*d*. net.

MIALL (L. C.).—NATURAL HISTORY OF AQUATIC INSECTS. Cr. 8vo. 6*s*.

SCUDDER (S. H.).—FOSSIL INSECTS OF NORTH AMERICA. Map and Plates. 2 vols. 4to. 90*s*. net.

Ornithology.

COUES (Elliott).—KEY TO NORTH AMERICAN BIRDS. Illustrated. 8vo. 2*l*. 2*s*.
—— HANDBOOK OF FIELD AND GENERAL ORNITHOLOGY. Illustrated. 8vo. 10*s*. net.

FOWLER (W. W.). (*See* NATURAL HISTORY.)

HEADLEY (F. W.).—STRUCTURE AND LIFE OF BIRDS. Cr. 8vo. 7*s*. 6*d*.

WHITE (Gilbert). (*See* NATURAL HISTORY.)

WRIGHT (M. O.). (*See* NATURAL HISTORY.)

INDEX.

PAGE

ABRAHAMS (I.) . . . 42
ABBEY (E. A.) . . 15, 47
ABBOT (F. E.) . . . 42
ABBOTT (E. A.) 6, 17, 38, 39, 42
ACTON (Lord) . . . 11
ADAMS (Sir F. O.) . . 36
ADDISON . . 4, 24, 25
ÆSOP. . . . 14, 48
AGASSIZ (L.) . . . 4
AINGER (Rev. A.) 5, 20, 27, 42
AINSLIE (A. D.) . . . 18
AIRY (Sir G. B.) . . 3, 34
AITKEN (Mary C.) . . 25
AITKEN (Sir W.) . . 30
ALBEMARLE (Earl of) . 4
ALDOUS (J. C. P.) . 40, 41
ALDRICH (T. B.) . . 17
ALEXANDER (C. F.) . 17, 25
ALEXANDER (T.) . . 10
ALEXANDER (Bishop) . 42
ALLBUTT (T. C.) . . 28
ALLEN (G.) . . . 7
ALLINGHAM (W.) . . 25
AMIEL (H. F.) . . . 4
ANDERSON (A.) . . 17
ANDERSON (L.) . . . 2
ANDERSON (Dr. McCall) . 28
ANDREWS (C. M.) . . 11
ANDREWS (Dr. Thomas) . 33
APPLETON (T. G.) . . 46
ARCHER-HIND (R. D.) . 46
ARNOLD (M.) 9, 17, 24, 25, 38, 39
ARNOLD (Dr. T.) . . 11
ARNOLD (W. T.) . . 11
ASHLEY (W. J.) . . 4, 35
ATKINSON (G. F.) . . 7
ATKINSON (J. B.) . . 2
ATKINSON (Rev. J. C.) 2, 48
ATTWELL (H.) . . . 25
AUSTEN (Jane) . . . 21
AUSTIN (Alfred) 10, 17, 24
AUTENRIETH (Georg) . 0
AWDRY (F.) . . . 48
BACON (Francis) . 4, 24, 25
BADENOCH (L. N.) . 30, 50
BAILEY (L. H.) . . 10
BAINES (Rev. E.) . . 42
BAKER (Sir S. W.) 4, 36, 37, 47, 48
BALCH (Elizabeth) . . 14
BALDWIN (Prof. J. M.) . 33
BALFOUR (F. M.) . . 7
BALFOUR (J. B.) . . 7
BALL (J.) . . . 47
BALL (W. Platt) . . 7
BALL (W. W. R.) . 15, 28
BALLANCE (C. A.) . . 28
BARKER (G. F.) . . 33
BARKER (Lady) . 2, 9, 47, 48
BARLOW (J.) . . 14, 48
BARNARD (C.) . . . 34
BARNARD (F. A. P.) . 4
BARNES (R. H.) . . 5
BARNES (W.) . . . 4
BARNETT (E. A.) . 9, 37
BARRY (A.) . . . 42
BARTHOLOMEW (J. G.) . 3
BARTLETT (J.) . . 9, 17

PAGE

BARWELL (R.) . . 28
BASTABLE (Prof. C. F.) . 35
BATEMAN (J.) . . . 4
BATES (K. L.) . . 24
BATESON (W.) . . 7
BATH (Marquis of) . . 36
BATHER (Archdeacon) . 42
BAXTER (L.) . . . 4
BEESLY (Mrs.) . . 5, 11
BEHRENS (H.) . . 8
BENEDIKT (R.) . . 38
BENHAM (Rev. W.) . 6, 25, 41
BENSON (Archbishop) . 42
BENSON (W. A. S.) . 2, 38
BENTLEY . . . 4
BERG (L.) . . . 10
BERLIOZ (H.) . . 4
BERNARD (C. E.) . . 4
BERNARD (J. H.) . . 32
BERNARD (H. M.) . 7, 35
BERNARD (M.) . . 15
BERNARD (T. D.) . . 42
BERNERS (J.) . . 14
BESANT (Sir W.) . . 4
BETTANY (G. T.) . . 7
BICKERTON (T. H.) . 28
BIGELOW (M. M.) . . 15
BIKÉLAS (D.) . . 21
BINNIE (Rev. W.) . . 42
BIRRELL (A.) . . 15
BIRKS (T. R.) 7, 32, 39, 42
BJÖRNSON (B) . . 21
BLACK (W.) . . 5
BLACKBURNE (E.) . . 4
BLACKIE (J. S.) 11, 17, 24
BLAKE (J. F.) . . 3
BLAKE (W.) . . . 4
BLAKISTON (J. R.) . 9
BLANFORD (H. F.) 10, 34
BLANFORD (W. T.) . 11, 30
BLENNERHASSETT (R.) . 47
BLOMFIELD (R.) . . 10
BLYTH (A. W.) . . 14
BÖHM-BAWERK (Prof.) . 35
BOLDREWOOD (Rolf) . 21
BONAR (J.) . 3, 5, 35
BOND (Rev. J.) . . 39
BOOLE (G.) . . 32
BOOTH (C.) . . 37
BORGEAUD (C.) . . 15
BORROW (G.) . . 21
BOSANQUET (B.) . 32, 37
BOSE (W. P. du) . . 43
BOUGHTON (G. H.) . 47
BOUTMY (E.) . . 15
BOWEN (H. C.) . . 31
BOWER (F. O.) . . 7
BRADFORD (A. H.) . 42
BRADFORD (G.) . . 24
BRADLEY (A. G.) . . 4
BRETT (R. B) . . 11
BRIDGES (J. A.) . . 24
BRIGHT (H. A.) . . 10
BRIGHT (John) . . 36
BRIMLEY (G.) . . 24
BRODIE (Sir B.) . . 8
BRODRIBB (W. J.) . 16, 46

PAGE

BROOKE (Sir J.) . . 4
BROOKE (S. A.) 16, 17, 26, 42
BROOKS (Bishop) . 42, 47
BROWN (Prof. C.) . . 33
BROWN (J. A.) . . 1
BROWN (Dr. James) . 4
BROWN (T. E.) . . 17
BROWNE (J. H. B.) . 14
BROWNE (Sir T.) . . 25
BRUCE (P. A.) . 12, 35
BRUNTON (Dr. T. L.) 28, 39, 42
BRYCE (James) . 11, 36
BUCHHEIM (C. A.) . 25
BUCKLAND (A.) . 6, 36
BUCKLEY (A. B) . . 12
BUCKNILL (Dr. J. C) . 29
BUCKTON (G. B.) . . 50
BUNYAN . . 4, 24, 25
BURDETT (C. W. B.) . 38
BURGON (J. W.) . . 17
BURKE (E.) . . 36
BURN (R.) . . . 2
BURNETT (F. Hodgson) . 21
BURNS . . . 17, 25
BURY (J. B.) . . 12
BUTCHER (Prof. S. H.)
. . 16, 24, 46
BUTLER (A. J.) . 17, 46
BUTLER (Rev. G.) . . 42
BUTLER (Samuel) . . 17
BUTLER (Archer) . . 42
BUTLER (Sir W. F.) . 4
BUXTON (Mrs. S.) . . 38
BYRON . . . 25
CAIRNES (J. E.) . 35, 36
CAJORI (F.) . . 28
CALDECOTT (R.) . 15, 48
CALDERON . . . 17
CALDERWOOD (H.) 7, 9, 32, 33
CALDERWOOD (W. L.) . 49
CALLAWAY (Bishop) . 4
CALVERT (Rev. A.) . 39
CAMERON (V. L.) . . 47
CAMPBELL (D. H) . . 7
CAMPBELL (Sir G.) . 4
CAMPBELL (J. D.) . 4, 18
CAMPBELL (J. F.) . . 47
CAMPBELL (Dr. J. M.) . 42
CAMPBELL (Prof. Lewis) 5, 16
CANTILLON . . . 35
CAPES (W. W.) . . 16
CARLES (W. R.) . . 47
CARLYLE (T.) . . 4
CARMARTHEN (Lady) . 21
CARNARVON (Earl of) . 46
CARNOT (N. L. G.) . 34
CARPENTER (Bishop) . 42
CARR (J. C.) . . 2, 17
CARROLL (Lewis) . 32, 48
CARTER (R. Brudenell) . 29
CASSEL (Dr. D.) . . 12
CATTEL (J. McK.) . . 33
CAUTLEY (G. S.) . . 17
CAZENOVE (J. G.) . . 42
CHALMERS (J. A.) . . 11
CHALMERS (J. B.) . . 10
CHALMERS (M. D.) . 36

	PAGE
CHANLER (W. A.)	47
CHAPMAN (Elizabeth R.)	17
CHAPPELL (W.)	30
CHASE (Rev. F. H.)	39
CHASSERESSE (Diana)	37
CHAUCER	16, 17
CHEETHAM (Archdeacon)	40
CHERRY (R. R.)	15
CHEYNE (C. H. H.)	3
CHEYNE (T. K.)	39
CHIROL (V.)	36
CHRISTIE (W. D.)	25
CHURCH (Rev. A. J.)	4, 16, 38, 46
CHURCH (F. J.)	26, 46
CHURCH (R. W.)	4, 5, 6, 12, 17, 24, 41, 42
CLARE (G.)	35
CLARK (J. W.)	25
CLARK (L.)	3
CLARK (R.)	37
CLARK (S.)	4
CLARK (T. M.)	10
CLARKE (C. B.)	10, 35
CLEVELAND (Duchess)	5
CLIFFORD (Ed.)	4
CLIFFORD (W. K.)	24, 33
CLIFFORD (Mrs. W. K.)	48
CLOUGH (A. H.)	18, 24, 25
COBDEN (R.)	36
COHEN (J. B.)	8
COLE (G. A. G.)	47
COLENSO (J. W.)	41
COLERIDGE (C. R.)	24
COLERIDGE (S. T.)	4, 18
COLLIER (Hon. John)	2
COLLINS (C.)	10
COLLINS (J. Churton)	24
COLQUHOUN (F. S.)	18
COLVIN (Sidney)	5, 26
COMBE (G.)	4, 10
COMEY (A. M.)	8
COMMONS (J. R.)	35
CONGREVE (Rev. J.)	42
CONWAY (Hugh)	21
COOK (E. T.)	2
COOKE (A. H.)	30
COOKE (C. Kinloch)	30
COOKE (J. P.)	8, 43
COOPER (E. H.)	2
CORBETT (J.)	4, 21, 48
CORFIELD (W. H.)	11
CORNISH (F.)	43
CORSON (H.)	24
COSSA (L.)	35
COTES (E.)	21
COTTERILL (J. H.)	10
COTTON (Bishop)	43
COTTON (C.)	15
COTTON (J. S.)	36
COUES (E.)	50
COURTHOPE (W. J.)	4, 16, 24
COWELL (G.)	29
COWPER	18, 24, 25
COX (G. V.)	12
CRAIK (Mrs.)	18, 21, 24, 25, 47, 48
CRAIK (H.)	6, 10, 24, 36
CRANE (Lucy)	47
CRANE (Walter)	47
CRAVEN (Mrs. D.)	9
CRAWFORD (F. M.)	14, 21, 24
CRAWSHAW (W. H.)	24
CREIGHTON (Bishop M.)	5, 17
CRICHTON-BROWNE (Sir J.)	10
CROSS (J. A.)	38
CROSSKEY (R.)	14
CROSSLEY (E.)	3
CROSSLEY (H.)	46
CUMMING (L.)	33
CUNLIFFE (J. W.)	24
CUNNINGHAM (C.)	36
CUNNINGHAM (Sir H. S.)	21
CUNNINGHAM (Rev. J.)	42
CUNNINGHAM (Rev. W.)	40, 41, 43
CUNYNGHAME (Sir A. T.)	30
CURTEIS (Rev. G. H.)	40, 43
CURTIN (J.)	21
D'ARCY (C. F.)	32
DABBS (G. H. R.)	18
DAHLSTROM (K. P.)	10
DAHN (F.)	21
DAKYNS (H. G.)	46
DALE (A. W. W.)	42
DALTON (Rev. J. N.)	46
DANIELL (Alfred)	33
DANTE	4, 17, 46
DASENT (A. I.)	12
DAVIDSON (Bishop)	41, 43
DAVIES (Rev. J. Ll.)	4, 43
DAVIES (W.)	6, 43
DAVIS (R. H.)	21
DAWKINS (W. B.)	1
DAWSON (G. M.)	11
DAWSON (Sir J. W.)	11
DAWSON (W. J.)	18
DAY (L. B.)	21
DAY (R. E.)	33
DEAN (A.)	10
DEAN (B.)	42
DEFOE (D.)	5, 25
DEGERDON (W. E.)	38
DEIGHTON (K.)	5, 19, 24, 27
DELAMOTTE (P. H.)	3
DELBOS (L.)	31
DELL (E. C.)	14
DE MORGAN (M.)	48
DEUSSEN (P.)	32
DE QUATREFAGES (A.)	1
DE ROUSIERS (P.)	35
DE VARIGNY (H.)	7
DE VERE (A.)	18, 24
D'ISRAELI (B.)	22
DICEY (A. V.)	15, 36
DICKENS (C.)	21, 24
DICKENS (M. A.)	22, 24
DIGGLE (Rev. J. W.)	43
DILKE (Ashton W.)	24
DILKE (Sir Charles W.)	30, 36
DILLWYN (E. A.)	22
DOBBIN (L.)	8
DOBSON (A.)	5, 14
DONALDSON (J.)	41
DONISTHORPE (W.)	36
DORR (J. C. R.)	47
DOUGLAS (Theo.)	22
DOWDEN (E.)	5, 17, 19, 26
DOYLE (Sir F. H.)	18
DOYLE (J. A.)	12
DRAGE (G.)	37
DRAKE (B.)	46
DRUMMOND (Prof. J.)	43
DRYDEN	25
DU CANE (E. F.)	36
DUFF (Sir M. E. G.)	6, 25, 36, 47
DUNCAN (S. J.)	22
DUNSMUIR (A.)	22
DÜNTZER (H.)	5, 6
DURAND (Sir M.)	22
DYER (L.)	2, 35
DYER (H.)	37
EADIE (J.)	4, 38, 40
EARL (A.)	33
EASTLAKE (Lady)	41
EBERS (G.)	22
ECCLES (A. S.)	29
EDGEWORTH (Prof. F. Y.)	35
EDGEWORTH (M.)	22
EDMUNDS (Dr. W.)	28
EDWARDS-MOSS (Sir J. E.)	38
EHLERS (E. S.)	29
EIMER (G. H. T.)	7
ELDERTON (W. A.)	11
ELLERTON (Rev. J.)	43
ELLIOTT (Hon. A.)	36
ELLIS (A.)	20, 25
ELLIS (T.)	3
EMERSON (R. W.)	4, 25
EMERSON (O. F.)	31
ERMAN (A.)	2
EVANS (Lady)	2
EVANS (S.)	18
EVERETT (J. D.)	33
FALCONER (Lanoe)	22
FARRAR (Archd.)	6, 39, 43
FARRER (Sir T. H.)	36
FASNACHT (G. E.)	25
FAULKNER (F.)	8
FAWCETT (Prof. H.)	35, 37
FAWCETT (Mrs. H.)	6, 35, 37
FAY (Amy)	30
FAYRER (Sir J.)	14
FEARNLEY (W.)	34
FEARON (D. R.)	10
FERREL (W.)	34
FESSENDEN (C.)	33
FIELD (Mrs. E. M.)	22
FIELD (Rev. T.)	12
FIELOE (A. M.)	14
FINCK (H. T.)	1
FISHER (Rev. O.)	33
FISKE (J.)	7, 12, 32, 37, 43
FISON (L.)	1
FITCH (J. G.)	10
FITZ GERALD (Caroline)	18
FITZGERALD (Edward)	18, 25
FITZMAURICE (Lord E.)	6
FLAGG (A. T.)	31
FLEISCHER (E.)	8
FLEMING (G.)	22
FLORY (M. A.)	3
FLOWER (Sir W. H.)	49
FLÜCKIGER (F. A.)	29
FONDA (A. J.)	35
FORBES (A.)	4, 47
FORBES (Rev. G.)	43
FORBES-MITCHELL (W.)	5, 47
FORTESCUE (Hon. J. W.)	4, 30
FOSTER (Prof. M.)	7, 34, 35
FOSTER-MELLIAR (A.)	10
FOTHERGILL (Dr. J. M.)	9, 29
FOWLE (Rev. T. W.)	36, 43
FOWLER (Rev. T.)	5, 32
FOWLER (W. W.)	2, 25, 30
FOX (T. W.)	38
FOX (Dr. Wilson)	29
FOXELL (W. J.)	43
FOXWELL (Prof. H. S.)	36
FRAMJI (D.)	12
FRANCIS (F.)	22
FRANKLAND (P. F.)	1
FRANKLIN (W. S.)	33
FRASER (Mrs.)	48
FRASER (Bishop)	43
FRASER-TYTLER (C. C.)	18
FRAZER (J. G.)	1
FRENCH (G. R.)	17

	PAGE
FREEMAN (Prof. E. A.)	2, 5, 12, 37, 40
FRIEDMANN (P.)	4
FROISSART	25
FROST (A. B.)	48
FROUDE (J. A.)	4
FULLERTON (W. M.)	47
FURNIVALL (F. J.)	18
FYFFE (C. A.)	12
FYFE (H. H.)	11
GAIRDNER (J.)	5
GAISFORD (H.)	10
GALT (J.)	22
GALTON (F.)	1
GAMGEE (Arthur)	35
GARDNER (E.)	2
GARDNER (Percy)	2
GARNETT (R.)	18
GARNETT (W.)	5
GASKELL (Mrs.)	14
GASKOIN (Mrs. H.)	38
GEDDES (W. D.)	17, 46
GEE (H.)	40
GEE (W. W. H.)	33 34
GEIKIE (Sir A.)	4, 5, 6, 11, 34
GENNADIUS (J.)	21
GENUNG (J. F.)	17
GEORGE (H. B.)	20
GIBBINS (H. de B.)	12
GIBBON (Charles)	4
GIDDING (F. H.)	37
GILLIES (H. C.)	29
GILCHRIST (A.)	4
GILES (P.)	31
GILMAN (N. P.)	35 37
GILMORE (Rev. J.)	16
GLADSTONE (Dr. J. H.)	8, 10
GLADSTONE (W. E.)	17
GLAISTER (E.)	2, 9
GLOVER (E.)	43
GODFRAY (H.)	3
GODKIN (G. S.)	6
GOETHE	5, 14, 18, 25
GOLDIE (J.)	37
GOLDSMITH	5, 14, 18, 25, 26
GONNER (E. C. K.)	11
GOODFELLOW (J.)	14
GOODNOW (F. J.)	11
GORDON (General C. G.)	5
GORDON (Lady Duff)	47
GORDON (H.)	33
GOSCHEN (Rt. Hon. G. J.)	35
GOSSE (Edmund)	5, 16
GOW (J.)	2
GOW (W.)	31
GRACIAN (Balthasar)	25
GRAHAM (D.)	18
GRAHAM (J. W.)	22
GRAND'HOMME (E.)	9
GRANE (W. L.)	43
GRANT (C.)	22
GRAY (Prof. Andrew)	34
GRAY (Asa)	7, 26
GRAY	5, 18, 26
GRAY (J. L.)	26
GREGORY (R. A.)	3, 33
GREEN (J. R.)	11, 12, 14, 25, 26
GREEN (Mrs. J. R.)	5, 11, 12
GREEN (W. S.)	47
GREENHILL (W. A.)	25
GREENWOOD (F.)	26
GREENWOOD (J. E.)	48
GRENFELL (Mrs.)	9
GRIFFITHS (W. H.)	29
GRIMM	48
GROVE (Sir G.)	11, 30
GUEST (E.)	12
GUEST (M. J.)	12
GUILLEMIN (A.)	33, 34
GUIZOT (F. P. G.)	6
GUNTON (G.)	35
GWATKIN (H. M.)	40
HALLE (E. von)	35
HALES (J. W.)	18, 21, 25, 26
HALLWARD (R. F.)	1
HAMERTON (P. G.)	3, 15, 26
HAMILTON (Prof. D. J.)	29
HAMILTON (J.)	43
HANBURY (D.)	7, 29
HANNAY (David)	4
HARDEN (A.)	9
HARDWICK (Archd. C.)	40, 43
HARDY (A. S.)	22
HARDY (W. J.)	40
HARE (A. W.)	26
HARE (J. C.)	43
HARKER (A.)	34
HARRIS (Rev. G. C.)	43
HARRISON (F.)	5, 6, 12, 15, 26
HARRISON (Miss J.)	2
HARTE (Bret)	22
HARTIG (Dr. R.)	7
HARTLEY (Prof. W. N.)	8
HASSALL (A.)	12
HATCH (F. J.)	11
HAUSER (K.)	5
HAWKINS (H. P.)	29
HAYES (A.)	18
HEADLAM (A. C.)	2
HEADLEY (F. W.)	30, 40
HEAVISIDE (O.)	34
HELM (E.)	35
HELPS (Sir A.)	26
HEMPEL (Dr. W.)	8
HENLEY (W. E.)	15
HERMAN (H.)	23
HERODOTUS	46
HERRICK	26
HERRMANN (G.)	10
HERTEL (Dr.)	10
HERTZ (H.)	34
HICKIE (W. J.)	39
HIGINBOTHAM (C. J.)	5
HILL (D. J.)	32
HILL (F. Davenport)	37
HILL (O.)	37
HILL (G. B.)	12
HIORNS (A. H.)	29, 30
HOBART (Lord)	26
HOBDAY (E.)	10
HODGSON (Rev. J. T.)	5
HOFFDING (Prof. H.)	33
HOFFMAN (W. J.)	1
HOFMANN (A. W.)	8
HOLE (Rev. C.)	9, 12
HOLIDAY (Henry)	48
HOLLAND (T. E.)	15, 37
HOLLWAY-CALTHROP (H.)	48
HOLM (A.)	13
HOLMES (O. W., junr.)	15
HOMER	17, 46
HOOD (T.)	15
HOOKER (Sir J. D.)	7, 47
HOOLE (C. H.)	39
HOOPER (G.)	4
HOOPER (W. H.)	3
HOPKINS (E.)	18
HOPPUS (M. A. M.)	22
HORACE	17, 25, 46
HORT (F. J. A.)	5, 39, 40, 41, 43
HORTON (Hon. S. D.)	35
HOSKEN (J. D.)	18
HOVENDEN (R. M.)	46
HOWELL (George)	15, 35
HOWES (G. B.)	35, 49
HOWITT (A. W.)	1
HOWSON (Very Rev. J. S.)	41
HOZIER (Col. H. M.)	30
HUBNER (Baron)	47
HUGHES (T.)	4, 5, 18, 22, 26, 41, 43, 47
HUDDILSTON (J. H.)	39
HULL (E.)	2, 11
HULLAH (J.)	2, 25, 30
HUMPHRY (Prof. Sir G. M.)	35, 49
HUNT (Rev. W.)	12
HUNT (W.)	3
HUTCHINSON (G. W. C.)	3
HUTTON (R. H.)	5, 26
HUTTON (Rev. W. H.)	5
HUXLEY (T)	5, 26, 32, 33, 34, 35, 37, 49
HYDE (W. de W.)	43
ILLINGWORTH (Rev. J. R.)	43
IMPEY (S. P.)	29
INGRAM (T. D.)	13
IRELAND (A.)	26
IRVING (H)	20
IRVING (J.)	11
IRVING (Washington)	15
JACK (A. A.)	17
JACKSON (D. C.)	34
JACKSON (F. G.)	47
JACKSON (Helen)	22
JACOB (Rev. J. A.)	43
JACOBS (J.)	14, 25, 47
JAMES (Henry)	5, 22, 26
JAMES (Rev. H.)	43
JAMES (Prof. W.)	33
JARDINE (Rev. R.)	33
JEANS (Rev. G E.)	43, 46
JEBB (Prof. R. C.)	4, 13, 16, 26
JELLETT (Rev. J. H.)	43
JENKS (Prof. Ed.)	37
JENNINGS (A. C.)	13, 38
JERSEY (Countess of)	48
JEPHSON (H.)	37
JEVONS (W. S.)	5, 32, 35, 36, 37
JEWETT (S.)	18
JEX-BLAKE (Sophia)	9
JOCELINE (E.)	26
JOHNSON (Amy)	34
JOHNSON (Samuel)	5, 16, 25
JOLLEY (A. J.)	39
JONES (Prof. D. E.)	34
JONES (F.)	8
JONES (H. Arthur)	16, 18, 26
JONES (H. S.)	2
JULIUS (Dr. P.)	9
KAHLDEN (C.)	29
KALM (P.)	47
KANT	32
KANTHACK (A. A.)	29
KARI	48
KAVANAGH (Rt. Hn. A. M.)	5
KAY (Rev. W.)	39
KEARY (Annie)	13, 22, 38, 48
KEARY (Eliza)	48
KEATS	5, 26
KEELE (J.)	26
KELLNER (Dr. L.)	31
KELLOGG (Rev. S. H.)	43
KELLY (E.)	43
KELTIE (J. S.)	38
KELVIN (Lord)	11, 31, 33, 34

	PAGE
KEMPE (A. B.)	33
KENNEDY (Prof. A. B. W.)	10
KENNEDY (B. H.)	46
KENNEDY (P.)	22
KEYNES (J. N.)	32, 36
KIDD (B.)	37
KIEPERT (H.)	11
KIMBER (D. C.)	35
KING (F. H.)	1
KING (G.)	13
KINGSLEY (Charles)	5, 10, 13, 14, 16, 18, 22, 23, 26, 27, 30, 41, 47, 48
KINGSLEY (G.)	38
KINGSLEY (Henry)	25, 47
KIPLING (J. L.)	47
KIPLING (Rudyard)	23, 27, 48
KIRKPATRICK (Prof.)	38, 43
KLEIN (Dr. F.)	7, 29, 30
KLEIN (F.)	28
KNIGHT (W.)	17, 28, 32
KUENEN (Prof. A.)	38
KYNASTON (Rev. H.)	43, 46
LABBERTON (R. H.)	3
LA FARGE (J.)	3
LAFARGUE (P.)	23
LAMB	5, 26, 27
LANCIANI (Prof. R.)	2
LANDAUER (J.)	8
LANDOR	5, 26
LANE-POOLE (S.)	6, 26
LANFREY (P.)	6
LANG (Andrew)	15, 26, 46
LANG (Prof. Arnold)	49
LANGLEY (J. N.)	34
LANGMAID (T.)	10
LANKESTER (Prof. Ray)	7, 27
LASSAR-COHN (Dr.)	8
LASLETT (T.)	7
LAUGHTON (J. K.)	4
LAURIE (A. P.)	1, 3
LAWRENCE (T. J.)	15
LAWTON (W. C.)	27
LEA (A. S.)	35
LEAF (W.)	17, 46
LEAHY (Sergeant)	38
LEE (M.)	23
LEE (S.)	25, 26
LEES (C. H.)	31
LEE-WARNER (W.)	13
LEEPER (A.)	45
LEGGE (A. O.)	13, 43
LEIBNITZ	36
LESLIE (G. D.)	27
LETHABY (W. R.)	2, 38
LETHBRIDGE (Sir Roper)	5, 13
LEVY (Amy)	23
LEWIS (R.)	16
LEWKOWITSCH (J.)	38
LIGHTFOOT (Bishop)	5, 13, 39, 40, 41, 43, 44
LIGHTWOOD (J. M.)	15
LINDSAY (Dr. J. A.)	29
LITTLEDALE (H.)	17
LOCKYER (J. N.)	3, 8, 34, 38
LODEMAN (E. G.)	10
LODGE (Prof. O. J.)	3, 27, 34
LODGE (R.)	5
LOWENSON-LESSING (F.)	11
LOEWY (B.)	33
LOFTIE (Mrs. W. J.)	2
LONGFELLOW (H. W.)	26
LONSDALE (J.)	25, 46
LOVER (S.)	23
LOWE (W. H.)	38, 39
LOWELL (J. R.)	15, 18, 27
LOUDON (W. J.)	33
LOUIS (H.)	38
LUBBOCK (Sir J.)	7, 10, 11, 27, 50
LUCAS (F.)	18
LUCAS (Joseph)	47
LUNT (J.)	9
LUPTON (S.)	8
LYALL (Sir Alfred)	4
LYDE (L. W.)	11
LYSAGHT (S. R.)	23
LYTE (H. C. M.)	13
LYTTELTON (A. T.)	44
LYTTELTON (E.)	27
LYTTON (Earl of)	23
MACALISTER (D.)	29
MACARTHUR (M.)	12
MACAULAY (G. C.)	20, 25, 46
MACAULAY (Lord)	27
MACCOLL (Norman)	17
McCURDY (J. F.)	44
M'COSH (Dr. J.)	32, 33
MACDONALD (George)	21
MACDONALD (G.)	29
MACKAIL (J. W.)	46
MACKNIGHT (J.)	37
MACLAGAN (Dr. T.)	29
MACLAREN (Rev. Alex.)	44
MACLAREN (Archibald)	48
MACLEAN (G. E.)	31
MACLEAN (W. C.)	29
MACLEAR (Rev. Dr.)	38, 40, 41
McLENNAN (J. C.)	33
M'LENNAN (J. F.)	1
M'LENNAN (Malcolm)	23
MACMILLAN (Rev. H.)	27, 44
MACMILLAN (Michael)	6, 19
MACMILLAN (M. K.)	23
MACQUOID (K. S.)	23
MADOC (F.)	23
MAGUIRE (J. F.)	48
MAHAFFY (Prof. J. P.)	2, 13, 16, 27, 32, 44, 47
MAITLAND (F. W.)	15, 36
MALET (L.)	23
MALORY (Sir T.)	25
MALTHUS (T. R.)	35
MANSFIELD (C. B.)	8
MARCOU (J.)	4
MARKHAM (C. R.)	5
MARR (J. E.)	34
MARRIOTT (J. A. R.)	6
MARRYAT (Capt.)	23
MARSHALL (Prof. A.)	36
MARSHALL (H. R.)	32
MARTEL (C.)	30
MARTIN (Frances)	4, 48
MARTIN (Frederick)	36
MARTIN (H. N.)	49
MARTINEAU (C. A.)	34
MARTINEAU (H.)	6
MARTINEAU (Dr. J.)	6
MASON (A. E. W.)	23
MASON (O. T.)	1
MASSON (D.)	5, 18, 21, 25, 32
MASSON (G.)	9, 25
MASSON (R. O.)	21
MATHEW (E. J.)	13, 37
MATURIN (Rev. W.)	44
MAUDSLEY (Dr. H.)	33
MAURICE (F. D.)	10, 27, 32, 38-40, 41, 44
MAURICE (Gen. F.)	5, 30, 36
MAX MÜLLER (F.)	32
MAYER (A. M.)	34
MAYO-SMITH (R.)	37
MAYOR (J. B.)	40
MAYOR (Prof. J. E. B.)	3, 6
MAZINI (L.)	49
MELDOLA (Prof. R.)	8, 33, 34
MENDENHALL (T. C.)	34
MENGER (C.)	36
MENSCHUTKIN (A.)	8
MERCIER (Dr. C.)	29
MERCUR (Prof. J.)	30
MEREDITH (G.)	18
MEREDITH (L. A.)	15
MEYER (E. von)	8
MEYRICK (E.)	30
MIALL (L. C.)	30, 50
MICHELET (M.)	13
MIERS (H. A.)	14
MILL (H. R.)	11
MILLER (R. K.)	3
MILLIGAN (Rev. W.)	40, 44
MILTON	5, 16, 18, 25, 27
MINTO (Prof. W.)	5, 23
MITFORD (A. B.)	10, 23
MITFORD (M. R.)	15
MIVART (St. George)	35
MIXTER (W. G.)	8
MOLESWORTH (Mrs.)	49
MOLLOY (G.)	33
MOLYNEUX (W. C. F.)	30
MONAHAN (J. H)	15
MONTEFIORE (C. G.)	38, 42
MONTELIUS (O.)	1
MOORE (C. H.)	2
MOORHOUSE (Bishop)	44
MORIER (J.)	23
MORISON (J. C.)	5
MORLEY (John)	4, 5, 20, 27
MORRIS (E. E.)	5
MORRIS (Mowbray)	4, 25
MORRIS (R.)	25, 31
MOKSHEAD (E. D. A.)	46
MOULTON (L. C.)	18
MOULTON (R. G.)	38
MUDIE (C. E.)	18
MUIR (J.)	1
MUIR (M. M. P.)	8
MÜLLER (H.)	8
MULLINGER (J. B.)	13
MUN (T.)	35
MUNRO (J. E. C.)	15
MURPHY (J. J.)	7, 33, 44
MURRAY (D. Christie)	23
MURRAY (G.)	8
MYERS (E.)	18, 46
MYERS (F. W. H.)	5, 19, 27
MYLNE (Bishop)	44
NADAL (E. S.)	27
NERNST (Dr.)	8
NETTLESHIP (H.)	16
NEWCOMB (S.)	3
NEWCASTLE (Duke and Duchess)	26
NEWMAN (G.)	29
NEWTON (Sir C. T.)	2
NICHOL (J.)	4
NICHOLS (E. L.)	33
NICHOLLS (H. A. A.)	1
NISBET (J.)	8
NOEL (Lady A.)	23
NORDENSKIÖLD (A. E.)	47
NORGATE (Kate)	13
NORRIS (W. E.)	21
NORTON (Charles Eliot)	4, 46
NORTON (Hon. Mrs.)	19, 23
NORWAY (A. H.)	31
OLIPHANT (T. L. K.)	27, 32

	PAGE
OLIPHANT (Mrs. M. O. W.)	5, 13, 16, 23, 25, 49
OLIVER (Prof. D.)	8
OLIVER (Capt. S. P.)	47
OMAN (C. W.)	4
ORR (H. B.)	1
OSBORN (H. F.)	7
OSTWALD (Prof.)	8
OTTÉ (E. C.)	13
PAGE (T. E.)	39
PALGRAVE (Sir F.)	13
PALGRAVE (F. T.)	3, 19, 21, 25, 26, 42, 49
PALGRAVE (R. H. Inglis)	35
PALGRAVE (W. G.)	19, 37, 47
PALMER (Lady S.)	23
PARKER (T. J.)	7, 49
PARKER (W. K.)	6
PARKER (W. N.)	49
PARKES (Sir H.)	6
PARKIN (G. R.)	13, 37
PARKINSON (S.)	34
PARKMAN (F.)	13, 47
PARRY (G.)	23
PARSONS (Alfred)	15
PASTEUR (L.)	8
PATER (W.)	3, 16, 23, 27
PATERSON (A.)	23
PATERSON (A. B.)	19
PATERSON (J.)	16
PATMORE (Coventry)	25, 49
PATTESON (J. C.)	6
PATTISON (Mark)	5, 6, 44
PAULSEN (F.)	10
PAYNE (E. J.)	12, 36
PEABODY (C. H.)	10, 34
PEACOCK (T. L.)	23
PEARSON (C. H.)	37
PEASE (A. E.)	14
PEEL (E.)	19
PEILE (J.)	31
PELLISSIER (E.)	32
PENNELL (J.)	3
PENNINGTON (R.)	11
PENROSE (F. C.)	2
PERCIVAL (H. M.)	18, 19
PERKINS (J. B.)	13
PETERSON (W.)	46
PETTIGREW (J. B.)	8, 35, 49
PHILLIMORE (J. G.)	16
PHILLIPS (F. E.)	23
PHILLIPS (J. A.)	30
PHILLIPS (W. C.)	3
PICTON (J. A.)	27
PIFFARD (H. G.)	29
PIKE (L. O.)	13
PIKE (W.)	47
PLAYFAIR (W. S.)	28
PLATO	26, 46
PLUMPTRE (Dean)	44
POLLARD (A. W.)	16, 17, 46
POLLOCK (Sir F., Bart.)	6, 16, 27, 36, 37
POLLOCK (Lady)	2
POOLE (M. E.)	27
POOLE (R. L.)	13
POPE	5, 25, 27
POSTE (E.)	34, 46
POTTER (L.)	27
POTTER (R.)	44
POTTS (W.)	28
PRESTON (T.)	34
PRESTWICH (J.)	11
PRICE (E. C.)	23
PRICE (L. L. F. R.)	36
	PAGE
PRICKARD (A. O.)	28
PRINCE ALBERT VICTOR	46
PRINCE GEORGE	46
PROCTER (F.)	41
PROPERT (J. L.)	3
PROWSE (D. W.)	13
PURCELL (E. S.)	5
QUESNAY (F.)	36
RABBENO (U.)	36
RAE (J.)	6, 36
RAMSAY (Sir A. C.)	6
RAMSAY (W.)	8
RANSOME (C.)	17
RATHBONE (W.)	9
RATZEL (F.)	1
RAWLINSON (W. G.)	15
RAWNSLEY (H. D.)	19
RAY (P. K.)	32
RAYLEIGH (Lord)	34
REICHEL (Bishop)	44
REID (J. S.)	46
REMSEN (I.)	8
RENAN (E.)	6
RENDALL (Rev. F.)	40, 44
REYNOLDS (E. S.)	14
REYNOLDS (H. R.)	44
REYNOLDS (Sir J. R.)	29
REYNOLDS (O.)	14
RHOADES (J.)	23
RHODES (J. F.)	13
RICARDO	35, 36
RICHARDSON (B. W.)	14, 29
RICHEY (A. G.)	16
RIGHTON (E.)	18
RITCHIE (A.)	6
ROBB (R.)	10
ROBINSON (Preb. H. G.)	44
ROBINSON (J. L.)	31
ROBINSON (Matthew)	6
ROCKSTRO (W. S.)	5
ROGERS (J. E. T.)	13, 37
ROMANES (G. J.)	7
ROSCOE (Sir H. E.)	8, 9
ROSCOE (W. C.)	19
ROSEBERY (Earl of)	5
ROSENBUSCH (H.)	11
ROSEVEAR (E.)	9
ROSS (P.)	23
ROSSETTI (C. G.)	19, 49
ROTHSCHILD (F.)	13
ROUTLEDGE (J.)	37
ROWE (F. J.)	20
ROY (Neil)	23
RÜCKER (Prof. A. W.)	9
RUMFORD (Count)	28
RUSHBROOKE (W. G.)	39
RUSSELL (Dean)	44
RUSSELL (Sir Charles)	37
RUSSELL (W. Clark)	4, 23
RUSSELL (T.)	34
RUTHERFORD (W. G.)	38, 46
RYLAND (F.)	16
RYLE (Prof. H. E.)	38, 4
SADLER (H.)	3
SAINTSBURY (G.)	5, 16
SALMON (Rev. G.)	44
SALT (H. S.)	28
SANDFORD (Bishop)	44
SANDFORD (M. E.)	6
SANDYS (J. E.)	47
SAYCE (A. H.)	13
SCAIFE (W. B.)	28
SCARTAZZINI (G. A.)	17
SCHLIEMANN (Dr.)	2
SCHMOLLER (G.)	35
	PAGE
SCHORLEMMER (C.)	8, 9
SCHREIBER (T.)	2
SCHUCHHARDT (C.)	2
SCHULTZ (Dr. G.)	9
SCHUSTER (A.)	33
SCOTT (M.)	23
SCOTT (Sir W.)	19, 25
SCRATCHLEY (Sir Peter)	30
SCUDDER (S. H.)	50
SEATON (Dr. E. C.)	29
SEEBOHM (H. E.)	1
SEELEY (Sir J. R.)	13, 37, 44
SEILER (Dr. Carl)	29, 35
SELBORNE (Earl of)	5, 25, 40, 42
SELIGMAN (E.)	36
SELLERS (E.)	2
SERVICE (J.)	41, 44
SEWELL (E. M.)	13
SHADWELL (C. L.)	46
SHAIRP (J. C.)	4, 19
SHAKESPEARE	17, 19, 25, 26
SHANN (G.)	10, 34
SHARP (W.)	6
SHAW (Miss)	14
SHELDON (W. L.)	32
SHELLEY	19, 26
SHIPTON (Helen)	23
SHIRLEY (W. N.)	44
SHORE (L. E.)	34
SHORTHOUSE (J. H.)	23, 24
SHORTLAND (Admiral)	31
SHUCKBURGH (E. S.)	14, 46
SHUFELDT (R. W.)	49
SIBSON (Dr. F.)	29
SIDGWICK (A.)	20
SIDGWICK (Prof. H.)	32, 36, 37
SIME (J.)	11, 12
SIMPSON (Rev. W.)	40
SKEAT (W. W.)	17
SKRINE (J. H.)	6, 19
SLADE (J. H.)	10
SLEEMAN (L.)	47
SLOMAN (Rev. A.)	39
SMART (W.)	35
SMALLEY (G. W.)	6, 28
SMETHAM (J. and S.)	6
SMITH (Adam)	3, 6, 35, 36
SMITH (Alexander)	17, 25
SMITH (C.)	19
SMITH (F. Hopkinson)	24
SMITH (Garnet)	24
SMITH (Goldwin)	4, 6, 14, 21, 28, 37, 45, 47
SMITH (H.)	19
SMITH (J.)	8
SMITH (Rev. T.)	44
SMITH (W. G.)	8
SMITH (L. Pearsall)	24
SOHM (R.)	40
SOMERVILLE (Prof. W.)	7
SOUTHEY	6, 26
SPANTON (J.)	3
SPENDER (J. K.)	29
SPENSER	19, 25
SPOTTISWOODE (W.)	34
ST. ASAPH (Bishop of)	40
ST. JOHNSTON (A.)	23, 47, 19
STANLEY (Dean)	44
STANLEY (Hon. Maude)	37
STATHAM (R.)	37
STEBBING (W.)	4
STEEL (F. A.)	15, 24
STEPHEN (C. E.)	9
STEPHEN (H.)	16
STEPHEN (Sir J. F.)	14, 16, 28

	PAGE
STEPHEN (J. K.)	6
STEPHEN (L.)	5
STEPHENS (J. B.)	19
STEPHENS (W. R. W.)	5
STEVENS (C. E.)	16
STEVENSON (F. S.)	6
STEVENSON (J. J.)	2
STEWART (A.)	49
STEWART (Balfour)	33, 34, 45
STOKES (Sir G. G.)	34
STORY (R. H.)	4
STONE (W. H.)	34
STRACHEY (Sir E.)	25
STRACHEY (J. St. L.)	37
STRACHEY (Gen. R.)	11
STRANGFORD (Viscountess)	47
STRETTELL (A.)	19
STUBBS (Dean)	45
STUBBS (Bishop)	40
SUTHERLAND (A.)	11
SWAINSON (H.)	2
SWETE (Prof. H. B.)	39
SWIFT (Dean)	15
SYMONDS (J. A.)	5
SYMONDS (Mrs. J. A.)	6
SYMONS (A.)	19
TAGGART (W. S.)	38
TAINSH (E. C.)	17
TAIT (Archbishop)	6, 45
TAIT (C. W. A.)	14
TAIT (Prof. P. G.)	33, 34, 45
TANNER (H.)	1
TARR (R. S.)	11, 34
TAVERNIER (J. B.)	47
TAYLOR (E. R.)	3
TAYLOR (Franklin)	30
TAYLOR (Isaac)	32, 45
TAYLOR (Sedley)	30, 34
TEGETMEIER (W. B.)	9
TEMPLE (Bishop)	45
TEMPLE (Sir R.)	4
TENNANT (Dorothy)	48
TENNIEL (Sir John)	48
TENNYSON (Lord)	17, 19, 20, 26
TENNYSON (Frederick)	20
TENNYSON (Lord H.)	15, 49
THEODOLI (Marchesa)	24
THOMPSON (D'A. W.)	8
THOMPSON (E.)	12
THOMPSON (H. M.)	36
THOMPSON (S. P.)	34
THOMSON (A. W.)	10
THOMSON (Sir C. W.)	50
THOMSON (Hugh)	14
THOREAU	28
THORNE (Dr. Thorne)	29
THORNTON (J.)	7
THORNTON (W. T.)	32, 37, 46
THORPE (T. E.)	6, 9
THRING (E.)	10, 28
THRUPP (J. F.)	38
THURSFIELD (J. R.)	5
TODHUNTER (I.)	6
TORRENS (W. M.)	5
TOURGÉNIEF (I. S.)	24
TOUT (T. F.)	5, 14
TOZER (H. F.)	11
TRAILL (H. D.)	4, 5, 36
TRENCH (Capt. F.)	37
TRENCH (Archbishop)	45
TREVELYAN (Sir G. O.)	14, 28
TREVOR (G. H.)	20
TRIBE (A.)	8
TRISTRAM (W. O.)	15
TROLLOPE (A.)	5
TRUMAN (J.)	20
TUCKER (T. G.)	46
TUCKWELL (W.)	14
TUFTS (J. H.)	32
TULLOCH (Principal)	45
TURNER (C. Tennyson)	20
TURNER (G.)	1
TURNER (H. H.)	34
TURNER (J. M. W.)	15
TURPIN (G. S.)	9
TYLOR (E. B.)	1
TYRWHITT (R. St. J.)	3, 20
TYRRELL (R. Y.)	16, 28
VAUGHAN (C. J.)	39, 40, 41, 45
VAUGHAN (Rev. D. J.)	26, 28, 45
VAUGHAN (Rev. E. T.)	45
VAUGHAN (Rev. R.)	45
VELEY (M.)	24
VENN (Rev. J.)	33, 45
VERNON (Hon. W. W.)	17
VERRALL (A. W.)	17, 46
VERRALL (Mrs.)	2
VICKERMAN (C.)	38
VICTOR (H.)	24
VINES (S. H.)	8
VIOLLET-LE-DUC (E. E.)	10
WAIN (Louis)	48
WALDSTEIN (C.)	2
WALKER (Prof. F. A.)	36
WALKER (Jas.)	8
WALKER (Louisa)	38
WALLACE (A. R.)	7, 30, 36
WALLACE (Sir D. M.)	37
WALPOLE (S.)	36
WALTON (I.)	15
WARD (A. W.)	4, 5, 16, 25
WARD (H. M.)	7, 8
WARD (S.)	20
WARD (T. H.)	21
WARD (Mrs. T. H.)	24, 49
WARD (W.)	6, 28, 41
WARE (W. R.)	3
WATERS (C. A.)	35
WATERTON (Charles)	30, 47
WATSON (E.)	6
WATSON (R. S.)	47
WATSON (W.)	20, 25
WAY (A. S.)	46
WEBB (W. T.)	18, 20
WEBSTER (Mrs. A.)	20, 49
WEISBACH (J.)	10
WELBY-GREGORY (Lady)	41
WELLDON (Rev. J. E. C.)	45, 46
WEST (M.)	24
WESTCOTT (Bp.)	38, 39, 40, 41, 45
WESTERMARCK (E.)	1
WETHERELL (J.)	32
WHEELER (J. T.)	14
WHEWELL (W.)	6
WHITCOMB (L. S.)	3, 16
WHITE (A.)	28
WHITE (Gilbert)	15, 31
WHITE (Dr. W. Hale)	29
WHITE (W.)	34
WHITNEY (W. D.)	9
WHITTIER (J. G.)	20, 26, 28
WHITTUCK (C. A.)	45
WICKHAM (Rev. E. C.)	45
WICKSTEED (P. H.)	36, 18
WIEDERSHEIM (R.)	35, 49
WIESER (F. von)	36
WILBRAHAM (F. M.)	41
WILKINS (Prof. A. S.)	2, 16, 45
WILKINSON (S.)	30
WILLEY (A.)	7
WILLIAMS (C. M.)	32
WILLIAMS (C. T.)	29
WILLIAMS (G. H.)	11
WILLIAMS (H.)	14, 31
WILLIAMS (Montagu)	6
WILLIAMS (S. E.)	16
WILLIAMSON (M. B.)	45
WILLINK (A.)	45
WILLOUGHBY (E. F.)	14
WILLOUGHBY (F.)	49
WILLOUGHBY (W. W.)	36
WILLS (W. G.)	20
WILSON (A. J.)	36
WILSON (Sir C.)	4
WILSON (Sir D.)	1, 4, 17
WILSON (E. B.)	50
WILSON (Dr. G.)	5, 6, 28
WILSON (Archdeacon)	45
WILSON (Mary)	16
WINCH (R. F.)	27
WINCHESTER (Bishop of)	6
WINDELBAND (W.)	32
WINGATE (Major F. R.)	30
WINKWORTH (C.)	6
WINKWORTH (S.)	25
WINTER (W.)	15
WOLSELEY (Gen. Viscou)	30
WOOD (A. G.)	30
WOOD (C. J.)	45
WOOD (Rev. E. G.)	14, 45
WOODS (Rev. F. H.)	1
WOODS (Miss M. A.)	21, 42
WOODWARD (C. M.)	10
WOOLNER (T.)	20
WORDSWORTH	4, 6, 17, 20, 26, 28
WORTHEY (Mrs.)	2
WRIGHT (Rev. A.)	39
WRIGHT (Miss G.)	1
WRIGHT (J.)	10, 21
WRIGHT (L.)	34
WRIGHT (M. O.)	28, 31
WRIGHT (W. A.)	9, 18, 25, 49
WULKER (Dr.)	10
WURTZ (Ad.)	10
WYATT (Sir M. D.)	8
YEO (J.)	3
YOE (Shway)	3
YONGE (C. M.)	6, 8, 9, 12, 13, 14, 24, 26, 28, 32, 38, 4
YOUNG (E. W.)	1
YOUNGHUSBAND (G. J. and F. E.)	3
ZIEGLER (Dr. E.)	3, 8

MACMILLAN AND CO., LTD., LONDON.

J. PALMER, PRINTER, ALEXANDRA STREET, CAMBRIDGE.

20/50/7/96

www.ingramcontent.com/pod-product-compliance
Lightning Source LLC
Chambersburg PA
CBHW031146120726
47905CB00006B/1842